NOTHING.
EVERYTHING.

NOTHING. EVERYTHING.

Virginia Montanez

NEW YORK LOS ANGELES

This is a work of fiction. Names, characters, places, and incidents are either products of the author's imagination or, if real, are used fictitiously.

Jacket design by Rejenne Pavon

Interior book design by A Raven Design
ISBN#: 978-1-960724-04-5 (pbk)
ISBN#: 978-1-960724-05-2 (ebook)

Published by Winding Road Stories
www.windingroadstories.com

For my parents and my children
who taught me how to love.
For my sisters who taught me how to laugh.
For Pittsburgh who taught me how to live.

Ellis Sloan Therapy Sessions

Practice of Dr. Willa Parrish
Gulf Tower
Pittsburgh, PA
May 2021

Dr. Willa Parrish: Ellis, good to meet you. I should tell you I loved your book.

Ellis Sloan: You've read my book? Is this a conflict of interest for you then?

Dr. Parrish: Not at all. Why?

Ellis: Well, you know who I am. Shouldn't therapists and their patients be strangers?

Dr. Parrish: So, when Oprah needs a therapist, she should do what exactly?

Ellis: Oh. Because everybo—

Dr. Parrish: Everybody knows Oprah.

Prologue

October 2020

Do you know what happens when your marriage of 17 years falls apart? When you have no choice but to walk away from your second kiss who became your first boyfriend who became your first love who became the man you married at twenty-two with the moon in your eyes and a catch in your breath?

Everything happens. And nothing happens.

Everything happens. You shout. Cry. You angrily, messily and aggressively throw his belongings into boxes. You shake out an entire jewelry tray of every gift he ever gave you and listen as rings, bracelets, pendants, watches and charms clink and slink their way around miscellaneous tchotchkes to rest on the bottom of a used moving box you Sharpied with "YOUR DUMB SHIT." He loads his car in sadness. You blame. He blames. And 'round and 'round you go on the Blame Carousel; where it stops ... doesn't matter. You quit writing your second book because the words all die. You move your children into an outdated duplex your real estate agent mother owns. You tell your kids their world is changing. Their world changes. Your world changes. Everything changes. Everything happens.

And yet, nothing happens. The world, disrespectfully, goes on. The mail comes. Your kids go to school. They come home. You cook dinner. You fight about homework. You Google how to find the area of a circle because you learned that back when your brain still accepted the input of new information. You teach it to your thirteen-year-old. She says, "That's not how my teacher taught us." You go to bed cursing Miss Jacobs and the existence of math. The sun rises. You wake up no longer remembering how to calculate the area of a circle. The world goes on. Nothing happens. The earth doesn't tilt off its axis under the weight of your crushing grief. The clouds don't rain blood—the least they could do to signify to the world that you, Ellis Sloan, are in soul-deep agonizing pain. Just a little blood rain. Is that asking too much for Ellis?

Ellis with the frizzy curly hair, grew up.

Ellis with the loud mouth and pegged jeans, got married and then got quiet.

Ellis with the four brothers, birthed two children.

Ellis Sloan née Marks got separated and became loud again while at the same time somehow becoming quieter.

Ellis Sloan with the dead marriage she's driving toward the Cliffs of Divorce, lives at the intersection of Nothing and Everything.

Everything.

Nothing.

This living life at the intersection of Nothing and Everything is brutal. It makes you want to buy every wall decoration at Marshalls painted with *Thankful. Grateful. Blessed.* Or *I Love Us* in looping script fonts, so you can take them home and light them on fire. *We are not thankful. We are not grateful. We are not blessed. There is no us. We are just really really angry and floating through the nothing while our brains are full of everything.* It makes you want to confront the women you see buying these decorative lies so you can say, "Honey, all it takes is one switch. One light switch turning on.

Or one turning off. To change it all. To upend you. To fuck it all up and leave you floating."

The intersection of Nothing and Everything is also where you swear quite a bit more than you used to.

Everyone is eager to tell you that you won't live forever at that intersection where all the lights are red. That feeling of being stalled out is temporary, they say.

There is Something, they say. While settled into their couches with their zero big problems, they assure you over text that something will come from the Nothing and the Everything. *Something is around the corner. Soon there will be Something for you, Ellis Sloan with the boy name and the frizzy hair and the two kids and the emotional baggage and the four brothers.* They try to help you get to Something—suggesting everything from the slow coal train of therapy to the screaming fast rocket of a one-night hook-up with a random stranger.

"Yoga!" "Lexapro!" "Marijuana!" "ESSENTIAL. OILS."

Unfriend. Block. Report. DELETE. ACCOUNT.

But sometimes, life does a thing.

And you go to bed in the Nothing and the Everything, and you wake up to Something.

And sometimes that something starts with an angry sleep-intruding shout at a toppled piano outside your open bedroom window at 7 o'god-damned-clock on a Saturday morning in October, four months after you walked away from your marriage.

Like I said. I'm much more sweary. I have ~~every~~ no intention of working on it.

Ellis Sloan Therapy Sessions

Gulf Tower
Pittsburgh, PA
May 2021

Dr. Parrish: Why don't you tell me why you're here.

Ellis: I don't know how to be happy.

Dr. Parrish: So, depression?

Ellis: No? I don't think. It's more like ... I've lost the instructions to myself? Now that the divorce is final and I'm on my own, I realize I don't know how to be happy anymore. I can't create it. I'm broken, but because I don't have the instructions, I don't know where the damage is so how the hell can I fix it? It's like I'm a Xerox with a paper jam and I'm blaring out this error code like J-72, J-72, but without the instruction manual, I don't know where to look for the little slip of torn paper that's throwing the whole machine out of whack.

Dr. Parrish: That was extremely well put.

Ellis: I used to be an author.

Dr. Parrish: You still are. You don't stop being a mom just because you stop having babies. You don't stop being a rock star just because you stop making records. You don't stop being an engineer just—

Ellis: I get it.

Chapter One

October 2020

Sleep is my escape.

It is a blissful drug that should be bottled with a "May Cause All Your Problems To Disappear" label. When your brain won't let you be—when it whispers what you hope are lies—*Maybe it wasn't him. Maybe it was you. Maybe you deserved it. What's the rest of life even got for you now, Ellis Sloan? Maybe you should just get a cat.*

But I don't want a cat. I like dogs. And Wren told me she learned from YouTube that if I die while at home, any cat I own would wait only one hour before snacking on my flesh like I'm made of Fancy Feast. She didn't say this with horror, but with blatant admiration. Then she asked if she could get a cat, and I don't honestly know what to do with that.

My asleep brain mostly leaves me be. My awake brain whispers questions only the devil would ask. *Does Wren even love you? Are you anything more than the human that feeds her and forces her to go to school? Are you failing her? Would Wren care if you died? Would she cheer on the Fancy-Feasting cat?*

Is Dunn okay? Does he blame you? Don't you think he's gotten quiet lately? Does he hate you? Is this going to screw him up for the rest of his life?

Sleep replaces those too-close thoughts with dreams too far away to do any real damage. Even the occasional nightmares (usually of Wren drowning in a high wave that sweeps her away from me) live on the edges of my consciousness—close enough to the rim that I can shove them into oblivion upon waking. If you don't grasp at retreating nightmares, sometimes they behave and slip into the fog before you can pull them back to see if you recognize them.

Sleep is peace. And lately, it's the only peace. So when the word "fuck" is shouted over and over, intruding upon my escape, I don't handle it well.

"Fuck!"

I crack open one eye enough to see my phone resting on my cluttered nightstand. 7:12 a.m. That's much too early for a Saturday. I clench my eyes shut tighter and wish there was a way to do the same for my ears. This is where Wren would say, "Like a pangolin. Pangolins can close their ears."

I had always thought a pangolin to be an ancient musical instrument. I've learned a lot from my 13-year-old.

"Fuck!"

I bury my head under my pillow and curse myself for leaving the bedroom window open for the night. But it had been a weirdly warm night and I refuse to run the air conditioning in October. We have laws of nature for this very reason.

Three more shouts of profanity slip into the room to find me, insistent on burrowing into my brain.

The first syllabic growl of a vicious swear forms in my throat, but I stop myself on account of Wren who has recently taken up swearing against my orders. My already fading parental power will lose further wattage if I say, "Listen, I realize I rage-screamed 'motherfucker' out my window this morning, but I would like to talk to you about your use of the D-word at dinner last night."

To which Wren would reply, "Dick, damn or dumbass?"

Mom of the Year. Mom of the Year Ellis Sloan with the boy name and the always wild hair and the bleary eyes and the scar that now snakes across her lower chin, and the Jurassic World t-shirt and the black yoga shorts that have never seen one single *asana* but have binged many John Hughes movies.

I whip the bedsheets off my body and stomp so hard toward the window I look like I'm trooping the *colours* for the Queen of England. My arms are a manic whirl as I shove the sun-faded curtains aside and yank up on the tattered, dented screen before throwing my head out the window only to collide with another burst of profanity erupting from below. That the world outside is only lit by the still-rising sun further stokes my anger.

"Hey!" I growl-shout down toward the street from my second-floor room. Without my contacts in, the morning-muted world is a blur. The shape of a man moves on the sidewalk below. There's a small white truck and what appears to be a piano of the "upright" variety, resting quite comfortably on its back. I don't imagine it's good for pianos, upright or grand, to defy their "This End Up" orders.

There are two other bodies standing down there. Men? So three men standing around a dead piano like they're about to lay it to rest in its grave. And descending to them from above—not the voice of angels, the eyes of God, nor the music of seraphim. No, give it up for the frizzy-haired bleary-eyed homicidal stylings of Ellis Sloan.

The three bodies below look up from their eulogy for the deceased piano. Three blank blurry canvases seeking out the intrusion.

"Do you mind?!" I shout downward hoping my words plop upon their shoulders with enough weight to convey my general desire to punch their blank faces. I don't need to see the faces to know they're exceedingly punchable; the heart just knows.

"Eller?!" a male voice I don't recognize calls up.

Well, hell. Someone down there knows me and not only that, they know me well enough to throw my terrible childhood nickname up at me.

Ellis Marks.

Ellis.

Eller.

Eller Beller.

Eller Beller in the cellar try'n to kiss an ugly feller, but the ugly feller said no to Eller Beller. He'd rather kiss a troll.

I hope whoever down there that called me Eller isn't a member of my mother's church because if this next thing I shout ever gets back to Poppy Marks, she'll burst into flames: "Who in the goddamned hell?!"

A voice from behind wriggles into my ears. "Wait, we can say that now?"

I raise my head too quickly, banging the back of it against the sill to momentarily stun myself blind. "Damn it." Three hard blinks do nothing to help me recenter. This morning was not meant to be so audibly sweary. I like to keep my blasphemy simmering beneath the surface like a good preacher's kid.

"Nice," Wren whispers with the same admiration she had for the corpse-munching cats.

"No." I turn to face her while rubbing what will soon become a nice-sized bump on the crown of my head. I return the authority to my voice and hope it stays there. "No, you can't say that." She once-upon-a-time was horrified if I even said *hell*, but turning thirteen gave her access to a new tier of YouTube videos and PG-13 movies, and now she wants nothing more than to let the obscenities fly.

"Why can you say it?"

"I'm the parent and before you go on about it, no, I don't have a different reason other than that, and I don't need a different reason other than that." One quick nod is meant to put the period at the end of the sentence and at the end of the debate. But Wren merely erases it.

"Why not?" she asks, her arms awkwardly crossed now. It is unnatural for her. Forced. Like an alien who was taught that crossing of arms meant defiance and it wishes to convey defiance to this human in order to keep its true lizard identity under wraps. "Why not?" she asks again.

"Because I'm the parent."

"You already said that." She narrows her eyes. "Are you concussed?" Wren reads too many medical sites. I make a mental note to restrict WebMD from her devices while she's at school.

"Eller?!" Again, that name. Shouted from below, the sound of it hollowing out as it enters the room from the open window. An auditory ghost calling out for its past.

"Fffff...." I catch myself as a huge smile spreads across Wren's face. The heathen. "...ffffffor gosh sakes, go get some breakfast ... consarn it."

"Pathetic. What's an Eller? Are you an Eller?" Wren's arms remain crossed and her eyes have further narrowed to slits.

"Go." I point toward the door.

"Because you're the parent?"

"Because I'm the parent."

"You already said that. Are you concuss—"

"Oh my God. Go." I shoo her.

As the door closes behind her self-satisfied chuckle, the ghost words hit my ears again. "Eller?! Come out!"

And in a snap, I am transported. A long-buried memory careens into my brain and smokes everyone out of the theater. There's only one showing today and it's *Ellis Marks, Age 10, 1990*. Only one ticket is available, and it has been sold ... to Ellis Sloan.

Please silence your phones.

Chapter Two

May 1990
Ellis, 10
Lincoln, 12

"Ellllerrrrr?! Come out, come out wherever you are, death breath!"

Ellis Marks crouched into a corner of her father's musty lawn shed. She was nestled between a stack of cracked snow sleds and an open bag of powder that smelled like a corpse. She'd seen her father sprinkling it on his garden plants and often wondered if he was trying to get things to grow or make things die. It seemed crazy to her that the answer wasn't more plain.

"Eller Beller kissed a feller ... and made him puke!" It didn't take but a moment for the sound of an obnoxious, delighted cackle to float into the shed. "I'm going to hit you so hard you're going to smell like this soccer ball for the rest of your life, Beller." Jerks always have such great voice projection and the words deftly found her ears. She knew it was only a matter of time before he would see the lock that was never latched—before he would open the double wooden doors to reveal her crouched in the corner like a trapped raccoon. Game over. *Here lies Ellis Marks, age 10, death by soccer ball at the hands of that walking zero Lincoln Hale.*

She scolded herself. The tree would have been the smart move. Wait for him to run past, then drop down quietly and sprint safely to home base three yards over where her four brothers and the two Delaney boys were probably already waiting. It wasn't going to look good that the only girl was dead last, and it would look worse if she never even made it back before being hunted down and smote in the spine with a soccer ball thrown with sufficient force to knock her breath out long enough to convince her she was dying.

There was a lot to curse as she sat wide-eyed in the dark. She cursed her poor decision. She cursed this stupid made-up game of soccer tag. She cursed her older brother Christopher for sprinting ahead of her on his stupid long legs. She cursed the entire animal kingdom for birthing whatever furry thing she heard scurry past her in the dark.

But she wasn't actually cursing. Swearing was off limits for the Marks children lest their father find out and make them memorize Bible verses about profanity before sitting them down and talking to them about love and light and God and goodness. Not swearing was always the easier path in the Marks household because the Marks household was run by Pastor David Marks of the Grace Christian Church on Margaret Road.

Ellis still had never uttered a single swear word. She couldn't even think one without feeling immediate remorse. Her brothers weren't as diligent as she. She'd heard Christopher shout, "I can't find my damn belt!" one morning, and by that evening his Atari was under her parents' bed and he had six new scriptures pinging around in what Ellis assumed was his otherwise empty brain.

And recently they had rented a VCR and took advantage of their distracted mother to add *Die Hard* to the pile of tapes—tucked safely between *Field of Dreams* and *The Karate Kid*, which Ellis had already watched four times. Her self-taught crane kick was a thing of beauty and she hoped to one day connect it to Lincoln Hale's quivering chin.

There was so much Ellis didn't get about *Die Hard*. So much that was truly dumb. But her brothers ate it up. And when John McClane said, "Yippee-kai-yay, motherfucker," two of them spewed food chunks and two of them went into coughing fits from going the other direction and inhaling. Ellis sat there in the potato-flavored spray and played the final scene of *The Karate Kid* in her mind's eye.

She couldn't imagine ever saying "fuck" and especially not the maternal-themed version of it like John McClane did. Thinking the word felt wrong. Saying it would probably feel like murder. But sitting there in the dark, on that day, in that corner of that dirty shed, the thought of murdering Lincoln Hale was enticing. Sure, it's one of the big sins, but how many scriptures could her dad make her learn if she was in prison serving several life sentences?

Not quite two years older than her, "the Hale boy" as her mother called him, was a ghoul. And he was just outside the shed door, she knew. Ready to fling it wide and spear her in the chest with a soccer ball and a gross cackle that would echo in her ears for days. She wouldn't have it. She pulled herself quietly from her crouch and shuffled to the shed doors, careful to avoid anything that smelled like death, anything currently alive, and anything loud enough to clatter out a confirmation of her hiding spot.

Her nose to the crack between the doors, she pushed one eye into the sliver of light to see Lincoln's chin a foot away. The chin she desperately wanted to crane kick. She didn't think. She acted. She threw her palms to the doors and pushed as hard as she could—every tease, insult, snicker and taunt loaded in her adrenaline cannon. The weathered doors exploded outward, swinging easily on hinges that were surprisingly well-oiled considering the shed's overall state of disarray.

She felt the moment of contact. Heard the crack followed by the shout. Saw the body awkwardly lurch backward before collapsing to the grass. She saw the dropped soccer ball roll away.

Then she saw blood.

She bolted with one thought racing through her brain as fast as she was running—*I am going to have to learn so many damn scriptures.*

Ellis Sloan Therapy Sessions

Gulf Tower
Pittsburgh, PA
May 2021

Dr. Parrish: Do you deserve to be happy?

Ellis: —

Dr. Parrish: Is that a hard question for you to answer?

Ellis: Well, do *you* deserve to be happy?

Dr. Parrish: My answer wouldn't be helpful to you.

Ellis: It feels impossible to answer. I know I should know that I deserve happiness, does that make sense? But I also know that I know I don't deserve it. I'm not saying it right.

Dr. Parrish: Why do you think that is? That you feel that way?

Ellis: That's what I'm hoping you'll tell me.

Dr. Parrish: I can't tell you anything.

Ellis: But—

Dr. Parrish: I'm going to try to show you though.

Chapter Three

October 2020

I text my mother.

Who did you rent the duplex to

And good morning to you!

Morning Who did you rent the duplex to

Incredibly, four minutes pass before she replies. *Inexcusable, Poppy. Unacceptable.*

To the Hale boy.

Lincoln Hale. Lincoln. Hale. I spend three minutes flailing around my bedroom, arms outstretched to the ceiling like I'm dancing for needed rain. Internally, I am yelling at Jesus, repenting to Jesus for yelling at Jesus, repenting to God in case Jesus is ignoring my calls, and questioning if I understand how the trinity works. I flop face-first onto my unmade bed with an overly dramatic bounce and let my body slink to the floor where I can sprawl my ruin out on my stomach. Lincoln Hale. Words and memories and feelings I've ignored since I was seventeen breach like zombies rising from the earth.

"Did you die?"

It's Dunn. Dunlin. I named both of my children after birds because their dad Oliver is a birder. That's a sentence I just typed. "Their dad Oliver is a birder." Had we a moment to do so, we'd ask, "What was loud, irreverent Ellis Marks doing falling in love with Oliver Sloan, the quiet history-loving birder eight years her senior?" We'll talk about that later. Right now, I'm dead.

"Not dead," I reply to my son with my voice muffled because my face remains smashed into the musty carpet. I should get it cleaned, but also, why? Cleaning a temporary home? Cleaning what only gets dirty again? Someone called that madness, didn't they? No thanks. Instead, I'll stay mostly sane and vacuum it every third Thursday.

Dunn turns and leaves the room. No offer of assistance. No questioning why his mother is spread-eagled on the floor looking like the opening scene of a crime procedural. While Wren faces all questions head-on with no buffer to shield her from the answers she doesn't want to hear, at sixteen, Dunn takes after me—head, meet sand. It's nice here. Knowledge doesn't live here in Bliss, where Oblivious is the president for life.

I turn my cheek to the carpet and drag my hand to look at the phone it still clutches.

> Christopher said he was looking for a place for a bit while he settles his father's estate.

> Not sure how long exactly.... I'll find a long-term renter once he leaves.

I told Chris to tell him to see you for the key....

I think he's coming next week. Be nice.....

Ellis?

The past is the past. Let it go.

Did you die? .....

Not dead. This is not punctuation --->
.... Stop it.

Wren enters my field of vision. She's changed out of her pajamas, but as usual, her clothes are horrible clashes of patterns that emit enough of a visual assault they seem to blink at you if you catch them from the corner of your eye. Quite possibly seizure-inducing. I'm still trying to teach her how to coordinate colors and patterns, but I've so far failed.

"Someone's knocking downstairs. Dunn is showering. Can I get it?"

"No!"

Wren slightly cowers at my shouted outburst, like a person who has been slapped once and is waiting for the next one to land on the backhand side. I should have known better. I curse myself and soothe in a soft voice. "No. No, I'll get it. Thanks, love. Gonna get up in a sec and go get it."

Wren ponders me for a moment. I've flipped onto my back but remain sprawled, staring at the ceiling, watching the blades of the wobbly fan whirl. She too looks at the ceiling then down at me. "Do you at least want me to poke my head out the window and shout down that you'll be there in one motherfu—"

"Wren!" There is no cowering this time. Just a smirk. She's messing with me and, in this instance, enjoys the banter because she was expecting the reaction. She walks away happily, with a soft skip and all her mysterious complexities—the fear she felt a moment ago completely erased. I call after her, "Your outfit is not leaving this house! Try again! Less patterns, less colors, less ... everything!"

Maybe I should stop buying her patterns. And colors. All black clothes. But the thought of Wren dressed in black unearths another Lincoln Hale zombie memory that wants to escape from its grave. I don't allow it. I shove that one back down too. But the thing about zombies is they're never buried forever. They'll always find a way to dig themselves out and force you to reckon with them, and often, it's not a happy reckoning.

If only there was a way to drive a knife into the brain of a memory, killing it forever.

I sigh at the ceiling. I guess I'll tuck my own fear away and answer the door like an adult. But after this I'm seriously considering a mayoral run for the town of Bliss: Population me, Dunn, and all the people who know that life's relentless shit is rarely worth dealing with.

Chapter Four

May 1990
Ellis, 10
Lincoln, 12

The living room of the Marks house was eerily quiet. Ellis took note of it and felt uneasy. It was church quiet. Library quiet. Outer space quiet.

Her parents sat on facing faded wing chairs adjacent to their lumpy living room couch which held the eldest three of their children and Lincoln Hale. All four sat slouched low with arms crossed defiantly. Ellis had a buffer of Nathan and Christopher shielding her from Lincoln at the far end near Poppy Marks, where he sat with crusted blood smeared across his nose and mouth. Ellis felt a grim satisfaction knowing she put it there. *Is this bloodlust*, she wondered.

A small stab of jealousy flared as she eyed her younger brothers. Lucas and Seth were relegated to the floor where they sat cross-legged near the large window, lounging easily and picking at the fibers of the worn carpet. They were clearly resting in the comfort of knowing their age would absolve them from any harsh punishment or blame. They were merely witnesses to the trial.

Standing beside Poppy's chair, Lincoln Hale's mother Jane cut an imposing figure to Ellis. A shadow across the room. Sentinel.

Tall. Strong. Confident. Chin-length black hair swept across her forehead then tucked behind her ear. Her clothes were black. Nearly always. The older children knew this because to them she was Mrs. Hale from school. The art teacher. The drama club advisor. She kept to black pants and black turtlenecks, only exchanging them for black skirts and blouses as the school year drew closed and the weather opened up.

To Ellis, who had been taking piano lessons from her for a year, she was two worlds. Lincoln's mother and Mrs. Hale. A wide smile and a slight scowl. A laugh and a *tsk*. Dark and serious. Bright and bold. Mysterious. Open. As she stood there in the Marks's living room, stretched to the full of her height, arms crossed easily over her chest, she was hard to read. Ellis chose to look away from her and instead looked down at her own legs where a bloodied knee poked out from her long shorts. She wondered if Lincoln was finding the same satisfaction at her blood as she felt from his.

Her father set his ever-present coffee cup gently on the coffee table and cleared his throat. Ellis sunk into her neck and hunched her shoulders to her ears. The trial would begin.

"Mrs. Hale," he started, "we thought it best we sit the children down and get to the bottom of this ... little tiff."

Ellis failed at holding in a derisive snort at the innocuous description of what she considered to be a declaration of war, but immediately quieted after a pointed glare from her mother.

Mrs. Hale, on the other hand, remained unreadable as she nodded her head once, never taking her gaze from her son who wouldn't look at her.

Ellis's father continued. "Now, children. Calmly. One at a time. Tell us what happe—"

This strategy proved unsuccessful when all four children on the couch sat forward and began shouting indecipherable accusations while throwing their arms and legs about in gestures ranging from aggressive pointing to kicking to air punching.

Ellis had been pantomiming a shoving movement when Mrs.

Hale's voice boomed through the room. "Children!" She gave out two loud claps of her hands, bringing total and immediate silence as Ellis, her brothers and Lincoln clamped their mouths shut and dutifully returned to their slouched arms-crossed postures as if their off-switches had been flipped.

David Marks's eyebrows shot up and he eyed their neighbor in wonderment. "Can you teach me that?"

Mrs. Hale merely motioned with an outstretched palm for him to continue. Ellis had thought her father was the judge, but now she was wondering if maybe he wasn't.

With her hands tucked neatly together at the waist of her faded floral dress, Poppy Marks leaned toward her husband. "Why don't you start with Lincoln? He is, after all, the one who is bleeding."

Ellis pulled herself to the edge of the couch seat and opened her mouth to remind her mother of the bloodied knee currently crippling her own flesh and blood, but she was quickly silenced by the outstretched hand of her father. He looked instead at Lincoln. "Tell us what happened."

"We were playing soccer tag and she hit me with the shed doors on purpose right in my face."

"It was not on purpose!" Ellis defensively searched the faces in the room for agreement or at least compassion but found none.

"You didn't open the doors on purpose?" Lincoln accused, suddenly a lawyer, making Ellis very aware that she was likely the defendant in this kangaroo court.

"I opened them on purpose. I didn't hit you on purpose!" Well, it was a little bit of a lie. Just a little. She had known he was there, hadn't she? She had known that the doors would probably hit him and that had been her intent, hadn't it? She said a prayer to God about her lie and slumped into the couch.

Her father held out his silencing hand once more. "That's enough, Ellis. If you interrupt him again, you'll have to go to your room until your turn."

She let out a grunt but stayed silent. Why leave the room to let

Lincoln spin lies her brothers probably wouldn't bother to refute on her behalf? A sad kick at the coffee table leg was her show of misery, to which not one of them seemed to have purchased a ticket. She felt abandoned.

"Go on, Lincoln," her mother encouraged with a traitorously kind smile.

"That's it. I was bleeding so I went home."

Ellis flung an arm toward the ceiling and waved it around dramatically. Nathan elbowed her and whispered, "You need to chill." But she answered him only with a glare and waved her arm more wildly. She would not stand for being falsely convicted. *This is America, is it not?*

She noticed her father sighed slightly before saying, "Okay, Ellis. Go ahead."

She leaned forward on the couch and exploded in a shout, "He is lying!" She glared at Lincoln across the bodies of her brothers. "You're a liar," she yelled with a growl in her throat.

This time, it was her mother who intervened. "Ellis! Stop accusing and tell us your side."

"After he fell, he got up and chased me and hit me in the back of the head with the soccer ball! So hard I nearly passed out! Look at my knee!" Tears burst from her eyes, and she felt the trail of shame they burned down her cheeks, but there was nothing she could do to stop them.

"Is this true, Lincoln?" Jane Hale demanded sternly of her son, her voice low.

Ellis swiped at her tears and awaited the deep satisfaction she would feel when he had to admit the rest of the story. She hoped it was so sweet it rotted her next cavity. She'd even get it filled without Novocain. *Just drill, Dr. Bowers. I can handle it.*

Lincoln found a spot on the yellow window curtains and kept his gaze there. He gave no answer or even an indication he'd heard her.

"Lincoln. Is that true?" his mother asked again, louder. "Did you chase Ellis down and hit her in the head with the ball?"

"No. She must have tripped when she ran away. She's lying."

The power of the lie hit Ellis fully in her chest. She didn't know it was happening until it happened, and the word was sitting in her mouth and then ejecting itself out into the world on her tongue. "Motherfucker!"

There was a beat of silence as the four syllables and its chosen punctuation mark sliced through the air one-by-one. Moth. Er. Fuck. Er. Exclamation point. A lot of very quiet things bounced around the room in the space of a second or two. A breath. A blink. A wide-eyed gape. An intake of air. A casual arm motion frozen. A mouth popped open in a perfect O.

But when you've done the thing. Said the thing. Threw the verbal grenade into the thing. Well, everything slowed down for Ellis Marks, and that one second seemed like a hundred lifetimes. Time screeched to a near halt. The sun set and rose a hundred thousand times in that one second. Glaciers melted. Species evolved. Suns died. Angels fell. Galaxies were born.

Ellis blinked.

Blinked.

Blinked.

And then a lot of loud things happened at once, and for as long as she lived, Ellis knew she would never forget a single detail of it. Some memories are painted in watercolor—a softer, more soothing representation of what had been a harsh reality. Some memories are pencil sketches that fade and smudge with time. And some are etched into diamond-hard surfaces in exact detail that will outlast any lifetime. This memory was etched. Forever.

Poppy Marks, the leader of the Wednesday Ladies Bible Study, ever and always the picture of grace and decorum, yelled—"Ellis Robin Marks!"—then slapped a hand over her own heart, letting out a sound that sounded like a gasp trying to hold down a rising gag.

Pastor David Marks, the picture of steadfastness and quiet resoluteness, burst from his chair so quickly he startled the family cat Cutesy who had been lounging in disinterest on the back of the couch. Cutesy leapt at his face—claws extended, fangs bared, destruction intended. A ferocious meow ripped through the room right before Ellis's father's face disappeared behind a launched ball of fluffy fury.

Lincoln Hale let out a "Holy sh—" then clamped a hand over his mouth to stop the rest of the swear from escaping. His eyes immediately grew wide, his eyebrows high.

Nathan exclaimed, "Oh, God," and then slinked low into the couch where he covered his face with one hand. A smile erupted larger and larger over Christopher's face until every one of his too-big teeth could be visually checked for tartar. He pulled the front of his t-shirt over his head and began laughing hysterically into it. Lucas and Seth, as if wired with shared operating instructions, leapt up and sprinted past their father who was trying in vain to pull the hissing cat from his face. The sound of a door slamming cut into the room a beat later.

But. Jane Hale. She managed to do the quietest and somehow most noticeable thing at once. As the room descended into chaos all around her—cat aflight, bodies flailing, shouting, running, slamming—she slowly lowered her head and raised a hand to cover what Ellis swore looked like a laugh about to explode out of her lips.

Ellis Sloan Therapy Sessions

Gulf Tower
Pittsburgh, PA
May 2021

Ellis: He was always quiet, you know? He was a graduate TA when we met at Pitt. A history TA at that. So, you know, quiet. Sedate. Here I come along, loud, brash, a mouth. We shouldn't have clicked. I mean, I was a preacher's kid from a big family with constant money struggles. His family owns wineries in New York. We should have been the north poles of two magnets—impossible to come together. But we did. It seemed that as the years ticked by, he got even quieter and expected the same from me. When I wasn't quiet—when I told the loud joke at a work event, he hated it. We'd come home and he'd punish me. Silence. Lectures. All those same punishments would happen if I went out with my own friends. He'd become this weird tinder box—ready to explode at the smallest thing. So I stopped getting together with my friends. They fell away, and I was fine with it. It was easier to keep him happy. To be nice, quiet Ellis on his arm while he talked with his professor colleagues about, I don't know, the Bolsheviks or some boring shit like that—

Dr. Parrish: Let me stop you a second. It's interesting you used the word "punish."

Ellis: I did? Oh. Well, I mean, it wasn't a "punishment" punishment.

Dr. Parrish: Did you think it normal for one partner to regularly punish the other?

Ellis: Well, he wasn't hitting me or anything.

Dr. Parrish: I know you know one can punish with words, Ellis.

Chapter Five

October 2020

Had I looked in the mirror before heading to the door, I would have noticed my hair. I would have seen the chaos of it. The knots, the sleep frizz, the disorganized mass of curls shamelessly jutting out in all directions, proud of how screwed up they managed to get overnight. Had I looked in the mirror, I would have seen my splotchy face, my errant eyebrow hairs. I'd have noticed my cheek lined with sheet marks and my puffy eyebags into which I could tuck the spare next-door key for safekeeping.

Had I looked in the mirror, I would have seen the stain of something brown on my beloved vintage *Jurassic Park* t-shirt, the pockets turned inside-out on my black yoga shorts. Actually, I would have seen my yoga shorts were inside-out and that a "Medium" tag was announcing the size of my ass and the state of my life to the world. *Medium.*

But I didn't because looking in mirrors is for women who don't have the knots and frizz and bags and chaos and scar. So, when I finally fling the front door open on Lincoln Hale, he stiffens into a momentary frozen pause and pulls back slightly, like a person who opened their credit card bill to be confronted with the consequences of their seasonal depression taking advantage of MasterCard's trust.

Me. The human equivalent of seasonal depression. Ellis Sloan. A sack of disorganized chaotic frazzle. Very, very Medium.

Him. My childhood's Lincoln Hale. To the rest of the world, Kennedy Hale. The only thing chaotic about him in this moment is the jumping around his eyeballs are doing as they hunt for a safe place to land. *The hair! The clothes! The eyebrow! Why's it doing that?!*

But there are no safe places on Ellis Sloan. *Not anymore, buddy.*

He finds his voice and injects familiarity into it. "It *was* you, Eller."

"Ellis," I correct, as I had done countless times in my teenage years with him—this risen zombie memory standing at my door.

He looks zero percent chagrined at my correction, which 100 percent annoys me. "Right. Ellis! The famous Ellis Sloan." He throws his hands to his chest. "It's me, Kennedy." As if I don't know him. As if we don't have a history. As if he's not famous for his role on the long-running, recently ended CBS show *Dewey* in which he played a dying librarian who discovers he can time-jump into the fiction books that have never been checked out. As if my mother didn't text me every Sunday to tell me the weekly episode's plot despite me never having watched one minute of the show.

Lincoln Hale informing me of his name is akin to a brother knocking on my door to say, "It's me, Nathan." *No shit, buddy. I'm aware.*

"Your name is Lincoln," I correct him out of the evilness of my own heart.

You'd think that would chagrin a person, but no, Lincoln Hale marches right on without so much as an awkward pause. The confidence his looks and talent gave him when we were younger was apparently now only stronger thanks to wealth and fame. "Yes! I always forget who knows me by my real name. I bet Beyoncé feels this way sometimes." He chuckles. The drums in my ear beat *douche.*

Wren suddenly appears at my side holding what is probably a cold Pop-Tart. Her new outfit of choice is slightly less likely to create a medical emergency in an elderly passer-by at the grocery store. "Beyoncé's real name is Beyoncé," she informs matter-of-factly while pointing her pastry at him. Then she looks at me quizzically. "He called you famous. Are you famous?"

"Absolutely not," I insist.

Lincoln looks at Wren, startled, but quickly composes himself and says, "Right. Of course. You know me as Lincoln, so Lincoln I am. Pick a president, any president, right?" No chagrin. March on through the cloud of awkwardness. *Hup-two-three-four.* He stuffs his hands in his jean pockets and rocks onto the heels of his shoes. "Been a crazy morning. Christopher said you'd have a key for me?"

"Yes, I saw you killed your piano. Poppy said you were coming next week."

"I'll call you Fillmore," Wren interjects. "What's Eller?"

Lincoln again darts his eyes between us—the two ladies Sloan—and decides to wade into uncertainty with Wren rather than certainty with me, because I'm the one who holds some of his past buried deep inside of her.

"Fillmore?" he asks Wren. "Can I object? And to answer your question, Eller is what we called your ... mom?" He ends his sentence with the word raised in a question and glances at me for confirmation that this slightly shorter version of me is mine.

I nod once. "This is Wren."

He smiles. "Wren. A bird."

Wren points at him deliberately and says with sincerity, "Very good." I nearly explode in a laugh. Her impression of a teacher praising a student was spot on, as all her impressions are, especially remarkable since she's never aware she slips into them.

He spends a beat trying to read her meaning but gives up.

"Eller Beller. That's what we all called her when we were growing up."

I don't interrupt. I don't even blink out of turn. But inside, I've charged the stage, grabbed the microphone, tapped it loudly three times until shrill feedback careened through the dark smoky room, and I shouted into it, *They did not all call me that! Only you called me that, Lincoln Hale!* Then I unfolded my middle finger to the audience of one, selfsame Lincoln Hale, and threw back a shot of something amber and burny before stalking off the stage with a growl.

Ah, perchance to dream. No, Ellis Sloan with the chaos is still Ellis Marks with the parents who taught her manners, several of which remain with her to this day.

"I'll get the key." I leave him to chat with Wren and hope against all the hope in the world that she does what only she can do —make an adult squirm under the glare of her uncomfortable questions and smart, always accurate direct observations. On one hand, I try to teach her good social skills, but on the other hand ... *get him, Wrennie.*

I venture a glance into the previously avoided hallway mirror as I pass, recoil in an appropriate amount of horror, skip a few stages of grief and then give my reflection a shrug of acceptance. The ark has been opened; this was what was inside; hope it melts his whole face off.

When I return, I hear a negotiation taking place.

"Garfield?" Wren offers.

"That's a cat," Lincoln rejects, leaning easily against the door jamb, his hands still in his pockets. Effortlessly cool. Show-offy bastard showing off his effortless coolness while I'm a chaotic Medium.

"But also a president," Wren says with a mouth full of Pop-Tart. I make a quick mental note to refocus a bit on eating manners with her.

"Roosevelt?" comes his counteroffer. "I like Roosevelt."

"Which one?"

"Does it matter?"

"It does. But not Roosevelt. Roosevelt is what you name a bird. Taft?"

"The fat one?"

"Don't body shame," she scolds. "But he was enormous. 350 pounds. That's as much as a reindeer. Hoover?"

"What am I, a vacuum?" He cuts his eyes with a slitted gaze to see my mouth already halfway open, and points at me. "Don't answer that." I'm pleased he recalls what kind of person I was. "Grant," he says to Wren.

"Arthur."

He pushes his shoulder off the doorjamb. "You know what? I'm going to leave it up to you. But not Arthur. That's an aardvark." He glances at me with eyebrows raised in expectation. Ah. The look I've come to know. An adult begging me to rescue them from Wren. She'll never engage a person if they are in a group, but may God throw his mercies upon souls if she corners you one-on-one. She once psychoanalyzed her guidance counselor so accurately I got a defensive email. And one of her fixations since she was seven when she visited a wax statue exhibit has been the presidents of the United States. Dozens of books in her room on them have been read more than once. Her ability to memorize anything meant, left to her own, she could have stood there for an hour trying to pick the perfect name for the man whose real name is Lincoln but who had a SAG card that said Kennedy.

"So, the key?" He lets his half-sentence fall away in the space between us.

I hold a closed hand out and dump six random but similar-looking door keys into his palm. "It's one of those. Probably. Likely. Should be."

He looks at the keys then at me, questions written on his face—all of them unanswerable—and thoughts written in his eyes—all of them judging what stands in front of him against what he long-ago left behind. His gaze settles a beat too long on the scar on my chin and I involuntarily try to shrug off the discomfort.

"Right," he says, snapping to while folding his fingers around the keys that I secretly hope don't work because I'm in the mood to create a little mayhem on this planet today. "Thanks, then. I guess I'll see you two ladies. I've got a piano to go rescue."

I smile the fakest smile I can as I begin closing the door on him.

"Bye, Truman!" Wren calls after him as he jogs down the porch steps, spreading the keys out on one of his palms.

"Who was that?" Dunn appears at the foot of the steps behind us, hair still wet from his shower.

"Kenned—I mean Lincoln," I correct myself with a shake of my head.

"No. It's Truman," Wren says.

Dunn pauses as he's about to bite into his own Pop-Tart, then rolls his eyes and mutters, "You guys are so weird."

Wren watches him head toward the kitchen and turns to me. "Are we weird?"

"Oh, Wrennie. Very much so. But we can still work on you. I'm done cooking."

"Cooking what?"

I smile at her. "Never mind."

When I'm back in my bedroom, I grab my glasses from my nightstand to peek out the window once more. This time, instead of thrusting my head out and screaming holy hell for all the neighborhood to hear, I try to conceal myself behind the curtains. Voices drift from below. The piano still rests on its back, and Lincoln is helping the moving men lift it into an upright position. It lands with a thud loud enough to make me cringe at the thought of the internal damage it might have sustained.

Lincoln stands at the keys with his hands on his hips, his shoulders lifting and then falling in a deep slow sigh. With his neck bent, he reaches his right hand down and effortlessly plays a bright, high melody that drifts upward and billows around me as he repeats it in a fast crawl down to the lower keys, apparently testing for damage. I shiver and remember another time I heard a similar melody played out absentmindedly like that.

Lincoln Hale takes up space in so many of the memories I wish to forget, but standing there watching him from above, I can't help but wonder if the piano below is the one I sat at many Wednesdays as a child—his mother Jane Hale's.

Chapter Six

August 1990
Ellis, 10
Lincoln, 12

"Have you practiced your piece this week, Ellis?"

Ellis nestled her open piano book into the grooves of Mrs. Hale's polished upright piano and settled herself onto the wooden bench. "Uh. Yeah. Some."

For as much as Ellis hated the guts of Lincoln Hale, she loved going to his house for her weekly piano lesson. While her own house was always swept up in varying degrees of disarray—at no fault of her mother's and at every fault of the five children aged seven to fourteen who lived there—the Hale house soothed Ellis.

It was three backyards and a quick cut through a narrow wood away, but to Ellis, it was another world. Lincoln's father worked a night shift at the airport, so he slept days and woke for dinner. Her lessons were on Wednesday evenings at 5:00. While Lincoln was off with Christopher and Mr. Hale slept and the rest of her brothers did their own sports and activities, Ellis walked alone to the Hales. She would feel a calm settle on her breath as soon as she saw the yellow brick house with the porch that stretched across it. It was no bigger than her house, but so much different.

Ellis guessed Mrs. Hale felt cooped being inside a school all day because on many lesson days, Ellis would find her outside when she arrived. In the spring, Mrs. Hale would be mulching or cutting the already-neat grass with a push lawnmower. Ellis always marveled at the grass with no weeds—grass you could sprint barefoot through without worry of bee stings or the cutting prickles of sharp weeds that only disappeared with winter's arrival.

In the summer, she'd find Mrs. Hale wearing her usual black clothing with a bright red silk scarf patterned in tiny silver stars and comets tied around her hair. She'd be tending to her garden, watering her lawn, planting green shoots in large porch pots that eventually overflowed like colorful waterfalls of rainbowed flowers until summer's dying gasps.

Ellis had once arrived to find Mrs. Hale perched high on a ladder using comically large fireplace tongs to remove a small dead animal from the roof gutter. Ellis had been unaware until that day how truly awful death smelled. She had pinched her nose closed as Mrs. Hale, safely returned to the ground, dropped the unidentifiable twisted corpse into a garbage bag before tossing the tongs in after. "'Tis a vile thing to die," she had said with dramatic finality.

Winters meant finding her sitting on her porch steps, her warm breath hitting cold air to halo out in puffs around her. She'd keep her eyes on the early dark sky looking for stars that sometimes didn't shine through Pittsburgh's heavy cloud blanket for a week. When it did finally break apart to reveal the heavens to her, she'd point a planet or star out to Ellis, who always pretended to care.

The inside of the Hale house was kept as neatly as the outside. Tabletops held one item or nothing at all, which struck Ellis as odd because wasn't that the purpose of tables? To hold things? At her house, tables near beds and couches were cluttered with six or seven vacation mementos or picture frames of gap-toothed school pictures.

There was nothing on the kitchen counters at the Hale's but a toaster and a crock of mixing spoons and spatulas. The iced tea

Mrs. Hale would offer to Ellis was poured into a short glass painted with little white daisies.

"Let's hear what we have, then. Go ahead now." Mrs. Hale took her place on a small round stool next to the piano bench. She straightened her back and closed her eyes to listen.

Ellis started tentatively and was only a few measures in when she heard, "No. B flat." Then a few measures later, "No. D major chord."

Ellis adjusted her fingers and tried again.

"No. D major, dear."

The third try was as unsuccessful as the first two, and Ellis let her wrists collapse discordantly to the keys with an audible sigh of frustration. Mrs. Hale flipped her eyes open to gently adjust Ellis's middle finger and thumb to the correct keys. "There. Close your eyes."

She did as bade.

"Play the chord. Again. Good. Again. Do you hear it? Shift your thumb one key either direction. Play it. Do you hear that? The change?"

Ellis stayed silent so as not to lie, because for as sure as she was that dead animals stink an otherworldly stink, she was sure there was no discernable difference between the two chords. Mrs. Hale's eyes popped open once more and she tilted her head at Ellis in question. "Do you hear it, Ellis?"

"No," she admitted dejectedly. "I just don't think I'm good at music."

Mrs. Hale shook her head with a small smile. "Everyone is good at music. We are humans and therefore we are nature, and nature is what gave us music to begin with. We are all good at music." She slowly emphasized every word of her last sentence.

Ellis eyed her blankly.

"Close your eyes again, child. Good. Listen to my words." Her voice returned to Ellis's ears softer and higher, with a soothing cadence. "There's music in the sighing of a reed; there's music in the gushing of a rill; there's music in all things, if men had ears; Their earth is but an echo of the spheres."

When she heard her teacher's voice catch at the air on "spheres," Ellis opened her eyes to find that Mrs. Hale's were closed. Written plainly across her face was a look of pinched sadness that Ellis understood even less than the meaning of the poem.

Ellis cleared her throat to break the uncomfortable and serious silence. Mrs. Hale erased her sadness with a quickly spreading smile and flipped open her eyes. They were wide and shiny. "That was Byron. Have you ever read Byron, Ellis?"

Ellis thought of the stack of R.L. Stine books on the cluttered table by her bed. "I'm going to say probably ... no." She ended with a comically definitive nod of her head.

Mrs. Hale let out a loud laugh, surprising Ellis who flushed with pride at being able to pull it from her. Her teacher quickly quieted though, pulling her laugh back into herself as if she hadn't meant to share it. "Ellis, music is music, just like math is math—but other things are math and other things are music. Do you understand?"

Ellis made no effort to feign understanding and shook her head.

"Well, this is music." Mrs. Hale flitted her left hand easily on the high keys, playing out a quick airy melody. "But the Byron I spoke to you? That's about how nature gives us music, too, if we only listen for it. And math? Well, there's math in nature—in the hexagons of beehives, in the petals of the flowers. In the daisies." She picked up Ellis's water glass painted with the very flower. "So, you aren't bad at music any more than a bee is bad at math. It is inside you. Naturally. You will train your ear to hear it. But you must practice, or perhaps you won't ever find it, okay?"

Ellis nodded and realized she had somehow been walked backward into a "practice more" lecture. Sneaky.

Outside, after offering a solemn vow to practice 20 minutes a day, she eyed the daisies basking in the hot sun in a neat weed-free bed near Mrs. Hale's walkway. She crouched down to rest on the balls of her feet, hugging her music book to her chest. She studied the white petals and wondered where the math was. She closed her eyes and wondered where the music was.

"What the hell are you doing?"

Ellis's eyes flew open to find Lincoln standing on the walkway a few feet away, his backpack slung over one shoulder. She stood quickly, embarrassed to have been found like that—hunched and shuttered. Earnest. Listening so hard for something she felt she was supposed to hear but couldn't. Looking for something she was supposed to find but couldn't.

With pursed lips, she threw her chin high. She had made a solemn vow to never speak to him after the lie he told that day three months ago. That lie everyone still believed. She was older now. Wiser. She was practically reading Byron.

She marched past him with her music book tucked tightly under her arm should he get the idea to smack it out of her hands. She saw his eyes roll. "You're just never going to say anything to me again? Ever?" he asked. She turned to be sure he saw the glare on her face and then continued her walk. Chin high, shoulders back. "Go ahead. Stay quiet. I have no complaints about that. You're not even—"

Ellis took off running toward home, leaving his remaining words to fall behind her, taking away their power so they'd die unheard.

His mother would be dead four months later.

Ellis Sloan Therapy Sessions

Gulf Tower
Pittsburgh, PA
May 2021

Ellis: I can't write anymore. I don't know how. I sit there. Nothing comes.

Dr. Parrish: And when you wrote *Luca Rex*, you just sat there, and it came to you? Out of nothingness? Neat trick.

Ellis: Well, not nothingness.

Dr. Parrish: Then what? What were you feeling that drove you to write?

Ellis: I guess it came out of sadness. Some anger. Confusion. Fear.

Dr. Parrish: Emotions you were reckoning with? Open to?

Ellis: Yeah.

Dr. Parrish: What emotions do you reckon with now? What emotions are you pulling out from their hiding places and confronting head-on?

Ellis: —

Dr. Parrish: Think about it. I'll see you next week?

Chapter Seven

November 2020

Looking forward to seeing your first ten chapters next Monday. Bea.

I am pouring myself a second cup of coffee after sending Wren and Dunn to the bus stop, him to high school, her to middle school, when the text message sends my heart into the weird adrenaline lurch hearts do when they confront danger. Except in this instance, it's not danger; it's dread. It's anxiety. It's me not wanting to disappoint Bea a week from today but knowing for certain that I will.

I consider not returning her text, but that never works with Bea. For one, she's dogged, as agents must be. Unfortunately for me, the doggedness that landed my first book deal, and the advance with my second, is also the doggedness that insists I stick to a writing schedule. But secondly, she's Oliver's aunt. She's family—sort of. I decide to be evasive.

I love that you still insist on signing your texts

Evading. Bea.

Intentional. Ellis.

Shall I fly down?

She's based in upstate New York, and I love her, I do, but for a sixty-something grandma type, she's terrifying and you definitely don't want her to "fly down" and look at you with disappointment in her warm eyes while wearing her usual attire that seems counterintuitive for a cold-blooded ender of souls—colorful patterned dresses under sweetly innocent cardigans. It's all a Mister Rogers-type facade meant to fool others into thinking they can win negotiations with her if they only keep a bowl of butterscotch candies and the final issue of *Ladies Home Journal* in the waiting lobby.

I don't believe Bea Bancroft has lost anything she wanted to win in her life.

Hell no

Okay, looking forward to seeing what you have in a week. My love to the people you love. Bea.

I stamp my foot onto the kitchen garbage can pedal to flip open the metal lid and then toss my phone in. The lid shuts with a satisfying snap and I smile in relief.

No, I'm not going to have ten chapters seven days from now. I'm not going to have even ten words. I have five words. A working title. *Ellis Sloan Untitled Book Two*. It used to be called *Book Two*. Then *Untitled Book Two*. At the rate I'm going, soon I'll have a 50-word book title and zero words of actual book.

I don't have any words, but I have hours and hours spent at my laptop, staring at a blank document with a mocking cursor rhythmically blinking out *you-suck you-suck you-suck you-suck.* I have whole mornings spent with my forefingers resting on the F and J keys, my middle finger resting below the E key that no longer has an E on it after I wore it away writing the 103,000 words of my first book. I have dozens of days I never could bring myself to sit at my computer at all because I knew no words would flow from my brain to my heart to my hands except me angrily typing the phrase "fuck all this shit" over and over until I slammed the laptop closed and instead napped while the kids were at school. I don't have ten chapters; what I have is a mildly successful first novel—that I hate—published two years ago. I have a $15,000 advance on my second novel, of which I have written zero words despite ten chapters being expected by Bea in a week.

I have a box of copies of *Luca Rex: For Now* that I'll probably donate to local influencer giveaways with my terrible autograph scribbled on the title page. I have a base of adoring teen to thirty-something mostly female fans who fell in love with my ridiculous angsty story of the teenage girl with the shitty life who met an angel who screwed her life up even more. I have a deep regret that instead of publishing a real book that told a believable story with complex characters using the humor I like to write with, I wrote a fantasy YA book that taught these girls that the bad things in life will eventually lead to good things.

I have a new life of bad things that will never become good things, and I have countless headaches, and I have an impending divorce, and I have the painful memory that moved in next door more than a week ago who I haven't seen since, and so I'm beginning to question if I conjured the whole thing in my empty brain for want of filler, but his midnight blue BMW remains parked against the curb along the sidewalk in front of the house, so maybe I don't have a hallucination, but I do have zombie memories that have become nearly supernatural in their resurrectionary strength since he arrived.

I have a lot of things, I do.

But I do not have a viable marriage to your nephew, and I definitely do not have ten chapters, Bea.

Signed, Ellis.

Chapter Eight

January 1991
Ellis, 10
Lincoln, 12

A body is not a person.

Mrs. Hale would be the first body Ellis Marks ever saw, but she felt like she had watched her slowly die for a few months.

It wasn't long after the lesson where Ellis heard Byron that a change happened. Ellis noticed first that she wasn't offered any iced tea in dainty glasses. She then noticed that the grass grew longer than normal. Flowers that overflowed their pots on the pristine porch started to wilt and die. Unswept tree detritus gathered in pockets along the walls of the front porch. The daisies in the bed withered to nothing and took their imaginary math with them.

Ellis saw a usually empty tabletop near the piano holding a tall glass with an inch of water next to a prescription bottle that never seemed to move. She saw her bright, tall, strong teacher slowly dim, shrink into herself, and weaken. Her eyes were rimmed with dark circles and her smile became shadowed with pain. She no longer seemed to hear the mistakes Ellis was making, and Ellis no longer heard Byron.

Ellis took hard to practicing, newly dedicated to making Mrs. Hale proud. To make her smile once more. To pull that elusive hard laugh. To erase a little bit of whatever stain had settled upon her teacher. One autumn day, Ellis left a lesson that had ended early and abruptly to find Lincoln quietly watering the porch flowers with his mother's metal watering can in a vain attempt to resurrect what was surely dead. She had walked wordlessly past him, her chin low this time, and he let her go with no taunt to chase after her. She left him standing there, quietly pouring life-giving water on black stems that could no longer drink salvation.

Some weeks, Ellis's Wednesday lesson became a Thursday lesson. Then a Friday lesson. Then they stopped. Ellis's mother answered her questions in short sentences. "She's under the weather." "Soon." "Maybe next week." "She's feeling tired." "She's resting."

Then one day, softly, with pain, "Honey, she died."

Just like that. She. Died. A person who was there, no longer was. Something that existed, didn't anymore.

While their father reassured him with words about the promises of heaven, Christopher had cried bitterly into their mother's lap, and Ellis didn't know if it was for the erasing of Mrs. Hale from the Earth, or for his friend whose mother had been the one erased.

Shaken at the sight of her brother in pain from a wound she couldn't see, Ellis retreated quietly to her room where she sat cross-legged on her bed and did not cry, for she felt she had merely watched a shutter that had been slowly closing for months finally blot out the last sliver of light.

She stared at the ceiling for a long time, listening to the activity of the rest of her family beyond her door. She didn't like the new and foreign heaviness she felt building inside of her, intruding on the ease of her life. She wondered what it was and how long it would last. Sleep would not come for her that night because she couldn't shake the nagging feeling that she had been at the beginning of something really good, only to have it end before she was ready.

Ellis Sloan Therapy Sessions

Gulf Tower
Pittsburgh, PA
June 2021

Dr. Parrish: Were you ever physically afraid of him?

Ellis: Only twice.

Dr. Parrish: "Only."

Chapter Nine

November 2020

I awake shortly into the second hour of the nap I took to avoid thinking about Bea's texts from earlier and her threat to gauge my progress, and likely my mental health, face-to-face. She and my publisher are expecting another book about Luca Rex and her angel, because I ended my first book hinting at forthcoming drama for the pair, going so far as to print a one-scripture coda on the final page— "... war arose in heaven." A harbinger. A claim. *There's more. Just you wait.*

But there's no more. Before I could decide what the war would entail, my marriage fell apart, and I died alive. The dead can't create, so I killed all the characters I thought I loved, and I buried them under six feet of cynicism. Luca's story was over because some stories are meant to just end and isn't that what life is anyway? Living story after story, some long, some short, each one ending at a transition point, often before we're ready, and sometimes long after we had hoped they would? I ended the *Luca Rex* story. She's gone forever. My only hope is to find a new story worthy of my contract, my advance, my agent, and my name.

But I look; I don't find. I've found nothing inside of nothing on top of nothing, adjacent to nothing buried beneath a thousand layers of nothing.

After I had tossed my phone into the garbage, I thought perhaps a dream would inspire me to write, so I collapsed onto the couch. But I was sent useless dreams, unless I'm writing a book about grocery shopping while buck naked. I'm desperate though, so I'll put that one in my pocket just in case. I'll call it *Cans in Aisle 5; Boobs in Aisle 6*.

I'm sleep-drugged and still sprawled on my couch staring at the ceiling, thinking up ways I can scrounge together enough money to pay back the half of the advance I mostly already spent on a divorce lawyer and affording life with two teenagers when a knock raps against the door. I lie still hoping it's FedEx letting me know they're leaving a package—even though I know in my brain I haven't ordered a thing lately. But the heart is the more hopeful organ.

I listen. It's quiet. Nothing.

Relieved, I exhale and close my eyes again.

A familiar voice calls from the other side of the door, "El?"

Fuck. Christopher. I bolt to my feet in a panic and then grab my head with both hands as darkness tries to close in on the heels of a headrush. Fuck. I fight my way out of it with a near stumble and look down to confirm I'm still in my pajamas despite it being eleven in the morning. Damn my own laziness. Damn my emptiness. Damn my brother. What kind of sociopath drops in without letting others know first? Other than our mother, of course. Poppy follows no one's rules but her own, and her rules say *I will show up when I want and you will be absolutely delighted to see me.*

I become like a kitchen roach caught in the flood of a light flipped on in the dead of night, except I don't know which way to scurry. Do I sprint to my bedroom and try to change my clothes, fix my chaos, and fly back downstairs to answer the door in under thirty seconds like Mary Fucking Poppins? Do I bolt out the kitchen door and run barefoot through the backyard and down the alley and hope no one phones Western Psych? Do I use the decorative living room mirror to gauge the level of my disaster and try to fix it the best I can with spit, finger combs and prayer?

"El?" The knock is louder, and Christopher's voice is mixed with a hint of worry. There is no time for me to rectify the state of my existence.

I spy my laptop resting on the coffee table and clutch it to my braless chest like a highschooler's textbook. My 34Cs are now being fully supported by a 15-inch MacBook that I once used to write something but that now contains nothing. "Coming!" I inject brightness into my voice in an attempt to remove the worry from his.

Chris has his life together neater than a stack of Pringles. He fled to California as soon as he graduated high school, got his nursing degree, his RN, worked his way through several hospital systems in various cities along the southern California coast, added additional abbreviations after his name, the meaning of which I don't even know, and stayed friends with Lincoln through it all. He returned home to work at a busy ER after Dad died five years ago. His apartment is neat, his car is spotless, his bills paid, and his friends loyal. I spent more than a decade seeing him twice a year, and now he feels perfectly comfortable showing up at my front door unannounced at 11:00 a.m. on a random Monday.

Someone better be dead.

With my laptop held to my chest and an excuse forming in my head to explain my appearance and general lack of togetherness to my extremely together brother, I fling open the front door with a huge, fake smile on my clearly bleary-eyed just-woke-up face ...

... to find Chris standing next to a grinning Lincoln Hale.

I wish I were the one who was dead.

Chapter Ten

January 1991
Ellis, 10
Lincoln, 12

A body is surely not a person.

Asleep forever in a coffin that looked creepy despite its shiny wood exterior and seemingly soft pillowy interior, Mrs. Hale wasn't wearing her usual black. It weirdly angered Ellis. She was sure her teacher would be unhappy with the orange and blue floral dress she was in. Ellis didn't want to use the word "wearing" because it seemed to her that you couldn't really "wear" something you didn't put on yourself. Mrs. Hale had merely been "dressed." Ellis imagined Mrs. Hale would have called the ridiculous dress her teacher's favorite word of all ... vile.

The black circles that had appeared under Mrs. Hale's eyes over the past few months were gone. But so was the brightness and the light and the boldness and the mystery and the openness. Everything that made her warm and glowing had burned out, leaving Ellis staring at a cold waxy statue of the woman who had told her to find the music and math in the world around her. This was not her teacher. This was not her neighbor from three backyards and a narrow wood away. This was not the woman she had made laugh. This was a doll who had been dressed and who would be planted beneath the earth in an outfit she hated for the rest of eternity.

It made Ellis furious.

Funeral homes were awful places, she decided. The smell. The ornate decorations. The weird curtains in places curtains shouldn't be. The hushed voices and the sad smiles and the tears and the muffled sobs. Green carpets and pink walls and gold doorknobs. She hadn't wanted to come and for sure didn't think she should be forced to look at a dead body, but her father had determined the whole of the Marks family must appear. He was, after all, the minister Lincoln's father had chosen for the funeral. He would talk of heaven and hope, and Ellis would try her hardest to believe him, for perhaps it was faith in the unknowable that would erase the new heaviness she carried with her since her teacher died.

So the entire Marks clan filed past the sign directing them toward "Viewing for Jane Kennedy Hale." Ellis saw the casket, what was inside of it, and immediately wanted to leave the room and even the whole building and the street block that held it. That was not a "who" in that coffin; it was a "what." And it terrified her.

She took note of the small thin man wearing a too-large brown suit standing near the corner of her teacher's final bed. Ellis guessed this was Lincoln's father. He looked weak, the opposite of Mrs. Hale who was tall, proud, and intentional in her words and actions in every single moment Ellis knew her until four months ago. This man seemed to have life happening to him, but Mrs. Hale always seemed to be happening to life.

After dutifully and wordlessly shaking the small man's hand as her parents had instructed, Ellis hurried out of the room with the death in it. She weaved through the clusters of adults quietly conversing in the hallway with sadness etched on their every word. A soft chuckle could be heard within one group, and Ellis felt a new surge of anger. In that moment, what could be worthy of a laugh? Far down the hallway, she saw Lincoln sitting with Christopher on a couch tucked against a wall.

Their eyes set into the opposite wall, they sat silently with their hands folded in their laps. Ellis never considered before that a parent could die—or that anyone she knew could die, for that matter. Imagining one of her parents becoming a doll someone else dressed and then buried low into the ground filled her brain with a dark noise she couldn't mute.

She sat with her brother and Lincoln and became as they were. Silent. Hands folded in her lap. Eyes on the weirdly pink wall. Heaviness all upon her. Dark noise bouncing in her head. She suspected this was all too much for a 10-year-old. She wondered what it was for a 12-year-old but didn't dare look at Lincoln's face to find out.

"I saw a table back there," Christopher said quietly to Lincoln. "You want some water?"

Lincoln only nodded and Christopher rose, leaving Ellis to sit in stony silence with his friend. A few adults walking past stopped to softly tell him they were sorry, but most smiled sadly at him and continued on with whispers floating from their lips.

Ellis felt compelled to at least break the silence. "Do you—"

Lincoln stood suddenly and walked away from the first words she had spoken to him since that word that day in her living room.

Ellis closed her mouth and watched him wander in the direction Christopher had gone. His hands were deep in his pockets, and he didn't seem to respond to the adults trying to speak to him as he weaved by them. She watched him duck into the hallway leading to the bathrooms.

Everything had changed. Life was serious and her vow no longer seemed as important now that she realized what life really was—a number line with an endpoint somewhere along it for everyone. No one got to be a line that went forever. People who are there won't always be. People could wither away to get buried below the ground like a dormant seed, leaving those left behind holding full watering cans but no way to reach them.

It seemed to Ellis wholly unfair that Lincoln, for as long as he lived, would never be able to reach his mother with his water.

Ellis Sloan Therapy Sessions

Gulf Tower
Pittsburgh, PA
June 2021

Dr. Parrish: Tell me about Wren.

Ellis: She's autistic. She's funny. She's complicated. She's frustrating. She's brilliant.

Dr. Parrish: I notice you check your phone often. Is that because of her?

Ellis: That's perceptive.

Dr. Parrish: Not my first autism-mom rodeo.

Ellis: She might need me.

Dr. Parrish: To?

Ellis: Rescue her from situations that might make her melt down.

Dr. Parrish: So, you spend your days watching your phone, waiting for a situation that you feel requires your intervention. And the school calls and says, "Come get her?"

Ellis: She's out of school now for summer, so right now I'm waiting to see if a text comes from my mother that she needs me, but she usually doesn't. But during school, her aide might call and tell me she's gotten upset, and if she requests to come home.

Dr. Parrish: And how often do they call and you go get her?

Ellis: Maybe once a month?

Dr. Parrish: I see.

Ellis: I hate when you say that.

Dr. Parrish: I know.

Chapter Eleven

November 2020

I hug my laptop more tightly to my chest, feeling exposed at being confronted not only by my brother, but Lincoln as well. Chris looks concerned at the state of my being, while Lincoln looks amused despite a plain effort to mask it.

I hide my mortification behind my fake and cheery smile. "Hey. What's going on? Everything okay?" I ask more brightly than an over-caffeinated Disney princess, my eyebrows nearly at my hairline, which only reminds me that my hair is probably ... not good.

"I should ask you that," Chris says.

"I'm good." I throw a nonchalant wave in the air. "I look a mess, I know. But I got to writing as soon as the kids left this morning, and it was flowing and I could not stop." I pause a beat to allow a retributive lightning bolt to blast me back to prehistory. When it doesn't happen, I pull a hand to my hair and feel how wildly it misbehaved today. A futile tuck of a handful of curls behind my ear does nothing but encourage them to pop out again with joyful disobedience. "Got a deadline to meet."

"Not that. I've been texting and calling you all morning."

I blink. Confused. "I didn't hear—" *Fuck. Oh no.*

I drop all pretense of being a person who has control and a life of purpose and a sense of self-worth and a bra under her shirt and a plot for a second book. "Shit!" I spin away from them and run into the kitchen where I toss my laptop onto the counter and stomp my foot on the garbage can pedal to dig my phone out. I am shaking drips of yogurt and clumps of wet coffee grounds from it when Chris and Lincoln walk in with clear concern. I know my face looks panicked and I do not care. Panic always wins the battle against self-consciousness.

My heart races out of rhythm as my shaky hands swipe open the phone screen. A quick glance through all the message notifications and calls I missed during my absence from consciousness show they were mostly from Chris. Two from my only friend Hadi explaining in graphic detail how angry he is at me for canceling on him. One from my mother reminding me of Sunday dinner. Another signed by Bea, telling me she sent an email with updated *Luca Rex* sales figures. One telling me the fabric store has 20% off today as they do every single day of the year because sales are lies stores tell to suckers.

There are no messages or calls from Wren's school.

I feel relief flood every inch of my body and it's euphoric and depressive, a weird wave to ride and it unsettles me. I hold my phone to my chest with a huge sigh and sink to sit on top of the garbage can lid. I am a living, breathing metaphor that has something to do with garbage and were I a better writer, I'd figure it out and write it here. But I'm no longer a writer. The words are all gone. But I can write a hell of a book title.

"Everything okay?" Chris asks, putting his hand on my shoulder and looking at me with the face of intentional concern he probably uses on his patients when they're fearful and worried.

I put my own hand over his and pat it reassuringly, returning his comfort. "Yeah. It must have fallen in when I cleaned this morning." Another lie. He probably knows it because my kitchen?

Not clean unless it was "cleaned" by a family of trash raccoons. "I worried maybe I missed something about Wren while I was writing. You know..."

Chris nods. He knows.

Lincoln is leaning with his shoulder against the wall, watching us, but does not speak.

"What did you need?" I ask Chris rather than try to find his messages with my shaking fingers. I'm still coming down from the adrenaline rush of fear that Wren had needed me, and I hadn't been there to rescue her.

"We," he half-turns toward Lincoln, "wanted to take you to lunch. Old times. Catch up."

I stare at them—my dear brother and this painful resurrection from my past. Wanting to catch up on old times with Lincoln Hale? I'd rather catch up to a train to hell and ride it into the bowels of Satan's lair. How are men so clueless? I smile; I don't mean it. "I would. But like I said, I have a deadline. I'll catch you next time for sure." I don't mean that either.

"You can't take a little break?" Chris asks. "Just 45 minutes." He looks me up and down. "Well, maybe an hour."

Ass.

"I simply can't," I say with the kind of confidence that would not normally exude from a woman perched atop a can of garbage. "When the words flow, taking a break is a bad idea. Gotta get those words from here," I point to my completely empty head where words no longer live, "to there." I nod that empty head toward the laptop I threw on the counter like it was a sack of potatoes. Seeing it on the counter makes me realize it was serving as my bra before panic over Wren set in. Awareness dawns that the only thing standing between my bare boob flesh and these two is my Jurassic Park shirt that's probably four washes away from becoming dinosaur-themed tissue paper.

I try to seem casual and unbothered as I awkwardly cross my arms over my chest, my self-hate growing by the moment. Maybe

I'll write a book about a girl who hates herself, continues to hate herself, then dies hating herself never having written a second book. And then her house cats eat her.

I glance at Lincoln and immediately look away when his gaze catches mine—eye contact with him feels entirely too intrusive. Why is that? Why can you look at a person's face, every inch of it—from one ear to the other, hairline to chin, and not feel a single emotion—not love, not hate, not anger. Nothing. These are mere body parts. But the second you find their eyes and those eyes are on yours, you go from being an observer to being mutually observed, and the emotions happen? For me, at this moment, those emotions are a little bit of hate. A little bit of anger. A little bit of confusion. And a little bit of nostalgia for what he used to mean to me.

Ugh. Gross. I abruptly stand from my garbage throne. (Book idea: *Game of Thrones*, but they're all trying to win reign over a land of garbage.) "Well, I'm going to get back at it. You two have a good lunch. Bring me cookies," I say to Chris. He knows I don't mean it.

I walk them to the front door and shoo them out into the sun as a car ambles down my one-way tree-lined street. The warm air from a week ago now holds hints of a chill, another reminder that time marches onward toward the deadlines I already know I won't meet. Chris kisses my cheek and Lincoln turns to say the first words he's spoken to me since the day he arrived. Actually, one word said with an easy wave: "Bye."

I smile at him; I don't mean it. "Bye now!" I sing-song out. I close the door and whisper "fucker" behind it; I mean it.

I march to the kitchen, grab the laptop with the empty document entitled *Ellis Sloan Untitled Book Two* and stamp my foot even harder on the garbage can pedal than I did earlier. It opens with a bang and the laptop makes a lovely plop sound as it lands on top of yogurt, coffee, and the remains of whatever I fed the kids for dinner last night. Tacos from a kit, I recall.

Vaya con dios, Luca Rex.

I return to my nap spot and fall into the couch once more, this time with my phone safely nearby. Staring at the ceiling I think of Bea again. Ten chapters. Six more days. I have nothing.

I'm empty.

Words are gone, stories won't come, yet memories won't leave me alone, knocking on my door, holding my eyes, echoing within me, demanding acknowledgement long after they should have run out of time and space to reverberate.

Chapter Twelve

October 1996
Ellis, 16
Lincoln, 18

Through this door is the rest of a life.

Ellis had been about to give up when she spied a bright yellow paper taped to a door near the rear of the Reizenstein High School library, Sharpied neatly with "PEER TUTORING." Bringing home a D in geometry that first six-week term had sent her parents into what could only be described as a fit.

Ellis first showed it to her father as he nursed his morning coffee at his desk, reading scriptures from his favorite Bible that had once belonged to her grandfather. The same way one might observe a lion stealthily approaching a gazelle in a nature documentary, she watched with dread as his eyes scanned downward until a nearly imperceptible twitch at the corner of his mouth indicated he'd found the D. He was silent for a long moment and then returned the paper to Ellis as he called her mother into the room with, "Uh, Pop?"

Handing the report card to her mother felt like handing her pornography, and to be sure, she felt her mother's reaction was probably close to what her reaction would be to being handed porn

—a lot of gasping, mild disgust, and side-eyeing so as not to visually absorb the depravity too directly into her eyeballs.

"Disappointed," her father said.

"Grounded," her mother said.

Her father had calmed down first and jokingly pretended to append Ellis's name to the bottom of the growing prayer list he kept on his desk. Her mother relished her anger a bit longer. Ellis was, after all, the first Marks child to ever earn a D in anything. Nathan even managed a B in Home-Ec for his only slightly crooked attempt at sewing a kitchen apron. It felt dirty to see the D staring back at her, printed in red ink while all the other grades were in black. The real scarlet letter wasn't an A, like in the book she read recently and loved. No, it was a D or, God forbid, an F. Ellis was sure if she ever brought home an F, her mother would molt out of her skin.

Her father, after a mini-lecture on individual academic responsibility in which he reminded Ellis of the "Everything thy hand finds" scripture, had joked, "A nunnery or tutoring, Ellis?" Since they weren't Catholic, Ellis was relegated to geometry tutoring and ordered to get at least a B. There would be no driver's permit until that grade improved, her mother explained as she signed the report card while attempting to not touch the paper that contained the offensive filth.

So there Ellis stood in the library facing a door behind which would hopefully be the start of a meteoric rise from a D to B in six-weeks' time, hopefully not twelve. Through this door was a driver's license. Through this door was freedom. With a long exhale, she pushed it open to find a depressing gray square room holding nothing but a mostly empty shelving unit and two round tables. One empty. One occupied by Lincoln Hale, bent earnestly over a book.

As recognition dawned, Ellis widened her eyes and spun wildly on her heels. A nunnery it was. Or the military. Or bus-riding for life. License be damned. *I'll get cats and live alone on the bus line and carry plastic shopping bags full of neatly folded stacks of other kinds of bags.*

"Hello?"

She pulled the door closed on Lincoln's called word and prepared to make her escape from society, but her geometry teacher Miss Peters approached before she could split. She was one of the youngest teachers in the school, but she kept her long hair braided down her back and wore an ill-fitting staid business suit for five rows of high school students six classes a day. "Ah, Miss Marks. Have a seat right in there."

Ellis considered bolting past her, out of the school, and not stopping until she hit an ocean into whose swallowing waves she could dramatically fling herself.

Her teacher's reassuring smile gave Ellis no reassurance. "Nothing to be nervous about. I'll get you settled in. This way now."

Her fate decided and her chance to escape gone, Ellis threw her chin to the ceiling and cursed silently toward it before following her teacher into the setting of her soon-to-be memory-etched mortification. Through this door, it all ends. Ellis watched as realization washed over Lincoln as gradually as the overly wide and knowing smile that spread across his whole smug face. "Ellis, this is Lincoln Hale. He's a senior and most excellent at geometry. He should be of great assistance to you."

Ellis didn't acknowledge him or her teacher and instead looked around the room. Gray floor. Gray empty walls except for one poster reminding the poor souls stuck in there to Just Say No. Truly a perfect setting for her foul mood—dark and colorless.

"We know each other," Lincoln offered, then leaned back into his chair while still smiling broadly at Ellis.

"Oh! Perfect! Keep your eyes on the clock. Head out before 3:30, okay? The lights will flicker to remind you. Then they'll go off completely and you don't want to be stuck in here when that happens."

Lincoln watched the teacher leave then turned his attention to Ellis, his wide smile not faltering a single millimeter. With the commanding air of a Godfather, he held out an inviting hand toward the chair across from his.

Ellis slid her backpack off her shoulders and slumped into it with visible dread then eyed him and his stupid frozen smile just as he sing-songed low and slowly, "Eller. Beller."

"I'm leaving." She stood to go but he threw his hand out to stop her, his mocking smile fading into a more genuine one.

"I'm kidding! Sorry. Kidding. Sit down. Ellis."

She did. Because what other choice did she have that didn't involve lifelong abstinence or off-the-grid feral living in a tent where she wrote unintelligible manifestos that were eventually submitted to a courtroom as evidence?

"Relax. We're cool. Christopher is going to get a huge kick out of this. What do you need help with? Let's see it." He pulled out a pencil that was wedged into the fold of the book he'd been so intently reading. Upon closer inspection, Ellis realized it was sheets of complicated music—legions away in difficulty from the simple songs she plucked tentatively out of his mother's piano. Maybe it was his piano now.

She'd never seen anyone reading music without an instrument in front of them. It struck her as odd. She lived her own spare time swimming deep among the letters that formed words that spoke their meanings nearly audibly to her. Little black music notes printed on paper couldn't possibly hold that magic or offer that escape.

She withdrew a single sheet of paper from her folder and slid it to him. Ellis watched the face she'd seen change so much over the last six years. She hadn't watched him progress from a short twelve-year-old menace with a disorganized mop of hair as dark as his mother's to what sat before her now intently perusing her homework—Reizenstein High's musical pride awaiting word on an audition from Juilliard for piano studies, who now easily towered a foot above her, his hair neatly stacked off his forehead revealing a face reflective of passing time, the same way Christopher's had changed. He was bent over the paper with his elbows on his knees and his hands clasped under the table.

Finally, he lifted his head. "Okay. 'Distance between points on a coordinate plane.' What don't you understand about it exactly?"

Ellis blinked at him.

He squinted. "Okay. What DO you understand?"

She only blinked again, her face as blank as the space in her brain reserved for understanding geometry.

"Oh."

"I got a D," she admitted miserably then dropped her forehead to the table, her hands dangling low beside her feet. The forward motion sent her long dark curls waterfalling around her head to surround her face like a collapsed parachute. Dramatic, yes, but truly the moment called for drama and if she couldn't bolt for the merciful waters of the Atlantic, the Hair Cocoon of Stupidity would have to do.

"Getting a D on a test is not that big of a deal," he offered.

She thought of her mother's righteous disgust at her porny grade. "No, I got a D on my report card."

"Yikes," she heard Lincoln breathe out low before adding brightly, "Once Christopher thought he was getting a D in biology. I thought he was going to cry. He ended up with a C though."

Ellis kept her head where it was and spoke deadpan into the tabletop, "How very wonderful for him."

She heard the soft exhale of a chuckle being suppressed. The tap of either his finger or his pencil eraser staccato-ed on the back of her head. "Sit up. Come on. This is easy. You'll see."

Resigned, Ellis raised her head and slouched against the table edge to clutch her hands beneath it, mimicking his posture exactly. They faced each other this way as mirrored images for a moment before she said, "But it's not easy. Not for me. I hate math. I like words."

"Geometry is the least mathy of the maths."

"My brain rejects it. Look." She grabbed the homework paper and sat back in her chair to stare hard at it. In jest, she furrowed her brow as if trying to absorb the information by osmosis then gave out a dramatic sigh. "See? Rejected." She slid the test to him and lowered her forehead to the table, her curls fanning protectively around her once more. "You and Christopher are going to sit and make fun of me later, aren't you?" she asked miserably from within her hair cocoon.

"Probably."

Ellis snapped her head up sharply to find Lincoln smiling. "You're a jerk," she observed.

"Actually, I don't know if you've heard this about me from anyone," he said, pausing meaningfully with a spark behind his eyes, "but I can be a real ... motherfucker."

She widened her eyes then dropped her forehead to the table again, this time with a much harder thunk, but she was powerless to stop the laughter that erupted from inside at the embarrassing memory. When she finally quieted, she lifted her head with a small sigh of resignation. "Ugh. All right. Help me. But if you talk to Christopher about tutoring me, tell him I'm secretly brilliant but acting dumb because of society's negative views on strong women." She suddenly understood why her mother told her she'd become too obsessed with *The Scarlet Letter*, to which Ellis had replied, "Would you prefer I dig into Dante's *Inferno* again?" Overhearing this, her father had shouted from his study, "Lord, please don't!"

Lincoln nodded his head once at her. Agreement struck. "Deal. This will take 15 minutes. Write the Pythagorean formula on here up top." He tapped his pencil point on her homework paper and looked at her expectantly.

Ellis blinked at him for a long moment, then inhaled and pointed a finger to her own lips to draw his attention to the words she would form from them. "I. Got. A. D.," she said with an exaggerated enunciation of each syllable.

He rolled his eyes and began writing the formula himself. It was equal in letters and numbers. He wrote it from memory and narrated what he scribbled. "D, meaning distance, is equal to the square root of the sum of x two minus x one squared and y two—"

Ellis let her forehead fall again to the table with an audible thump. Her headache would be blistering tomorrow morning.

"Now what?" she heard Lincoln ask.

"I just really hate you," came her reply from beneath the protection of her hair.

He let out a full laugh and it bounced around the small room to ricochet into her ears. Inside of her hair, she smiled down to the table at the sound and remembered making his mother laugh like that once and how it had made her feel whole and proud and ready to do about anything to draw it from her again. And like she did then in Mrs. Hale's neat living room, she grabbed the song of laughter, latched tight to the feeling it gave her and tucked it close to her heart so she could pull it out later to once again feel its warmth.

Ellis Sloan Therapy Sessions

Gulf Tower
Pittsburgh, PA
June 2021

Dr. Parrish: Tell me about Dunn. Did he realize the problems in your marriage?

Ellis: I think I hid them from him pretty well.

Dr. Parrish: And, growing up, if your father was weirdly sullen some days, or yelling behind closed doors at your mother other days, you wouldn't have noticed that as long as your mother kept smiling through it?

Ellis: —

Dr. Parrish: If you heard your father yell at your mother in public would you have taken notice and felt fine about it? Especially as you became a teenager? Would that have been normal? If your mother became quieter and quieter, you wouldn't have picked up on it at all?

Ellis: I get it.

Dr. Parrish: My point, Ellis, is this: Who were you really hiding the realities of your marriage from?

Ellis: Myself?

Chapter Thirteen

November 2020

The tableau must be arranged.

When my kids are in school, I spend the hours between 7:20 a.m. and 2:15 p.m. as unproductive as a haughty housecat, but I become a whirl of activity once it registers that Dunn will be home in 15 minutes, and I still look like a haggard alley animal, and the house looks very recently ransacked.

Presenting an air of calmness, neatness and order to Wren and Dunn has become an obsession since the three of us moved into the duplex four months ago. Me and Oliver splitting up might very well be the most disruptive event in their lives for a long time, so while the bathroom drawers might hold disorganization, and the kitchen might have multiple junk drawers and cabinets hiding stacks of mismatched dishes, and while the closets might look like I earn my living selling secondhand miscellanea at flea markets, on the surface, to a teenager, the house is in order. It is clean. Things are in their place. The chaos was hidden. *What chaos? There's no chaos. Look at all this order. Everything is good. Everything is fine. Your mother does not toss expensive electronics into the kitchen garbage can while you're at school.*

Every school day from 2:15 to 2:30, the bathroom is cleaned of tossed clothes and towels. Toiletries put away. The shower curtain Dunn never closes is slid into place. The beds are made, dirty dishes placed into the sink, the counters wiped, the blankets I napped in folded neatly as if they hadn't been used for days, and my clothes changed from woman-who-quit-trying to woman-who-pretends-to-try-real-hard.

When Dunn walks in the front door each school day at 2:30, I will have taken pains to arrange myself in a tableau—a physical representation of the person I want my children to believe I still am even though I haven't been her for a long time because bit by bit Oliver was chipping away at me and I didn't realize it until I looked around and found I was already walking amongst my own ruins, no idea who or what was left standing. I still don't know.

When 2:30 comes, I will have slathered tinted cream on my face, dabbed a blush of color onto my cheeks, and brightened my eyes with concealer and mascara. My curls will be forced into obedience with the help of spray gel. I then might sit myself at the small writing table I keep in the living room, perched straight-backed at my laptop typing meaningless drivel into a Google document I've entitled "lkskdjfls." Author Mom is here working hard on her next masterpiece! Author Mom is a word wizard! Look at her typing 120 words a minute to get out all the words in her head!

Or I will sit in the colorful floral wing chair, one of the few things I took with me from the old house. I'll poke my nose into a book I'm not reading and have no intention of reading. Educated Mom is here, and she is reading. She cares about life and learning new things! When I'm Educated Mom, I'm careful to sit in a chair —never on the couch. Couches speak of laziness. Sitting on a couch is a plop. Chairs speak of purpose. Sitting on a chair is a deliberate lowering of oneself to complete a task other than slack-jawed napping.

Today, after erasing the unsettling intrusion of Chris and

Lincoln, I realize at 2:30 that I have forgotten to arrange myself into a Mom In Control Of Life tableau, and my laptop is still swimming in garbage. The engine roar of Dunn's school bus rumbles by announcing his imminent arrival. I have mere seconds before he walks in and finds Real Mom standing there looking lost and unproductive. Being caught fishing an expensive laptop out of a bag of garbage does not speak of control and order and cleanliness. It speaks of a mom who maybe lost her shit a little while you were at school.

I sprint into the kitchen and stomp my foot on the garbage can pedal so hard the nerves on the top of my foot crackle. The sound of the front door opening hits my ears just as I pull the laptop out. A frantic swipe with an already dirty dish towel takes care of the unidentifiable sludge, and I toss it into the sink when Dunn appears and drops his backpack on the table.

"Dunn! You're home. I lost track of time. Was about to take a snack break from writing." *I'm ready, Satan. Take me.* "What would you like?"

"I got it." He reaches for the Doritos bag on top of the fridge. I notice he's much taller than me now, and I remember a time when he needed a short wooden step stool to reach the countertop, much less the top of the fridge with such ease. I see hints of my brothers' and my father's strong, straight features shadowed in his own and it warms me. Much the opposite of the rounded edges of Oliver's. I'm glad at least my family's genes kicked his family's ass.

"Good day?" I ask him as I do every day.

"Yup," he answers as he does every day. Sparkling conversation the two of us have. Positively heartwarming. (Book idea: *The Art of Meaningful Three-Word Conversations with Your Teenager*.)

"How's the art project coming?"

"Good. I like it."

"Algebra?"

He smiles at me.

"Algebra?" I ask again.

"Working on it."

"Work harder."

He grabs his backpack and I follow him to the stairs so I can call after him as he heads for his room, "One more chance and then I'm getting you a tutor."

I hear his door close right before the word "tutor" leaves my lips.

One child fooled by Author Mom, who nearly blew the tableau. I have one hour until Wren comes home, provided I don't hear from the school that she needs me to come earlier.

I grab a stack of unopened mail resting under the fruit bowl on the kitchen counter. I will make sure I am busy at my writing desk when Wren arrives home. Finance Mom is here keeping life in good working order! Writing checks and licking envelopes and making pretend budgetary notations in a fake spreadsheet she entitled "j29!klj." Busy business! Accomplishing accomplishments! Stapling staples!

I am a lie I tell my children to keep them feeling secure while I figure out how to get my footing in a life that turned to quicksand beneath me.

I just need to fake it long enough until I figure out how to pull myself out and find a solid path forward.

Then I can stop hating myself.

Chapter Fourteen

October 1996
Ellis, 16
Lincoln, 18

"I hate myself." Ellis had started the tutoring session as she had the last one—her forehead on the table, her arms dangling at her sides, her hair shielding her from view.

"Oh. Bad?"

Ellis pivoted her head to place her ear to the table then shoved her hair out of her face. She looked at Lincoln as he took the seat next to her. She could see he was nearly ready to explode in a laugh at the sight of her. "I continue to hate you also," she said.

"What the hell happened? You were good. Ready."

She had thought so too. But she forgot the part where she was achingly bad at math, and if there was a way to screw it up, she'd find it even on the darkest night through the thickest fog with nothing to light her way but a dying match.

Ellis kept her ear to the table and reached above her head to feel around blindly for her folder. She slid it around her head to Lincoln. "It's in there." She groaned and returned her forehead to the table. She was beginning to become intimately familiar with the smell of it. She heard Lincoln whistle in mock appreciation. "Sixty-five," he said.

Ellis groaned again.

"What did you do here, then? Okay. Oh. I see. Wow."

She groaned louder.

"You forgot to take the square root after you did the—? And you didn't realize your answers were too—? How?"

In a low wooden tone, she answered his questions in order. "Yep. Nope. Because I'm too stupid to live." She pressed her ear to the table again and swatted away her hair to reveal her face. "I'm thinking about quitting school and selling drugs."

Lincoln shook his head. "You'll need math for that. You'll get ripped off. Drug dealing is mostly math."

"The nunnery it is. Hail Mary, full of grace, right?" She lifted an arm in the air to perform an exaggerated and incorrectly executed pantomime of the sign of the cross and then pivoted her forehead to the tabletop once more.

A kick from his shoe rattled against her chair leg. "Stop that. She wrote here you can redo new questions for the ones you got wrong, so there you go."

Fully upright again, Ellis's shoulders sagged and her face fell flat. "For half-credit. You know what half-credit of the ones I got wrong added to the 65 percent of 20 questions I got right is going to get me to grade-wise on this? Because I sure don't."

"Get 'em all right? About 82."

"Literally couldn't hate you more."

"You're very hateful."

She pointed at him. "The nunnery could fix that I bet."

"But the vows."

"What vows?"

"I saw a movie. There's vows. Poverty."

She scoffed. "I'm already poor."

"Chastity."

"Boys are jerks." She extended her upright palm in his general direction.

He raised his eyebrows. "Obedience."

Ellis blinked.

He smiled slowly.

She slapped the tabletop with her open hand and exclaimed, "Let's do some geometry!"

"Atta girl."

Ellis finished the first problem while Lincoln watched her step-by-step progress when the door cracked open and they looked up to find Christopher's head poking into the room.

"There are my nerds! El, Mom called the school. You're supposed to come home with me and Linc. Dad had to take the car so she can't come get you. I'll be in the gym." He took a quick glance around the depressing room. "I've never been in here. Is this the school prison?" he asked with a laugh.

"Yes," Ellis replied as she returned her focus to the practice test. "Break me out, smuggle me a shiv, kill the warden, or go away."

"Wait, am I the warden?" Lincoln asked defensively.

She kept her eyes on her work and smiled down at her paper letting her silence answer his question.

She heard Christopher close the door behind his own laughter.

"It's cool you can make Chris laugh," Lincoln said after a moment.

Ellis paused her work and considered what he had said, then shrugged. "I guess." Making her brothers and her parents laugh was easy and now second-nature to her. She was always seeking to pull waterfalls of their laughter from them to fill empty air or too-serious moments. Nathan, the most serious of them, was a special challenge, and when she could get him bursting out in full-throated laughter, she felt an odd urge to hug him, but never did. "Want me to make you laugh?" she asked suddenly.

"What?"

She leaned back in her chair and crossed her arms. "Know where I learned 'motherfucker' back then?"

"Well, it's been a while. I think Chris said *Die Hard*?"

"Yep. I didn't know what the word meant. In fact, I didn't understand much at all about that movie. I was ten, you know."

"So?"

"I shortened it at the last second because I was so mad, I could barely think, but I nearly called you a 'yippee-ki-yay-motherfucker.'" She smiled big at him. "I thought it was one word."

Lincoln laughed so hard at Ellis's story that the librarian, who they thought had left for the day, poked her head into the room and scowled them back into library-appropriate quietness. When the door clicked quietly closed, Ellis quickly spun on Lincoln and demanded with her face lit up in hilarity, "Can you imagine that living room if instead of me shouting motherfucker at you, I had screamed yippee-ki-yay-motherfucker? I know one thing for sure; your mother would not have been able to hold that laugh in like she did."

He grinned at the memory. "You saw that too?"

"If I close my eyes, I can still see her standing there covering her mouth with her hand, her eyes wide, watching my dad try to pry Cutesy's claws from his face skin. He had to use antiseptic on the scratches for like a week! He never loved her the same after that. Poor Cutesy; done in by her primal fight or flight instincts."

"Boy, she chose wrong, didn't she?"

When they finally regained control of a second round of stifled laughter, Ellis sighed to steady her breath and looked at him thoughtfully. "I didn't like you; but, boy, I really did like your mom so much."

He bit at the inside of his bottom lip as if working to control something he didn't want to show. "I really did too."

They sat in silence for a long moment, letting the energy of the room return to a more peaceful level worthy of the memories of his mother that softly spiraled around as if she'd floated into the room to visit them for a while. Finally, Lincoln said, "Eller?"

"Ellis."

"Ellis?"

"Yep?"

"Get to work, jailbird."

She did as the warden bade and knew she wouldn't dread their next session so much, if at all.

Ellis Sloan Therapy Sessions

Gulf Tower
Pittsburgh, PA
June 2021

Dr. Parrish: You like to toss out a joke when things get heavy in here.

Ellis: Yeah.

Dr. Parrish: It's clearly a cope. I know you already see that. I can tell.

Ellis: I do.

Dr. Parrish: Growing up the only girl of five, I can imagine emotional displays weren't encouraged or common.

Ellis: No. My brothers would tease me if I cried. Emotional displays didn't get me a single thing. Laughter got me everything.

Dr. Parrish: And of course, that humor gave you some attention from your parents who were dividing theirs among the five of you.

Ellis: Bullseye. It's not a revelation. I know why I'm this way.

Dr. Parrish: Do you like being this way?

Ellis: Sure. Emotions are stupid things that make you feel wrong things and do rash things. And what's the alternative? Feelings? Crying? Pointless. And gross.

Dr. Parrish: I see.

Ellis: What are you writing on there?

Dr. Parrish: Just—so much.

Chapter Fifteen

November 2020

The world has gone mad and lost all its manners. Shortly after Wren arrives safely home, a knock at the door sounds for the second time today and both times no one texted to tell me they were coming. At least this time, Finance Mom is here, and she looks presentable in her dark blue jeans and Kelly green sweater and face made up and her curls forced into the places curls are supposed to be—not disco dancing atop her head.

Finance Mom has her glasses on. She used to call them her reading or writing glasses, but now they're her pretendin' glasses. *Because if she's wearin' 'em, she's pretendin'.*

Finance Mom opens the door and finds, for the second time this day, Lincoln Hale. Only now without Christopher. Alone. Standing at my door with that ever-present easy half-grin pulling at the corner of his mouth, the same one that used to make me desperate to spread it into a full smile and then a laugh with my jokes and dramatics.

He eyes my hair and clothes quickly, and I nearly want to slam the door in his infuriatingly pleasant face. He'd been greeted twice, hours earlier even, by Bra-less Jurassic Park Mental Mess Woman;

he wasn't expecting Finance Mom who pretends to have all her shit together in neat binders with cascading color-coded tabs.

"Yes?" My smile is fake—all business, because I am Finance Mom, here to pay your cable bill and check for better car insurance rates.

He pushes a black square bakery box toward me that I immediately recognize from me and Chris's favorite spot for lunch, Oakmont Bakery. "Your cookies."

I still in confusion. "My ... cookies?"

"Chris said he needed to get to work, so he asked me to give you the cookies."

"He ... got me cookies?" I can't hide the surprise from my voice or face.

"I don't know why you're so surprised," he says with an easy laugh. "I think I've heard you ask him for cookies at least two dozen times in my life."

His reference to the past sparks the air between us.

He pushes the box into my hands as Wren appears beside me holding a book about Greek mythology, another of her fixations. "Hey, Wilson," she says in greeting with an awkward swiping wave, like a windshield wiper.

Lincoln smiles but shakes his head. "Rejected. Not Wilson. That's a volleyball."

"Why did your parents name you after a president?"

"Why'd yours name you after a bird?"

Wren opens and then closes her mouth. They look from each other to me in expectation.

I'll not be interrogated about decisions I made when I was in my early twenties. "I'm going to go put these in the kitchen," I say and pivot away, expecting him to bid Wren goodbye so she can close the door and follow me in an effort to snag cookies before dinner. But instead, from the kitchen, I hear their conversation continue with Wren observing, "I bet she doesn't even know why she named me Wren."

"I bet she does."

"I'll call you Harrison."

"I like it."

"Which one?"

"Which one?" I hear him repeat as I open the box of cookies, still confused as to why my brother sent them and why he sent dozens and dozens of them. I could nearly cater the cookie table at a small wedding with these.

"Yeah, the one who died after a month or the one who was afraid of lights?"

I erupt in a snicker at Wren and quickly cover my mouth with my hand, hoping they didn't hear me.

"Do you mean afraid of heights?" he asks her.

"No. He was literally afraid of lights. Lights." She loudly enunciates the word, again becoming the teacher to him, her student.

"Changed my mind. Not Harrison," he says.

"My brother's named after a bird too, you know." She's not letting him go, and out of the goodness of my heart—Saint Mom is here to relieve Finance Mom—I grab a paper plate and haphazardly dump half the cookies onto it and return to the front door.

My arrival to push the plate of cookies into Lincoln's hands interrupts Wren's explanation of what a dunlin is. "Enjoy," I say. "Christopher bought way too many for us three. I don't know what he was thinking."

Wren grabs a thumbprint in each hand from the top of his plate before I can stop her, and runs awkwardly up the stairs calling, "Bye, Harrison," over her shoulder. A beat later, she yells out, "Dunn! There's good cookies down there!"

"She's pretty funny," Lincoln says after Wren's energy leaves the room to follow after her.

I smile, and I mean it, because it's true and it's just about my favorite thing about her. "She is. Well, thanks for dropping the cookies off." *You're dismissed*, is what I'm really saying. But he doesn't read my silent thoughts like he once used to and instead studies my face for a moment, lingering on the scar on my chin that wasn't there when he knew me. I look past him at nothing. I don't want to spend too much time on the face that pulled at me a lifetime ago. He clears his throat. "It's no problem. I'm right here anyway." He tilts his head to indicate the door to his side of the duplex.

I have so many questions I could scream at him. *Why are you here? Why did you come back to this little place when you have a huge important life out there? Why did you do what you did? Why didn't you come? Why did you keep the house so dark? Why did you throw me away?*

But instead, I merely say, "Right," for lack of literally anything more I wish to say to him at this point in my life, partly because it's long-gone history that no longer matters and partly because, even as an adult, I might not like any of the answers.

Dunn lands with a hop at the bottom of the stairs and gives a small nod of greeting toward Lincoln while eyeing the plate of cookies in his hands.

"Yours are in the kitchen. From Uncle Chris," I tell him.

"Best uncle. The others need to step up their game," he says before leaving in search of the treats.

"Only two," I call after him then turn to Lincoln. Nutrition Mom has big plans to feed her kids fish sticks and canned corn for dinner while she stands in the kitchen and tries to find the appetite she lost months ago when she realized she could no longer write.

"Dunn?" Lincoln confirms.

I nod. "Dunn. Dunlin." I can't help a grin in spite of myself. "The other bird."

Lincoln chuckles then quiets. "All right. Thanks for these." He lifts the plate a bit then steps out of the doorway and turns toward his own door.

"Sure," I say and close mine quietly on him.

I text my brother.

Thanks for the cookies????

20 minutes later, his reply comes.

Ha. I figured it was time. Just this once.
Don't start thinking it will be a habit.
Lunch with me and Linc soon, okay?

Sure.

I don't mean it because I don't want to let the messy past intrude on my chaotic present. I'm trying to clean things up, not make them more complicated. I brush away the feeling of old familiarity that emerged between me and Lincoln and head toward the broom closet to grab a bucket of cleaning supplies.

Mrs. Doubtfire Mom is here and she's going to half-heartedly scrub the toilets until fish stick time, so she doesn't end up sitting on the couch letting the past freely unfurl inside of her, reminding her of a beautiful, brilliant boy who had once made her feel like he was capable of lifting her all the way to the very stars his mother pointed out to her.

Chapter Sixteen

October 1996
Ellis, 16
Lincoln, 18

From the back seat, Ellis recognized the gray Dodge sedan being driven by Lincoln as one that once belonged to his mother. It seemed morbid to her that he was still faced daily with a tangible reminder of her absence.

The drive from the school was a short ten minutes, which Ellis found merciful because she was being forced to listen to Lincoln and Christopher discuss the various physical attributes of a choice selection of girls in their class. She interrupted them as Christopher launched into his opinion of someone named "the other Cassie, the thinner one."

"I want to tell you how cool it is that of all the things you could have chosen to be in this wide wonderful world, you two chose to be sexist pigs."

She saw them exchange a synchronized eyeroll.

Lincoln said defensively, "We aren't sexist," at the same time Christopher responded with, "We aren't pigs."

"Oh. So, Chris, you admit you are sexist, and Lincoln, you admit you are a pig." She looked out the window at the passing scenery. "Glad we got to the bottom of that trough."

"Girls don't talk about guys? Sure," Lincoln said with doubt.

"We do," Ellis admitted. "We'll say, 'He's cute' or 'He's so athletic' or 'Did you see him with his shirt off?' We don't say," she threw her voice into a low gruff tone with an unidentifiable accent, "'Did ya see the pants bulge in those jeans? Board me like the Thunderbolt, stud muffin.'"

Christopher threw his head against the headrest in a loud, full laugh. "Honestly, El. Your mouth."

Ellis shrugged nonchalantly. "Sorry we can't all be as delicate as the precious flower you two call 'Cassie, the thinner one.' Is that her *Dances with Wolves* name?"

Christopher shook his head. "No. Her *Dances with Wolves* name is Cassie With The Big—"

Ellis quickly covered her ears. "You're a pig!"

Lincoln caught her gaze in the mirror with his own laughing eyes as he slowed in front of the Marks's house. She looked away with a grin. Lucas and Seth were home from school already, racing their bikes along the driveway and blindly out into the street with childhood's assumed immortality as their only helmets.

"Tell Mom that me and Linc are going to Eat'n Park," Christopher said to her.

Ellis grabbed her backpack and caught Lincoln looking accusingly at her brother before giving him a weird insistent nod. Christopher seemed to understand the silent command and turned in his seat as she moved to leave the car. "Do you want to come get some food with us?"

Ellis was surprised at the invitation but shook her head and stepped one leg out onto the curb. "Hell, no. I'm going to go lock myself in my room and practice not screwing up the Pythagorean formula, because I learned today that the nunnery is not an option for disobedient heathens like me." She leaned back into the car and put her hands on each of their shoulders. "You pigs have fun." To Lincoln she said, "Pray for me, Pythagoras." And to her brother, "Bring me cookies."

Christopher rolled his eyes, and she knew he would not bring her cookies. He never brought her cookies. She could no longer remember how it started, this request she made only to Christopher when he would leave her. *Bring me cookies.* Once, when he was 15, he was getting ready to walk out the front door with their mother to go to the dentist for wisdom teeth extraction, and she had reminded him not to forget about her cookies.

Her mother had delighted in sharing the story over dinner that night, much to his embarrassment, that when he came to from the surgery, Christopher immediately asked the amused dental nurse for cookies. This was followed by a 30-minute ride home during which he kept druggedly pointing to random houses and shouting desperately, nearly in tears, "Pull over! I bet they have cookies for El in there!"

And that was all that mattered to Ellis. It didn't matter that when conscious and in full control of his faculties, he never brought her cookies. What mattered was that when he was in a drug-induced stupor, when his emotions couldn't be held down with pride or feigned indifference or lies, all he wanted more than anything was to bring his younger sister the cookies she always asked for.

She knew when her mother recounted that story, the whole family laughing riotously, her father falling out of his chair in a silent wheezing fit of hysterics at Nathan's imitation of what he imagined Christopher had sounded like shouting out the window, that she would never stop asking him for the damn cookies. It was their spoken exchange to convey what they didn't feel comfortable expressing aloud—the acknowledgement of the connection between them.

Nathan had been gone for nearly two years now, and Lucas and Seth had each other. Ellis and Christopher, at only 19 months and one school grade apart, were easing into a friendship of their own, and she couldn't think about him leaving like Nathan did and she couldn't think about how the house had seemed to sag in on itself after he left, and she couldn't think about what Christopher's absence would do to the house or to her parents who probably didn't realize how much they dimmed their internal lights for months after Nathan had gone.

"Good luck tomorrow," Lincoln called to her as she stepped from the car.

"I'll try to remember your cookies," Chris said.

Ellis walked toward her house knowing her brother would not bring her the cookies because he never did but feeling the same fullness in her heart for him as if he always had.

Ellis Sloan Therapy Sessions

Gulf Tower
Pittsburgh, PA
June 2021

Dr. Parrish: You didn't take anything when the marriage fell apart?

Ellis: I mean, not much. I packed his stuff and made him leave. Then a month later, I packed our clothes and left. Moved into a duplex my mother owns and had some basic furniture taken from the house. The kids' beds and stuff. We sold the house, and he moved onto campus housing but ended up taking a sabbatical. Went back to his family home in New York for much of the time. But, no, I didn't take much. I felt desperate to leave every reminder behind. I didn't even want to see the couch, you know? Everything was a bad memory. Connected to a bad memory.

Dr. Parrish: Surely there were good memories.

Ellis: Of course. There were many. I loved him. Dearly. Despite. But it's life. The good memories were normally followed by bad ones, so I couldn't just separate them, could I? It all had to go.

Dr. Parrish: Good things lead to bad things?

Ellis: Well, yeah.

Chapter Seventeen

November 2020

There are three days until Bea is expecting to find ten chapters of a second *Luca Rex* book in her inbox. Three days until I disappoint my agent, my aunt-in-law. Three days until she starts to worry that I've lost it while I've just spent months questioning if I ever even had it.

Author Mom acts like she not only had it, but continues to have so much of it, she's run out of Tupperware containers to put it in. Author Mom is a big liar. Author Mom doesn't even own Tupperware. Author Mom owns plastic restaurant takeout containers that would melt if she ran them through the dishwasher (top rack) but once.

But it's Saturday and Author Mom has been replaced with Saturday Mom, who fills her kids' days with activities until Sunday Mom shows up with her purse full of anxiety.

"Wren! We'll be late!" I call up the stairs while adjusting the collar of my white turtleneck sweater in the wall mirror that I generally avoid. But we're going out in public; let's not look like an island castaway at least. As I tuck my hair behind my ear, I spy my hand in the mirror. My bare ring finger. I remember I thought it would take me the rest of my life to get used to its absence after I dropped it into a box of Oliver's shit four months ago. Instead, it took two weeks. Just like that. Time erased. As if it was never there.

"I'm sorry! I'm sorry!" The shrill panic in Wren's voice breaks me from my trance. She rushes down the steps in her ever so slightly awkward gait, worry plain on her face. Years of learning her oddities tell me she's a bit on edge this day. I'll recalibrate accordingly.

"Love, it's fine. Relax. I wasn't yelling at you. Just, you know," I gesture, "toward you. You have five minutes. Plenty of time. Shoes, jacket, headphones."

"We won't be late?" She is anxious and fearful, ready to cry.

"No, hun. We'll get there on time. Shoes, jacket, headphones. Say it for me."

I watch her open the coat closet while repeating her tasks in order to herself, like I taught her. "Shoes, jacket, headphones. Shoes, jacket, headphones." She grabs her shoes. "Jacket, headphones. Jacket, headphones. Jacket, headphones."

I eye Dunn sitting on the couch in his own jacket, his shoes already on and say in a low voice, "She's a bit off. Careful. Be kind." Then in my normal voice, I add, "Have fun driving with dad. Then dinner at Poppy's with all the cousins."

Wren, now in shoes and her jacket, walks past us toward the kitchen, a serious and focused look on her face, still methodically chanting to herself the final task on her list so as not to forget it. "Headphones. Headphones. Headphones."

My phone chimes at the same time Dunn's does and we are mirror images as we grab them and read the same message.

> So sorry. Something's come up.
> Reschedule for tomorrow?

Dunn's face and posture fall in sync, and Saturday Mom must become the fortress of protection between an absent father and a yearning son. I'm always aware that when I protect Dunn, I'm also protecting Oliver and I hate it. He doesn't deserve the protection, but Dunn does, so I become the increasingly damaged fortress separating my son from Oliver's failings.

I send a forgiving text to the Oliver/Dunn thread and then smile at Dunn, keeping my mannerisms and voice intentionally nonchalant. "Always something, huh? Probably at the school. Must have been really big for him to have to cancel on you. But he'll be here tomorrow and Wren and I can switch our tickets to tomorrow."

"Hey!" Wren reappears, still without her headphones. "No. We have tickets. It's the new water exhibit!"

Dunn sinks himself further into the couch and opens a game on his phone. "Just go, Mom. I'm fine here alone."

"I don't know," I say to him.

When Wren lets out a small growl of disappointment, I turn to her. "Where are your headphones?"

"They weren't in the kitchen. I think I left them in the car yesterday."

"Go check to be sure."

She scowls but does as I tell her. I can feel Dunn's disappointment hovering in the air around him. It's nearly imperceptible, but I can see it. I can see him taking his emotions and balling them up. Shoving them low. Slamming the door on them. I can see it because I know it when it stares back at me in the mirrors I avoid. "Come on, bud. You want me to take you out driving?"

"In the Honda?" he says with much the same tone as one would say, "In the busted chicken wagon?"

I smile. "It's not a minivan."

"It's not dad's Audi either."

"You've become spoiled."

Dunn scoffs slightly and looks around our small living room at my comment. I see it through his eyes and I'm hit with a new wave of sadness at how much his life changed when I packed them and moved out of the old house where he had a huge bedroom, a basement full of diversions, and a swimming pool to while away lazy summers with neighborhood friends. Here in this duplex resting on a small lot between two other identical duplexes, we have three small bedrooms, a little square front porch we now share with Lincoln, an outdated kitchen with a slanted floor, and an underperforming dishwasher that sounds like it runs on a kinked hose and a race-car engine.

"Yours doesn't have a back-up camera anyway," he says as if it settles the matter.

"True. But have you heard about rearview mirrors? Retro and probably coming back in style soon."

The corners of his mouth hint at a grin. I'm desperate to pull it fully out because it's rare to see since he's drawn some sort of curtain over himself, his smile, his features, his laugh.

"Let me take you driving. Wren will get over the disappointment. She—"

As if on cue, Wren pushes open the front door. But she's not alone. She's shadowed by Lincoln, who follows her into the living room. He is standing in my house again, breaching the hull once more, and I freeze mid-gesture in my confusion at his presence. He's dressed casually in jeans and a blue jacket thrown over a faded Pirates t-shirt.

"Wren knocked," he says as if it's explanation enough.

I merely stay frozen in my gesture. Maybe if I don't move ...

Wren jumps in, clearly eager to explain the situation to her frozen mother. "Clinton will take Dunn driving. He said so."

"Who's Clinton?" Dunn asks inside his own confusion.

Wren points to Lincoln. "Him."

"Not Obama?" Lincoln asks her.

"Wait. You guys told me his name was Truman," Dunn says accusingly.

I unfreeze. "No. He's Kennedy. I mean Lincoln." It's happening again. It's all gone off the rails. I hold up my hands and shake my head in frustration. "Oh my God. Everyone just stop naming presidents for a second so I can think." They do and I look from Wren, who is eager, to Lincoln beside her, who is amused, and finally to Dunn, who is still visibly confused.

Eenie-meenie-miney-mo. I point at Wren. "Talk."

"Clinton ... this person right here ... said he will take Dunn driving for us so we can go. So let's go and not be late."

I look to Lincoln in expectation, but he only eyes me. "Well?" I say to him.

"What? Oh, my turn? This is fun. So, Wren knocked and said a whole bunch of stuff, then she called me Obama, hence my confusion at Clinton, then she said Dunn wanted to go driving and that he needed someone to take him and that you couldn't because you have tickets to a show ... or something. There were a lot of fast, loud words."

"Science center water exhibit," Wren corrects him, then adds, "Mom, I said please."

"She said please," Lincoln affirms with a nod of his head.

"I'm sorry," I offer meekly to him with a side glare at Wren. I can't yell at her because it upsets her too much, but I'm definitely going to grit my teeth when I speak to her "calmly" about this later. "She shouldn't have done that. We're good here."

"But the museum," Wren moans. Her eyes glisten and I expect I will deal with an emotional collapse at broken plans. But the plans don't always work out. I had planned to have parental backup at this point of my life—someone to do the Dunn things while I took care of the many Wren things. Instead, Oliver fled to New York, and I have to find a way to make sure both of my children are happy, an impossibility when the happiness of one throws a hurdle in front of the other, and I have no partner to pull it out of the way. Single motherhood. A whole lot of impossible logistics.

"I don't mind at all," Lincoln says with a glance at Dunn, who then looks at me for a silent cue as to how to respond to the offer.

I'm at a loss. On one hand, I wouldn't ever let Dunn go driving off with someone he's never really met, but on the other hand, I do know Lincoln, and there was a time in my life when I knew him so well, I'd thought perhaps I could love him. Then on the other hand that was a lifetime and a whole different Ellis ago. I stand with my proverbial hands full with an impossible situation ... that Lincoln solves with one phrase spoken to Dunn. "Ever driven a BMW?"

Dunn bolts into a standing position as if a cannon has been fired inches from his ears. He is suddenly very alert and very animated, more so than I've seen him in a long time. Like he pulled his curtain aside a little. "I'm going with Truman."

Wren looks ecstatic that her plan worked, then says to Dunn, "Call him Clinton," at the same time I say with what I hope is determined finality in my voice, "His name is Kenn— Lincoln!"

Lincoln looks at all three of us, one by one, and I let him hold my eyes this time. "Do I get a say in my name at all with you three?" he asks.

Wren slowly shakes her head with pursed lips and closed-eye sincerity that nearly makes me break into laughter.

Dunn is at the door in a few strides. "Mom, go. I'm going to drive a BMW. Is it the blue one out front?" he asks Lincoln who throws him a thumbs-up in reply.

Dunn smiles big and then rushes out with an eager Wren tagging close behind him. "I'm waiting in the car!" she calls to me. Lincoln and I are left standing alone, the front door gaping wide, awaiting our own exit from whatever just happened in my living room.

"I'm sorry," I say.

A swipe of his hand brushes my words from the air. "Don't be. I wasn't doing anything. Reading."

I wonder if he actually reads, or if he's like Educated Mom who just pretends. I recall who he once was, how smart, and decide he's probably really reading, unlike me who doesn't like to let others' words in anymore because doing so reminds me I'm no longer capable of turning my own out.

I grab my jacket and bag. "Still. She shouldn't have. She can be too bold. You're sure?"

"I am."

I bite at the inside of my cheek in uncertainty.

He reads my mind. "You want references? Guy named Christopher Marks. You need the number?" He makes as if to reach into the pocket of his jeans to fish out my own brother's number.

I chuckle. "Touché. Take him to the high school. Lot of wide open places there."

"Ah, the high school. I haven't been there since—" The sentence trails off and I don't want to pick it up. He stands at the door and presses his back to it, indicating with a beckoning wave for me to precede him. "Hey?" he asks as I pass by. "Is he going to wreck the car by any chance?"

I lift my shoulders in uncomforting uncertainty. "This'll be his third time driving. I'll pray for you."

I reach into the air and perform the wildly incorrect version of the sign of the cross I had once done in front of him long ago, then bounce down our shared steps ahead of him. The echo of his chasing laughter follows me to my car and shadows me for hours, whispering remnants of our past I haven't heard since I left them to die. It gives me a headache radiating up my neck.

Chapter Eighteen

November 1996
Ellis, 16
Lincoln, 18

Ellis sat alone in the tutoring room. This would be their sixth session and she had never beaten Lincoln to it, so she had been surprised to find it empty.

She had nearly decided to walk out when he finally came in clutching a set of stapled papers. He eyed her seriously, like a lawyer visiting an arrested client who was probably guilty. He sat next to her without speaking and took an eternity to scoot his chair into the table at the desired distance.

Ellis shifted her weight with unease. "What?"

"I have your test here." He glanced down at the test in his hand and then placed it face-down on the table in front of himself. "And I have to tell you—one second." He grabbed the test from the table as well as the pencil that was tucked behind his ear and walked to the small shelf of reference books and counseling brochures. He picked up one on eating disorders and then returned it before grabbing another on smoking.

He turned to her. "Do you smoke, Ellis?"

"Of course not, you ass."

"Then you don't need this." He tossed the brochure down. "So mouthy." He threw her a reproachful look and then stuck his pencil in the sharpener mounted to the wall above the shelf. By the time he had grinded his pencil, blew on it, grinded it again, scowled at its unevenness, grinded it again, and again, and finally was satisfied with the result, the pencil was half the size it was when he came into the room, and sharp enough to pierce a cow's nostril.

He walked at a near crawl to his chair and lowered himself into it once more. "Tell me," he started, "how did you feel about your performance on today's test, Miss Marks?"

His tone made Ellis consider the real possibility that she reached new depths of failure. "I thought ... I did...," she looked at her knotted hands in her lap, "okay?"

"I see." He tapped his pencil point on the back of the test, leaving behind a few pinprick dots. On the fourth tap, the freshly sharpened point snapped clean off and he raised his eyebrows at her.

Reading his intentions, she warned, with a finger pointed at his face, "Don't even think about it. Why do you even have my test?"

"Mrs. Peters asked me to take a look at it with you." He paused for a drum of his fingers on the back of the test. "She wanted me to ... show you your mistakes."

"Oh."

"Yeah."

"Should I plunk my head down on the table now? You know what? I'm going to do it now. I'm never going to learn to drive. I'm going to live in this room until my skin fuses to this table." She began to lower her forehead when Lincoln grabbed her shoulder.

He held her in place as he slid her test into her line of sight then flipped it over.

79.

Ellis blinked for a few beats of her heart then jerked herself upright in clear surprise, flipping her draped curls out of her eyes with a shake of her head. Happiness lit every one of her features as much as her heart felt lit up too.

Lincoln gave her arm a light punch. "See that? Look at you."

Ellis exploded in unbridled joy at seeing a good score after getting low Cs and even one D that nearly sent her screaming from the classroom when the teacher handed it to her. But this time, she would shout with happiness. "Ahh!"

Lincoln flinched as her unexpected burst of glee filled the room and bounced off every hard surface that couldn't absorb the sound, which in that cold gray room was everything but the two of them. He smiled and watched her look at the test in near reverence. "This is my highest score. In geometry." She met his eyes. "I'd kick your ass in English. But this is my best geometry score yet."

"'Yet,'" he parroted. "Getting there."

Ellis returned to her chair and smoothed out the papers she had accidentally crumpled in her dramatics. She suddenly had a thought and slitted her eyes at him. "Wait. What did you get in this class?"

"I took it in 9th grade."

Her eyes grew wide and she held out a palm in front of his face, shushing him to silence. "Never mind. Please don't tell me. I want to feel good about myself for like ten minutes."

"You sure? I'll tell you. I got—"

"No." She pointed a finger at him.

"I don't mind. I got a—" His eyes sparkled from within.

"Lincoln Hale. No."

"It was a—"

Ellis threw her arm out and covered his mouth with her hand, pressing her palm against his lips. He instinctively reached a hand up as if he would pull hers down, but instead lowered his to rest in his lap. "I'll kick your chair out from under you," she seethed low with a hint of mock menace. His cheeks and lips moved against her hand, indicating a small grin.

"Got it?" she asked. "Just shh."

He held himself still for a few beats and a slight brush against her palm indicated he had opened his lips slightly. He pulled in what seemed like a deliberately controlled breath through his nose that he exhaled as a warm rush of air that whispered along her knuckles, sending a shiver into her. His dark eyes magnetized to hers, holding them, making it impossible for her to look away. When finally he nodded his head, Ellis smiled in satisfaction and removed her hand, but her face quickly fell when she saw his expression. It confused her. Too serious. Too taut for the light moment she had intended to create. His jaw was set and clenched, rippling near his ear. Her hand felt warmer than it should and she drew it into a fist in her lap if only to acknowledge the heat radiating from it. She wondered if she had done something wrong.

An uneasiness descended on the room and fell most heavily into the space between them, a contrast so stark from their usual engaged lightness that Ellis's neck grew tight with tension. He seemed to notice it too, because he cleared his throat as if trying to hit reset on the moment, to rewind it to before the air became laden with something they hadn't encountered together before.

"So let's look at your test. See what you got wrong."

Ellis adjusted herself in her chair and grabbed her pencil, unsure of herself, and a bit embarrassed, but mostly confused as she tried to pin down what shifted between them. It was invisible, but at the same time so tangible she felt the intense need to run from the room to escape it.

Instead, she compartmentalized. She placed a wall around the heaviness until later when she could inspect it alone in hopes of dissecting and interpreting it. For now, she began looking through her test to see which problems she had worked incorrectly.

"Hey?" he said softly after a moment, tapping her knee with his pencil eraser.

She didn't look up from her paper because she didn't want to see his expression for fear it would tear down the walls she just built around the weirdness. The odd uncomfortable weight of something floating heavy and low between them was still there, and the same weight seemed to be sitting heavy and low in her stomach. "Yep?"

"Ninety-seven."

Stunned, Ellis lifted her hand a full foot in the air and dropped her pencil dramatically to the table. She turned in her chair to find him eyeing her with a smirk. As the heavy air slowly lifted between them, she smiled at him and said softly, at the same time he did, as if he knew for certain the word he could and would and had wanted to pull from her—"Motherfucker."

A note would find its way to Miss Peters's desk the next morning, written in lovely cursive flourish on the librarian's personalized notepad watermarked with little cartoon squirrels reading tiny books entitled *I'm Nuts About Reading*:

> *Please advise your Wednesday peer-tutoring students to watch their volume. The laughter and carrying-on has reached unacceptable levels as of late.*

Ellis Sloan Therapy Sessions

Gulf Tower
Pittsburgh, PA
July 2021

Ellis: Ninety-seven percent of the time, he treated me perfectly.

Dr. Parrish: And the other three?

Ellis: —

Dr. Parrish: Doesn't sound like a lot does it? Ninety-seven sounds high. But, break it down. Apply the math. Twenty-four hours in a day. Ninety-seven percent is twenty-three about, right? It seems to me if I take care of, say, this table right here really well except for the one hour a day I choose to throw rocks at it, it's going to get damaged regardless. Even if I only threw small pebbles. Over time, those one hours of damage would add up, especially if I don't repair the damage each time it occurs. Ellis, if there's no ongoing repair taking place, the only way to not damage something is to be careful with it one hundred percent of the time. It sounds like you spent a lot of years excusing the bad three for the good ninety-seven.

Ellis: I hate math.

Chapter Nineteen

November 2020

When Wren and I return home, the BMW is parked on the street in front of the duplex once again. I'm scared to make eye contact with it but force myself to walk a quick lap to see if Dunn did a little damage that Finance Mom will need to call the actual insurance company about. It's pristine.

The front door to my side of the duplex flings open before I can use my key and Dunn excitedly pulls me in by my wrist. Wren tosses him a roll of her eyes and sheds her coat on the floor. My head hurts too much to care; maybe Mrs. Doubtfire Mom will care tomorrow. She heads to her room to read the books I bought her about the science of water.

"That good?" I ask Dunn who looks ready to burst.

"I drove a BMW with a stick shift. Manual! I got stalled out twice, but I got it and it's pretty easy. We went—"

I hold up a hand. "If you're going to end that sentence with the phrase 'miles per hour,' I should advise you it's best not to tell me."

"No. We went all around the school and then he let me go on the road next to the school too. My first time on the street. Look." He shoves his phone at me and swipes through several pictures of him smiling in the driver's seat. Clearly Lincoln was the photographer. "Did you know he's famous?"

That's my cue to walk into the kitchen and find something to punch my still-raging headache back to where it came from. "I'm aware."

He trails close behind me. "I never watched the show. I think older people like you like it."

"Cruel."

"But, like, he's really famous. More than you."

"I'm not famous at all."

"Are you sure? A few girls in my school who I don't even know, seniors, have asked me if you were my mom."

"Please tell them I killed Luca." I toss four Advil into my mouth.

"Huh?"

I throw back a swallow of water. "Kidding." But not really.

My tall, quiet teenager, who normally says a total of twelve words to me on a good day, follows me from the kitchen all the way upstairs to my bedroom, narrating the life and works of one Kennedy Hale as if he's the official biographer. "... and he went to school for music. Did you know that?"

"Yep."

"But then switched to acting. Wonder why."

I toss my shoes into my closet where they land on top of a pile of other shoes because chaos hidden behind doors is my entire brand. "Ask him. Probably a girl."

"Maybe. He's had lots of girlfriends according to what I've read."

"Truly fantastic for him," I deadpan.

"Now that his show is over, did you know there's stories that he'll be in a movie next?"

I want to shoo him out of my room and I want to let my Advil work because my skin seems to be forming the first prickles of a fever, but I don't. The despondent face he wore this morning in disappointment at his father, and the way he's been since the split—his mood capable of darkening unexpectedly as if a storm rolled in from the sea on a perfectly sunny day—is for a moment replaced with a spark of genuine joy that lights a small fire inside me. I don't want to watch it burn out just yet.

"What else did you learn? Have you been sitting here for hours studying Lincoln?"

"Why do you call him that?"

I reach under my bed to produce a long plastic storage container and pull my junior yearbook out of stacks of random memories I haven't looked at in years. I flip to one page and point to myself, my wild curls earning a snicker from Dunn. "Me," I say. I flip to the pages near the front of the book, where the pictures are larger and the seniors' portraits are glowing with the promise of lives beyond Reizenstein. I point to another face. "Uncle Chris." I flip a few more pages. There is Lincoln's face. It's beautiful. It always was. Young, but already nearly a man. A half-smile that I memorized and adored. Eyes glowing as if we'd just shared a joke. I rest my finger on his picture. "Lincoln."

"Whoa."

"Yep. We grew up four houses away from each other. I'll show you next time we're at Poppy's." I slap the book shut and move to drop it into the container, but Dunn grabs it from my hands before I can.

"Gonna look at it later. Want to see something cool though?" he asks, plopping himself onto my bed and pulling me down next to him.

Not really, son. "Sure do."

He holds his phone in front of me again, a YouTube video set to play. "I found this interview he did at his house in California. I guess that's where he lived?"

"Still does. He'll not be here long."

"Anyway, look." Lincoln is seated on a white couch, his skin glowing warmly from a splash of yellow sunlight falling across his features. He's dressed simply in a white t-shirt and gray chino pants. I'm struck at how sparse the background is. Mostly empty space. Behind him is a wall-spanning built-in shelving unit with most ledges empty and the others holding only one item. The coffee table in front of him and the side table are empty. Not even a lamp or a stack of coasters. I immediately know what I'm looking at. Jane Kennedy Hale's influence. Her minimalism. Lincoln had recreated the stark simplicity of the Hale house, but on a grander scale. I don't know why it makes me smile, but it does. As he's talking about the upcoming season of his show, a second camera angle reveals a black baby grand piano along a large stretch of windows overlooking the ocean that glistens in the far distance beyond a valley of civilization.

"Yeah, his house looks cool," I agree with a smile. Internally, I'm now more flummoxed as to why Lincoln is here when he has that place and life waiting for him in California.

"Mom. Not that. No. Look." Dunn spreads his fingertips out on the screen to zoom in on a spot behind Lincoln's shoulder. One of the shelves of the built-in holds a lone item, sea green, resting at a tilt. My breath catches. It's my book. It's *Luca Rex*. My pained head grows loud with rolls of thunder.

"Are you sure you're not famous?"

"I promise. I've only written one book." *And never to write another*.

"Anyway, I thought that was cool. I'm going to ask him about having your book next time we drive."

I'm suddenly at attention. "Next time?"

"He said he'll take me after school on Tuesday. That's cool with you, right? I mean, I'll stick with the lessons and drive with Dad when he's here, but I really want to drive the BMW some more."

Well, here we are. I cannot stop it any longer. The past has managed to push past every hurdle I've thrown in front of it, scaled every wall I've built around it, forded every moat I've filled to drown it, and crawled from every grave I've dug to bury it. It is here and it will be reckoned with.

I'm resigned and too sick to protest. "Sure. That's cool."

I send an elated Dunn off with my old yearbook and collapse onto my bed, my neck suddenly stiff, my head hammered by jolts of pain, my skin clamming up coldly and then lighting itself on fire. I don't need a thermometer to tell me I'm feverish. I already knew I wasn't writing ten chapters tomorrow, but being sick puts the nail in the coffin of my deranged hope that something amazing would spark and I'd type it out at an astonishing 300 words per minute.

I text my mother to tell her I'm not feeling well and that we won't be at family dinner tonight. I text Hadi to cancel our regular Saturday night hang—for the second week in a row.

Movie night is canceled due to pestilence

No

Sick

Don't fucking lie to me

Not a lie. Death beckons.

Fine. See you next week. I'm feeling like Goonies

They never say die

Exactly. ur a trash friend

You love me

Even in my pain, I smile at my phone. Hadi Reza.

He's brash and rude and confident, all necessary to succeed at his investment job in New York City, and he's going to absolutely shit a whole brick wall when he finds out who moved in next door and is now teaching my son to drive a manual-transmission BMW.

I feel myself weighted with sleep, memories of the first time I drove a car swirling in my head. I'm too sick to stop them, so just this once, I give them permission to remind me of what I'd long tried to forget.

Chapter Twenty

January 1997
Ellis, 16
Lincoln, 18

Ellis felt the push of the door to the tutoring room against her limp body, sliding her a few inches along the cold gray floor. She was on her back and the bottom edge of the door was sharp against her thigh, but she didn't resist. A few additional shoves sent her body to an angle and Lincoln's head appeared around the door's edge.

"What the hell are you doing down there?"

"Dying."

"From what?"

"Stupidity."

Another hard shove against her body allowed him to enter the room. He casually tossed away his book, which Ellis knew by now would be the music of Tchaikovsky or Beethoven or Mozart. It sailed above her and landed on the table with a thwack.

"What now?" he asked, towering over her. "I swear you're the most dramatic person I ever met."

"Polygons."

"Pretty easy. Triangles is where you might have some problems."

She rolled onto her stomach with a moan, the dirty floor cool against her nose tip and forehead. "I already have problems, ass."

She felt a nudging kick at her foot. "What?"

"I thought I was so close to getting this damned grade high enough to start driving, but polygons are trying to sabotage me. My dad is already suggesting I can spend the summer teaching archery and sailing at church camp in Virginia instead of driving."

"You know archery and sailing?" He sounded surprised.

She thought of her last four summers spent at the camp where she mostly let the religion roll off her, and the sun and daily adventure and temporary friendships absorb into her. It was nice getting away from her brothers for two months, but now she'd outgrown being a camper, and would be a counselor. It didn't sound nearly as fun. "You should realize by now that I'm a complex individual with a range of talents," she said woodenly into the floor.

Ellis heard the door open and wondered if he had left but refused to look. She would lie here alone on her stomach until the lights flickered and then walk home even if it took hours and maybe her mother would think she'd gotten kidnapped, and then when she reappeared safe, her mother would feel such relief she would let Ellis learn to drive despite the C she was currently holding in 11th grade geometry. *She Came Back to Drive: The Ellis Marks Story*—an ABC Afterschool Special.

"Linc, you coming? Mr. Mac is—" It was a girl's voice. "What the hell? Is she okay?"

"She's fine. I swear."

Ellis put her cheek to the floor and looked up to find a red-haired senior she recognized from the hallways but whose name she didn't know, staring down at her with concern. "I'm fine; just stupid," Ellis said, "at math. I'd kick your ass at English." She knew it would pull a laugh from Lincoln and it did, filling her with satisfaction.

"Okay, then." The redhead dropped her concern and turned to Lincoln. "You ready for rehearsal? Mr. Mac is looking for you."

Ellis returned her forehead to the floor. They were discussing the spring play, *Our Town*. Lincoln had been cast as the Stage Manager. Ellis spoke into the floor. "Go. Have a good rehearsal. I'll be here next week. Maybe I won't even move from here until next week."

She heard the door close. Five more minutes. She'd sprawl here for five more minutes and then go call her mom to take her to the town library where maybe there was a book about polygons or a book about good jobs you can get without a high school diploma or, barring that, a book about childhood emancipation from accountability-loving parentals. The door opened once again and the kick at her shoe returned. "Get up."

"No. Go to rehearsal. Was that Cassie With The Big—"

"Ellis Marks."

"Lincoln Hale," she mimicked his tone and cadence.

She sensed a movement before strong hands grasped her under her arms and easily lifted her to a standing position like a tantruming toddler. She whirled around and found her nose in his chest.

"Let's go driving," he said down to her.

"Are you nuts? Go to rehearsal. I'll get grounded again."

"Geometry will still be here in twenty minutes. It's a sunny day in January in Pittsburgh. There's no snow on the ground, and I have a car sitting outside. I'll take you driving."

"But—"

With an exasperated roll of his eyes, he pulled her backpack from the table and grabbed her hand in his. She let him drag her through the library and out into the hallway where they walked past the redhead who looked from their joined hands to Lincoln's face in surprise. He rushed past with Ellis awkwardly stumbling behind to keep up with his long strides. "I'll be in rehearsal tomorrow. She actually is sick. I need to drive her home. Tell Mr. Mac. Thanks, Cass!"

His grip was firm as he led Ellis out of the main entrance and into the cold. The sun hinted at warmth, but the air was still biting. She'd left her coat in her locker. Undeterred, Lincoln continued his march to the parking lot, which was mostly empty, not letting her hand go. She smirked knowingly at the back of his head. "So that really was Cassie With The—"

"You're the worst."

"I'm just saying I noticed them too, is all."

"Chris is right. The mouth on you."

She sent a satisfied cackle into the air and let him drag her to his mother's old car where he finally released her hand. It grew immediately cold. He tossed her backpack in the back seat and opened the driver's door. "In you go," he said with a wave of his arm like an eager chauffeur. "Either that or we go back to that damn gray windowless room." He looked at her shivering body briefly. "Get in and it will be warmer."

"Fine," Ellis agreed, wanting to escape the cold.

In the passenger seat, Lincoln inserted his key in the ignition. The keychain was a small, faded keyboard, the black keys having turned to gray, and the white now a scuffed tan. "Start 'er up."

"How?"

Lincoln twisted fully in his seat to look at her incredulously. "Are you kidding me right now?"

"I don't know how to start a car! Why would I know that?"

"By existing? Christopher has been driving since he was 15."

"What? How?"

He shrugged. "We used to take this car around the block."

"But your mom—" She stopped herself, remembering his mother would have already been dead. "Sorry."

"It's okay. So, you want to put your foot on the gas—pedal on the right—not too hard though, and turn the key forward while giving the pedal a little push with your foot. So everything forward and down. Then let the key and pedal go. Go ahead."

Ellis did as he said, but was heavy with her foot, and didn't let the key go quickly enough, pulling a loud angry rev from the car.

"Jesus. Little easier next time."

"I told you this was a bad idea!"

"Chill. Shift to drive. The D."

"I know that," she spat.

"I can assume nothing with a person who doesn't know how to start a car."

She threw him a sarcastic smile and moved the gear stick as she'd seen her mother do until it nestled into the correct position. The car gave a tiny jolt indicating it was ready to roll and she let out a small nervous chirp. Internally acknowledging the fact that she was about to operate a death machine against the orders of her mother, father, and the Commonwealth of Pennsylvania, she gripped the wheel tightly with fear, but also a hint of excitement. Perhaps this was what her mother meant when she would whip out the "if your friends jumped off a cliff" line. Here Ellis was, about to jump off a proverbial cliff because her friend was sitting in the passenger seat telling her to. *She Drove Off a Cliff: The Ellis Marks Story Part 2*—an ABC Afterschool Special.

"Lift your foot a bit. More. More. There. So we're moving and—"

Feeling a small push of panic rising in her chest, Ellis slammed her foot down, bringing the car to a jarring halt that threw them against their seatbelts with a sudden, painful lurch. "I got scared!" she blurted at the same time he let out a drawn out "why?"

"I'm sorry," she squeaked, holding fists to her cheeks.

"Look, Ellis, worst case, you get the brake and gas confused and send us into the stadium gate right there and we die. No one can punish you when you're dead."

Her internal fear shifted from mere grounding to fiery death. "I hate you."

"You always say that, but you still show up."

"So I can get my grade up and learn to drive."

"Ergo," he opened his palms toward the dashboard, "here we are. Literally learning to drive. Lift your foot again."

"How are you so calm about this? About everything? All the time?"

He grew quiet and shrugged. "I guess ... sometimes you realize what's big enough to be worth worrying about."

She looked at his profile and wondered what he thought of in that moment. Maybe his mother. Maybe his upcoming audition at Juilliard. He looked at her, and she smiled, feeling warmed by the glowing light of friendship that lit the spaces between them these days. She wiggled her eyebrows at him. "Okay. Lifting my foot. Pray."

"Already been praying, babe."

The word "babe," thrown so casually, sparked inside her head. She focused her eyes out the windshield and with an inhale for bravery and a prayer of her own for protection, pulled up her foot, sending the car into a slow roll.

"Okay, Andretti, you're coasting at a blistering five. Bring it up to a ten maybe?"

After fifteen minutes of driving the car up one length of the parking lot and down again, practicing slow turns that Ellis screeched nervously throughout, reaching a top speed of "a screaming 17 miles an hour," as Lincoln narrated in his play-by-play, then parking the car diagonally across three empty spaces "like a drunk-off-her-ass grandma," they snuck back into the school, careful to avoid Cassie With The— and Mr. Mac or anyone else who might report that Lincoln Hale had in fact been able to rehearse and junior Ellis Marks was not in fact so ill that she had passed out onto the floor of the tutoring room and that the two of them had in fact been spotted snickering and zigzagging around each other in a low crouch through the library rows before closing the door of the tutoring room behind themselves.

Ellis Sloan Therapy Sessions

Gulf Tower
Pittsburgh, PA
July 2021

Dr. Parrish: Do you realize you touch your scar when you're feeling vulnerable?

Ellis: I— No. I never realized.

Dr. Parrish: Is that a painful memory?

Ellis: In more ways than one.

Dr. Parrish: We should look at that.

Ellis: Why? It's the past.

Dr. Parrish: How many more times do I need to say "the past builds our now" before you'll believe me?

Ellis: At least seven.

Dr. Parrish: The past builds our now. The past builds our now. The—

Ellis: You're going to accidentally summon a demon, you know.

Chapter Twenty-One

November 2020

So this is death.

"What's wrong?" I hear Lincoln's muted voice through the bed comforter I'm burrowed under and through the brain fog of whatever random casserole of over-the-counter drugs I swallowed in want of relief. What is he doing here, in my bedroom? Is it today or tomorrow? Is it still yesterday? Is it day or night? The pain that shoots up my neck and stabs easily through my brain sends a wave of nausea crashing through me.

"I'm dying," I groan out in answer.

The covers are pulled from my head and I slit open one eye to see him standing over me, awash in sunlight. It's blinding and painful. It's daytime. Which day? I remember going to bed Saturday night and stumbling blindly through Sunday, serving easy meals and helping with homework as best I could. I remember regular retreats to my bedroom to heave over the toilet and to throw back whatever meds I could find to get me through the next hour or two. I remember falling into bed. I don't remember the kids going to bed. He frowns down at me. "You're dying? From what?"

"Death, I think." I close my eyes to shut out the light that hurts.

"You're dying from death?"

"It has been known to happen."

"What are the symptoms of death?"

"My head hurts. I'm puking. I'm cold. I'm heavy. My head really hurts. My neck so much."

I feel the back of his hand against my cheek, and I can't tell if his skin feels cold or hot. My senses are jumbled. He immediately pulls his hand away and I crack open one eye to find him typing rapidly into his phone.

"Wren and Dunn?" I ask.

He keeps his focus on his phone screen. "School. On their way. Dunn texted. He got Wren on the bus and then got a ride to school. With Joey? He told me to check on you. Now shh."

I have got to tell my children to stop going behind my back to seek help from Lincoln Hale, my God. "When was this?" I try to find my place in time. I don't remember getting Wren up for school or picking out her clothes or reminding her about teeth and deodorant and about being kind and helpful and advocating for herself when she felt frustrated. I didn't do her hair. Did she have her water bottle and her headphones for the bus to drown out the noise? Did she take her folder? Did she have a lunch? Did anyone remind her to try to stay on task? All the duties of motherhood gnaw at me and I tense my neck to try to sit up, sending more daggers of ice and fire into my head.

"About a minute ago. Stay still."

So today is tomorrow and no longer yesterday. I'll rest until it's tableau time. I pull my comforter over my head only to feel it yanked cruelly down again a moment later. When I open my eyes the narrowest slit I can manage, I find Lincoln's nose a half-foot from mine but I cannot jerk away because I know the pain it will electrify through my skull.

"Close your eyes," he demands, still hovering.

I do, grateful for the darkness.

When I reopen them, he is standing again, typing into his phone. I shiver. When I feel the covers replaced once more over my head, I strangely wonder if this is what it's like for corpses when the sheet is pulled over them to tuck them into the first moments of their final and eternal sleep. I feel him reach under the cover for my hand. He holds it for a moment and then I feel him do the same to my right foot. I think he might have a fever. His hands feel hot. Or maybe cold.

I think I should tell him to take his temperature, but I feel a deeper heaviness settle on me and I don't fight it. Thankful for a merciful respite from the cold and the blinding pain and his hot—or maybe cold hands, I let the weight push me below the surface of consciousness into oblivion.

When I open my eyes again, I am stretched across the back seat of a moving vehicle. I'm still wearing the t-shirt and leggings I slept in. I have no shoes or socks, but a blue jacket is thrown over my bare feet. A warm hand cradles my neck and another is under my head, supporting it. Lincoln's face hovers above. He looks down at me but doesn't smile. I close my eyes on the punishing rays of sunlight filtering into the window at intervals. Death is quite painful. It is the opposite of peace. We have all been lied to.

Rest in pain, Ellis Sloan.

I let myself slip away once more.

Lincoln is carrying me. He's walking too fast, nearly jogging, and it hurts very much. My head screams. My skin is on fire. But I'm cold. Definitely cold now. "Please stop," I whisper. "My kids?" I don't know what I'm asking him. To stop running so it will stop hurting me? To take me someplace where I can be a mom who isn't dying? I feel myself becoming untethered from consciousness again and I want to fight it. This all feels like something I should be here for, but I'm helpless and I feel my leash to this place and time break free and fall away. I don't reach for it.

I'm in a narrow bed, uncovered and shivering. My feet are

numb. The room is bright with fluorescence. Snippets of words register in my brain. I drift in and out.

"I'm not sure."

"Sloan."

"I don't know."

Vivid flashbacks of a memory long held down burst to life. These lights. This bed. This room. These sounds. The beeping. There's shouting. Words I don't understand give tinny echoes off hard, unforgiving surfaces. Lights whirl past overhead. I'm covered in my own blood. I can taste it. Scared. Reaching my hand out for Seth. For anyone. Is Seth okay? Am I to be alone while I die? Is he? Was he? No one holds my hand. It stays cold and it trembles in a vain reach toward emptiness and absence. I fade out again.

Then in.

"I saw NyQuil."

"Rash."

I reach for a hand. It comes for me. It's warm and I squeeze it because it feels like my only connection to realness. I think it might be the tether holding me here. I want to stay here and see my kids again. I squeeze it harder and feel the same pressure returned in kind. A silent message of comfort.

"Her brother will know."

I become unmoored and slip away.

"My sister."

My hand is empty, and I am too weak to do anything more than widen my fingers on the bed in search of the tether. *Keep me here, please. Don't let me fall away again.*

"El?"

"A line."

"Tap."

"Three. Two. One."

There are too many hands on me now. I'd only wanted one to hold. This is too much. I'd like it all to stop. I'd like to go back to the car and have my neck cradled warmly with my head resting in a strong open hand, and then I want to crawl into my bed and not be here where it's loud and bright and cold and where it feels like I'm at the beginning of a goodbye. I'm rolled onto my side. I think my brain will explode. I hope that it does.

Rest in peace, Ellis Sloan.

I awaken in heaven.

Chapter Twenty-Two

March 1997
Ellis, 16
Lincoln, 18

"Ellis, we're ready!" Christopher's shouted announcement breached the door to her bedroom.

"Be right there!"

The reflection that greeted Ellis in the full-length mirror on her closet door was a slightly different version of herself than she'd remembered the last time she cared enough to study who she was in her body. Over the last six months, a slightly older clone had gradually erased the last traces of her preteen years. Her skin was calm. Her wisdom teeth performed a miracle that closed the slight gap between her upper front teeth. Her dark brown curls were now mostly tamed by trial and error with various cheap products she'd snagged at Hills on shopping jaunts with her mother. Her face was different too but in a way she couldn't quite figure out. Maybe more angles. Her jawline more evident. Less roundness. She didn't have an artist's eye to decode the metamorphosis, but the shift had taken place.

"Ellis! I swear!" Christopher again.

"Okay! God!"

"Don't take the Lord's name in vain," came her father's call from somewhere deeper in the house. Ellis rolled her eyes and internally uttered every invocation she could think of. *God. Jesus. Jesus Christ. God Almighty. Good God. Holy crap. Holy shit. Holy bananas. Holy cow. Mother of God. Mother—*

She stopped herself on that one, partly because it wasn't the Lord's name—what was the point of defiance if you weren't going to truly defy, and partly because the word made her think of Lincoln. With Ellis finally nearing the needed B grade to set off on a new path of freedom that would find her begging her mother to use the family's only car, they'd manage to work tutoring around Lincoln's busy schedule. Around the activity that came with his acceptance to Juilliard, which was reported in the local newspaper for a reason she couldn't understand. Around his play rehearsal schedule. Around his hangouts with Chris. Luckily, they didn't also have to work it around Ellis's schedule because hers was school, eat, sleep, lather, rinse, repeat and toss a weekly church service and occasional friend hangout in there.

They met on Wednesdays. They sat in the gray prison. They laughed. They took advantage of good weather to sneak out to driving lessons. Ellis was worried she'd need to pretend to be terrible at it once her mother finally decided to "teach" her. She knew how to start a car. She knew how to back out of a parking space. Lincoln had thumped her back in congratulations when she finally reached 25 miles per hour, nearly causing her to swerve into a parking lot curb. She'd yelled at him about being a "death-wishing lunatic." He yelled that she was "being too Ellis." She looked at him and yelled, "What the hell does that mean?" and he pointed ahead and shouted, "Curb!" The car bounced harshly over it. They stormed their separate ways after equally impressive door slams but found themselves laughing uproariously the very next Wednesday as Lincoln mimed in slow motion their angry yelling and wild flailing when the car had hopped the barrier.

She punched his arm when the Juilliard acceptance came. He

tried not to smile; she pointed into his face and said, "Don't smile. I mean it. Don't do it." He finally smiled proudly.

She helped him learn his lines; he helped her to not set fire to homework on congruent triangles the day she snuck in a lighter and held it to the paper to make him laugh. He had wrestled it out of her hands, managing to toss it into the small trash can just as another set of tutoring students entered the room. An announcement about smoking in the school carrying a punishment of a week's suspension was included in the principal's message the next morning.

It was what it became. A friendship. Confined to the hours of 2:45 to 3:30 p.m. most Wednesdays. Outside of that, the high five as he passed her, once per day, in the crowded hallway. A wink at her with an easy, "Hey, Eller," when he came to pick up Christopher for whatever amusements the two of them set off in search of.

Tonight, her family would see him in the spring drama club production. She had thought perhaps she and Christopher would go alone, but her mother insisted it be a family event to show support to Lincoln. Poppy had long ago decided that whenever possible, the Marks family would fill in the maternal support gaps left by Jane Hale's absence.

Ellis spent opening curtain to closing curtain transfixed, watching him move about the stage with a confidence she didn't think she'd ever have, sending his words and every ounce of their meaning right up to the ceiling. He was, in a word, magic. That's the word she settled on. Magic. Believable magic. Pushing his emotions to the surface, sending a perfect expression out to the audience to pull a laugh when the laugh was expected to be pulled. Finding a soft voice to bring a hushed stillness over the entire auditorium. He was the captain. This was his ship.

When the standing ovation was over, the lights raised, the crowds herding themselves out into the hallway where Ellis had once been dragged along by a hellbent Lincoln, she mostly stayed in the background of her family when they found him after the show. Poppy gushed and her father placed an arm around Lincoln's shoulder to say, "I'm proud of you. What a talent you've been given." Lucas and Seth high-fived him and Christopher bumped his fist. Ellis merely smiled, feeling uncomfortable and awkward interacting with him when he was playing the role of Christopher's friend, not hers. They didn't mix those friendships. This was Chris's time. She respected it.

Lincoln threw her his usual wink. At some point, Ellis had learned to read his face. *I'm glad you're here.*

"Where's your father, dear? I'd like to say hello," her mother said.

Lincoln tossed his gaze over the heads of the crowd milling in the hallway. "Oh, I'm not sure. He's here somewhere."

Ellis's parents walked away in search of him.

"You want me to stick around?" Christopher asked him.

"Nah. I came with my dad in his car anyway. I'll go home with him. See you tomorrow though."

When they'd settled into the station wagon for the ride home, Ellis was ignoring Lucas and Seth's loud conversation about who from their classes they had seen, but she heard her mother mention she hadn't been able to find "Jeff" after all.

Ellis looked out her window into the parking lot she'd driven without her parents' knowledge many times now and spied what looked to be Lincoln at the edge, near the trees where she'd jumped the curb, getting into his mother's old car.

He drove off alone, and a dark, cold anger immediately found Ellis's heart.

Ellis Sloan Therapy Sessions

Gulf Tower
Pittsburgh, PA
July 2021

Ellis: He left me once. Us. Me and Dunn.

Dr. Parrish: Left you how?

Ellis: Dunn was young. Maybe nine months old. He just checked out of the marriage. I didn't understand why. We weren't fighting. I was being good, you know? Quiet. Just mothering Dunn. Then he called me and said he couldn't do it anymore. I was at work. I was working in marketing for an ad company, writing copy and stuff while my sister-in-law was nannying Dunn. And Oliver said he was thinking of leaving me. Just like that. "I'm thinking of leaving you." Who does that? It wrecked me. My boss had to comfort me.

Dr. Parrish: What did you say to Oliver?

Ellis: I hate this.

Dr. Parrish: That's what you said?

Ellis: No. I left work and told him to meet me at home and I initiated sex with him.

Dr. Parrish: I see. And that made him not leave?

Ellis: No. He still packed some stuff and left us to go to his family's estate. But we worked it out. He said it was just an adjustment, becoming a father. When we met, we had plans to travel the world, the two of us, see all the history he's so obsessed with, but he's eight years older than me. We felt like we had to start the family right away. So we did. He was only gone from us a month though.

Dr. Parrish: "Only."

Chapter Twenty-Three

November 2020

Memories of blood and terror no longer chase me.

Even with my eyes closed, I can tell that it is bright and warm. The shivering has stopped, and the pain is gone. The tether must be gone too, never to be grasped again. Out of reach for eternity. Galaxies away and floating further beyond.

My eyelids are heavy, and it takes effort to pull them open, but I do because I want to let the warmth and light in. I feel a flush rise in my cheeks. My heart races. My heart still beats?

A face appears in my vision. Hovering. It's surrounded by a glow of white light. I blink.

"Ellis?"

I blink again and focus on the face, trying to draw out its murky features into something recognizable and concrete. Anything I can hold onto as real.

"El? I'm here."

A hand is gripping mine. I blink again. A familiar face finally emerges from the fog of my confusion. "Christopher?" I ask, slowly reorienting myself with consciousness and my tethered place to Earth. And my brother.

"Damn. You scared me. Us." His smile is awash in plain relief.

The haze thins slightly. "Where am I?" I ask softly, my throat dry. My tongue thick.

"My hospital."

"What happened?"

"You been sick, kiddo?"

I don't nod because I suddenly remember how much that hurts. "Little."

Christopher shakes his head slowly. "False. You've been very sick. Meningitis."

It's a scary word, and it does to me what scary words are meant to do, scare. Christopher gauges my reaction and immediately soothes with a hand on my shoulder. "Viral. It's a bad case, but it's viral. That's the good kind. We did a lumbar puncture. A spinal tap. But, El, you let yourself get very dehydrated on top of it. Dangerously, dangerously so." He nods toward the air above my head.

I follow his gaze to see several bags of clear liquid suspended from metal hooks. The path of the tubing leads to my arm where a needle disappears into a bandage. I flex my fingers. It hurts. Pain. I'm alive.

"We've got some meds in there to help with your pain, get your fever down and replenish your fluids." He winks. "Did I tell you you let your fluids get dangerously low?"

I smile softly at him. "Don't lecture."

"Oh, but I'm gonna. You were burning up and delirious and I'm not even going to ask you what meds you mixed. Your fever was over 104. You really did scare us all. How do you feel?"

I take stock of myself. I tense my neck to only encounter manageable pain. My skin no longer prickles or stings. "A lot better. Wren and Dunn?"

"It's only early afternoon. We called Oliver. He's going to be there after school for them. He's still in town."

I'm immediately unsettled. "Does Wren have a lunch? When

can I go? She only eats packed lunches. The school food— She can't—" I brace my hands alongside my body to try to sit up.

He pats my leg. "Don't sit up. Just rest for a bit. Wren is fine." He glances at the IV bags and then at his watch. I finally notice he's in his full ER scrubs. "You need to lie still for one more hour. You're improving rapidly, and since it's viral and since you're going to drink plenty of fluids when you get home—" he eyes me down the length of his nose, like a teacher scolding a student, "I'm sure you'll be out of here and home before dinnertime. You're not being admitted. This is the ER. No hospital Jell-O for you."

I lick my dry lips. "Hospital Jell-O doesn't sound too bad."

He chuckles. "I'll get you some water for now. It's green Jell-O anyway."

"It shouldn't exist."

"Amen. Okay, I do have patients other than my sister. Mom planned to come earlier but I told her you'd be discharged soon. She'll be here to take you home. She's freaked and probably sent you a thousand texts. Your phone's there." He points behind me toward a small table. "I'll be back in thirty minutes. Stay still and rest." He walks to the door where he stops to wash his hands at a small sink. I watch him while I try to piece together the gaps in my memory. I remember fragments of the ride to the hospital. My head and neck cradled.

"Chris?"

He smiles at me with raised eyebrows while drying his hands.

"Did I come in an ambulance?"

"Lincoln tossed you in an Uber—and I mean that nearly literally; he was freaked when he couldn't wake you—and brought you here. When he felt how hot your cheek was, he texted me. I had a feeling it was meningitis based on what you told him, so I had him look at your eyelids for a rash, which you have. I told him to bring you here rather than to Mercy by ambulance. I thought he'd drive you, not come in an Uber. It's a whole story. We'll tell you when you're well and rested. We'll get that lunch you promised us."

I smile at him and watch him head out the door.

"Chris?"

He pops his head back in. "Yep."

"Bring me cookies."

He winks and disappears again, and I lie there wondering what it looked like to any nosy neighbors when CBS's Kennedy Hale tossed a barefoot unconscious woman into the backseat of a car and sped away with her.

I smile at the ceiling and then reach for my phone.

Heaven will wait.

Chapter Twenty-Four

March 1997
Ellis, 16
Lincoln, 18

Ellis told her mother she was walking to a friend's house. It was a lie whose guilt she brushed away easily as she threw her jacket on and stepped into the chilled night air. The sky was cloudless, yielding its whole canvas to the stars. *Mrs. Hale would have loved this.*

She walked alone through three yards, two barking dogs, and the narrow moonlit wood to Lincoln's house. Anger's uneasiness had settled upon her, and she wished to brush it away as she had the guilt of the lie. She knew she wouldn't sleep until she found answers to the questions pressing so heavily on her heart. She found the house dark and Lincoln's car in the driveway. On the porch, she held her fist suspended in the air for a solid ten seconds before finally rapping her knuckles against it. It was done. Now to wait.

When no answer was returned, no light lit, no movement telegraphed from within, she sighed and slowly backed away from the door. She turned on her heel and had been about to lower her foot to the first step when the door creaked open behind her, startling her enough to cause her to lose her footing. She awkwardly stumbled down the second step and desperately grabbed onto the railing to stop herself from plopping down the final four on her rear. *She Came to Save the Day, But Fell on Her Ass: The Ellis Marks Story Part 3*—an ABC Afterschool Special.

"Eller?"

"Ellis," she corrected automatically, regaining her footing. She turned to see Lincoln step out of the dark house onto the porch. His hair was wet, and he was out of his costume in a t-shirt and loose lounge pants tied at the waist. She imagined this was what he slept in and knowing the fact felt a step too intimate. She barely even knew what her brothers wore to bed. She regretted having come.

"What are you doing here?"

How quickly she went from all-in to desperate to get out. She began backing down the steps with her hand on the railing. "You know, it's not important. I'll see you at school Monday, right? Night."

"Ellis." It was the same voice he used when she would make a lazy mistake on her work. Authoritative. She hated it but froze her retreat. He lowered himself to sit on the top step, motioning for her to sit next to him with a nod of his head. She did.

They sat that way for several long and quiet minutes. A car slowly rolled by. An airplane engine could be heard overhead. It trailed away leaving them again in the silence of the moon broken only by the faint rustle of the wind in the pines. Ellis wasn't bothered by the quiet that settled between them. Silence could be a scratchy woolen blanket one is desperate to throw off. This silence was soft, as it often was when they were together. Warm even on the chilly night. There was no need to crawl out from under it with any urgency.

Lincoln broke it first. "Why are you here?"

She leaned back on her palms to look at the moon. "Well, I was going to ask you something."

"What?"

She pulled herself forward again and rested an elbow on her

bent knee, plopping her chin atop her fist. "I was going to ask you, how did you feel about your performance?"

She heard a chuckle inside his throat for she had parroted the question he often asked her about geometry tests.

"Pretty good," he said.

"You screwed up a line though, right?" she scolded. She'd run lines with him enough to know what the audience didn't realize. A word mix-up and an entire skipped line of dialogue.

He leaned onto his palms as she had done, and grinned. "I did."

"I'll give you an A." She looked at him. He was watching the moon. "Minus."

"Minus? Wow. Tough."

They smiled and Ellis leaned back again. "That's not all I was going to ask you," she said after a moment.

"Okay."

"Your dad didn't come."

He let a beat pass between them. "Is that a question?"

"Did your dad come?"

Silence was the answer.

Ellis nodded. "I had a third question."

"I'm not counting."

"How do you sleep in this house alone at night?"

He watched the moon become shrouded behind a lone passing cloud and only shrugged.

"Do you always keep it so dark?"

There was no response, and she didn't push. Her arms were beginning to go numb so she leaned forward again. He did too. Their bodies were mirrored, as they often found to happen without immediately realizing they were doing it. "I had one more question."

He looked at her.

She reached into her inside jacket pocket and pulled out the folded program from the play. "Would you sign this for me?"

He pushed at her hands and rolled his eyes.

"No, I'm serious," she insisted. "Would you sign this?"

"Shut up. And I don't even have a pen."

Ellis smiled wide and reached into her jacket again, this time producing a marker which she held into the air like a sword. "Voila!"

"What else you got in that pocket?" He grabbed at the front of her coat.

"Drugs. Really good ones." She swatted his searching hand away. "Now sign," she ordered, holding the paper and marker out to him.

"No."

"Sign it and I'll do ten extra problems this weekend. Blow Miss Peters's mind so hard on Monday her braid will come all the way undone." She looped the marker through the air. "Like a magic spell. *Braid-us unfurlus*!"

He eyed her skeptically but took the marker and paper and signed his name neatly to the front of the program. "This is dumb."

"It's not. You'll be famous one day, you see, and I'll have Lincoln Hale's first autograph. I'll sell it and sail the world alone." She took the program and marker from him and stood. "I'll go now. Let you go to bed and lie awake in a dark house thinking about that mistake you made." She gave his shoulder a pat and hopped down the steps.

"Eller?"

"Ellis, you persistent ass," she said, turning to him.

"You're a pretty good friend."

She smiled and let his kind words spread through her. "I really am. But I won't tell Christopher you said this. He's, like, super possessive of you." She turned to leave.

"Ellis?"

She froze and turned once more.

He looked up at the trees and then to her. "Come sit out here again some night if you want?"

"You bring some snacks. I'll bring the drugs."

He let out a full laugh and Ellis drank it in like she always did. She knew she would sleep soundly that night, for the anger she felt at his father dissolved away when the laughter she heard floating through the cold air told her that maybe Lincoln would be able to sleep some this night too.

And so she did on cool lazy nights when her homework was done and dinner eaten and her family comfortably settled into their evening routines. She walked to the Hale house, through three backyards and through a narrow wood, as she often had as a child, only now through the dark. Only now to sit on the porch with Lincoln, not at the piano with his mother. The house would stay dark, and he would laugh at her jokes and stories. And she would inhale the music of it until it was inside her, pushing on her heart, seeking to enter the quiet space where she kept the memory of his mother's laugh.

She let his in and hoped they'd find each other again there.

Ellis Sloan Therapy Sessions

Gulf Tower
Pittsburgh, PA
July 2021

Ellis: Maybe we got married too young. He's the only boyfriend I've ever had.

Dr. Parrish: Ah, your first love.

Ellis: —

Dr. Parrish: No?

Ellis: I'm not sure.

Dr. Parrish: Did he want children?

Ellis: —

Dr. Parrish: No?

Ellis: He said he did.

Dr. Parrish: I asked if he wanted them, not if he said he wanted them.

Ellis: I no longer know the answer to that question.

Dr. Parrish: Did you push to have children more than he was prepared to do so?

Ellis: —

Dr. Parrish: Ellis, we're not putting blame anywhere. We're trying to understand truths. Hiding from them won't get us anywhere.

Ellis: I pushed. Insisted.

Dr. Parrish: So you took control.

Ellis: Yeah. I guess I did.

Chapter Twenty-Five

November 2020

Dunn texted a few times to check in, his second message a bit more serious than his first. I reply with breezy joking messages to ease his mind and ask him what he wants for dinner. If he responds, I'll scold him for using his phone at school. He knows this. We are now engaged in a battle of wills.

On her way to school, Wren sent a meme I don't understand but am sure she found absolutely hilarious. I reply with an eye-roll, the emoji I've learned is usually the correct response. I then text her aide to be sure everything is well.

Oliver texted to say he had heard from Chris that I was sick. A later text asked what time the kids got home from school. A third text asked about a key for the front door. A final text said never mind because he had gotten the information by texting Dunn (busted!) and by calling Wren's school. The key issue was resolved because the front door had been left unlocked. I respond with "thanks."

My brothers and their wives used our group text to send their thoughts and love. Nathan with a staid, "Get well, brat." Lucas with, "What in the world??" and Ash, "Kick its ass, El!"

Bea texted, "Dying is a cowardly way to get out of writing a book. One more week." I send her the middle finger emoji. Nothing will happen in one week. What is empty will remain empty because I am the only one who can fill it and I'm still empty.

Hadi texted, "What the F. U. C. K?! I'm still in town. On my way." I respond, "Don't come. I'm fine." I know it's too late though and he's probably already zooming down the Parkway East yelling holy hell at other drivers daring to take up space in his chosen lane.

Poppy Marks had apparently spent the morning activating her prayer chain in such a dramatic fashion that her church friends assumed I wasn't just at death's door but was actively breaking it down with the vengeance of a wronged superhero. I'm only halfway through the 38 texts she sent me of forwarded messages of despair and handwringing and prayer screenshots when Christopher pokes his head in.

"El? They're telling me there's a guy out there in the waiting area wanting to see you. He's ..." He pauses as if uncertain where to take his sentence.

I nod knowingly. "A lunatic? It's Hadi."

"Ah. The famous Hadi. You want me to go send him away? You need to rest."

"As if anyone has ever sent Hadi away. I'll see him for a minute. Arab in his thirties. He'll be in a suit. Little shorter than you. Can't miss him."

Christopher heads out in search of Hadi just as my phone vibrates in my hand. A new text message appears from a number I'm unfamiliar with.

I forgot your socks and shoes.

I glance at the phone number again in confusion. It's an out-of-state area code.

Mom???

Lincoln. No matter what Wren says.
Lincoln.

I wiggle my feet under the sheet and can feel they are covered in rubber-soled hospital socks.

No worries. I prefer being carried like a pharaoh anyway.

In like a rag doll, out like royalty.

I smile at the screen and try to conjure the memory of him carrying me into the ER, but it's buried in a part of my brain that's too murky for me to access.

It's my brand

Talk soon.

"Ellis Robin Marks Sloan the Third!"

I don't even have to pull my eyes from my phone screen. "Hadi," I say. I text "yep" to Lincoln and look up.

His perfectly tailored blue suit and coral shirt are striking against his glowing olive skin. He is standing in the doorway with his hands on his waist—an accusatory stance if I ever saw one. Behind him, Christopher appears slightly breathless. "Buddy, you cannot run in a hospital."

Hadi swipes dismissively at the air. "It's the emergency center. It's the very place in a hospital one can run. Watch some Grey's." He approaches my bed with dread etched on his face. "Are you dying?"

"She's not dying," Chris replies from behind with a tone that can only be described as a verbal eye-roll.

Hadi bends at his waist to stick his face into mine, his black eyes wrought with worry. As always, he smells of verbena and I want to hug him for his comforting consistency in my life. "Did you *almost* die?" he demands low and slow.

"No," I say at the same time Christopher says, "Maybe."

Hadi rears in horror and spins to face my brother. "What?" he nearly shouts.

"Meningitis."

Hadi whirls again, his face more horrified than when he spun away. "Meningitis!"

I roll my eyes. "Relax."

"Viral," Chris interjects from the doorway where he's leaning against the jamb watching Hadi's dramatics. "She'll be fine. But she's had a lumbar puncture, so she needs to rest," he says, laying down a hint Hadi clearly sees but intentionally doesn't pick up.

He instead keeps his eyes on me and throws a hand in the air to motion for Christopher to approach. Chris does with a sigh and keeps his arms crossed defensively as they stand shoulder-to-shoulder beside my bed, looking down at my prone form. I suddenly feel like I'm looking up at mourners at my own wake. It's entirely unsettling, being viewed like this. I make a mental note to have Nathan's wife Celeste change my will to be sure my eventual funeral is closed casket no matter how well I age.

Hadi puts his hands out and gestures widely above me in circular motions. "How did this happen to her?"

Christopher pokes himself in the chest. "You're asking me?"

"Who else?"

"Maybe the grown woman who let herself get sicker and sicker for days and didn't tell a soul and then got dehydrated on top of it and kept taking NyQuil even though her fever hit 104 and wouldn't come down?" He does an exaggerated imitation of Hadi's gesture over my bed. "Maybe ask her?"

My soft chuckle is enough to bring a dull pain to my neck. Hadi narrows his eyes at him. "Victim blaming."

"Victim blam— Listen to you. I don't even know you."

"Introduce us, El," Hadi says while still looking at Christopher.

"Christopher, Hadi. Hadi, my brother. Be nice." I'm not sure to which of them I direct that last part. Maybe both. They throw indifferent nods of their heads to acknowledge each other's respective existences on Earth.

Hadi starts again. "There. Now I know you. Tell me everything. What does she need? When can she go home? What are those meds?" He points to the bags hanging above my head. "Who is taking her home?" He looks at me. "I can take you home." Back to Christopher. "Do you have care instructions for me?"

Christopher opens his mouth to speak and then abruptly clamps it shut and walks out of the room, never uncrossing his arms.

Hadi looks at me bewildered, but I smile. Now that we're alone, the shield he always seems to be holding out in front of himself lowers and I can see the fearlessness and confidence disappear from his face. He grabs my hand. "Are you okay? Really?"

"Hadi, I'm fine. I feel so much better already. Chris says I can leave in an hour or so." He opens his mouth, but I rush on to stop the things I already know he's going to say because we often seem to share a brain. "Poppy is coming to get me. You're free to go to New York, and I'll be good as new in a day or two. I'll see you next weekend. We'll watch *Goonies* like you wanted. I won't cancel. Promise."

He sighs. "You can't do this. Not take care of yourself and this happens. Or worse." He blinks and a shine forms in his eyes. "I don't work without you, okay?"

"That's silly."

He is vehement. "No. I am serious. You're all I have. If you die before me, I will be erased out of existence like Marty McFly nearly was."

I smile at his invocation of one of our favorite movies. "You have nothing to worry about. I promise, McFly."

"I should get a medal for being dramatic enough that I got a meningitis patient to comfort me from her actual death bed."

"I'm not dying and don't make me laugh. It hurts." I wince.

He stands to kiss my cheek and rests his hand on top of my head. "Your hair is a fucking nest. Couldn't love you more."

"Same. Now go. Have a good flight. I'm going to rest so Christopher will let me go home."

"He's a bit of a dick, that one, yes?" he asks with a comical tilt of his head.

I only smile. I'll not speak badly of either of them.

"Okay. I'm going to go make my assistant hate life. I'll let you rest. Love you. Hate you. Don't ever do this again. Oliver can't win, and if you die, he wins." He begins buttoning his suit jacket as he turns to leave but abruptly pauses when he sees Christopher standing a step or two inside the room, watching us. And listening. Hadi remains frozen for a moment, and I'm sure it's because he realizes the "dick" line was overheard. But he quickly regains his confident posture and snaps his fingers toward Christopher twice. Shield up. "Take care of her," he orders and then brusquely walks out of the room with a tug at his cufflinks and the haughty air of a man who owns the hospital and everything within a five-mile radius of it.

Christopher whistles in mock appreciation. "Lunatic is right." He checks my IV bags. "Looks like you're getting out of here soon. Doc will be by shortly."

"Great. Oh, I don't have shoes, I'm told."

"I'll put you in a wheelchair."

I nod. Suddenly a thought occurs to me. "Hey," I say, "how did Hadi even find out I was in here?"

Christopher smiles. "Only thing I can figure? He must be on Poppy's Prayer Chain."

I don't even mind the pain that pulsates through my head as my brother and I explode in shared laughter.

Chapter Twenty-Six

March 1997
Ellis, 16
Lincoln, 18

"You're so quiet tonight. You good?" Ellis was on her third cookie when she finally asked the question she'd been holding back since Lincoln walked out of his house to sit on the porch step with her. The change in clocks let the days grow longer, so a small glow of light still burned its fire low in the trees. Directly above them, the stars had taken the stage. He'd been slowly twirling an Oreo in his hands for ten minutes, watching it spin, flipping it, and not eating a bite.

He gave her no answer, keeping his eyes on his hands and the cookie they toyed with.

"Do you want me to go?" she offered. "I can go."

"No. I don't want that."

There was a strange hardening of his features she couldn't read. His eyes small. His jaw tight. It wasn't worry. She knew what that looked like from the previous day when she nearly rear-ended a mail truck on one of their driving excursions, and easy-going Lincoln became one of those grandmas who frantically stomps her foot down on nothing, hoping a passenger-side brake would magically materialize.

"I'm going to guess, then. Christopher? Did he do something annoying? I only ask because he annoys me every day and it'd be cool if he was portioning that out a bit."

He didn't smile. A huge concern to Ellis, who had perfected the art of easily getting those grins to turn to chuckles to turn to full laughs that drew looks from librarians, classmates, and once, Christopher, who had been surprised to see her able to do it.

"Your dad?"

"Nah. You know I don't give a shit about him."

A breeze carried his words to her, and they surrounded her heavily. Sadness. That's what she was seeing. And she knew. He finally seemed to notice the cookie in his hands. He dropped it to the steps, letting it bounce down to be carried away by a lucky yard critter after they had said goodnight. "So, your mom," she said in answer to her own question.

Tension contracted his features and his shoulders. It was a direct hit. Bullseye. No question. She watched him work his mouth. Pulling his lips inward and then biting at his cheek. She was gutted for what he was trying to hide.

"Is there something I can say? To, like, help you right now?"

He brushed his hands on his jeans, removing the last of the cookie crumbs. "It's her birthday. Was her birthday? I don't know."

"Oh," is all she could say wishing there was more, but what do you say to a person missing another person, and not because they've gone on a trip, or simply moved away, but instead, left forever? Ellis felt too small against the size of his loss to be any good.

"You know what?" Lincoln finally said. "You can go. I'm just not good company right now. And you've got your test in two weeks. You should study."

"Stand up."

"Why?"

"Just stand up, please. I do everything you tell me to do at all times."

He shot her a look for her clear lie but drew himself to his full height, seemingly under great weight. She grabbed his hand and led him toward the front door of the always dark house, then pushed it open. Shadows played with the light filtering in from windows. "Can I turn a lamp on? Or will you disintegrate and die?" She was pleased to hear him stop a chuckle that had built in his throat. A start.

He pulled slightly away from her, and the room lit up. Ellis saw it for the first time in years. Exactly how it had been. They hadn't changed a thing. Touched or moved a thing either, it seemed. It gave her the strange sensation that she'd stepped back in time and was once again the ten-year-old girl sitting with her teacher, poking her fingers at the wrong keys between sips of iced tea from short drinking glasses painted with daisies.

She led Lincoln to the piano and sat down on the stool her teacher used to perch herself upon during Ellis's lessons. Back straight. Chin high. Ears open. Eyes closed. Heart lit until it died. "Sit down," Ellis ordered with a point at the bench.

He did with a sigh, then rested his hands atop each of his legs. "Why? What?"

"It's so weird to be sitting in this spot. You're in my spot and this is her spot, right? It's like," she snapped her fingers once, "I'm back there. Back in time. Plucking out 'Twinkle Twinkle Little Star' while she tried not to cringe. But I kept screwing up the notes, so it was more like 'Twinkle Little Star Twinkle.' I was really bad."

He finally gave her a small, crooked grin. It was another opening.

She scooted herself closer to the piano, to the exact spot Mrs. Hale had always scooted. "Listen, Linc. This sucks. I hate it for you. It feels like you're too young for something so ... big? But, do you ever feel her around you like I do sometimes? Like that day in the tutoring room when we were laughing about her reaction to Cutesy?"

He only looked down at the piano keys and gave a small shrug.

"What was her favorite song to make you play? I know she had to have asked you to play for her. She'd have needed to hear something beautiful after my weekly musical assaults."

"Beethoven. 'Pathetique.'"

"Play it for me? Then I'll go home and do stupid geometry." She straightened her back as Mrs. Hale had always done, folded her hands into her lap and closed her eyes. And then she waited. In sadness for her friend. In mourning for her teacher whose place she occupied on what should have been her birthday spent with her son now on the brink of adulthood.

The first soft notes finally floated up and found her, and she came to understand why Mrs. Hale always closed her eyes. It injected the music with more power. If sadness was music, this was it. Slow. Deep. Gradual. Like a low crawling fire taking its time to spread. Like a ballet dancer stalking across a stage, her movements full of despair and her face wrought with pain. It was a song of sorrow. Regret. Misery. And it was beautiful.

She didn't intrude on him with a peek but let him have the time alone to play without anyone's eyes touching him. But as she let the music creep low and sad around her, she hoped he wasn't fully alone, because surely, she thought, prayed, begged while sitting there listening, if we're to say goodbye to people, to never see them again, nor touch or hug them again, to go the rest of our lives knowing there's no spot on Earth they still walk, then at the very least, if her father's God was as merciful as he preached him to be, Lincoln should be given the transcendence needed to reach his mother in the beyond with the music she had taught him.

For it was Mrs. Hale's birthday and she had said her earthly goodbye to her son six years earlier. She deserved to hear from her stool at the seat of heaven his gentle song screaming out in yearning for her.

Ellis Sloan Therapy Sessions

Gulf Tower
Pittsburgh, PA
July 2021

Dr. Parrish: And you wrote *Luca Rex* while all this was happening in your marriage?

Ellis: I wrote *Luca Rex* because of my marriage.

Dr. Parrish: How so?

Ellis: When we met, I had told him I was working on a novel. Not *Luca Rex.* Something from before. I never finished it. I've been writing novels since I graduated high school. I started another and couldn't finish it. Another that I quit as well. I was a huge disappointment to him. He lost his temper one night and threw my laptop into the sink and ran water over it.

Dr. Parrish: Why was he so invested in you finishing a novel?

Ellis: Listen, he's an author too. He's got books in the university library system, not to mention countless journal pieces. Mostly U.S. History. Academic books. Students use them as sources for their papers. It doesn't pay much. When I got my writing contract, I think he saw it as a way out. Sell my book, make a fortune, he quits his job, and we finally do the traveling we said we would. He'd be free. We'd be free.

Dr. Parrish: His family doesn't support him?

Ellis: No. He's got a big inheritance coming at some point though.

Dr. Parrish: So you finished the book then. Got a new laptop?

Ellis: Yeah. Everything was backed up.

Dr. Parrish: And that made things better? Finishing the book?

Ellis: If anything, I think it angered him that I'd done it. Because he couldn't hold it over me anymore. Yell at me about letting him down. Letting his aunt down. Plus, the fact that it was a commercial success bothered him, I think. He was the author out of the two of us. I was the failed author. Not anymore. I'd done it. He was quiet. Never congratulated me. Nothing. Just ignored it. Said, "Is that so," when I told him I'd finished it. That his aunt had loved it. "Is that so?"

Dr. Parrish: How did you respond to that?

Ellis: I hid everything.

Dr. Parrish: Meaning?

Ellis: Copies of my book. Any enjoyment I got from the book tour. Fan mail. I kept it all hidden as best I could.

Dr. Parrish: Why shouldn't you have enjoyed those things, Ellis? You'd worked for them.

Ellis: It didn't seem fair to him. I didn't want to make him more upset. My happiness made him unhappy. I loved him. I'd never intentionally hurt him. Why start?

Dr. Parrish: You never intentionally hurt the person you felt was punishing you. I wanted to say that out loud so you could hear it.

Chapter Twenty-Seven

November 2020

We should first rewind to understand how I came to be where I am right now. Sitting at a small round table in the Oakmont Bakery cafe on a late Monday morning. My children in school. My ex again tucked away safely in New York. Lincoln, in his usual jeans and t-shirt, to my right. Hadi, always in a perfect suit, to my left. Christopher, in hospital scrubs, across from me. Hadi smiling widely at Lincoln in plain adoration. Christopher scowling at Hadi. Lincoln eyeing me in amusement. Me questioning all my life's choices that led me to this eyeball version of a Mexican standoff.

The upside of having meningitis is that it earns the sufferer the level of sympathy necessary to motivate a cold-hearted literary agent to text an author to tell her a one-week deadline to submit the first ten chapters of her second book was now three weeks.

The downside of having an older brother who is a nurse is that he knows, medically, the main reason you landed in the hospital with a case of viral meningitis is that you stubbornly allowed yourself to become dehydrated. Therefore, Chris gave me only one week of house calls and check-in texts before he asked about rescheduling "that lunch."

I give up on everything so easy; why are other people so damn persistent? It's infuriating. But there was no getting out of it. Lincoln was here; he had saved me by ragdoll-ing me into an Uber, and he showed up on Tuesday while I was still in bed and miserable to take Dunn driving as promised.

Dunn had returned and plopped on my bed to fill me in on everything he'd learned: Lincoln had my book because we were once friends; he read it and liked it. He was considering taking a movie role that would film in Japan. The BMW is a rental (here I make a mental note to yell at Lincoln). He has two cars in California. Their next driving lesson will be the next day after school with another set for Saturday. Driving a stick shift was easy now. Poppy was downstairs making them dinner and Aunt Maddie had dropped off clean laundry. Dunn was a complete chatterbox after months of near silence. If I hadn't felt like fresh roadkill, I might have enjoyed his animated soliloquy more.

I began to feel mostly like myself by Thursday, and good enough to perform my Mom In Control tableau by Friday. Then Hadi arrived from New York on Saturday and things got interesting. Because when your kid walks in the door and shouts, "We're here," your friend is going to want to see who "we" is. And when one half of "we" is Kennedy Hale, your friend is going to whisper to you, "Is that Kennedy Fucking Hale I am seeing?" And when the answer is, "Yes. Please be cool," your friend is going to be very uncool and seat the two of you next to each other on a couch, demanding answers like a lawyer. Dominos fell and Hadi discovered the lunch scheduled for Monday, insisted he would be coming even if it meant spending time with Christopher again.

And now here we are, eyeballs bouncing around, sitting in uncomfortable chafing silence. It seems not one of us knows what topic of conversation to broach.

But Hadi starts with, "So, Kennedy—"

I shake my head. "No. Lincoln. He's Lincoln."

"Well, either way he's an assassinated president, right?" We all can't help but snicker at the remark.

"You can call me whatever you want," Lincoln says with a wave of his hand. "Wren sure does."

Hadi straightens. "Wait. You know Wren? Of Wren?"

"Of course. We're buds. I think." He eyes me for confirmation that he's not mistaken. I nod. Wren thinks highly of him. It's why she continues to pester him about his name. It gives her something to talk to him about.

Hadi is forlorn. "She's a tough nut to crack. She hates me and all I do is love her."

I smile and pat his arm. "That's not true. You only see her once a week. You're still figuring her out."

"I know. I'll make her love me yet. I'll buy her love like I did Dunn's. All I had to do was buy him various Apple products. Boom. Love bought."

"Not everyone can be bought," Chris mutters before stabbing a bite of salad into his mouth.

"It's called a joke," Hadi points out to him.

"Who's laughing?"

Lincoln catches my eyes and widens his own. I can read him like I used to. *Oh, boy*.

I roll my eyes. *I know. These two*.

He winks and it's the same. It's the same wink. The one he always threw at me. So casual. I look away. I don't want to see it. There's nothing good for me behind it.

As much as I enjoy their barbs, a peace accord must be brokered between Chris and Hadi. "You two should get along better than this. You're grown men. You both love me. You both take care of me. You both love my children." I pause and look from one to the other. "And apparently, you're both on Poppy's Prayer Chain."

"What in the hell is Poppy's Prayer Chain," Lincoln asks, looking into all our faces.

I laugh, bending over my bagel, sending my hair falling around my face. When I flip my head back, pushing the curls into place once more, Lincoln is watching me with nostalgia plain on his face. I really can still read him. *You used to do that all the time.*

"Poppy's Prayer Chain," I explain, "is my mother's little text group of, probably, I don't know, how many would you say, Chris?"

It is Hadi who pipes up before Chris can answer. "Forty-four people."

"So, you are on it, Hadi," I exclaim in plain delight.

"Of course I am. Poppy and I talk. Have for a few years now."

"How and why are you talking with my mother?" Chris asks, clearly as stunned as I am.

"Well, you don't own her, Christopher." Hadi says the name with overly aggressive syllabic elocution. "We met once, maybe your old house, El, and we agreed to exchange numbers because we were worried about Ellis and decided we would want to be letting the other know how she was because Ellis is a stone cold ice queen. She doesn't share much. So Poppy and I share for her. Our wagons," he lifts his hands in front of himself and holds his fingertips together to form a loose ring, "circling."

I hadn't known. But it made sense now. How if I was a little restrained with Hadi one Saturday, a text from Poppy about having everyone over for dinner would hit my phone on Sunday morning. And if I'd had a rough week with Wren, Hadi would show up for our Saturday hang armed with extras of my favorites and would agree to a movie I loved more than he did.

"Oh," is all Chris can say. "That is ... actually pretty cool."

"It's actually extremely cool," Hadi says with his usual confidence before taking a bite of his turkey on rye.

Lincoln finds my eyes again and his are serious. I understand and send a message. *I'm fine. I'll be fine. Soon. It's not your concern. Look there; I've got wagons.*

Hadi continues, "Anyway, at some point, I started getting the prayer chain texts. Poppy added me without asking. Hell, I read them and pray for 'em. God is God right? Then I got the Ellis texts and lost all my shit." He shoots me a look meant to wither me to rueage.

"All of it," I agree.

"Uh-oh, Linc," Chris suddenly says with a nod toward the air behind me. Hadi and I turn to look, but Lincoln doesn't. It's late in the morning so the cafe is mostly empty, but one table is occupied by three young women. They're whispering conspiratorially to each other while looking our way and then hovering jointly over a phone screen before looking back at us.

"What?" I ask, turning to Chris.

"I think they recognize Linc."

Lincoln shrugs and sips at his coffee. "It's fine. I'm used to it. No big deal."

"Oh, here they come," Hadi says with the eager delight of a four-year-old talking about Santa's reindeer.

Lincoln sets his cup down as they arrive between his chair and mine. He lifts his eyebrows at me. *Here we go.* With fascination, I watch him change from Lincoln Hale to Kennedy Hale. It's his smile. He shutters it and himself somehow before turning to them. They're not getting the real Lincoln. It's remarkable. Like a chameleon changing its colors while you watch but you can't figure out what exactly is changing and how the hell is it doing it.

"Hello," he says with kindness that's genuine, even if the smile isn't.

"Uh, yeah, hi," one replies dismissively before the trio turns to me. "Are you Ellis Sloan? The author?"

I'm—Wait. What?

Chris and Hadi simultaneously inhale food or drink into their windpipes causing twin eruptions of hacking fits behind their fists. Lincoln eyes me and his shuttered smile is quickly replaced with his genuine one. *Well, well, well.* I'm in shock and without words.

Great. Not only can't I write them; I can no longer speak them. My next book will be a blank journal with one line of text:

I don't know. You figure it out. The end.

While the still comically reeling Hadi and Chris gulp water to clear their airways, Lincoln takes note that I'm not currently a functioning human being and answers for me. "You're correct. This is Ellis Sloan. The author."

The trio of fans begin to fidget with excitement and elated looks, talking rapidly over each other, heads jostling for eye contact with me. I hold one set of eyes, drop them and find another while they gush. That's the only word that works here, so yay, I at least found one word. They gush.

"We love your book so much!"

"Luca is hilarious!"

"I love how you used synesthesia—jumbling up all of his senses!"

"You look a little different from your picture."

"We hope we aren't bothering you."

"We just had to say hello."

"Can we get a picture with you?"

Finally recovered, Hadi leans his head toward Chris and says just loud enough that I can hear him, "I have literally never been happier."

Their heads come nearly together as Chris responds while still raptly watching the scene unfold. "Same. Inject this into me."

"You're the nurse. Inject it into me."

As for me, I can't unfreeze myself. I'm two seconds away from either a massive life-ending stroke or these lovely young women thinking I'm the rudest bitch alive. As he's done a few times over the last several weeks—and it's honestly so irritating—Lincoln saves me, rising from his chair while holding his hand out in request for a phone of theirs. "Of course she will. I'll take it." He sends me a look. *You gonna move or what?* When I don't, he pulls me up by my elbow, his grip finally snapping me out of my personal Blue Screen of Death.

I reboot and brighten my features at the excited trio. "Oh, yeah. Happy to take a picture. What are your names, then?" Bea had taught me this. Always ask their names and then repeat them. It does wonders to fans and sucks them in for life. They will buy anything you write after that, she'd said.

"Elaine."

"Billie."

"Katie."

"Elaine. Billie. Katie. Got it and I'll never forget." I tap my forehead. "It's in there."

They titter excitedly and their happiness warms me. Bea remains a genius. An evil soul-crushing genius, but a genius nonetheless.

With the picture taken, my smile probably stony and terrible because I generally avoid cameras, and Elaine, Billie and Katie giving me their final kindnesses, begging for a second Luca book (*not happening because books require words and we're fresh out of those here, folks*), Hadi holds his hand up to them.

"Ladies. Ladies. Before you go. This guy right here." He points to Lincoln who is seated and trying to bury his face in his cup of coffee. "Do you know him?"

They look at Lincoln who is positively chagrined for the first time in all the times I've been with him and send their answer to Hadi in blank expressions and uncertain shrugs. He nods and waves them away, as only Hadi can do. "That'll do. Off you go then."

When we're alone again, Lincoln pushes at my upper arm the way he used to when I'd solved something difficult and says the same thing he'd say then: "Look at you."

I reward him with what might be my first genuine smile since the day he arrived, and I'd shuttered my real one away from him as

I watched him do with those women. I can tell he notices it's me this time. *Oh. I remember you.*

Hadi grabs my hand on top of the table and squeezes it. "This is my favorite day ever. I could get sick and die tomorrow."

"Don't worry, Hadi," Chris reassures. "If you get sick, you'll jump right to the top of Poppy's Prayer Chain. Those geriatrics will storm the very gates of heaven for you."

I again throw my head forward in laughter, my hair falling to shield my face. I don't care if it does pull at Lincoln's sense of nostalgia the way his wink does to me. It feels good to laugh and let the real me feel it fully, rather than the half chuckles I've been forcing before quickly silencing them for fear the universe would hear and send punishment.

"Speaking of Poppy." Chris is looking at his phone screen.

"What?" I ask. Did the universe hear me laugh? That was fast.

He reads, "Christopher dot dot dot dot dot dot—" He smiles at me. "Why does she insist?"

"I've tried, man."

He restarts, "Christopher, while at lunch today please invite the Hale boy and Hadi to Thanksgiving. If they wish to decline, they'll need to speak to me. Period. In person. Exclamation. Dot dot dot dot dot. Dot."

I don't betray a movement, but internally I sink a little. The universe really will force me to reckon with Lincoln.

Chris eyes both. "Either of you willing to tell Poppy Marks no to her face?"

"Not fucking me," Hadi says, already typing rapidly into his phone. "I'll have Remy change my schedule. Remy's my assistant. Remy hates his life. Oh look, Remy just texted." He flashes his phone screen at us. "'I hate my life.'"

"I'll bet he does," Chris mutters.

Lincoln finds me. *Well?*

I've already resigned myself. I hate that I don't hate him. That I can't. There's a reason we were once such good friends. That kind of connection doesn't ever go away, I guess. We'd once upon a time clung to each other. Inhaled each other. Believed in each other. *It's fine.*

"I guess not me either then," he says to Chris.

Well played, Universe. Well fucking played.

Chapter Twenty-Eight

April 1997
Ellis, 16
Lincoln, 18

Elation.

Ellis exploded out the classroom door sending it smashing with a bang against the wall. Elation. This was elation. A word she learned and knew and read but never felt. It's a noun you can't see. It swooped through her heart and up to her brain, lighting sparklers and floating lanterns all along the way.

The crowded noisy hallway was abuzz with between-bell activity. Students jostled for locker access, merging in and out of the lanes of moving body traffic to get to their next class in the three minutes they were allotted. A few of the startled jumped as Ellis burst into the hallway and careened to a stop in the middle of it. She was an unmoving island in the rushing river of bodies streaming around her. She looked up the hallway one way and gave a small hop to see above the crowd. When she didn't see her target, she whirled around to look the other way, her chest heaving with excited breaths. Elation.

In her hand was her test. 86. Circled. With an exclamation point. *86!* 86 was good. But 86! meant something more than a number. More than a percentage. An exclamation. A celebration.

This was all she needed. She could drive now. Get her license. Spend the summer like a normal teenager.

He should be in the hallway right now. She always passed him at this time of day, between this set of classes. But she had been 20 seconds late into the hallway because Miss Peters stopped her on the way out to offer congratulations.

Ellis spun and searched desperately for his face in the close faces, those in the middle distance, the far away. The buzz of voices intruded into her brain—snippets of conversation and shouts and the general rush of white noise that bounced off the lockers and tile and created a wall of sound that wouldn't dissipate until the next bell rang and those final few brave stragglers ducked into classrooms with the echoes of three minutes of hallway life dying behind them.

When she spied him afar, the noise stopped. The movement of the bodies around her slowed as if the rushing river was dammed to a trickling creek. He was walking toward her, a textbook in a hand swinging freely alongside his body. Smiling. Tossing his head back in laughter as he elbowed Christopher.

And then he saw her, and she knew he did because he slowed his walk as a look of concern gradually erased his laugh and then came for his smile. Confused, Christopher slowed too, looking at Lincoln in question.

Ellis threw away every caution she had ever tucked into her heart and took off running, her eyes on Lincoln's. There were no thoughts. Only feelings. Empty brain. Full heart.

She watched the concern fall away slowly from his face as he spotted the paper clutched in her hand. His eyebrows rose to indicate a knowing smile was chasing close behind. He shoved his textbook against Christopher's chest and let it go without caring if it would be caught or left to fall. Ellis ran, her shoulders knocking against oncoming bodies, and saw him open his arms toward her as she neared. A laugh once again on his face. She grew a lifetime between those last three long strides. Eller Beller left standing in the wake of Ellis Marks.

When a teacher called out, "Miss Marks, no running," Ellis pushed the words out of her way, and she leapt.

She leapt knowing he would catch her. She leapt not caring who would see. There's no room for embarrassment in a heart overflowing with gratitude and relief and pride and other emotions she couldn't identify because they too were nouns she couldn't see. She vaulted easily off the ball of the foot of the right leg that had propelled her up countless trees—the same legs that had safely carried her away from the chasing taunts of 12-year-old Lincoln Hale.

She leapt readily for the outstretched arms of 18-year-old Lincoln Hale.

She crashed against his chest in mid-air and felt his arms encircle her waist to immediately stop her fall to Earth. She threw her arms around his neck and clung, suspended a foot off the ground with no plans to ever come down. His arms tightened around her. He squeezed her body against his and a rush of fire burst out from her heart in every direction.

She was surprised to feel that feeling. That warmth she once felt in her hand at touching his face now seemed to live and grow inside of her. There was a knot in her throat she couldn't swallow down and a push of something unidentifiable pounding at her heart. She recognized it as tears yearning to be cried and was confused by it as she buried her face into his neck. She was happy. Why did she feel sad? Why did she feel scared and safe at the same time? Why didn't the nouns you can't see line up in order and identify themselves so that you could know them, and deal with them?

Lincoln loosened his grip on Ellis's waist, yielding power back to gravity to send her in a slow controlled slide down his chest. She landed once again on Earth, but their eyes remained locked.

"Guys. What the hell?" Christopher looked at his sister, who was looking at Lincoln with worship in her eyes, and then at Lincoln, who was looking down at Ellis with a look much too serious for the halls of Reizenstein High School between periods in late April.

"Tell me," Lincoln said to Ellis, his arms still around her waist.

"86."

"86!" The exclamation point. Ellis felt a new rush of pride at hearing it come from him. An exclamation point was a noun you could see and hear, and also feel.

"Am I having a stroke right now?" Christopher asked a random passing classmate who kept walking.

Ellis realized then how it looked. What she had done. Leapt at Lincoln. Let him hold her and hug her and she put her face in his neck and breathed him in and let his heart touch hers. Mortification washed over her, and her face burned with hot shame. She stepped backward and pushed against the prison of his arms, but he refused to let her go, only tugging her closer until she was against him again. Confused, she looked at Christopher who only shrugged in his own loss for answers.

"Eller," Lincoln said.

"Ellis. Let me go." She pushed against arms that only pulled her closer.

"Eller. Go to prom with me."

Her mouth popped open. She heard Christopher mutter, "I'm going to the nurse." And with that, he dropped Lincoln's textbook at their feet and walked away, leaving his sister where she stood—in his best friend's arms, a burning in her heart, a smile on her face, and a feeling that she would forever look at this moment as one with a before and an after.

She was ready for after.

Ellis Sloan Therapy Sessions

Gulf Tower
Pittsburgh, PA
August 2021

Dr. Parrish: He didn't like your friends. So who are your friends now?

Ellis: My family. Brothers. Their wives. But I have one friend still. Hadi.

Dr. Parrish: How'd he manage to survive?

Ellis: Hadi can't be sent away. He's survived worse. His parents and only sibling, an older brother, died in a car accident when he was in his early twenties. Can you imagine? We shared a table in an over-crowded coffee shop in Market Square one day six years ago. I was editing *Luca*. He was working. Laptop to laptop. I can't even explain what happened. Like, our souls knew how to interact? Almost like me and Oliver at first. Hadi has an impossibly busy schedule working in New York but living here on the weekends. We make time for each other most every Saturday. Oliver hated it. Stayed in his study. But Hadi stayed in my life no matter how many times I tried to cancel. Oliver would still punish me with silence or anger, but Hadi was worth it. He made me feel loved. Still does even though he's engaged now.

Dr. Parrish: Did you find it unusual that your friend made you feel loved and worthy, but your husband didn't? What did you do to deserve Hadi's love?

Ellis: Nothing.

Dr. Parrish: What did you do to deserve Oliver's?

Ellis: Everything.

Dr. Parrish: Nothing. Everything.

Ellis: Oh, wow.

Chapter Twenty-Nine

Thanksgiving 2020

"I feel like we should say a prayer before we go in there, yes?"

It is Hadi who eyes my mother's nearing house with trepidation from the back seat of my car, the backup-cameraless chicken-wagon Honda, where he's squished between Wren and Dunn. Thanksgiving dinner at the Marks house has been at 4:00 p.m. every year since I can remember. When I told Hadi this, he had said, "So we'll arrive at 3:59:59?" Instead, we arrive at 3:30, the autumn sun already lowering in the sky, touching the tops of the trees in the backyard.

"What are you afraid of?" Wren asks him.

"Do you know how many people are in your family, child?"

"Like, twenty-four," Dunn answers for Wren.

"It's about twenty too many, is what I'm saying, Sir Dunlin."

From the passenger seat, Lincoln says, "It is a lot. Let's drink the wine first. Pop it, Hadi."

"I'm going to start calling you Buchanan," Wren says too loudly.

"Me? Why?" Lincoln flips down the visor to eye her in its mirror.

"Because he was an alcoholic who kept getting dysentery."

"I don't even know what to do with that," Lincoln responds dryly.

"Embrace it," she replies. "If anyone should be scared to go in there, it's me. It's loud as fu—"

"Language!" I scold as I park the car along the curb in front of the house, the driveway already full of minivans—Seth's, Lucas's, and Nathan's. Even with Nathan and his family of six out of state and Chris staying single and childless, Lucas and Seth had managed to sire or acquire enough children to keep Poppy's house raucous. Lucas, a high school teacher with an impressive five children, and Seth, a City of Pittsburgh firefighter with his six, of which four were adopted, were seemingly locked in a child-accumulating competition into their forties.

"High five me. Right now, young lady," Hadi says to Wren, encouraging her terrible mouth. She obliges, much to his plain delight, and then leaves the car to skip the entire front yard up to my childhood home. I see Chris give her a fist bump in greeting at the door. Nathan's teenage son Jack knocks at Dunn's window, and they too take off together.

At the front door, the casual havoc of our family gatherings swirls behind Chris. Seth's wife Maddie throws us a wave as Lucas's wife Ash shouts hello in pursuit of her toddler hellbent on entering what was likely an already-chaotic kitchen. I hear Nathan laughing but don't yet see him. I'm so used to this whirlwind that I'm immediately comforted by the mixture of voices and laughs and sounds that my heart recognizes.

We are barely a foot inside the door when Poppy rushes at us from the kitchen and through the paths of several running children, her arms outstretched and her face so awash in excitement that her eyebrows come close to touching her gray hairline. Hadi moves backward as if to escape out the door, but I see from my peripheral vision that Chris grabs him by the arm to hold him in place.

She goes for Lincoln first, crushing him in a hug as much as a short 120-pound woman can crush a six-foot man. "Dear, when last were you here with us in this house?"

"It's been a bit, Mrs. Marks."

"I'm sorry about your loss." I'm struck to see my mother fighting off tears. She knows, as we all do, that Lincoln didn't speak with his father and that his death and the estate settling were likely merely transactional in nature to him.

He responds with a smile and soft thanks.

Poppy next turns to Hadi, who is still held in place by an amused Chris. "Hadi. My prayer warrior. Hug me."

Lincoln and I catch each other as he pulls off his jacket to hand to a waiting Seth. I widen my eyes comically. *Oh my God. Prayer warrior.*

He crinkles his eyes. *Hilarious.*

And that is how it goes. Small groups of family descending upon the three of us as we work our way from the front door to the Thanksgiving table that is actually a folding table pushed against my mother's dining room table and then covered with several white tablecloths. It stretches from the living room into the dining room. Nathan and Celeste reach us first because I haven't seen them since summer when my life fell apart right in front of them. I always feel like I should salute him. He's a military man for life—currently commanding at Scott Air Force Base in Illinois. But he grabs me in a hug as does Celeste, the female version of him. Tall, thin, and as military-minded.

Hadi is introduced around with Chris as his sentinel shadow, waiting for him to try to bolt again, and Lincoln is re-enfolded by my brothers who slap his back before pulling him away for beers and laughs. I link my arm through Hadi's to lead him away from Chris. "It's going to be okay, prayer warrior. Let's get a drink. Take that edge right off."

"Is there an edge? Where? Can you just push me over it instead?"

Three of my nieces run screaming past us as a dog I don't even recognize chases after them. Hadi widens his eyes at me. "Make it three drinks. Big ones."

"You're going to make him talk with the women?" Chris asks. "Hadi, we're going to drink beer and quiz Lincoln about his amazing life. If you go into that kitchen with El, the wives and Poppy will put you to work chopping cucumbers for the salad."

"Sexist," I say to Chris.

Hadi kisses my cheek. "I'm not making the salad."

"Traitor."

"Aunt Ellis!" As Chris and Hadi walk away, Seth's oldest daughter Georgia grabs my hand and pulls me to the living room clearly in want of a corner of quiet. She's 15, studious, and as confident as Hadi, which seems an impossibility to me. I don't recall any confidence when I was 15. She pulls me down to the couch with seriousness on her face. "Listen. I need you to come to my school."

"What did you do and does your father know?"

"Aunt Ellis, do you know how popular your book is at school?"

"Oh, really?" With Seth still living close by, she attends the same school my brothers and I had, Reizenstein.

"Yes! Can you come in a few weeks to talk to my Literary Legends Book Club."

I explode in a laugh. "Literary Legends! Child, please." I attempt to stand, but she only grabs my wrist and pulls me down again.

"No, that's just the name. It's a book club. We read everything. And we read *Luca Rex* and every single one of them loved it and when they found out I was your niece, well, if you come, I have a good shot of being elected president next year."

"There's a presidency? Why? How many people are in this little book club? Like ten?"

"104."

"Oh."

"Exactly. Please? I'll do anything!"

"I don't know. I haven't done anything with that book, publicity-wise, in more than a year."

She is undeterred and pulls me into a begging side hug that hurts my bad shoulder. "Please, please, please, please, plea—"

"Holy shit, child. Fine."

"Language!" I hear my mother call from somewhere beyond. Georgia and I snicker low at each other.

"How's your next Luca book coming? Can I get a sneak peek?" she asks.

Sure. If you want to peek at zero words. My Google document is basically a night light. A SAD machine. Next Thanksgiving we'll all sit around and talk about how my contract got canceled and my life has lost all direction and about how I spend my days riding the bus in circles. "Maybe soon I'll let you," I lie to her. I no longer wait for the lightning bolts. God gave up on me.

Maddie pokes her head around the wall from the kitchen. "Ellis, your mama said stop swearing and also, dinner in 20." She glances from her daughter to me. "Georgia bug you about the book club thing?"

"Yep. We'll get it scheduled. I should probably find where Wren ran off to hide."

Georgia smiles. "I saw her head to the basement. Quieter down there. But she hugged me, so I feel like I had a real win today."

I pat her knee and go.

I don't find Wren in the basement. It's empty, which means the teen contingent moved to the backyard while the day's fading sun still provided a barrier against the cold air. She may have braved up and joined them. Sound doesn't hurt her as much outdoors where the voices aren't walled in to echo and reverberate. Remembering she'd often hide with her phone in the cold, green, linoleum-floored basement laundry room, I decide to take a quick peek there.

She is not there. But under the harsh glow of the fluorescent lights, I find, clinging to each other, crushed against each other, arms and heads moving desperately, Christopher braced with his lower back against the dryer, locked in a passionate kiss with Hadi.

And that is when my world breaks.

Chapter Thirty

May 1997
Ellis, 17
Lincoln, 18

"Christopher said it's your birthday?"

Ellis sat as she always did, next to Lincoln on the top step leading to his dark house. They had been chatting about school and movies and music and the upcoming graduation ceremony that would see Lincoln and Christopher taking those next steps away from her and her life.

She avoided thinking about not having Lincoln to sit with at night in the dark and quiet, and not having Christopher there to be what she needed him to be, a presence. A voice that bounced along the walls of the Marks house reminding her he was there, even if she couldn't see him. It wasn't a place in her life she could yet reckon with, knowing her brother's closet would sit empty of his clothes and his voice would warm some faraway rooms and hearts. And knowing the Hale house would sit empty most every night. Her friend gone away. Her brother gone away further.

"Yep," she said.

Lincoln smiled. "Happy birthday."

She returned his smile.

"Get anything good?"

"Birthdays don't mean anything in our family. It's just addition." She ticked a finger in the air as if keeping score. "Plus one."

"That's right. I never did get invited to a single birthday party for Christopher as long as I've known him."

"There hasn't been a single birthday party for Christopher. You know, my dad says it's because birthdays are 'pagan in origin,' but I secretly think my parents are too poor to buy five kids gifts every year, so they came up with that excuse to save money."

Lincoln let out a laugh and she let it warm her.

"So, prom," he started.

"Yep." A thrill of excitement rushed quickly through her body.

"You have a favorite flower?"

She considered it. "Not really, I guess. No. Should I?"

He shrugged. "I don't know when people normally settle on a favorite flower. I asked Chris what yours was and he said, 'Why the hell would I know?' He had a point."

"You know, I think I like daisies. Maybe daisies."

"Daisies?" He seemed taken aback.

Ellis lifted an elbow to her knee and rested her chin on her palm to talk up to the trees. "I know we don't talk about your mom too much, but I remember this one lesson where she talked about daisies. Remember she grew those? And those glasses she had? I loved them and those little daisies. She told me there was math in them. I never saw it. But she made me want to. She quoted Byron. And then she told me I needed to practice more." She chuckled at the memory which seemed to have faded and muted. Like it was a copy of a copy of the original. An echo. "But she talked about the daisies. Yeah. I think I'll say daisies."

Lincoln's expression clouded with seriousness, and she regretted bringing up Mrs. Hale. She hadn't meant to sadden him again.

He held her eyes for a long moment until she felt the need to apologize, and was nearly ready to do so when he asked, "You know on prom night?"

Ellis felt a flip in her stomach. Or maybe her heart. She nodded.

"I don't want you to be worrying about it, okay? There's always the whole question about, you know, kissing or whatever."

She didn't speak.

"And I don't want you to be nervous or worrying that I'm going to do something that night, okay?"

An unexpected flash of disappointment raced through her, and she internally scolded herself for it. "Sure," she said easily.

"I don't want you to be nervous, so I'm just going to do it now."

Ellis froze at the same time everything inside of her heated in ways she hadn't felt before. She remained frozen when he leaned into her, closer than he'd ever been. She closed her eyes at the overwhelming pull at her heart when she felt his hand slide up her jaw, his fingers loosely brushing the back of her neck. His thumb on her ear. His lips met hers softly and she slowly melted from the warmth of everything she felt, from her skin to her soul.

Later, she walked home atop a dream.

Ellis Marks was kissed for the first time on her 17th birthday, three days before prom, on a cool May night sitting on the top step to Lincoln Hale's porch in front of his too-dark, too-quiet house.

That night would be the last time she spoke to him in person for 21 years until the day he would stand below her open bedroom window shouting profanity at his mother's fallen piano.

Ellis Sloan Therapy Sessions

Gulf Tower
Pittsburgh, PA
August 2021

Ellis: He was devastated by Wren's diagnosis. His younger brother Edward is autistic and the family—well, it was long ago, before we know what we know now and have the interventions that we do, but his family hid Edward away more and more as the years passed. Our wedding was the first time I met him. They'll hide him away in another part of the house or his room with his aide during dinner with guests. They were ashamed. I didn't think much of it because they were in New York; we were in Pittsburgh. It's easy to ignore something you aren't seeing every day. But as Wren grew, I could tell, you know? Something wasn't quite right. He insisted there was nothing wrong. Lucas, my younger brother, he's a teacher. He sat me down one day after she'd melted down at my mother's house in front of everyone. Screaming. Crying. Rocking. She was nine. Too old for that. He told me what he'd noticed. Had noticed for a while. So I had her diagnosed. A real diagnosis. I told Oliver and he faded into the background of her life. Which is crazy because she's brilliant. The conversations they could be having about history? Important stuff? While other dads are trying desperately to find ways to relate to their daughters? He had it. But he couldn't handle it because all he'd known about people like Wren is shame. So he let her go.

Dr. Parrish: Do you think she noticed that? Him pulling away from her?

Ellis: I need a little break.

Dr. Parrish: Sure.

Chapter Thirty-One

Thanksgiving 2020

I don't think I'm exaggerating when I say my world spins. Like, my world? It spins. It spins off its axis and falls to the ground and bounces away under the dryer where I'll never get it back and now must create a new world for myself, one in which what I'm seeing makes sense. It feels like an out-of-body experience when you see something like this that doesn't fit into the space you carved out for people in your life.

Chris is my straight brother. Hadi is my best friend who is annoyed by Chris, who is in turn annoyed by Hadi. Those are their boxes they fit into perfectly. But here they are. My brother. And Hadi. Holding each other. Breathing into and of each other. What the fuck is happening? Who am I? Where am I? Who are they? What is this place? Nothing makes sense. When they notice me, they harshly shove each other away and immediate terror surfaces on Chris's face.

"El," he starts.

I hold up a hand. I'm currently building a new world because my old one is broken apart under the dryer. I need a minute before I can hear words. "Just. Give me a second. I need to sit down." I awkwardly spin one way then another like a two-year-old ballerina. "There are no fucking chairs in a fucking laundry room," I mutter to no one.

Hadi snaps into action and flips over a tall empty laundry basket. "Sit," he says, his fear and uneasiness from minutes ago erased. I sit. As I once did upon a garbage can, I now sit on a laundry basket. *Once Upon a Laundry Basket would make a great book title* is the kind of thing that runs through my head during world-building. I'm starting to understand Wren's obsession with Minecraft.

"El," Chris tries again, his voice sounding like it will break.

I'm not there yet. Still building. Sorting. Making new boxes for everyone. Transplanting the shrubbery. Reroofing a few buildings whose tops were blown off into the stratosphere at the sight of my brother holding Hadi. I hold my hand up again. "Wait. One minute. Nearly ready. Super close."

I sit there on that old, cracked upside-down laundry basket in the basement of my childhood home and run it all through. Chris in high school. Chris not going to prom or any dance. Chris leaving immediately for California as if escaping life here with us. Chris rarely talking about his dates. Chris holding Hadi's arm. Beautiful Chris raised in a house of tough boys led by a pastor who likely believed homosexuality was a sin. In fact, I recall more than one family discussion on just that. Chris weeping on our father's dying body.

I look at them, my new world taking shape and needing a building block only they can hand to me. "But how? You just met."

Hadi rolls his eyes, clearly at ease in the wild situation that unfolded. "I drove him to work after our lunch with Lincoln, remember? You and Lincoln went home, and I took him to work?"

I do remember. That lunch. They'd seemed to connect—their heads bowed close, joking with each other—but it didn't hold a meaning for me until now.

"So we started talking and texting, me in New York, him here, and well, here we are. Making out in your mom's murdery laundry room like we're star-crossed. Romeo and Mercutio."

Chris can't laugh at the joke or pull his eyes off me.

I stand, my world rebuilt. All new. Everyone in a new box. Delightful planters of daisies returned to everyone's windowsills. Except Oliver's. His entire house is made of snakes and a dark cloud that rains scorpions hovers low over it at all times.

"El, please." Chris, wracked with emotion, takes a step toward me, reaching out a hand. I stop him with my words and my own hand before his face can break any further. There's just no need for anyone to shatter when I've so recently rebuilt everything.

"Listen to me. Both of you. Wait. I need to breathe a second." I inhale and exhale while they watch me like I'm a firecracker about to explode. "Okay. Wits, gathered. Listen to me. You," I point to Chris. "I love you. So, please, get that damn look of terror off your face. I'm just trying to orient myself to this new reality. When you're ready to talk to me about all this, you can. Let's leave it at that. Boom. Done."

Chris slowly shakes his head at me and says my name with a crack splitting his voice.

"What?" I ask.

"I don't know what to say."

"Say nothing. This is a beautiful thing. Don't ruin it with damn emotions." I turn to Hadi. "You."

"Bring it, love," he says with his arms crossed and his face bright.

"Whatever this ends up being, I know you'll be as good to him as you've always been to me."

"Of course, but I plan to sleep with him." He puts all the emphasis on the last word.

Chris widens his eyes and lifts his hands to his hair while I throw myself forward at my waist in laughter. Hadi. Always perfect. "Okay, now it's boom. Done. I'm going to walk out of this room and you two finish whatever I interrupted, but holy shit, do a mirror check before you come up." I clap my hands twice. "Get it together, boys. We still have dinner to get through."

When dinner is finished and cleared, another search for Wren leads me to the front porch where I instead find Lincoln sitting in the wide swing, banished from helping in the kitchen because of his guest status. His black sweater in the darkening evening blends him into the scene.

"Little chilly out here," I say as I step out from the house, the glass storm door snapping its latch closed behind me.

He only smiles then pats the swing. *Sit with me.*

I do. It feels odd sitting here with him, like my mother and father often did while they drank their coffee on cool summer mornings before the earth heated up and the air grew thick with water. I can hear the voices of the teenagers floating through the thin cool air from the backyard, even in the early darkness of the fall. We settle into silence, like we used to.

"You good?" I finally ask.

"Yeah. I haven't had a real Thanksgiving in—" He stops his sentence and changes direction as if he took a wrong turn with it. "Thanks for the invite."

"Poppy invited you."

"True. But you let me come."

"Poppy can still ground me, I think."

He chuckles. "Man, you were grounded for so long."

"Ages."

"The living room brought back some memories for me."

I let out a soft laugh at this. "Motherfucker."

"Exactly."

"The mouth on me, right?"

We quiet again as Jack and Dunn run from behind the house and head down toward the minivans, likely going the full circle around the yard.

"What are they all playing?" Lincoln asks.

"Who knows. Maybe tag."

"We should teach them the soccer ball version of that."

I slit my eyes at him and he playfully nudges at my shoulder with his. We listen to the echoes of the kids' shouts. I hear Wren yelling something and am happy she's found the space she needed to have some fun with her cousins.

"Ellis, I'm going to put my arm around you and don't freak out; it doesn't mean anything. I just need to say something to you."

"Okay?" I draw the word out as he settles his arm around me and uses his leg to set the swing swaying lightly.

"I loved our friendship."

I don't say anything because I don't yet know where he's taking me.

"I'm sorry."

"For lying to your mother?"

"No. Well, yes. But I fessed up to her on that, as you know. But not that. I'm sorry about that night."

Oh, that memory. I want it to stay down, even all these years later. "It's history." I shrug. "We were kids. We've lived a lot of life since. Just saying the word prom at this point in our lives sounds childish, doesn't it? Listen: prom. How ridiculous. It's practically like saying Underoos. Or even, listen, ready? Truly outrageous, Jem."

"Shrinky Dinks," he enunciates.

"Polly Pockets."

"He-Man, Master of the Universe." He laughs then quiets with a shake of his head. "You're so good at distracting people when they want to talk to you. But I've wanted to apologize a long time."

"I got over it, right?"

"Regardless, I'm sorry." He pulls at my shoulder. "Forgive me?"

"My father used to say it's a sin to not forgive. You can thank David Marks for this one. I forgive you." I toss him a perfect execution of my grossly imperfect cross that I may have to celestially answer for one day. "Forgiven."

He lifts his arm from around me and settles his hands into his lap. I shiver and stand. I hate that I still want to know what happened that night, like it's a mystery I need the answer to. But he didn't offer that answer up, and I suspect if it would have given me some comfort, he'd have dispatched that comfort to me.

I let my unanswered questions stay there on the porch and go in search of my daughter, feeling like a small spot of damage that I'd carried within me for a long time was finally patched up to heal. It'll be up to me to not pick at the scab simply because I'm dissatisfied with the extent of the repair.

Chapter Thirty-Two

May 1997
Ellis, 17
Lincoln, 18

Ellis couldn't have known.

She couldn't have known that was the last time she would see Lincoln Hale for decades. She couldn't have known that the new feelings, the new experiences, the new Ellis was fleeting. She couldn't have known they would be wrenched away so quickly. Brutally. That the dull burn of her lips would be chilled with a cold cloak tossed unfeelingly across her heart.

She couldn't have known when she came home later that night, her footsteps light, her heart electrified, that turmoil and pain burned deep within others in her life. She couldn't have known that some pain eventually, desperately reaches for a reckoning. That the lightness of her happiness had an equal and opposite weight of darkness.

She couldn't have known that growth didn't only come from time, it grew out of pain too. That pesky thing called character wasn't a gently germinating seed; it was a product of white-hot liquid metal being hammered and cooled by life's hard and unforgiving arcs.

She couldn't have yet known that every scar was once a wound.

And she couldn't yet have known what scars others hid, nor what new wounds awaited.

Ellis Sloan Therapy Sessions

Gulf Tower
Pittsburgh, PA
August 2021

Dr. Parrish: Tell me ten things you like about yourself. Why are you laughing?

Ellis: You're serious?

Dr. Parrish: Completely. Go ahead. List them.

Ellis: Out loud?

Dr. Parrish: Preferably. So I know you're really doing it. So your brain can hear it.

Ellis: Why?

Dr. Parrish: There's science behind it. Ten things. Give me one.

Ellis:

Dr. Parrish: Just one. Something you like about yourself.

Ellis: This feels self-indulgent.

Dr. Parrish: So? Let's hear one. Are you a good writer? A good mom? A good friend? Do you think you have nice eyes? Give me one. Here. I'll start. I have great hair. Easy. Now you.

Ellis: I guess I like that I'm funny.

Dr. Parrish: You think you're funny?

Ellis: Cute. Yes. I think I'm funny.

Dr. Parrish: I agree. Give me another.

Dr. Parrish: Ellis?

Dr. Parrish: Nothing? What are you feeling right now? Why is this making you tear up like that?

Chapter Thirty-Three

December 2020

Shit. Shit. Shit. Shit.

It's afternoon on the Saturday after Thanksgiving. I open my front door on the deceptive grandmotherly dress, posture and countenance of that nightmare in a cardigan Bea Bancroft, come to suck out my whole soul with one withering glance and a flick of her forked tongue.

"Bea, love! What a surprise. What brings you here, you miserable hateful crone?"

She smiles at my verbal U-turn. "Ah, always with the words, you are, dear. It's a surprise check-in. My ears have been burning and my texts have been going ignored. In a way, you manifested me." She snaps at the air once.

"Can I manifest a change to your flight home to NYC for two hours from now? Off you go. Security is a bitch." I attempt to shoo her away.

"No. My flight leaves in four hours." She brushes past me, and I close the door behind her. The mantle of evil, cleverly disguised as a cardigan, has entered my home. I may need to burn it all down for want of an exorcism.

"Wow. So, literally back and forth. JFK. PIT. JFK." I call out the airport codes.

She settles into the wing chair as if invited to do so. "I don't mind. I enjoy airport hubbub."

"I know I joke, but are you the actual devil?"

"Only when I need to be."

"I know. I've seen you make people cry." I drop down onto the couch. "What's up? Taking a break from kicking fallen angels into hell? Getting your horns sharpened in the Strip District?"

"By my math, you have one week from Monday to meet your first deadline after you've already let three or four of my deadlines pass over the summer, which I allowed on account of you setting fire to your life."

I hold up a hand. "Uh, uh, uh, you shrew. I was forced to set my life on fire."

"How's the writing going?"

"Amazing! Truly fabulous! Stars aligning!"

"You lie."

"Is the devil also omniscient? I thought that was God's trick."

"The industry is hitting a bit of a saturation point right now, Ellis. They desperately want your second book. I've been sending you sales figures via the email. Have you been reading those?"

"Do you want me to lie to make you feel better? It's a sin, but I bet that's your power source."

"You should read those. It's an odd thing we're seeing. Maybe a late word-of-mouth blip, but they'd like to ride it if they can. But I'm not going to lie. They've whispered about the possibility of dropping you."

There it is. I knew it was coming. I put away my irreverence. "Would I have to return the half of the advance they already gave me?"

"First, no. But you obviously wouldn't get the remainder. And second, it makes me nervous that you asked that question."

"Just covering my bases."

"Mom!" Wren's too loud call comes from upstairs.

"Come down!" I call, realizing her presence is what I need to buffer me from Bea, and maybe send her running to catch her flight. "I'm working on it, Bea. But would they be upset if the next book wasn't Luca?"

"It would need to be an amazing book for them to let Luca go at this point."

I scowl. "*Luca* was dumb, Bea, and you know it. Drivel. Meaningless unrealistic fluff. Do you know not one scene I wrote in *Luca* passes the Bechdel test? Not one!"

"The what test now?"

"Bechdel. Google it. Are there any scenes where two women have a discussion, and they aren't talking in some way about a man? No? You failed the test. It's gross that I failed the test with *Luca*."

"Your sales aren't gross though, is what I'm trying to say. People love Luca and seem to be doing so more and more. Try for another *Luca*. Just sit down and write one opening scene for me for next Monday. Only looking for a start."

"Wow. You really want me to write a *Luca* don't you. Being all kind and un-witchy."

"I thought I was the devil, not a witch?"

"You can wear two unholy hats, Lucifer. I'll try. For you. But I'll probably email you a blank document with a twenty-word title. Brace yourself now for it."

"Will do. Don't disappoint me though. I'd hate to make you miserable." She stands.

"Oh, you monster, you've only ever made me miserable, and you know it."

"Another lie."

Wren lands with a loud moan on the stair landing at the same time Lincoln and Dunn walk in the front door after their latest driving session, which they embarked upon over my loud objections, Lincoln promising if Dunn wrecked the rental BMW, he'd cover the cost of the damages.

"Mom!" Wren moans again, tears in her eyes. She's a fire I'll need to put out. Dunn and Lincoln toss a wave to Bea after I introduce them all briefly, then head into the kitchen, probably in search of snacks and for Dunn to further pepper Lincoln with questions about literally anything. Lincoln is the subject and Dunn is his best student.

I settle Wren into the couch with instructions to hold herself together for a moment, then walk Bea to the door. She turns on me. "Is that—?"

I hold my palm out to her face. "Bup! Bup! Bechdel test!"

"But wasn't that—"

"Bechdel! Shh! Don't ruin it. Go. I'll read the emails you have sent via the electronic mail over the world wide web."

"Fine. Go write."

When Bea is once again off to fly with her screeching howl into another poor soul's circle of existence, I turn to a miserable Wren, a paper clutched in her hand. "What is it?"

"Music class." Her least favorite.

"Ah. Your favorite."

"Stop it!" She can't handle sarcasm when she's upset. I scold myself for trying it.

"Calm. Don't speak to me that way, please."

"I'm sorry! I'm sorry!" She's turned the wrong direction here and is now fearfully apologizing. I settle next to her with a sigh and take the paper from her.

Dunn and Lincoln return to the room.

"Okay," I say as I read. "Because you told Mr. Michaels you didn't feel like you can handle the symphony field trip he wants you to write a paper on the history of the Pittsburgh Symphony to earn the field trip credit."

"A five-page paper!" She says it as a wail.

"Wren, you've been writing a history project for months now with no problem. You can do five pages on the symphony."

"It's all in the margin size," Dunn offers unhelpfully. "And font. Twelve point five is your friend."

Lincoln, surprisingly, sits next to Wren on the couch. "The symphony, you say? What's the problem with going to it?"

Wren answers before I can do it for her. "I can't handle the noise."

"Why not?"

"She has autism," Dunn says.

Lincoln and I find each other. He says, *Oh, I didn't realize.*

How could you not have?

"I don't have autism, Dunn! I am autistic." She looks ahead at nothing in particular. "It's not something you have. It's something you are. I am it. It is not me."

Lincoln considers this for a moment while I let my pride at Wren flow. I've worked so hard to remove the stigma for her. We talk about it. She talks about it. She accepts it. She has grown to love what it means for her brain. The amazing things she can do with it. How she can hear things differently and experience the world in a richer way. Until those hurdles come and she sometimes can't bear them. Like now.

"And what does that do to you, regarding the symphony?" Lincoln asks her.

It takes her a moment to respond. "It's too loud. The instruments. I don't like some of them."

"Too loud, or it's mostly certain instruments?"

"I don't know. I like the violins. And the flutes. We listened to some different symphony parts in class. But lots of parts I didn't like and me and Lindsey had to leave the room."

"Lindsey is her aide," I explain.

"What if I take you all to the symphony instead of you going on the field trip? Then you could leave when you wanted if you hated it and still get the credit and then you won't have to write the paper? I have a season ticket package. Four seats."

"Why?" Dunn asks. "You don't live here." Bless that kid to

Midas' riches for asking the question I wanted an answer to. I throw him an invisible hug I hope he can feel.

"I like to support it still, is all, even though I moved away."

"He's a musician, you know, Wren," Dunn says. "Piano."

I'm conflicted because I don't think Wren will be able to handle sitting through a symphony performance. "You want to write the paper, Wrennie?"

"I bet you'll like going," Lincoln says. We eye each other the same message. *What are you doing?*

She shrugs. "I guess we can try to go."

"Perfect!" Lincoln stands. "What's the show?"

I read from the paper. "*Manfred*? Opens in two weeks."

"Done."

He heads for the door, but I stop him. "Wait. What do we wear for your seats? Do I need to shop? Please say no."

He looks me up and down. I'm currently in Author Mom attire, or maybe Finance Mom. I can't remember whether I was typing gibberish into *Untitled Ellis Sloan Book Two* or stapling blank small paper to blank large paper when Dunn and Wren awoke. Regardless, I'm in my dark blue jeans and a soft blue sweater. "That's fine," he says. "Wear whatever. Who cares? It's not the opera."

"Don't even mention the opera," Dunn warns.

"I hate it. It makes me cry it hurts so bad," Wren offers in explanation.

"Gotcha. I don't have a subscription to the opera, so you're good. Okay. Symphony in two weeks." He opens the front door and points to Dunn. "See you Tuesday." He points to me. "I heard that scary grandma. Go write."

I ensure Dunn has already begun his march upstairs and that Wren is still looking miserably at her lap, upset that none of her options were desirable, then I hold my hand close in front of my chest to send Lincoln my middle finger for his eyes only.

He pulls the door closed on his own laughter.

Chapter Thirty-Four

May 1997, Prom Night
Ellis, 17
Lincoln, 18

Ellis knew.

As soon as she saw the seriousness on her father's face when he walked into her bedroom, she knew. She knew whatever it was would be bad and that it had to do with her. And it was and it did. If it had been something good, it would have been her mother. But bad news came from her father because he could stay calm. Didn't project. Didn't absorb.

She didn't hear the words with her ears but instead felt the terrible meaning of them blanketing her heart. Or maybe it was that she saw the words—letters forming phrases coming out of her father's mouth. Heavy words that fell with a great weight on her chest. Gray, softly spoken words that contained enough power to deafen her from the inside out.

But in her deafness, her heart still understood the meaning:

Lincoln had come to the door, you see, Ellis. He was upset and in an urgent rush. I know you've showered and Mom did your hair and you're wanting to put your dress on that we got for you at the department store bargain basement and that looks absolutely wonderful on you, but Lincoln said he can't take you and to tell you he was sorry and then he ran off with more apologies and got in his car and sped away. I can see your devastation and I'm going to sit here for a minute on your bed with you and let you process and feel this.

"I don't understand," she finally said.

"Ellis, listen. We know Lincoln, your mother and I. We know him in ways you and Christopher don't, is all I can tell you. I tell you this so you can understand that he's not a hurtful person. He's had struggles you haven't. He's suffered."

"His mom."

"Of course, but life isn't just one problem. You'll see that as you grow. It's often problem after problem, and sometimes? Those problems interact and stack on each other."

"But why tonight? What happened? I don't understand."

"I won't lie. I don't either. I just know by his face, it was one I've seen before, and well, it's the face that means he wasn't going to be able to be here for you, even if he was here for you, do you understand?"

"Not really." She wouldn't cry. She wouldn't. She'd known how to shut that display off for years and so she did. Turned the valve and hardened herself against whatever storm was trying to topple her over, crashing her to the ground to make visible emotions spill out of the cracks. She wouldn't. She'd turn her back to it.

"We can't ever know what someone is struggling with under the surface. People seem like they're perfectly well and happy, but underneath, there's all kinds of chaos and pain. Things they don't show. I want you to understand I think he's struggling with something this night. I don't think it's about you. There are bigger things at work is all. I know you're sad."

"I'm mad."

"Well, I am too. No father wants to see his daughter this way. To tell her something like this. I'm just trying to give the young man the benefit of the doubt he's earned with us over the years."

"I don't think I can do that."

"You don't have to. But remember our job as humans. It's to forgive so we can grow and can free others to grow in their mistakes too."

"Dad, I can't hear this right now. This can't be a thing that turns into *my* lesson to learn."

He stood after a comforting pat at her knee and left, pulling the door closed silently. Ellis pulled pins from her curls and let them fall to the carpet, then crawled beneath her covers. She'd stay that way for hours, running every conversation they'd ever had through her head. Every laugh. The kiss from three nights ago. She stayed there as activity sounded from beyond her door. Other doors opening and closing. A called command from her mother. Dishes clattering.

Her room darkened with the slow creep of night, and she turned no lamp on to light her sadness or to wash out the glowing red fire of her anger. Much deeper into the night, she heard Christopher come home long after the house had quieted. He'd not wanted to attend the dance and instead spent it with a group of like-minded classmates. She wondered if he knew what his best friend had done to her, but she'd never speak of it to him. The mortification would be too much. Everything needed to be shut off. Every valve.

She faced a summer with Christopher in the house, a constant reminder of his best friend. A summer with Lincoln's presence reminding her of this night. She'd not be free from it. She finally fell into what would be an often-interrupted sleep after deciding she'd speak to her father in the morning about heading to church camp and working after all. It would get her away from everything she didn't wish to face. But most importantly, it would get her away from he who she didn't wish to ever gift with another moment of friendship.

She would not let him use her as a tool to dig for relief from sadness. She would not sow in his heart the seeds of another single laugh.

She would not grant forgiveness that was never sought.

Ellis Sloan Therapy Sessions

Gulf Tower
Pittsburgh, PA
August 2021

Dr. Parrish: What did that mean for you? Watching that unfold at the symphony?

Ellis: It meant—I don't know. That other people could love Wren? Is this an awful thing I've said? I hate myself.

Dr. Parrish: Explain it a little more before you so readily fling your body into the self-hate pool. Also, you said it again.

Ellis: Ugh. Okay. I will say ten things I like about myself as punishment on my way home, I promise.

Dr. Parrish: It's science, not a punishment. Go on. What's so wrong with what you said?

Ellis: It's just, well, Hadi loves Wren, yeah, and my family does. But Lincoln was different with her right from the start? I don't know how to say this. Her autism wasn't a barrier he had to climb over? Not like everyone else had to, and not like I assumed people who will come to meet her for the rest of her life would need to. Wren is hard. She's also wonderful and amazing. But raising her, I'm terrified she'll be alone. Won't be able to make friends because I think people will meet her and see that difference in her eyes. Her movements, mannerisms, language. And walk away from her because that's the easier option. I guess it showed me there are people out there who it won't be an issue for. They'll keep going until they get to who she is, like I've had to do. Like Oliver hasn't.

Dr. Parrish: So that did what to you? When you saw how he could interact with her like that?

Ellis: It gave me a little hope for her. I guess I felt ashamed because I didn't realize I had no hope for her up to that point. I think I expected her to become like her uncle Edward. Oliver's brother.

Dr. Parrish: You've told yourself you've been protecting her by the ways you've held her back?

Ellis: Yeah.

Dr. Parrish: Are you sure you aren't protecting yourself a little too?

Ellis: From what?

Dr. Parrish: Well, Ellis, we don't have to pick up and try to put back together that which never has the chance to fall down.

Ellis: I'm stealing that.

Dr. Parrish: I'll add it to your invoice.

Chapter Thirty-Five

December 2020

Sitting here in Heinz Hall, I am underdressed.

Thank you, Lincoln, you ass.

Sure, back there, in the seats I'd like to occupy, with my people, I would fit in with my jeans and sweater. But Lincoln directed us here. Four rows from the stage. I am surrounded by that which I scorn. Men in what I assume are cashmere turtlenecks and suits that cost more than my car, stand with one hand in a pocket and laugh with close-mouthed haught at stupid jokes about Mozart's role as a political revolutionary.

Walking down the slope of the long aisle felt like leafing through one of Poppy's old JCPenney catalogs. At the beginning were Dockers and casual sweaters. Some church clothes for children. A little further and we've stumbled upon two-hundred-dollar suits and dresses that were probably only pulled out of closets twice a year. Then near the end, grandmothers of the bride in sparkles. He had guided us around gaggles of older women wearing enough sequins to light the way of a ship through a dark harbor. He led us around chattering groups of women my age wearing shimmery short dresses with heels so high Dunn asked me, "How don't they fall over?"

"The rich don't have to live by the laws of physics," I had explained to him, leaving him confused and Lincoln, in front of him, throwing an eyeroll over his shoulder with, "Classist."

Normally Wren would have interrupted to explain one of the laws of physics to her brother, but she wasn't speaking, which I knew meant nerves, which I knew meant she was touch-and-go. I felt a hint of dread poke at my heart.

I am seated between Wren and Dunn, with Lincoln sitting on Wren's left side. Wren looks tense. I attempt to soothe. "You okay, Wrennie? You want to leave?"

Wren doesn't respond. She is surrounded by the kind of noise she hates—voices of every timbre and volume ricocheting around a room designed to efficiently carry sound. Instruments of all varieties are being tuned and tested on the stage.

I watch the patrons milling around us, secretly fascinated by them and wonder about their lives when they leave here. They're probably not going to a three-bedroom duplex with slanted floors. "Hey," I say to Lincoln. "You see that Fitzwilliam there?" I nod toward the tall thin man standing at the opening of our aisle.

"What the fu—" Wren's small grin despite her nervousness stops his reply. He restarts, "What the heck is a Fitzwilliam?"

"Fitzwilliam. Old rich guy."

He rolls his eyes then slits them at me. "Wait. Am I a Fitzwilliam?"

I consider this a moment. "No. You're not quite old enough yet. You're still a Yardley."

Lincoln laughs loud enough that the Sparkle Grandma in front of him rotates her head to give him a scolding look. When he merely winks at her, she whips around fast enough to dislodge a cataract. "What about the Fitzwilliam?" he asks me.

"I wonder. Do you think his outfit costs more than my car?"

Dunn leans in front of me. "Mom, Lincoln's watch costs more than all your clothes, your car, and everything we own."

In plain shock, I look at Lincoln who pretends to be enthralled with the contents of the program in his hands, holding it two inches from his face and flipping pages way too fast to be absorbing anything. "Why do you even know that?" I ask Dunn.

He shrugs. "I know stuff. I like watches. I can Google."

I reach across Wren and grab at Lincoln's right arm, but he yanks it away before I can snag it. "Why?" he asks. He points at the head of the nosy Sparkle Grandma in front of us with laughter holding his eyes then puts his finger to his lips. "Behave."

"It's a Rolex." Wren suddenly joins the conversation.

"And why do you know that?" I ask her with even more surprise than I had at Dunn. I'm full of so many questions, but the lights flicker to encourage final seat-taking and Wren grips the armrests on either side of her chair.

Lincoln notices her posture. "Listen, Wren. Give this a chance. Thirty seconds. You can even count. And if you feel like you're about to lose it, kick my leg and I will literally throw you over my shoulder and we'll go get dessert somewhere."

"That is going to look a lot like kidnapping," Dunn says, leaning in front of me.

Lincoln and I can't help but chuckle at the imagery, but Wren bunches her face. The lights further dim to darkness, and I lean to Wren's ear. I know to whisper more softly than I think I need to. "Girl, you're stronger than 29 seconds."

She nods dutifully and I know that more than anything on this earth, she wants to make it to 30 seconds. I pray to the ceiling that she does, but I brace myself for what I'm sure this is about to become—an intrusion on the audience's enjoyment when the four of us stand to leave 27 seconds into the first number while the teenage girl in the group covers her ears. Dunn and I are used to those moments, but Lincoln is probably about to learn, and regret bringing us.

A light applause drifts through the air as a man dressed in black bends at the waist in a quick nod toward the audience and takes his spot before the musicians. He raises his arms and his wand. I inhale. I am prepared for whatever happens now. I always must be prepared.

Wren spends the first 15 seconds looking very much like she's about to ask for rescue from Lincoln. The cellos are pulling hard strokes in one direction across their strings, creating a repeating low drone of a note that I can see is unpleasant to Wren who is pressing a finger to her right ear. Lincoln holds out an open hand in front of her above her lap. *Wait*, he telegraphs to her with it. *Wait*.

She waits, with one finger on her ear, the other preparing to come for the left ear. She waits through the joining in of the woods, which I can see she doesn't much enjoy, her hand now shaking from the harsh pressure she's exerting on her ear. I recognize it as a physical manifestation of a rising panic. But she waits through a growing wall of sound as seemingly every instrument has joined the fray. Lincoln's hand remains in front of her. *Wait.* I wonder how much longer she can hold on. I don't want her to suffer. I wonder if I should end it now.

She's trembling. I will end it now. Rescue her.

Lincoln begins to slowly lift his hand a few inches to indicate a crescendo is occurring, and it does, and then he quickly closes his hand into a fist just as a note bursts out in final staccato from the orchestra. Then there is silence. The conductor is still. The air breathes. I watch as Lincoln flattens his hand and lowers it slowly to hover above Wren's lap. She looks at him and he motions to her with his other hand that she can let go of her ear as a light airy sound swirls through the hall. Violins and flutes play out high, and like dandelion seeds, their music floats on the breezes of cellos, evoking brightness and birdsong.

Lincoln shows a thumbs-up and returns his hands to his lap, allowing the music to speak. Amazingly, Wren seems to be listening. Tense. Ready to spring. But listening. Opening to it, rather than slamming herself shut.

Lincoln is studying her responses. He seems to take note that she tenses when brass instruments are taking up too much of her senses. Sees her relax as violins pull in front, as cellos intone low and steady and long—not harsh percussive bursts. He sees, as I do, her face soften as flutes chirp brightly and then sing out sweetly. Her small smile when violins push out soothing, undulating waves. Sees her flinch when a cymbal intrudes unexpectedly.

Dunn isn't slouched or looking bored, so I assume he's either not hating it, or is on alert, awaiting my command to abort the plan. Dunn has spent most of Wren's life poised to escape situations that fell apart. I smile at his profile; he doesn't notice.

Lincoln is again indicating to Wren an imminent crescendo and she braces for it. He taps her knee, and she looks at him. He gestures for her to cover her ears. She does, drowning out the burst of trumpeted blares that fill the room. His outstretched hand comes in front of her. *Wait. Wait.* He slowly brings it down to hover low above her legs. She removes her hands and is again awash in light violins, soothing strings, high notes flitting out of flutes like morning birds.

I turn my attention to the stage and finally allow a little of my tension to release from my shoulders. The movement on stage is mesmerizing—the passion and intensity of the conductor backdropped and surrounded by bows and arms dancing in sync. I venture a breath and let my ears truly hear the music. It's a waterfall of peace that washes over me. It absorbs into my skin until I'm feeling it inside, pushing high, falling low, beating rushed, then unhurried.

Wren has relaxed into her chair with the softness still on her face, her mouth slightly open below transfixed glowing eyes. I know when my girl feels right. She feels right. Lincoln's hand darts in and taps her knee. She covers her ears with a quickness, and I am forced to reckon with the emotions now swirling alongside the blaring music he protected her from.

My child. I feel sadness of what she can't handle, what she might never experience, what limitations life might hold her to. I'm sad that things are hard for her and I'm sad that others can't see how strong she is. She held on, she did. It has been six minutes.

She is being guided through a symphony with hand gestures and it is working. Lincoln knocks his fists together in front of Wren and I expect her to reach for her ears. Instead, she grips the armrests and a few beats later, hears cymbals crash loudly. She had been expecting it; she could handle it. Gratitude and relief mix into my sadness, and I feel them too strongly all at once—the nouns we cannot see move us the most. I quickly swipe at a tear, hoping I'm not seen. I feel a tap on my knee and see Lincoln's hand retreat from it.

Above Wren's head, his eyebrows are furrowed and a slight nod upward asks me an unspoken question. *You okay?*

I roll my eyes at my own behavior and offer a small reassuring smile, swiping away a second tear. I nod. *I'm fine. Just being really stupid.*

Dunn pokes an elbow into my arm, and I lean toward him. "Are we leaving?" he asks quietly into my ear. I shake my head no. *Not yet.* "Are you crying?" he asks, concerned.

I don't know when the last time he saw me cry was. Or even if he ever has. I reassure him with a smile and whisper, "Just happy. For Wren. Now, shh."

Wren lasts 23 minutes of Tchaikovsky's *Manfred* symphony. Twenty-two-and-a-half minutes more than was her goal. When she finally taps her foot against Lincoln's shin, I wildly wonder if he really will toss her over his shoulder and I secretly kind of hope he does just to see how the Sparkle Grandmas react. He instead motions to an usher seated in a chair at the foot of the stage, facing the audience. She pops from her chair and hurries to our row where she crouches in the aisle to assist in extricating us as quickly as possible.

We are saved an embarrassing walk up the aisle by a door alongside the front row that leads to a narrow and winding hallway that eventually spits us into the quiet lobby. A few ushers and sales staff mill about quietly. Straggling patrons head for restrooms or to take calls. A group of bored teenagers who escaped the show occupy a bench, their faces in their phone screens. Lincoln pats the usher on the back and whispers down into her ear. She smiles and leaves to head toward the doors to the hallway. "Thank you!" I call out to her.

I hug Wren and she lets me. "Ah, Wrennie. Look at you." She shrugs me off, having allotted me what will probably amount to all the physical affection she'll allow for a month.

Dunn holds his fist out to her, and after a moment she taps it with her own, unable to stop a smile from lighting her face.

Lincoln smiles down at her, crossing his arms over his chest. "You survived more than 20 minutes of *Manfred.* I think Tchaikovsky and Byron would approve."

Something inside of me shifts. "Byron?"

Lincoln finds my eyes. Mine are questioning; his are suddenly serious.

"Byron," he affirms. "*Manfred* is a Byron work. Tchaikovsky scored it with this symphony."

I'm confronted anew with memories of my youth. Of my piano teacher. Of her melancholy face as she quoted the poet to me.

"What's it about? *Manfred*?" asks Wren. Back when I read and absorbed words into my brain, Wren never walked past without asking me that question. *What's that about?* I've explained the plots of dozens of Stephen King novels to her on account of I'm the best worst mother in the world. When I explained *Pet Sematary*, she had said, "Oh, cool!" I still haven't let her read *Luca Rex*. On account of it's a pile of hot garbage, and I'm 100 percent certain she'll mock me for having written such overwrought drivel.

Lincoln considers her question. "Well, it's dark. And it's about a tortured soul. And about guilt. It's about the people left behind after."

"After?" Wren asks.

His eyes are on me again and I can't read him. I sense he wants to say something more, but he remains quiet, so I pull at the memory of his mother, trying to sharpen the edges of her that have softened and blurred with time. But I know the path that lies beyond those memories leads me to other painful ones, so I leave it.

We exit the quiet lobby to step into the night air, the city glowing yellow with the warm lights of Christmas. I walk alongside Wren, a few steps behind Lincoln and Dunn. I watch Lincoln's back as he tucks his hands deep into his coat pockets and hunches his shoulders against the oncoming winds that always seem to rise from the rivers to swirl low through the streets of Pittsburgh.

Thoughts of his mother won't let me go, whirling around me with whispers of daisies and music and Byron and her black clothes and her brilliant red hair scarf dotted with stars and comets.

Wren's yell to Lincoln ahead snaps me out of my trance. "Hey! Where are we getting dessert?" she demands a bit more loudly than necessary. I'm ready to remind her about volume and manners but Lincoln pulls one hand out of his pocket and thrusts his arm up into the night air as if he's unsheathed a sword before battle. "I know a place! Onward!"

Dunn looks wholly embarrassed to be walking next to him, but Wren shouts out her own "Onward!" startling a few passersby, and I laugh deeply. I can't remember the last time I felt this lightness, as if the weight of my own suffocating existence was lifted just enough to let me breathe for a while. I know tomorrow will likely knock me off my feet in punishment, but here on this sidewalk, braced against the cold wind, my proud and loud daughter at my side, heading for dessert (which the guy wearing the Rolex that costs more than my whole life will be paying for), I decide I'll let tomorrow worry about its own things, like the fact that I let Bea's deadline pass a week ago and sent her nothing, and was rewarded with silence.

Home again and in my bed, I read the program from the show, curious as to the Byron connection because I can't shake the bizarre coincidences that all had to line up for the poet to have intruded on my life again. I flip to the donors list and run my finger down it, but I don't have to go far to find the donation that's listed simply as

In the lasting memory of the eternal Jane Kennedy Hale

Chapter Thirty-Six

May 1997
Ellis, 17
Lincoln, 18

She didn't know why she walked there that night.

She'd be leaving in the morning, and she had gone into her room to see her suitcase sitting on her bed, open and awaiting her to fill it with what she needed for two months in Virginia. Her mother had stacked clean clothes on her bed, waiting to be transferred and tucked neatly into the suitcase. The transition of her life weighed too heavily on her.

Christopher would be gone when she returned, off to southern California where the winters didn't live, and the summers held on for every season. She'd return to an emptier house and emptier parents who were watching their children leave one by one. She would return to thoughts of her own future and plans to be made and colleges to consider and memories to create. For so long, nothing changed. Every year, in and out, was nearly the same as before. She and her four brothers and their parents. Church. Sports. School. Fights. Punishments. Seasons. Ages ticking up by one. Then one. Then one. The years following suit.

Then stitch after stitch, the seams of her childhood started to come apart and here she stood, a latched suitcase and an airplane ticket away from another being snipped. Rather than face the emotions whispering uncertainties in her ear, she chose to walk out of her room and away from them. Out into the warm May night air. She knew where she was walking but wouldn't admit it to herself even as she rounded the house toward the backyard. She let her legs carry her through the yards and through the narrow wood. The mourning-like drone of crickets surrounded her with noise matching her internal disquiet.

The Hale house was dark. Of course it was. Always dark. Sadness and anger settled in the air around Ellis, and she welcomed them. She acknowledged the weight they held, and she let them sit there, pressing on her, digging into her chest and burying themselves in deep. She eyed the glass on the windows and felt the intense desire to hurl a rock through one of them.

Instead, she approached the house and quietly climbed the porch stairs until she stood at the door. A shuddered deliberate inhale seemed to feed and strengthen her resolve, but also her anger. Should she pound on the door until he came out? Should she demand answers she thought she deserved? What if the answers hurt? Did she want painful truth or this equally cruel unknowing? Deep down, she knew the truth would probably not set her free. The truths intentionally hidden in the dark are rarely beautiful once the light of day shines on them.

She set her jaw and held her fist in front of the door and prepared to knock, not knowing what she'd say and with what level of anger she'd say it. But she knew she needed to hold on to this one stitch for a bit longer before she left tomorrow and it fully gave way. Her knuckles nearly rapped the door when she heard the first notes of muted music from the other side.

She cupped her hands around her eyes and peered into the narrow strip of glass framing the front door to see Lincoln seated at the piano, the moonlight washing the room in a gray eerie glow. She crept along the house to another window where she could watch him more closely with his back to her as he pounded the keys—his hands and fingers racing up and down their whole stretch. The music was muted through the window, and she didn't know the song, but she could see, hear, and feel every emotion he was pushing out of himself and into his hands. He was hunched, his head bent low over the keys.

She watched him for minutes as he pulled thundering gloomy storms from the keys before his hands raced impossibly fast to create airy brightness up high. She saw him lift and shift his weight slightly as he pushed harder and faster into the music, his arms shooting outward then pulling in closer, his hands seemingly driven by electricity. At intervals, he lifted his hands higher and higher before he dropped them mercilessly to the keys. He built the song to frantic heights and then finally walked his fingers quickly from high to low, playing out a final mourning note. Ellis saw him sag. The music went out of the air, out of the room and out of him. He kept his head down and brought his arms out to grasp the sides of the bench, his body heaving—what with, she didn't know.

She didn't understand what she had watched. It wasn't just music. It was so different from the song he'd played for his mother on her birthday. Something had been coursing out of him and it seemed dark and distraught and nothing she should know anything about. She crept slowly down the steps, leaving behind the house and leaving behind Lincoln to find his way out of whatever raging tempest gripped him.

It all seemed suddenly too much for her, the weight of it— of him, of that, of this. She was but seventeen and felt more ready to leave in the morning, the space between them stretching vastly longer even as she stood there in place. She would leave this all behind and when she came back, Lincoln would be gone, and it won't have mattered or meant anything.

She left the truth sitting in the dark Hale house, at his mother's piano, fighting something too big for Ellis, and she sensed that not knowing that truth would be easier than learning about whatever could grip a person to bring them to such a dark and frantic maelstrom as she saw him caught inside. She stepped into the dark woods and brushed away the tug of loss that pulled at her as she allowed the full unraveling of a stitch in her life she'd once been so desperate to hold on to.

Ellis Sloan Therapy Sessions

Gulf Tower
Pittsburgh, PA
August 2021

Dr. Parrish: Maybe this isn't a story about him giving you hope, Ellis. Maybe this is a story about Wren showing you she's strong enough to be worthy of that hope when she's given the chance to prove it.

Ellis: So you're saying—

Dr. Parrish: Let's start creating even more chances for her to push her comfort zone a bit wider, and in turn yours too, instead of spending all your time trying to avoid that because of your fear or even expectation that it will fail. How will she know she can do it if you won't give her the chance to try?

Ellis: So, I'm failing her.

Dr. Parrish: Absolutely not. You know you've done the work. Be proud. Let's try to take the next step now on this path you've cleared for her. Let's keep pushing.

Chapter Thirty-Seven

New Year's Eve 2020

"Hadi, Chris, hug me."

"Are you drunk right now, Ellis Robin Marks Sloan?" Hadi scolds me as he shrugs into the winter coat Christopher holds open for him as they prepare to step out into the frigid snowy air. "When do you ever hug?"

"You forgot 'the Third,'" I say to him, referring to his favorite addendum to my name when he's had it with me. "And I'm not drunk. I'm just happy for you two. Seeing you like this."

I can't remember ever having had a good time on New Year's Eve. As a child, I ignored it. As a teenager, I spent it in the basement watching old Carol Burnett skits with my brothers and father. We didn't much enjoy watching her, but we did love watching my father laugh so hard he'd begin to wheeze silently, often eventually ending up on the floor in hysterics. As an adult, I spent it watching Disney movies with Wren and Dunn before going to bed to wait for Oliver to come out of his study.

New Year's Eve is as over-hyped and disappointing as low-fat dessert recipes. Just put the butter and sugar in them and sit on the couch by yourself while you eat them alone and wait for midnight to show itself so you can go to bed. *You're not fooling anyone with your almond flour and stevia, Jessica.*

Chris still hadn't talked to me other than letting me know that Lincoln had known about him for a long time, which led me to inviting them all to New Year's Eve to give Chris a chance to settle into himself and to see who he is with Hadi when other people he loves are around him.Dunn left early to sleep at a friends and Wren sent her own self to bed at ten but only after telling us to keep our volume down because we were being too loud while playing board games. The four of us had spent the night being as irreverent with our banter as ever until Hadi said, "Well, we are all going to hell for sure."

"Seeing us like what?" Chris asks, wrapping a scarf haphazardly and loosely around Hadi's neck and then taking his hand.

I point to their hands. "Like that." I point to Chris' face. It's open. Bright. Happy. "Like that."

"She's for sure drunk," Lincoln says from behind me where he's on the couch, bent over the coffee table, returning board game pieces to their proper boxes and sorting color play money into their correct slots or rubber bands.

"I am not! I had two. I always only ever have two." I don't tell them why, but it niggles at my brain. Chris knows. I smile at my brother. "I wish you'd stay. Until midnight."

Hadi intercepts my request. "Absolutely not. It's our first New Year's Eve and we haven't seen each other for a week, and I have things I wish to be doing to your brother at midnight that you shouldn't be witness to."

"Holy shit, Hadi," Chris says, dragging him by the hand on to the porch and down the steps as Hadi calls quite loudly, his voice carrying easily through the quiet snowy night that will soon ring out with echoes of celebration, "Really specific things, Ellis! You can't even imagine them! There's this one where—"

I laugh as Christopher covers Hadi's running mouth and pulls him roughly to him, only to replace his hand with his own mouth. An effective silencing technique if I ever saw one. Sufficiently squelched and finally released by Christopher, Hadi throws his arm around my brother's waist, and I watch the two of them walk away toward Chris's car.

I close the door on the bitter air, and I'm warmed. By Hadi. By Chris. By the rickety furnace I keep telling my mother will die soon. By wine.

"I love them," I say.

"I can tell," Lincoln offers as he returns the lid to Pictionary, a game we all were awful at—I drew a pineapple and Hadi's exasperated guess was, "Fucking Bart Simpson?" He leans back into the couch and says introspectively, "You know, I had fun."

"You say that like you didn't think you would."

"Well, it's an awful holiday."

"Stick your fist out." When he does, I bump it with mine and plop down next to him. "Thank you and amen."

"What? No—?" He throws his arm up and slices at the air in a poor attempt at my sacrilegious sign of the cross.

I feign disapproval. "That's terrible. Hadi's right. You're going to burn in hell."

He throws his head back and laughs to the ceiling like he always does. It's not nearly a challenge to pull those from him. He's always so ready to give them to me. I can't imagine what it's like to live life like that at this point. Out loud and alive and open. I guess having millions of dollars and the fawning adoration of nearly an entire gender over the age of thirty helps a bit.

"Shh," I hiss. "Do you want Wren to come down and yell at us?"

"Absolutely not."

We sit in that comfortable silence we've been able to find once more, ever since Thanksgiving.

"How much longer do you think you'll be here?" I finally ask.

"Sick of me?"

"Obscenely so."

"Then forever."

I chuckle.

"Soon. Maybe next month? I'm not in a hurry to pick my next project and I'm enjoying being away from California. Still need to figure out about shipping my mother's piano out there. Guess I should get on that."

"I had wondered if it was the same one."

"It is. One of the few things I took. Had everything else thrown into an estate sale."

"Man, I hated playing piano. I'm pretty sure I was terrible at it."

"I heard you play a few times from the porch while my mom taught you. Listen to me, okay, El? You truly sucked."

I elbow him in his ribs. "You had your mother's genes catapulting you to proficiency." I zoom my hand upward through the air. "My genes barely allowed me to master 'Hot Cross Buns' on the recorder."

"That's true. Okay, I'm going to head out."

I shoo him up and toward the door with a wave of my hand. "As Hadi says, 'Off you go, then.'"

When he pulls the door closed behind himself with a small salute, I busy myself with clearing the dishes and glasses, loading the insanely loud dishwasher, and placing the board games where they belong—on the top shelf of the messy coat closet that Mrs. Doubtfire Mom pretends not to see. Fifteen minutes later, as I'm shutting off lights and locking doors, my phone buzzes with a text from Hadi.

Happy New Year, my love.

I look at the time on my phone. It's 12:01 a.m. As usual, I'd missed the turn of the year. *Eh. Who gives a shit?*

Happy New Year. So what you needed to do to my brother took one minute? What an athlete you are, Hadi.

Trash! We were driving. At Chris's just now.

I send him the see-no-evil monkey and the hear-no-evil monkey emojis then flick down the switch to darken the final corner of brightness in the house. Just as I'm about to put my foot on the first step upstairs, a soft knock taps at my front door.

There is not a span of time with a name that can describe what seemed to be a microscopic slice of existence I experience from the moment I open the door with confusion, to the moment Lincoln reaches one arm out to hook me around the waist, pulling me against his body, pressing his mouth to mine.

My breath leaves my chest and my thoughts beat a similarly quick exit from my brain.

He ends the chaste kiss as quickly as he sprung it on me and I take a step backward, grabbing at the door frame near my thigh to steady myself.

"Happy New Year, one minute late," he says with his cocksure half-smile, then leaves me there speechless, breathless, and searching for even a single thought beyond *what the fuck just happened?*

I close my door at the same time I hear his latch shut and walk myself slowly upstairs, bringing my fingers to my lips then lower to my scar. I trace the familiar path of it.

Just this once. This one time. This one day. Right here. Now and probably never again. This holiday isn't so terrible.

Tomorrow will probably be pretty awful.

Chapter Thirty-Eight

January 2000
Ellis, 19
Lincoln, 21

"Marks's residence. Hello? Hello?"

"Ellis?"

"Yeah. Who's this?"

"Lincoln."

"Oh."

"I know Chris came home for Christmas too. Just looking for him."

"Yeah. He's not here. Went with Poppy and Dad to the store. I'll tell him you called. Bye."

"Ellis?"

"Yeah?"

"I read about the writing award you won. The short story contest."

"Yeah."

"Congratulations."

"Sure. Thanks."

"Happy New Year."

"Right. You too. Bye."

"Goodb—"

Ellis Sloan Therapy Sessions

Gulf Tower
Pittsburgh, PA
August 2021

Dr. Parrish: And you two never discussed that kiss?

Ellis: Of course not. It was meaningless.

Dr. Parrish: You thought that at the time, I'm sure. But now that he's gone?

Ellis: I don't dissect it. Why bother?

Dr. Parrish: And he didn't leave that month or the one after, despite what he'd said?

Ellis: Listen, I know what was happening. We settled back into our friendship. There was a reason we had become so close all those years ago. We're kindred. Our souls don't know how to not connect. Like me and Hadi. He settled into the fold of my family. He'd been alone for a long time, since his mother died. I see that. So, no, he didn't leave, because people do that—latch on to my family. They're a chaotic bunch, but you know, they're … a comfort? He was latching on to them. Spent Christmas with us at Poppy's. Then stayed all winter. Taking Dunn driving on days when the snow wasn't an issue. Chatted with me and Wren. Fought with Wren about his name. She'd settled on Trump for weeks and he was hilariously livid about it. Me and Hadi started involving him and Chris in our Saturday movie hangouts. See? He settled into my family. I don't think he realized his life in California was starting to feel lonely until he came back and got sucked in by Poppy and the Markses.

Dr. Parrish: How'd you feel about it? Him being there?

Ellis: He was my friend. He, Hadi and Chris distracted me from my emptiness of words. I ignored Bea all winter long and she let me. Radio silence. I knew what it meant. What was coming.

Dr. Parrish: So spring rolls around. Take me to the big panic attack.

Ellis: —

Dr. Parrish: I know you don't want to, but let's try to get some progress happening, Ellis.

Ellis: Wren had had a meltdown at school. A big one. There was an unexpected fire alarm. False alarm. But she wasn't ready for it. The noise. The chaos. She was hysterical and they couldn't calm her down. Not when she's rocking like she was. I needed to get her.

Dr. Parrish: Absolutely.

Ellis: It was storming horribly. One of those ones? You know? Instant flooding. Inches in an hour. And I couldn't find my keys. I think maybe Dunn had driven us somewhere and tossed them wherever when we got home. They weren't anywhere. So I knocked and got Lincoln. He said he'd drive but—

Dr. Parrish: Ellis? Go on.

Ellis: It was instant paralyzing dread once I realized. What it would do to me. What he would see. I had worked hard to keep myself out of that exact situation since that day in the rain with Oliver. Like, fifteen years? And here it was. Rising up to tower over me. To try again to take me down with it. I hadn't killed it. It was just lurking and waiting. It won that day.

Dr. Parrish: You always get me with the words you choose, Ellis.

Chapter Thirty-Nine

March 2021

"Wait! Can I drive?"

This question stops Lincoln, who already has his hand on the driver's door handle. The rain is pounding the cartop so hard the water splashes six inches into the air like a miniature Vegas hotel fountain. It's the kind of rain that immediately soaks you if you're caught in it, and with my question literally giving him pause, umbrella-less Lincoln is caught and soaked. But he pauses despite the drenching. What's wet is wet, so what's the point of even shielding himself, I suppose. He squints at me and blinks repeatedly, the driving rain making it hard to keep his eyes clear. Even through the sheets of water, I can see his confusion.

"You want to drive?" he nearly shouts to be heard over the rushing wall of white noise the rain is creating. A gust of wind rips the small, flimsy umbrella from my hand and we turn our heads to watch it cartwheel awkwardly down the sidewalk like a city tumbleweed. I'm soaked in seconds.

We return our gazes to each other above the car. If it wasn't so serious a situation, I'd laugh. If it didn't involve Wren needing me, I'd giggle at the ridiculousness. If it didn't mean driving through a rain hard enough to create pools of standing road water, I'd throw my face to the sky, close my eyes and open my soul to the cleansing. What a sight we must be. Standing on opposite sides of a car. Soaked through. Water dripping from our noses, our eyelashes, our chins. His hair now flat, my drowned curls plastered to the sides of my face. Having a little discussion about who is going to drive as if a monster storm wasn't surrounding us with tentacles of windy rage.

"Yes, can I drive?" I repeat the question with a shout.

"Why?!"

My umbrella, now mangled, whips past us heading down the sidewalk in the opposite direction. We watch it careen away then eye each other once more. "I'll just drive!" I shout, as if I'm merely doing him a favor.

A crack of lightning explodes.

"Jesus!" Lincoln hunches his shoulders and winces at the sound. "Get in the car, Ellis!"

"No! I need to drive!"

"Can you drive a stick?" he shouts.

I freeze. In many ways. My heart freezes and I die. My body freezes and I shiver and die again. My brain freezes and I die a third time. I cannot drive a stick. I have as good a chance of getting a helicopter off the ground as I do driving this damn BMW to Wren's school. The hills. The lights. The rain.

Lincoln finally opens his door, folding himself into the car. I hear his door slam closed.

And he waits. For me.

But he doesn't realize.

Ellis Sloan froze three ways and died.

Right there in the rain.

My teeth begin to chatter, and I don't know if it's from the cold seeping into my bones through my wet clothes or icy fear lacing its fingers through my heart.

"Ellis!" Lincoln is leaning over to shout at me, knocking on the passenger window from the inside. I can barely hear him. "Ellis! Get in!"

Another crack of lightning, this one exploding close enough to resurrect me from my trinity of deaths, compels me to pull open the passenger door and fall inside just as a rip of thunder rolls across the ground.

"Jesus, Ellis!"

I can feel Lincoln's bewilderment and frustration, but I say nothing in defense of myself. Too much breath. Too many words.

Now we sit in the echo. The echo of his epithet, the rushing of my fear, the hollowness of his confusion, and the water—pounding water. All ricocheting inside the car as he exasperatedly pushes the start button, leaving behind a wet splotch from his dripping finger.

The car plays out a gentle welcoming *bing-bong-bing-ding* startup tone and I'm struck that it's not the correct soundtrack for this moment. This moment should be accompanied with screeching. Scratching. This moment should be backdropped with shrieking discord from a punk band.

"You're a lunatic, Ellis Marks. Jesus." Lincoln mutters it low. Slow. To himself maybe. And maybe to Jesus.

His use of the name he once knew me by burns in my ears. I don't respond. All of my energy is directed toward stopping the panic that is rushing through my insides from showing up on my outsides. I should look for something to dry myself so I don't arrive at Wren's school looking like I was rescued from open water. I should push my matted hair from my cheeks. I should wring out the hem of my shirt. I should pull the visor down and look in the little rectangle mirror and see what visual horrors I'm about to inflict upon the office staff of Shaw Middle School. Not that I ever show up there looking like a Kardashian, but I've never shown up looking like a drowned sewer rat either. I'd like to find a nice middle ground between those two things.

I should do the things that functioning adult humans do after they've gotten caught in the rain. The things Lincoln, a functioning adult human, is doing right now. But I don't. I let the wet be wet and the drips drip. My full focus must stay on the panic. It pounces when I'm not guarded. Perhaps if I don't move, it will leave me be. If I'm quiet. If I don't breathe. But my panic feeds on stillness. On movement. On quiet. On noise. It feeds on my breath. It feeds on my suffocation. It's an insatiable parasite that grows stronger the harder I fight to control it.

I stare at the strip of glossy decorative wood inlaid on the black rubber console in front of me until my eyes glaze and I'm staring through it, into it. The world around that one space fades away from me. It's just me, that strip of wood, and my panic. A new trinity.

Lincoln's body enters my frame of vision, blocking my view. I blink the dryness from my contact lenses and refocus my eyes. He has opened the glove compartment in front of me and is rummaging through it. He pulls a few random papers and receipts out before tossing them back in and closing the small door with a bit more force than needed to latch it shut.

I jolt slightly at the sound and my panic takes notice, rushing ever faster upward and outward. I'm aware I'll not be able to hold it down much longer. Some lurking monsters can only survive if they surface and are therefore hellbent to do it.

Lincoln is twisting his body to dig around behind my seat, his seat, under his seat, under mine. Every compartment lifted. Opened. Closed. He sighs and grips the top of the steering wheel with both hands. "How do I not have a single napkin in this car?"

I remain quiet and stare at the water sheeting the windshield. Poor visibility, as they say in weather reports. *Be careful out there. It's a nasty one. Back to you, Bob and Jill.*

Lincoln rubs his hands across his face and shakes a few drops of water off his fingers. "Where am I going?" He turns to me.

A new confusion sweeps across his face when he sees mine. He wasn't expecting the wetness welling in my eyes. I hold them open wide. "It—" It comes out a croak. I clear my voice. "Shaw Middle School."

Lincoln keeps an uneasy gaze on me, holding my eyes while he shifts the gear and works the pedals. I don't remember him activating the windshield wipers, but they're moving as fast as I imagine they can go, unable to move the water quickly enough to do much good. I feel a slight lurch of momentum and he turns the wheel to bring the car into the road.

My panic feels the motion too and throws an electric charge of adrenaline to my heart. I try to take a deep breath like I tell Wren to do when she's having trouble calming down. *Just breathe,* I say to her. *Just breathe,* I say to myself now. But the air I breathe into my lungs is not an antidote; it's a booster shot. Everyone knows this to be true, but they continue to sell the lie of "breathe through the panic." There is no antidote to panic. You have to let it tire itself out while you choose whether or not to suffocate. It doesn't care either way.

My heart races off-rhythm making it impossible for me to draw in a full breath. I resort to shallower half-breaths while trying to hide from Lincoln that I'm in a struggle with my whole all everything right now.

He remains oblivious to the internal war I'm waging. His full concentration is on driving through rain so hard we might as well be driving on the ocean floor. When he shifts to a higher gear, my breath catches quietly, unnoticed. I'm close to breaking. I crawl a hand inconspicuously to grip a small compartment in my door. It's probably meant to hold loose change, a pack of gum, a tossed candy wrapper. But for now, it's holding me together.

I shift my eyes to Lincoln and find he is my opposite. Breathing easily like a human, not erratically like the panic-addled lunatic Ellis Sloan. He's the picture of composure. One hand at the top of the wheel, the other resting loosely on the gear shift. His legs move interchangeably, and if I understood manual driving, I'd better understand what he's doing with his feet. A stop. A go. A traffic light's glow is barely visible through the halo of water and spray falling in blankets onto the windshield. The occasional bolt of lightning or reverberating thunderclap sends me into an internal spiral that I keep hidden. I focus on my breathing. Tight. Hard. Panicked. My ears are screaming. My mouth is sewn shut.

He obeys the GPS and turns on to the main business route through town. One gear. Another. Another. Each one indicating a notching-up of speed. A faster rushing of water. A further diminishment of visibility. *It's looking to be a pretty nasty commute this afternoon, Bob and Jill. Remember, folks! Turn around; don't drown.* I want to tell Lincoln to drive slower. To please be careful. But I cannot. The seams on my mouth stay put. I feel the car jerk as a pool of road water takes hold of a tire with a sickening swerving motion. And that's the end. That's where I lose the fight. Panic wins; Ellis Sloan with the broken whole all everything loses. I bend slowly at my waist in defeat and lower my head to rest my chin on the tops of my knees. My arms come up to wrap and encase my head completely.

The monster surfaces.

I let the shivering take my body, and the memory take everything else.

Chapter Forty

May 2004

"Careful!"

Ellis regretted the tossed word before it had left her lips. She could see Oliver visibly tense at the exclamation. She bit at her lower lip in a show of nerves and muttered a "sorry" to him.

"Sheets of rain" is how Seth's new wife Maddie described it as she bade Ellis and Oliver goodbye after hosting them for Sunday dinner. "Careful driving, loves. It's fixin' to rain sheets," was her exact phrasing. And what an apt description it was for what Ellis saw outside the windshield. Veritable planes of water being dumped on the car and the earth. Gusts of wind borne from a black sky pushed the water into visible ripples in the air. They'd made it to their car mere moments before the sky let loose its full measure of rage.

"Should we wait it out here? Probably be over pretty quick," she had asked him nervously as the downpour escalated.

"Nah. We're already in the car. It's not that far to home." With a reassuring pat of her knee, he started the car and backed into the road.

Ellis hated the rain. The hard rains of the Pennsylvania hills and mountains were relentless in the late spring especially. Bursting in and out of the landscape quickly, but with enough force to flood roads and basements multiple times a season. No, it wasn't the Pennsylvania storms that made Ellis hate rain. It was Tennessee. It was a small bridge—maybe even small enough to qualify as a mere overpass. It was December and it was rainy. Ellis had been heading home with Seth from visiting Nathan who was stationed in Florida at Eglin but had a two-day break. City-by-city they crawled their way up the map. Occasionally they encountered a snow flurry or traffic heavy enough to send them into profane steering wheel-pounding rage fits.

But this rain—this Tennessee rain through which Ellis had been sleeping soundly in the passenger seat while Seth drove, was beginning to freeze. And Seth wasn't expecting that. He didn't realize. Until the tires hit the bridge, searched for traction, and found none.

Ellis woke to immediate disconcerting terror. To Seth yelling "fuck" over and over while the world outside was spinning too fast for her to find any point of focus. Just twirling sky and landscape. A merry-go-round of fear. He yanked the steering wheel sharply left and right, a desperate but futile fight against physics.

Ellis's screams as the car spun and careened across the bridge were eerily swallowed into silence when the front bumper of a pickup truck that had been a bit behind them smashed into her door, plunging her into immediate and soul-deep darkness.

It's weird how one can go through life unafraid of a thing, and then spend the rest of their life terrified of it. Before the accident, Ellis had driven and been driven through countless storms of varying ferocity. Rain and snow and ice and wind. Everything nature threw at her, Ellis handled as if it wasn't a threat. The perceived immortality of youth is always eventually shattered, and for Ellis it shattered completely that day on the icy bridge in Tennessee.

Years later when she told Oliver on their third date about the noticeable scar that ran along the bottom of her chin, about the larger more jagged ones that crisscrossed her right shoulder and right leg, he'd been what he should be. Soothing. Compassionate. Caring. He painted on a furrowed brow and shook his head with empathy and sadness. *How hard that must have been for you. What a scare. I'm so glad you were okay.* He had gripped her hand on the table of the restaurant and gave it a squeeze. *I'm here for you, Ellis.*

But that day in the car. That day in the rain. That day after dinner at her brother's house where the sky was *fixin' to rain sheets.* That day she'd said "careful" despite all his angry requests that she never criticize his driving. That she not grip a door compartment in a silent show of fear. That she not pull in a fearful breath he could hear. That she not be so "fucking irritating" while he was driving.

That day after all the fights about driving and directions.

That day she glimpsed a monster she'd never seen surface before.

Ellis Sloan Therapy Sessions

Gulf Tower
Pittsburgh, PA
August 2021

Ellis: I thought I would die. It felt like someone flipped my switch off. Near-instant blackness. I spent a week in a hospital in Tennessee. Seth wasn't that hurt. I took the brunt of the truck. Seth feels guilty about that to this day. He says it's why he became a firefighter. That accident. Those people cutting me out of our car while he watched.

Dr. Parrish: What were your injuries?

Ellis: I have some scars, obviously. Here. The one on my leg is pretty jagged still. Same with my shoulder; it's never felt the same since. I had some internal bleeding. Broken ribs poking at lungs. Broken leg. The usual. Lacerations and bruises. Fear. My body was young. I healed.

Dr. Parrish: Fear.

Ellis: Yeah. I don't know how to make it go away.

Dr. Parrish: Sometimes it doesn't ever.

Ellis: Ever.

Dr. Parrish: Don't get hung up on that word. I'm just saying sometimes we seek to erase that which we can only confront and control.

Ellis: You should write a book.

Dr. Parrish: I'm not the author here.

Chapter Forty-One

March 2021

"Jesus. Fuck."

I hear Lincoln spitting out words that do nothing to calm me and everything to further panic me. I don't hear him. I hear Seth. I hear my panicked brother in the rain, the world spinning around us, yelling *fuck* until blackness swallowed me.

My head remains at my knees, encased in the protective cage of my arms. At some point, I started rocking. Nudging my body forward in the seat to let it shift backward again and again. I set it to the rhythm of the crashing waves of my internal fear. Shivering. Rocking. Moaning. My eyes are squeezed closed so tightly I see jagged streaks of angry burnt reds swimming behind them, bursts of yellow intruding with every hard beat of my heart. I cannot stop the shivering. Sometimes my panic has surfaced as sobs on the side of the road, parked in the rain, my confused children strapped in the back seat while I waited out the storm. On this day, the panic wracks my body with such intense shaking that my teeth are knocking together loud enough Lincoln can surely hear them even above the din of hard rain on my coffin of glass and steel.

Part of me wants to look to see what's making him swear in that fearful way. The normally brave Lincoln allowing threads of fear to weave themselves into his voice must be a harbinger of disaster. The realization that doom is imminent sends another flare of panic through me. Nature wants to finish what it started in Tennessee. What it tried to finish that day with Oliver. I feel a knot rise in my throat—a sob pleading to be freed. I swallow it down and moan long and low as the car pushes into another slight swerve.

"Fuck. Fuck. El. Fuck."

Then I feel it. A hand. Tentative. On my back. Just a slight pressure. Fingertips. No palm. A questioning touch. A whisper of uncertainty. A seeking of something.

"Fuck. Fuck."

The touch is gone, and I feel shifting gears interrupt the rhythm of my rocking. I'm so cold. Everywhere. From the center of my being to the outer edges of my expelled breath. It's all cold. I move my hands into my wet gnarled hair and grasp huge handfuls of curls. I squeeze harshly at them, willing the pain I inflict to warm me like the hand did. It does not. But I keep them there—squeezing. Pulling. Letting the hurt remind me I'm alive. Focusing all my fear and panic into hurting myself. If I hurt, I'm alive. If I hurt, I'm feeling something other than panic, fear and dread.

If I hurt, I deserve it.

He spits out more words.

"El?" A question.

"El." A statement

"God." A prayer.

"Fuck." A resignation.

Another shift of gears and the hand is back. Fingers sprawled to cover as much area as possible. It's no longer a question. It's pressure. A statement of intentional thereness.

And there I sit. Bent at the waist. My hands pulling at my wet hair. My eyes clenched. Moaning. Shivering.

The hands presses.

Suddenly through the fog of my fear, I realize it's not the rain

Lincoln is swearing about. It's me. It's this. It's the surfacing. It's my emotional mess. My collapse in his presence. That, and not the weather. Me, and not the storm. Ellis, and not an oncoming truck.

I'm his storm.

Me, the woman trapped in memories she knows will never let her go.

Chapter Forty-Two

May 2004

It was so unexpected to Ellis. She'd angered Oliver before, sure. She'd seen the loss of temper. The face turned red. The time he threw his keys at her. Or punched a wall. Kicked over a chair.

She and Oliver so rarely fought, but when they did, he often ended up offering halfhearted apologies intersected with "but," and excuses intersected with "you." "Sorry I yelled at you, but you asked the question with an attitude." "Sorry I lost my patience with Wren and yelled loudly at her, causing her to collapse in fright and sensory overload, but you knew I was tired."

But on this day of sheeted rain, a monster as ferocious as the one bursting from the clouds emerged. It began with an angry sigh. A clenched jaw. A slightly readjusted grip of the steering wheel. An inhale. A sudden darkness on his face. Then an all-out assault of the gas pedal. The car lurched violently through the rain. The force of momentum hit Ellis as hard as the surprise did and pushed her body against her seat back.

"What are you doing?! Oliver!" Ellis shouted the words, terror beginning to rise in her chest. She could hear it in her own voice. A guttural tremor. If he heard it, he didn't show it. Or didn't care. He steeled his jaw and his grip and kept a persistent foot on the gas pedal, only pulling it up to brake at the final moment he could without slamming into cars in front of them.

Ellis could see nothing but gray. Gray sky. Gray rain. Gray road reflecting the sky. The world outside was a rushing colorless void and the man driving her through it seemed to be ready to die and planned to take her with him.

Ellis was crying now, sobbing out begging words as memories of Tennessee flooded her body with panic. But he remained in a zombie state, unhearing. He entered the main route through town, a two-lane road with a speed limit of 40, and immediately brought the car to 67. Ellis watched the speedometer numbers creep higher and higher as they careened around cars, pickups, and delivery trucks. One lane. Another. Sudden braking sent the car hydroplaning precariously before he regained control only to accelerate dangerously again. Angry honks followed their path, a perfect soundtrack to her inner horror.

He turned sharply on to a side road, narrow and wooded with barely a berm to provide cushion from disaster. Long deep puddles pooled at odd intervals, catching the tires, forcing blinding sheets of water onto the windshield.

The terror she could hear behind her own begging further panicked Ellis until she was in an endless loop of dread tumbling with bursts of memories she'd worked hard to hold down. She heard her brother screaming *fuck*. She felt the spin of their car on the bridge in Tennessee. She saw the truck closing in on her window. She felt that first push of metal into her shoulder and knee. She felt the jagged edge of something sharp slice open her chin.

She unleashed a full-throated scream when, finally, Oliver lost the battle against the water. A brake into a curve through six inches of standing water took hold of the car and spun it until Ellis saw headlights rushing directly at her. She closed her eyes and shielded her face with her arms knowing what would come next. Shattering glass. Slicing metal. Pain. Darkness. Then fear that would live with her forever, only stronger.

But the darkness didn't come. Instead, she felt the car swerve sharply and come to a rest. The engine cut off but everything inside of her was still running at full throttle. Inside, she was still screaming. Outside, she shivered and wept, too scared to look to see where they had come to rest. Out of the corner of her eye, she saw Oliver open his door and leave the car. She heard and felt the slam. A moment later, her own door was yanked open and the driving rain pelted her right leg and shoulder, the same ones that had become blood-covered in Tennessee. "Get out and drive," Oliver spat out angrily, rain pouring on him.

Ellis lowered her arms from her head, still heaving from panic, and looked up at him incredulously. He was unrecognizable, anger having turned his face into something foreign and sinister.

"Get. Out. And. Drive," he said, emphasizing every word. Ellis looked at their surroundings to see the car had skidded into a small shoulder, sparing them from oncoming traffic after they spun out. A car drove past, splashing Oliver with buckets of water. "Fuck! Get the fuck out and drive! I'm not doing it if you're going to be so fucking ridiculous!"

So Ellis did. She shakily climbed over the gear shift to the driver seat, her legs and arms feeling numb. Oliver slumped heavily into the passenger seat and slammed his door so hard she was sure the window glass would shatter. She drove slowly with her husband not looking at her the whole way. She drove terrified, praying for the rain to stop. She prayed to wake from what she was sure was a nightmare.

Safely at their house, watching Oliver storm inside, slamming the door behind so hard that the bright wreath of faux daisies fell from its hook, Ellis realized the nightmares wouldn't always live in her sleep. Sometimes, they'd inflict their evil on her while she was awake. She covered her jutting stomach with her hands, as if to somehow reach and soothe the boy inside who would be born in two months.

Ellis Sloan Therapy Sessions

Gulf Tower
Pittsburgh, PA
August 2021

Ellis: So how do I control the fear? I've canceled things simply because there's a chance I'll have to drive through a storm. And now that Dunn is driving on his own?

Dr. Parrish: You're pushing your fear onto your son?

Ellis: Yeah. I don't want to. Will I be this way every time it rains forever? Maybe I should move to the desert.

Dr. Parrish: Let's not run all the way to Arizona from this, and let's not focus on forever. It's daunting, and I would argue, not even a real concept. Time is finite. The fear will always be with you to some degree; let's work on controlling the degree. I do think you'd have had an easier time healing from the accident if Oliver hadn't terrorized you just a few years after it.

Ellis: Terrorized.

Dr. Parrish: Do you have a better word?

Ellis: I guess not.

Dr. Parrish: So, we have fear. It brings panic. We know this. Let's address it while it's below the surface instead of you trying to deal with it once it, as you said, rises up to tower over you. The good news is, we have lots of ways to work on trauma.

Ellis: Trauma? No, I don't think it's tr— Ah. Just going to point to your diplomas. Touché.

Chapter Forty-Three

March 2021

This is how the rest of the ride goes.

The shivering. The moaning. The rocking. The hand comes to warm me, the hand leaves to shift, the hand returns to warm, leaves, returns. Always returns to the same spot on my back. And the rain never relents no matter how many times I mutter "please please please." All my fear awaits that next slip. That slide that means we no longer have tires on the road. That the water has won and we, the mere humans, have lost.

But it never comes. The hand comes. The hand goes. It presses. Gives warmth, absorbs cold. Leaves, always to return. To sprawl wide its generosity.

I'm aware of the hand leaving and the car stopping. A final shift of a gear. The endnote of *bing-bong-ding* as the car's engine powers down. The nearly imperceptible settling of three thousand pounds of machine. I stay bent with my hands entangled in my hair. And I shiver. My body wracked. There's no warmth anywhere. I can't find it.

A word. My name.

"Ellis."

A beckoning.

I won't sit up and face this. I won't. I feel the hand again, but this time it reaches to my own hands and works to gently unlace my stiff, gnarled fingers from the tangles in my hair. One by one, my fingers are released from their imprisoning strands. Resigned, I let my freed hands fall and ignore the dozens of pulled strands crisscrossing my palms. I tuck my arms under my chest, seeking warmth from them. There is none. I draw in a ragged breath and make plans to stay this way for the rest of my life like a crash test dummy that served its usefulness. My plans are thwarted when I feel his hand clasp my shoulder to give it a tug. A slight pull upward.

A soothing tone. "Come on. We're here."

I let him pull me slowly to an upright position. Shame and embarrassment wash away every last trace of now-retreating panic. I'm further mortified when I realize I'd been crying behind all the shivering and rocking and moaning. Lincoln is left to come to terms with what I am—a basket of clinical insanity sitting in the passenger seat of his car. Wet, crying, shivering, terrified.

And I hate myself for it. I let the self-hate leaven and fill every space left empty by the dissipated panic. I hate every part of me. I hate that I collapsed. I hate that I lost the battle. I hate how afraid I am. I hate that I cried. I hate that he saw it. I hate that I'm embarrassed. I hate how calm he is. I hate that he comforted me and that I needed it and wanted it and I hate that he's looking at me with concern shadowed across his face. I hate that he ran his hand through his hair three times, and it looks just fucking fantastic now.

"Ellis." A beginning.

I can't bear anything he's about to say. Not one word or question. Not a syllable. I place my words into the path of his own. "I'm sorry. I'm sorry. I'm sorry. I—" I run my palms up and down my face, wiping away tears mingled with rainwater, but leaving behind strands of my hair sticking to my cheeks. I am trying to wipe away my falling-apart and cover it with my mask of calm, but my tremulous breathing and a defiant tear tell on my lie. I swipe it away only for another to run a relay behind it. *Fuck.*

Another and another and another and I let my face fall into my hands. Defeated. To be able to crawl away and hide. To disappear from this mortifying moment and the memory that begat it—the memory that will resurrect panic every time it rains—I would give anything. But it will never leave me. It lives in me and with me and will only die when I do.

Lincoln grabs a hold of my wrist and pulls me to him, wrapping his arms around me awkwardly over the center console. I let him warm me while I again try to dam the tears that refuse to stop. *Still a few showers lingering at this hour, Bob and Jill.*

"Do I need to go get her?" he says into my ear.

I pull out of his arms. I'm aware of the state of my everything. My eyes are probably red. My chin is quivering like a scolded four-year-old. My hair, we won't even talk about it because I don't imagine there are words sufficient. My clothes look like I put them on straight out of the washer.

As I take another look, I tell ya, there's still some ugliness out there, Bob and Jill.

I shake my head. "I'm okay. No. You can't. You're not on her list. Security list. I'm fine. I'm sorry. It's—I'm okay. I'm stupid." I force a weak smile and take the first deep breath I've managed since he said the car was a stick shift. Fucking manual transmissions. Why are they still making these? Women aren't out by the rivers scrubbing their clothes up and down a wood washboard with a bar of soap, so why are men still driving around shifting gears that could be shifting themselves? I have a lot of strong and sexist thoughts on car transmissions and housekeeping for someone coming down from a reputation-ruining panic attack. "I'm going to go get her. Really, I'm okay."

"I don't—" He considers me with a brief perusal that darts his eyes around the whole of my face. "Yeah, I don't think you're okay."

"I'm very close to okay," I offer. He slits his eyes skeptically, but I ignore it. "More okay by the second," I say, aware that the weird smile I've widened from ear-to-ear would be better suited for a murderous ventriloquist puppet. It's a smile of all eyebrows and teeth, but no light.

Lincoln sees right through my fearful shadows like a searchlight, but sighs. "Okay. Might want to—" he reaches to flip down my sun visor and swipes open the mirror cover, "take a quick look in there before you go in."

I do.

Boy howdy, Bob and Jill, have we got ourselves a real mess. You can't imagine the aftermath we're seeing right now in some places.

I look like I was recently and violently birthed by a barn animal. Wet. Puffy. Matted. Snotted. Red. Strands of wet, pulled hair crisscrossing my face. "I don't suppose you have a brush in here?" I ask as I consider the methods available to counteract the horrors revealed by the mirror.

"I don't even have a napkin in here, babe."

I hurriedly run my fingers down both sides of my head and use my shirt to wipe my nose and swipe away the errant hair strands and last few tears. At least those have stopped. I tuck my gnarled and knotted wet hair behind my ears and turn to Lincoln whose look of concern is now dancing with slight amusement. He bites at the inside of his upper lip and raises his eyebrows at me. *Oh my.*

"The hottest thing you've ever had in this car, I know," I say.

"I had a rotisserie chicken in here last week, so, maybe not," he replies easily with a shrug.

I open the door with a small smile and go for my daughter. Soaked. Exhausted from panic and incredibly embarrassed. And probably about to have to convince the school staff that I don't need an ambulance or a priest. I brush that all away for now and grab hold of something I notice hiding behind my heart—gratitude. It's warm and comforting, and for this moment, it's what I need. It reminds me of the other time in my life he'd comforted me, though I didn't appreciate it then.

Looks like we're through the worst of it, Bob and Jill, but I think we'll be cleaning up from this one for a few days.

Chapter Forty-Four

December 2014
Ellis, 34
Lincoln, 36

A body is not a person.

Pastor David Marks of the Grace Christian Church on Margaret Road died like he lived—calmly, without anger—not at his shortened time nor the disease that was taking him. He died on a cold day surrounded by love. He died with fresh snow on the ground and the flower bulbs he planted along the porch in October still awaiting their chance to live. He died in his bed at home with the hands of his children laid upon him and his body supported by the weight of his small but stoic wife. He died hearing whispers of love and feeling the wet cheeks of his children brushing against his face. He died quietly. He died with grace. He died with his eldest son Nathan praying reverently over him, and his next-eldest son Christopher resting his head upon his father's fading heart, weeping.

He died with his younger boys, Lucas and Seth, holding each of his hands. He died with his only daughter's palm soothingly stroking his hair.

Ellis walked out of her parents' house after her father took his last breath and she walked into the backyard woods to cry, alone, where the only witness was a brave scampering squirrel who was unaware of the extent to which she suffered.

Days later, after the platters of sympathy food had been delivered, the grandchildren informed and comforted, the tears cried and the arrangements made, she found herself in the same funeral home she had been in years ago when her piano teacher died. The walls were still pink. The carpet changed, but still green. The air still heavy with discomfort, disquiet, and palpable weariness of spirit.

She had insisted her father be buried in his favorite suit. It was blue. While he lived, it set off his bright eyes and warm skin. In death, those eyes would not shine again. The coffin was open. All traces of his sickness had been erased, but like her piano teacher, this was merely a doll; it was not her father. She didn't know where he'd gone, but he was not there in that body waiting to be planted like his bulbs. Like Mrs. Hale. Like they all would be eventually.

Huge wreaths of flowers overflowed the room and the hallway leading to it, a testament to his ability to draw people into his life and never let them go regardless of distance or time. Ellis walked among the flowers with Oliver's arm protectively around her waist. Every pocket of his jacket and pants were stuffed with tissues he kept offering to her, but she had already cried everything out in the woods, alone with a squirrel. And then shut off the valve.

Ellis never understood the funeral home flowers but guessed they were a desperate attempt of those left behind to acknowledge loss without uncomfortable phone calls. The same held true for the trays and dishes of food that kept arriving at her mother's house to the point that she had begun handing them off to Ellis and her brothers to freeze. *You have suffered a great loss. Here are gaudy wreaths of flowers adorned with satin pageant sashes, and here are 65 lasagnas. May he rest in peace.*

Hadi, her friend of only a year, already knew Ellis better than to send flowers. Instead, he'd return from London soon, armed with what she needed—a good wine she couldn't afford, a decent-sized box of burnt almond torte, and a willingness to watch a movie he hated but that she adored—*The Cutting Edge.* He wouldn't make her talk about her father, and he wouldn't try to pull emotions out of her. He'd let her exist inside her grief quietly.

A spray of daisies caught Ellis's eye and she led Oliver to them. Their white fans of petals surrounding yellow circles were a stark contrast to the dark reds and pinks in the other arrangements. The daisies spoke of warm summers and happiness. The rest spoke of cold lonely darkness. Ellis removed the card from the daisies and flipped it over.

- Lincoln -

She tamped down the weird rush she felt at seeing his name injected into her time of personal pain, invoking long-disregarded memories yearning to be picked up, dusted off, and looked at once more. One more chance to stir. To create meaning. She tossed them aside instead.

"Who's that?" Oliver asked, pulling her closer to his side and smiling sympathetically.

She shook her head as she returned the card to the daisies. "Just a friend of Christopher's," she said, not wanting to explain it further.

She was surprised to feel the wetness of a tear rolling down her cheek. She took the tissue Oliver held out to her then pulled away from him and wandered off to find her mother.

She didn't know if she set off to offer comfort, or in search of it.

Ellis Sloan Therapy Sessions

Gulf Tower
Pittsburgh, PA
September 2021

Ellis: It's so weird as I look back on it. He was the calmest, most sedate person you could ever meet. To the point it was boring. He was room-temperature white bread, and I was a Mento tossed into a liter of Diet Coke. But like I said, I realized soon after our wedding how explosive he was. But the thing is, he was my first relationship. I thought for a long time that's how relationships worked.

Dr. Parrish: Did you address it with him? After the explosions would settle down.

Ellis: Every time. I stood up for myself, I'd like to think. But we had the same fight again and again. And I told him every time that I felt like I would break eventually or that he would go too far. It got to be very *Groundhog Day*-ish and to the point where I threatened to leave unless he started seeing a therapist or talked to a doctor about medication.

Dr. Parrish: He agreed?

Ellis: No. He said he wouldn't be controlled like that. He didn't speak to me, and I know you think I'm exaggerating this, but I assure you I am not—he didn't speak to me for eight days after I told him to go to therapy. I can't even tell you how miserable that made me.

Dr. Parrish: Eight days of silence.

Ellis: Well, he sent me a text.

Dr. Parrish: What did it say?

Ellis: It said, "Do you not hear Wren crying?"

Chapter Forty-Five

March 2021

Well, I don't have anyone to blame but myself.

This I know as I sit here on my couch, Wren asleep upstairs. Dunn over at Lucas's to head to an early soccer workout with his cousin. It's my fault. For lots of reasons. It's my fault because I didn't write. It's my fault because I fell into complacency over the winter. Forgetting my guard. Stupidly lowering it when I should always hold it high and ready, like Hadi does.

But I didn't. I let myself think I was happy, but really, it was Happy Mom, the plastic shiny front hiding everything—my loneliness, my fear, my panic, my worthlessness. I put my writing away. I enjoyed the winter with my brother, Hadi and Lincoln. I smiled. Laughed.

The universe saw it and came for me. Hard. All in one day.

The phone call from Wren's school. The car ride with Lincoln in which I collapsed into ruins. Lincoln got Wren and I home and while I was in the kitchen fixing her a snack of cheese and crackers, I made eye contact with the stack of mail I hadn't yet braved up enough to open. The corner of one letter was the address of the family court. The final divorce decree. Done. Over. I thought I'd be happy. I thought freedom would envelop me and whisper about how I didn't have a bad marriage pushing me down anymore. But it didn't free me; it crushed me. Scared me. I ran our marriage through my head. His easy laugh when we first met. The way he'd shake his head at my loud antics. Our wedding at the vineyard. Our knowing smiles. Happy moments. Saddened there would be no more.

But the universe wasn't done. Not until the email came through. From Bea. Informing me the publisher wished to cancel my contract due to lack of progress.

And that was it. That was one thing too many.

Wren went to bed, and me?

I ... am drunk.

No. I am not. I am never drunk. I have two drinks and I stop. Every time. Every Saturday night with Hadi. Every holiday. Ever since that day in San Diego. I don't go past two. I will not be punished for three. Or four. I am a pilgrim. I am the preacher's kid. Two drinks. I am not one to—

You know what? I'm drunk.

I drank. I drank four. I drank it away. After two, I wondered what number drink drinks you right past the pain, and the answer, I found, is four. At least for me. Four. Four drinks drank away the divorce decree that I didn't open, but rather tucked into a folder at my writing desk where I no longer write. Wren's meltdown. The car ride of terror. The look of concern on Lincoln's face. The emotions I showed him. The fact that I'm no longer an author to the point that I can't even play Author Mom because there's nothing to write that anyone wishes to pay me to read.

So here I sit on my couch, my head pressed deep into the back cushion, my insides soaked in four big glasses of warmish red wine. My brain is sloshing about in a wet murky fog. My heart is either slowing down or speeding up. Who can tell on four? My skin is burning and numb at the same time. My ears are buzzing. And buzzing. They won't stop buz—

Oh. That's the doorbell. The doorbell is buzzing. Who would dare buzz the doorbell after four? I flop my head to the side and attempt to focus my vision on the door. It is a parallelogram. I don't remember doors being parallelograms. Is this new architecture? Maybe that's a trapezoid.

Wren would know. I don't dare wake her to ask. She has never even seen me on two. Imagine the judgment if she saw me on four.

Bzzzzzz. "Eller?" Lincoln. Softly.

"Don't call me that." No clue if I said that out loud or if I left it inside to drown in the soupy fog of my spongy brain.

"Ellis?"

Ugh.

"I can hear you in there."

Motherfucking Lincoln.

"Did you just say, 'Motherfucking Lincoln?'"

Damn. I guess I'm saying some stuff out loud. I say, "Go away," and hope to God it was aloud.

Bzzzz.

"You've been ignoring Chris and Hadi's texts. Hadi told me to kick it down if you didn't let me in. I bet Wren won't like it."

Using my daughter against me. If he hadn't been so achingly kind that very afternoon, to both of us, I'd grab the pepper spray in my purse and unleash burny fire on him. Instead, I ignore him.

"Doing it!" I hear a thud at the door. He will indeed wake Wren.

"Stop! I'm fucking coming."

I am at the door, and not only could I not tell you the door shape, but I also could not tell you how I got to the door. Did I walk? Did I crawl and then hoist myself up with the doorknob? Maybe on four I can fly?

I don't open it for him, but only unlock it and then return to the couch to wearily plop myself down into the indentation I left behind.

Lincoln lets himself in and observes my state, then walks wordlessly past me toward the kitchen.

I call out to him, "You know what my problem is?"

He says nothing. I hear a kitchen cupboard close and the faucet turn on.

"My problem is ... I'm not good at finding things." I say this with certainty. Confidence. I have Sherlocked this mess and I have *ah-hah-ed* right to the truth and there it is.

"You're not good at finding things? That's your problem?" he calls from the kitchen.

"I can't find things. When everyone else is finding things, I?" I stab a finger toward my own face. "Don't find the things."

He is standing at my knees. Looking down at me with a glass of water in his hand. "What things? What don't you find?" He pushes the glass toward me. "Drink."

Fuck him for telling me what to do. I place the full glass on the couch cushion next to my leg and watch with great satisfaction as it topples over. The wet splotch blooms and grows, the couch hungrily drinking it in. It reaches my jeans and dives in.

"Woman," he breathes out long and low.

"Fuck you."

He sighs. "What things?" he asks again as he lowers himself to the adjacent chair. "Hey," he says when I don't respond. "What things can't you find? Or don't you find?"

I turn my head to see him. His face covered in stupid concern for stupid Ellis who is drunk on four. I wonder what his number is. I wonder if it's exponential. I wonder why I care. Fuck him. Fuck his sympathy. Fuck his stupid presidential names. I close my eyes. "I couldn't find the comet."

"Did you check under the bathroom sink? That's where—"

I open my eyes. "No, you fucking moron. Not that comet. THE comet. An actual space comet. Like Haley's. Hale Bopp." I slice my flattened hand through the air. "Comet. NEOWISE. Remember the comet?"

"Ah." He leans back to rest in the chair and ponders me in a way I don't wish to be pondered, with crossed arms and a tilt of his head. "You're quite a sweary drunk. It tracks."

"I'm not drunk. Fuck you." I close my eyes again. I hear a soft chuckle. I will punch his face as soon as I can feel my arms again, I swear to God. Four makes me extraordinarily angry.

"So you couldn't find a comet."

"Because I can't find things."

"So what?"

Pain enters me, but it's not the kind that hurts your bones, or muscles or joints. This pain worms into my heart where it creeps like a vine. It crawls to my throat where it forms a knot before heading to my eyes where I feel it trying to squeeze out tears. I remember walking a beach with young Wren, everyone around us picking shark teeth from the rocky sand and not being able to find her a single one. She was so disappointed. I remember standing in the dark behind Poppy's house, trying to find the comet to show Dunn. I couldn't find it. I searched so long with different star mapping apps. He seemed disappointed as he slowly walked to the house. I couldn't find a good husband. I couldn't find the words to write. I swallow and let the pain spread as it wishes. I don't even care that a tear manages to fight its way to life, running its new path of freedom down my cheek.

"I've never even seen a shooting star. Your mom told me I would find the math in nature. That I would find music in nature and inside me. I never did, and I looked hard. I don't find things. Not the good ones."

A deep silence falls on the room and I feel the weight of it add to my already heavy body. Lincoln's face is blank save for a ripple near his ear relaying that familiar clenching and unclenching of his jaw that makes me want to shake him by his shoulders.

I frown at him. I wish I could read him. But I'm too drunk on four. None of his letters make words.

"Math in nature?" he asks quietly.

I sigh. He doesn't get it. He's just repeating everything I say. "You don't get it. Just go." I flop my heavy arm wildly toward the parallelogram and it lands with a thud in my lap. Everything feels heavy. My eyelids are leaden. My arms are rocket boosters. My head, the biggest pumpkin you ever saw. I let it sink further into the couch cushions. Maybe the couch will absorb me like it did the water.

The quiet of the room settles heavily on me like a weighted blanket.

I don't move. Moving starts all the bells and whistles and buzzing again. Stillness quiets it. I like the quiet. Four is so noisy.

Is he still here?

"I'm still here."

Damn it, Ellis. "Let me show you out then. Off you go!" I summon the strength of ten mothers lifting cars off their children to lift my head from the couch. It takes another forty mothers and the power of Jesus Christ to pull my body to a standing position. But all the car-lifting mothers and omnipotent saviors in the universe are no match for Ellis Sloan's four. The weight of the four pushes me forward. I feel myself tilting, about to become the test dummy in an experiment called "Effects of a face-first fall through a glass coffee table."

My second-to-final thought before my body smashes through the glass is *what a dumb way to donate your body to science.*

My final thought before my body smashes through the glass is *this shit right here is going to hurt.*

Then I scream and fall into a memory, and not a good one. Because I can't find good ones.

Because I can't find things.

Chapter Forty-Six

July 2020

Ellis Robin Marks Sloan's marriage to Oliver Michael Sloan ended on a Friday in late July.

It wasn't the day she filed for divorce, or the day she packed his belongings while her children weren't home to see the physical representation of their family cleaving apart. It was the day that brought the night that she went to bed alone and did not know where her husband was, and it was the night she lay awake and realized for the first time in all the times she'd angered him that she wasn't wishing he would come home; she was scared that he would.

It was there, sitting on her bed, chest heaving, ears straining, every creak of the settling house jerking her upright in fear, that she knew. It all had to end. She'd been fully broken. This couldn't be her existence. Fear couldn't be the future. The forever.

It had started with an innocent statement from Georgia to Oliver. Seth had forgotten to tell her it was a surprise. She hadn't known. "I'm so excited to meet Edward, Uncle Oliver." That was the statement that started the first domino. Were there a gravestone for her marriage, it would read:

Here Lies the Marriage of Ellis Marks and Oliver Sloan 2003 to "I'm so excited to meet Edward, Uncle Oliver"

The first domino hit the second, a sharp look from Oliver to Ellis whose stomach fell as quickly as her dread rose.

"Meet Edward?" Oliver asked, confusion and anger warring for territory across his features.

Silence settled over Maddie and Seth's large kitchen. Ellis could hear Nathan clearing his throat—a nervous habit he'd had since they were kids.

It wasn't often that Ellis and her brothers were able to gather with their children and spouses. For years, Christopher had been absent. Then the Air Force took hold of Nathan and Celeste, pushing them scattershot across the globe. But when fortune smiled down on them that week in July, they were all there at Seth's house. Only Poppy hadn't yet arrived.

"Meet Edward?" Oliver asked Ellis again while her brothers, standing with their wives around the huge L-shaped island in Seth's kitchen, attempted to pretend they weren't noticing what was unfolding.

Ellis set her wine glass down. "Oliver. Your book party—"

She could see him putting the puzzle together. He'd written another book—this one on war presidents. Ellis was planning, as she did with every book, a launch party to which she'd invite her family and some of Oliver's professor friends. And she'd invited Edward. His brother.

The third domino fell—the change to his physical bearing. His clenched jaw. His hand tightening around his glass. A twitch at the corner of his eye. He was standing near the kitchen sink and Ellis went to him. Slowly. Weaving between her brothers and their wives as the voices of the children drifted in from outside.

She looked into his face, seeing the darkness already creeping in. "We'll talk about it at home. Nothing's set in stone. Are you ... okay?" she asked, putting her hand on his arm while an audience pretended not to watch. It was a loaded question and he looked at her as if she pulled a trigger point-blank. *Are you okay* is what she asked when she feared things were going to fall apart. When she worried he was approaching the line that once crossed meant he was too angered to rein in his explosions. "Are you okay" meant, *Are you about to knock over something or throw something? Are you about to scream at me in front of these people?* To Oliver, the question was an attack. To Ellis, the question was an entreaty *—please don't.*

The fourth domino fell—Oliver walked wordlessly from the kitchen and out the front door.

The fifth domino fell—Georgia, with a tearful apology to Ellis, left the kitchen to look out the window to watch her uncle drive away in the car that had brought his family there.

In the kitchen, reeling, Ellis turned from the sink to face her family, embarrassed, but gave them a small smile, hoping they wouldn't notice what she hid behind it. Maddie caught her eyes with a sympathetic expression and Ellis hated to see it because it meant she was deserving of sympathy. That someone was saddened on her behalf, or even worse, mourning for her and who she had been and what was left in that person's place.

Ellis looked into her four brothers' faces, watched Lucas and Seth shuffle uncomfortably while Nathan busied himself with gathering empty cups. Her sisters-in-law had grown quiet, fiddling with their hands or drinking glasses. Ellis couldn't bear it. Finally, Maddie clapped her hands once before walking into the dining room then returning with her arms overloaded and piled with the desserts she had made. "Let's do this," she said with a smile and tone of triumph, trying to force the awkwardness that was Ellis's marriage out of the air of the kitchen.

"Hell, yes," Christopher said and then headed for a drawer to grab spoons and forks that he began distributing as Maddie pulled foil and plastic lids off the tops of cookies and pies and cakes and brownies. Seth disappeared into the dining room to rescue the baked goods Maddie hadn't been able to carry. He ran into the kitchen in feigned slow motion, imitating a firefighter carrying someone from a burning building.

Ash, Lucas's wife, grabbed a fork from Christopher. "Sugar is the cure. Sugar has never once let me down," she said with a wink at Ellis before spearing an apple pie in dead center and scooping an enormous bite into her mouth.

"Do not double-dip that fork in that pie," Nathan pointed to her.

"What are you gonna do, Colonel?" Ash taunted as she hovered her fork above the crater she had made in the crust.

Leaning against the kitchen sink, Ellis watched. An outsider would see her oldest brother, standing tall and broad in his Air Force shirt, his military haircut trimmed to perfection, pointing aggressively at the emboldened wife of their youngest brother, and wonder if a domestic disturbance report would be filed later at the police station. But Ellis knew behind Nathan's command was humor, and behind Ash's irreverence was a good-natured badass whose job as river rescue diver allowed her to unflinchingly take on the military-forged stoicism of Nathan.

"I'm terrified, truly," Ash whispered in mock fear to Nathan, inching the fork lower to the crust.

Christopher, now standing next to Ellis, elbowed her playfully in the ribs as they joined in laughter at the exchange. Ellis knew what this was. It wasn't just her four brothers and their three wives cheerfully eating dessert. It wasn't just the playful banter of a brood that had grown into adulthood together through marriages and births and deaths and troubles and celebrations. It wasn't just the teasing and camaraderie of a group who had stepped above their labels of brothers and sisters-in-law to become real friends.

It was her family, deliberately circling their wagons around her. It was their way of protecting her from the embarrassment and anxiousness they knew she was feeling.

As she stood there watching Nathan trying to wrest Ash's

swooping fork from landing into the center of a perfect, untouched dish of brownies, surrounded by love and literal laughter, Ellis only felt sadness and anxiety rest its heavy burden across her mind.

Christopher seemed to feel her mood shift because even as he laughed at the antics in front of them, he put his arm around Ellis's shoulders. She tilted her head to rest against him and wrestled with the realization that she was always the one in the family who needed to be encircled by the wagons. She was always the one who needed the protection.

It seemed that of all the things in the world her brothers might need to protect her from in life, her husband should never have been one of them. And on that day her marriage died, it was 13-year-old Wren who became her fiercest protector of them all. Because when they finally returned home, dropped off by Christopher, Oliver's car was parked in the driveway.

And the sixth domino would fall that night.

Ellis Sloan Therapy Sessions

Gulf Tower
Pittsburgh, PA
September 2021

Ellis: He always told me I was trying to control him.

Dr. Parrish: Were you?

Ellis: Honestly, early on in our marriage, I was. I didn't know how to be in a relationship. It was my first one. I tried to control things for sure. But things got hard, and we went to counseling. He'd grown up watching his mother control his father in ways that astounded me. Like, she'd really gone overboard. It was his father's family winery, but she ruled it and made the decisions. And in his personal life too. Told him what to wear. Constantly ragged on his driving. Belittled him. Read his emails constantly. Stuff like that. Off the charts bonkers. And he readily admitted that affected him and he never wanted to become like his father. Under the complete control of his wife. He didn't want me telling him how to drive or how to interact with our children or even giving him pointers on his writing. He'd never let me read a thing until it was published.

Dr. Parrish: So what did you do as a result of the counseling?

Ellis: I pulled back. Let him make more decisions. I worked on my shit.

Dr. Parrish: What did he do as a result of the counseling?

Ellis: Well, he— He—

Dr. Parrish: Right.

Chapter Forty-Seven

March 2021

How am I still falling?

The smudged planed glass of the tabletop is rushing at me with the speed of a rocket and crawling toward me as slow as evolution. A life spent at intersections is now resting at the intersection of rocket and sloth. It's a surreal and disorientating place to be. It feels like that falling you do right before you jerk awake, but instead of jerking awake, I keep falling. And falling.

In a blink, I defy the laws of gravity and I am floating, watching the face-beckoning tabletop move further away. I guess I really can fly on four. I wonder what I can do on five and I wonder if it involves lightning.

I only get to enjoy my new superpower for a moment because gravity has entered the chat and with a harsh thud, I am placed on my feet and my face is now inches away from Lincoln's. I feel his hands gripping my shoulders and I'm aware that if he moves them away, I will fall again.

"Did I fly?" My voice is breathy and full of wonder.

The edges of Lincoln's eyes wrinkle in a chuckle at my question. I'm so close to him. To those lines around his eyes. I hadn't noticed them before. Their shallow sweeping valleys. Their gentle arcs fanning to comforting points of rendezvous at the corners. Then they're gone, smoothed out by his return to seriousness. "Yep. You flew. Face-first toward the table. Let's sit you down before you try to fly toward some power tools."

I use the last of my strength to resist the pressure of his arms pushing my body away. I hold my ground and move my face closer to his. My drunk pride, which would normally be sober mortification, leads me to ignore the fact that he seems to pull back slightly. "Smile," I order. I feel the grip of his fingers on my shoulders loosen slightly, but his hands remain where they are to shore me up. I can't remember the last time I was shored. I've only felt beached lately.

I can see he tries to stop himself, but the command to smile wins, sheepishly this time, and I once again dive drunkenly into the comfort of the lines around his eyes. I want to know what he lived as they gradually appeared on his face over the years. The loves. The joy. The sadness. Betrayals. Fear. Elation. The nouns we can't see. I knew him before the lines and then he lived a life without me in it, and this was the only story I might get to hear of it. The one these lines might tell me.

I reach a hand toward his face and he slightly deepens the pressure of his fingers on my arms before he's forced to pull one hand away with my arm creeping further up. I softly trace my fingertip along one of the warm arcs from the corner of his eye to near where his temple meets his dark hair. But the line disappears along with his smile, and I am left with a sadness I can't explain. I feel stillness. I hear quiet. I don't move my finger from his temple. That is where it wants to be on four. On that line, by that eye, on that face, in this room, at this weird intersection of being both shored up and beached to die.

When he slowly wraps my hand in his to pull it down away from his face, I nearly want to cry. I find his eyes. He releases my hand to bring his own to my chin and lightly touches a finger to my scar. "What did this to you?"

I don't answer. I won't tell him. There are things he's never told me—things I deserve to know. This is one he's earned no right to ever hear. I'll keep it folded away.

The touch disappears and I feel his other hand leave my shoulder and I'm no longer shored up. The chill that burrows to my bones sends a shiver all the way to my toes. I am as sad and empty and alone and cold on four as I am on zero. I feel myself tipping again.

"Mom?"

"Wren!" I widen my eyes in panic and lurch my arms out toward Lincoln in mid-flail. He catches my shoulders again and I'm once again instantly warmed. He pulls me close, his face shadowed on mine to deliberately shield me from Wren's view. She is standing at the bottom of the steps. I desperately try to telepath my thoughts into him. *She can't see me on four. Please.*

With the help of gravity, he lowers me to the couch. He spies the empty water glass still tipped on the cushion next to me. He leans down toward me and reaches a hand out to grab the glass while bringing his lips near my ear. I hear his whisper as he pulls himself up. "I know."

Lincoln straightens to his full height and turns to face Wren quite brightly. More brightly than I've ever seen him. Too brightly. *Bring it down a notch, bud.* "What's up, Wren!" He is a used car salesman selling the lemoniest lemon on the lot on the last day of the sales quarter. It's the smiliest I've ever heard him speak.

"I heard talking, ... Jefferson." I can sense her suspicion. Or her gathering of information to form a theory to test a hypothesis to research the data to write a paper which she will publish in peer-reviewed scientific journals, the whole premise of which will be *My Mother: Just, Wow.* "And I'm thirsty." She says it as an accusation. How dare she not have been provided water before she needed water, is her unsaid question.

I pipe up as sober as I can sound. "Okay, honey. I'll get you shom wllater." I brace my palms near my hips, preparing to hoist myself up knowing full well I'll be kissing the coffee table shortly. But A for effort, Ellis. And maybe B for Blood loss and C for Call the ambulance. Time will tell where on the alphabet we end.

"No!" Lincoln glares down at me then says more quietly, "No." He holds a splayed hand stretched out, bidding me to stay. My eyes meet his but there are no lines for me to rest inside for comfort. He's too far away and too serious. He shifts his open hand into a stern point. "You ... stay." I relax on the couch. "I made you, uh, carry all those things for me. I'll help her." He is now trying to telepathically message me something with his eyes and eyebrows and as far as I can translate, it is *if you try to stand and balance on two legs, you will surely die.*

He's not wrong.

"Who's not wrong?" asks Wren.

MOTHERFUCKER.

I freeze and wait to find out if I said that one out loud too. M for motherfucker, because isn't that how this whole thing started so long ago?

Blessedly, Lincoln cuts in. "Me. I'm never wrong. It took her a while to realize that, but the important thing is she finally got there." He chuckles as if he's expecting Wren to join in with his joke, but he's only met with the silence that he knows by now often meets the jokes Wren encounters.

"Got where?"

"To the ... you know what? Never mind. So I'm Jefferson today, then? Cool. Water!" He's back to selling the car. "You wanted some. Let's take care of that. This way."

I close my heavy eyes and listen as he guides Wren to the kitchen. I hear a cupboard bang open.

"Not that one. Not that one. It's purple. No. Does that look purple to you, Jefferson? Look back there. Behind the— No."

Plastic and glass are clinking and clunking as he tries in vain to find what doesn't seem to want to be found, probably because Wren left it to roll under her bed.

"Listen," he sighs, "is this one okay?"

"No."

"I will give you twenty dollars for this one to be okay."

I smile. Imagine thinking you can just give Wren—

"Deal."

MOTHERF—

I silence my thoughts or maybe my mouth. I can't be trusted with my internal voice on four.

"Excellent. Here's your money." A pause. "And here's your new okay cup."

"Mom always gets me the water."

Another pause.

"Aren't you fourteen?"

"I'm thirteen."

"So not six?"

Silence. Silence. I wonder what's happening in there. Are looks being exchanged? Is a battle of wills being waged? Does he stupidly think he can win?

"Fine. Gimme." Wren.

Brat.

I hear the freezer. The ice. The water. The *hrmph.* I open my eyes and smile at her as she passes, but she only shoots me a glare. Her footsteps thud up the stairs until I hear her door closing with a bit more force than normal.

And that's the last thing I hear as I let the four drown me into oblivion to swim among painful memories until the morning. But the last thing I feel is my body enveloped in a chill, and the strange sensation of a spot of warmth radiating from the scar on my chin.

Chapter Forty-Eight

April 1, 2020

Her scar felt like it was on fire, and Ellis knew it was only her imagination.

Oliver was an inch from her face, screaming maniacally and wildly into it. She could nearly feel the rage burning off him. She tried to soothe him, but he was undeterred, his entire body hooded in anger. Ellis pushed her lower back against her low dresser, to cower away from the madness he was hurling at her at a level she'd not seen before.

He'd waited until the children were asleep before finally unlocking the door to his study to go to their bedroom. Ellis had been pulling her nightgown out of a drawer when he came in, already wild-eyed and heaving. Oliver found her where she stood and stalked her. Pushing himself against her, demanding answers but not giving her breath or space to provide them.

Awful words. Hurtful words. Words meant to shame. To belittle. To scare. He threw them at her. His chest hard against hers. She tried to explain. That Edward had overheard about the party from his parents and had called her. Wanting to come. But Oliver wouldn't listen. Or wouldn't hear. Wouldn't let the words into his ears. Instead, he sent his own words out on his tongue. Over and over until Ellis had her hands up, her palms facing the torrent, the backs of her hands shakily braced against her face, guarding her chin. Her scar. Her trauma. She realized panic was taking her. Her breath became erratic. She began to beg. "I can't. Please please please. I can't. I can't do this. Please."

There in her own bedroom, Ellis began to crouch away from him, her eyes clenched, waiting for what might come. What escalation would put a stop to his profane ranting?

"Stop it! Stop it!" It was a scream that could inject ice into the hottest of veins. It was Wren. Rushing at Oliver. Pushing herself in front of him, screaming gutturally and long. Shoved at his chest. Shoved at his stomach. Kicked at his leg. "Stop it," she shouted again and again, even as her stunned father stumbled from the force of her body. "Stop it," she screamed even after he had stalked out of the room, and she fell to the floor to rock herself in search of comfort while her mother tried in vain to give it to her.

Over and over, she screamed, as broken as her sobbing mother was.

The shadow of Dunn fell across the floor. It was then Ellis knew.

It had to end. It all had to end. The damage was spreading beyond her, and the only way to protect everyone else from it was to tear apart her family. To uproot her children's lives. To acknowledge she already walked among her own ruins, but there was still time to save Wren and Dunn.

He slept elsewhere. She spent the night terrified he'd come for her and hurt her with his body instead of his words. She packed everything he owned. She raged at his attempted apology three days later. She found new facades to cover the damage until she could figure out a way to repair it.

Surely, there must be a way to repair it.

Ellis Sloan Therapy Sessions

Gulf Tower
Pittsburgh, PA
September 2021

Dr. Parrish: You're not a religious person it seems? But it's interesting because *Luca Rex* clearly has a pretty large vein of theology running through it.

Ellis: I don't know that any of my brothers latched hard on to the religion we were raised in. And keep in mind that *Luca Rex* was written because of the very fact that theology failed me. Because I'd sent a plea up that things would get better, and an answer never came. What? Are you trying to tie this all in to God?

Dr. Parrish: Of course not. I'm a lapsed Catholic... What is that? Is that supposed to be the sign of the cross? Cute. But let's follow the path, okay? What if some divine answer had come to you five years ago, and, in that moment, Oliver apologized? Would you have sat down that night to write the story of a girl who sought an answer only to be answered with silence?

Ellis: Probably not.

Dr. Parrish: If an answer came to you that kept Oliver from losing control last July, where would you be right now?

Ellis: In my bad marriage.

Dr. Parrish: If you hadn't gotten strong enough to walk away from that marriage and instead an answer came down to you to show you how to survive it longer, as you'd often wished, would you have found Lincoln's friendship again, learned all the long-hidden truths you have now learned—freeing truths, I might add—and then shared what seems to have been a healing night with him? Would you be sitting here with me week after week, as you like to say, fixing all your shit?

Ellis: So you're saying—

Dr. Parrish: You have spent a lot of your life watching for the bad that followed the good to the point that you never noticed the good that was finally being created from the bad.

Ellis: I'm Luca?

Dr. Parrish: Yes, you're Luca, Ellis. You managed to write and publish a book about an entire concept—bad creating good—yet never recognized it happening in your own life. That's weirdly impressive in a way.

Ellis: In a head-in-the-sand kind of way?

Dr. Parrish: Well, yeah.

Chapter Forty-Nine

April 2021

"You have got to be fucking kidding me."

Standing here in the Reizenstein High School library tutoring room once again, I'm shocked to find myself surrounded by color. There are no gray floors. There are no gray walls. Gone is the faded, torn poster reminding teenagers that resisting highly addictive drugs is as easy as merely saying no to them. The wall-mounted pencil sharpener has been replaced with a sleek electric one, and the shelving unit no longer holds dusty pamphlets on smoking, eating disorders and depression. In their place are two tethered laptops and a plastic placard informing the students how to access the digitized holdings of the library catalog.

The round tabletops upon which I spent many a Wednesday thunking my forehead in overdramatic despondency are now shiny wood rectangles. The once-gray floor is a colorful mosaic of vinyl tiles forming a soothing ombre pattern running from orange to blue in a sweep from one corner to the other. And the walls. Bright. Bold. Yellow. Sunny. This is not the geometry prison of my youth. This is a fucking sensory delight.

For months since she'd cornered me at Thanksgiving, I'd

manage to beg off Georgia's monthly invites to the ridiculously named Literary Legends Book Club, offering a myriad of excuses that involved Wren, headaches, Dunn, and "writing" (if lying is a sin, Satan is going to make me his left-hand demon once I finally get down there), until finally Seth texted me and told me time was up.

So, I showed up. Even though I'm no longer an author with a contract. Even though I'm nothing but a fraud. Even though my closets and cupboards and facades hide the chaos of my internal self. Even though my jokes hide the fact I've become unmoored, floating through my existence without an anchor to even attempt to throw overboard. I dressed myself in Famous Author Mom attire left over from my book tour—a tan corduroy buttoned skirt that hit my mid-calf with a slit up the front of my right leg that ended a few inches above my knee, to make walking possible because women's clothes are ridiculous. A soft cream sweater. A tartan patterned scarf. My hair loose and slightly wild because some battles I can't fight every day. I stood in front of 90 students in something called a "project room" that did not exist when I attended, and answered their adorably naive questions, and awkwardly accepted their gushing compliments. I lied and said I was working hard on writing the next Luca book, and the devil smiled with pride and patted the empty chair of firesnakes next to him.

Then I snuck away because I was hearing this small, formerly gray room calling out to me. I'd crept through the dark library, pushed open the door, flicked the light on, and said aloud to no one, "You have got to be fucking kidding me."

I slide one of the purple cushioned chairs to the center of the room. No hard chairs in this paradise. I sit in the center of the changed room. I think. I remember. I let it all run through the movie of my mind. Even though the room holds no resemblance to what it was, the emotional pull is weirdly as strong as if it had never changed. The shape of the room. The click of the door. The hum from the air vent. Its place on this earth. It's all familiar enough.

I'd left my junior year here so angry and embarrassed. I'd

floated well enough through my senior year, holding on to decent grades and a loose set of friends I didn't feel a lasting connection to, and I'd headed to Pitt for college and nearly immediately met Oliver. *Boom boom boom.* I blinked. Children were born. Life got difficult. My father died. Christopher came home. My marriage ended. And now here I sit. Baggage-laden and no longer who I was the last time I was in this spot.

"No way."

I whip my head up to see Lincoln poking his own around the door's edge, his eyes taking in what mine already had.

"Lincoln. What are you doing here?"

He steps into the room, still looking at the walls, floors and shelves. "Seth. He and I snuck in and hid in the back. He wanted to see Georgia talk, and I wanted to see the school again. The inside." He crosses his arms and eyes me. "You're not the only distinguished alum, you know, Ellis Sloan."

"I know. I saw the display case. County councilman Garibaldi is an alum! Very exciting."

He chuckles and pulls a chair away from the table to sit in the middle of the room across from me, our knees nearly touching. "Would you look at this room," he says.

"I'm livid."

We hold each other's eyes. I know he's doing what I did, so I let him. Running everything back. From the moment I first walked into that room with dread. Our sneaks out to drive. The scoldings from the angry librarian. The fights. The laughs. The quiet moments when his mother would come up in conversation. Me leaping at him in a hallway in elation. Our story ending for a long time with no goodbye. No explanation. Just a falling away.

He finally speaks. "Would you scoot your chair to the table and thunk your head down on it for me—real dramatic-like? One good solid thunk."

I chuckle at the memories. "I was really something."

"You are," he says, then draws a deep breath. He lets it out with a sigh and considers me with his head at a tilt. "You did good. Your talk."

"All lies," I say matter-of-factly. He knows my contract was axed. I had stupidly texted Hadi as much after I'd drunk my four, and he and Christopher had sent a text to Lincoln to check on me, and yes, Hadi confirmed, given him permission to get the door open by any means possible. We hadn't discussed my drunken torment or oversharing since, as I'd done a good job avoiding the subject and Lincoln himself.

"Not a lie," he says with a slow shake of his head.

"Well, I'm not an author anymore, am I, Lincoln?"

"Okay, that one is a lie. You've always been an author for nearly as long as I've known you. Your words, you know? No one picks them like you do. I listened to you talk tonight. The way you find your phrases? You're still an author. You're not at the end of anything. Early on I spent a lot of years between acting jobs. I know the floating you're feeling. It's not permanent."

It's like he's in my mind, seeing what I'm feeling. Just dead on. But I don't respond. It's too painful. Failing as an author hit me as hard as my failure as a wife did, and what I assume will be my eventual failure as a mother to Wren. At least I seem to be hitting the Dunn thing out of the park. *Run the bases, Ellis Sloan, because that kid is a miracle of patience and kindness these days.*

"You told me you don't find things."

I roll my eyes. "Oh, God. I was drunk, Lincoln. Who knows what manufactured emotional bullshit I was carrying on about."

"Truth comes out of drinking sometimes. I broke up with a girlfriend once because I got drunk and told her I hated her dog." He lets out a quiet laugh at the memory. "I mean, it was a terroristic little rat for sure, but I'd never have said it sober."

"There's no coming back from trashing a person's dog."

"You know, there just really isn't."

I cock my head at him. "But what's your point?"

"My point is, you'll find it. You'll find what you're looking for. Your next story to write. I'd bet my mother's piano on it."

"You don't want to do that. You'll lose that bet easily."

"Stop that," he says like he used to when scolding my dramatics in this room years ago, and I can't help but pull my smile wide at him. He does the same and says, "Yeah, I heard it."

I throw my gaze around the room and then return to him. "Time doesn't always erase everything, I suppose. I guess even the things we think are gone are just waiting for the moment when we're ready to see them again. Notice them again. Lying in wait until we pass by close enough to stir them up."

His face grows serious across from mine. "Like I said. An author."

I grin in spite of myself, feeling some comfort from his attempts to shore me up again.

An odd hollow metallic click sounds out and we are enveloped in total darkness in the windowless room inside of another larger room. A box within a box. I freeze, my eyes finding nothing but black in what was a literal heartbeat ago a room as bright as heaven.

"Uh-oh," I hear from Lincoln.

"Was that the main shutting off?"

"Maybe. I don't know. Could be the janitor shutting the library switch off. I can't imagine they're finished with the meeting, right? Seth would be looking for me. I came with him."

I can't stop a laugh from bubbling up at the hilarity of the situation we have managed to find ourselves in.

"We're going to be locked in this school and probably arrested for trespassing in the morning and you laugh," Lincoln says from the darkness.

"Ellis Sloan and Kennedy Hale. The Prides of Reizenstein. Arrested for trespassing." I laugh again.

"Cute. My phone is in Seth's car. Where's yours?"

"My bag. Somewhere in this ocean of blackness. I think on the table or maybe I dropped it to the floor by the door." I'm holding my eyes open wide, but they still find nothing. I hear the rustle of Lincoln moving. Another laugh escapes me. "I'm sorry. I can't help it. It's too perf—"

My words die in my throat when I feel Lincoln's palm brush the top of my bare knee that the slit in my skirt left exposed. I don't know if the touch is accidental, but having found my knee, it becomes intentional, his fingers widening across my leg. When I don't breathe or move or speak, he pushes his hand forward a few inches, his touch soft, until he reaches the scar that runs up the side of my leg. Were that the lights were on. Were that I could see his face. Were that I had to, in any way, acknowledge the emotions of the moment, I'd have made a joke meant to halt everything. But in the darkness, no eyes to intrude into mine, no judgment, no vulnerability, nothing but a touch on my knee that I hadn't realized I craved, I simply do nothing. Like listening to his music with my eyes closed, I feel his touch while surrounded by inky blackness. In the absence of sight, there is only that which I hear—his breath, and that which I feel—his hand.

He pulls it away. I should speak. I should tell that joke. I should scold him for his errant fumbling finding the wrong target in the dark so that Chris and Hadi can tease him later. But I don't because the hand comes for me. It finds my shoulder. It runs along the side of my neck. To the back of it. In my hair. It pulls me forward until his lips find mine. In the dark. Of the room where our friendship began. Where 16-year-old Ellis Marks sent his laughter high.

Whereas the New Year's kiss was a sweet pressing, this is urgent searching. A pushing and a pulling. From both of us. In the dark, I don't care. In the dark, I can pretend I'm not crumbling apart. In the dark, I can just let everything fall away and stay in the moment—clutching at him while his hand finds my other knee and pushes higher.

He pulls away, our spent breaths colliding to intertwine in the space between us. In the light of day, I'd scold myself and hold myself down in my proper place. In the dark, I want to let go and chase after everything that eludes me. Find what hides.

"We should get out of here while we can," he says, and I find ten different meanings behind it.

"Yeah," is all I say.

We fumble through the dark until I find my bag and pull out my phone to force an eerie spotlight into the room. It shadows Lincoln's face. Hard. Stony. His breathing still not settled. Nor is mine.

Like we had long ago, so many times, we creep through the library, this time in the glow of the last sliver of the day's light. The hallways are still lit, students filtering out from the book club meeting. Lincoln and I wander away from each other, him to find my brother and me to head to my car alone.

And as I was sure it would, light pulls the regret out from the darkness, forcing me to look at it. What have I done? What did we do? Acting as we did, there in that room. Throwing free all the reins we normally leashed ourselves with. Letting memories push us to each other like that.

I take the long way home because at least the car will provide a cover of darkness for my embarrassment. There's no fluorescence to light my unmoored course. No glow to shine on my uncertainness of self. No lamp to reveal the pain of my failure.

I return to my empty house. Dunn again spending the night away, and Wren sleeping at Poppy's. It is dark. I reach for the switch by the door but pull my hand away before I flip it up. Sometimes, you just want things to stay hidden. I head for the couch, and sitting there alone, I decide I'm not going to live in the memories anymore. I reach for the movie projector inside of myself that has been lighting them since Lincoln arrived, and I darken them all back to the past once again.

Please deposit your trash in the receptacles near the exits. Come again soon.

Chapter Fifty

April 2021

I sit in the dark of my living room for an hour, still in my Famous Author Mom outfit, my shoes left near the front door until Mrs. Doubtfire Mom shows up tomorrow to whisk them away before Dunn and Wren return. Order will be restored.

It's peaceful in the dark because it mutes my awareness of everything inside of me as much as it does my awareness of my surroundings. I don't let myself think about the school. About him. About the past. About my unknown future. My anchorless drifting. I just exist in the dark. An empty being. Muted. Waiting.

A knock sounds at my door and I'm not surprised. I knew it would come, and the intentional softness of it tells me he knew I'd be sitting here waiting for it. Not in my kitchen. Not in my bedroom. Right here. Waiting.

When I pull the door open on Lincoln, he's barefoot and his eyes don't find mine. They are on my lips. My jaw. My throat. Dragging slow along my scar. I am being drunk like water after a week gone without. Wholly consumed without being touched. His fingers splay out stiffly alongside his legs before he draws them into tight fists.

He's coiled.

Well, fuck it. Fuck it all. Fuck Oliver for whatever the hell I am now. Fuck the bad book I wrote and all the good ones I won't. Fuck the mail I can't open, the divorce decree I won't read, and all the fake roles I play every day to prove I'm surviving. Fuck the past and the future. Fuck whatever the reason was that Lincoln left me stranded so long ago. Fuck the good things I can't find and the bad things I do. Fuck the panic that lurks deep inside of me.

Fuck all the rain that ever fell in Tennessee.

I grab the front of his shirt to drag him inside, against me. I kick the door closed behind him because a woman who is out of fucks is the kind of woman who will barefoot kick a door closed so she can drag a man to her. I hear a whisper of my name, his breath warm on my ear, his lips barely brushing it. "Ellis Ellis." It pulls a shiver from me. He says my name like a spell. Like he's summoning a force. It's the third "Ellis"—the one he whispers against my lips that cracks the final splinter in my will as I realize it is me he is summoning.

He is a man. I am a woman. This is a need. This is science. This is nature. *This is not a having, Ellis. It won't matter tomorrow.*

Like he once did long ago when I'd leapt at him in the crowded halls of Reizenstein High, he circles his arms around my waist to lift me a foot off the ground, his mouth seeking out all the places his eyes already feasted. When he hits the first step to take me upstairs, he adjusts my legs to wrap around his waist in a grip. When he hits the third step, he pulls away. "Wren?"

"Not here."

At the fifth step he pulls away again. "Dunn?"

"Not here."

When he hits the seventh step, it's my turn to pull my lips from his. "This means nothing."

"Sure."

When he hits the eighth step, I tear away again. "At all."

"Whatever you say."

When he hits the ninth step. "I'm serious. It's just need. Not a having."

"Need. Not having. Got it."

When he reaches the final step, I brace my arm on the stairwell wall to halt him and say with my forehead pressed against his, "We're friends, right?"

"Do you want me to drop you?"

I kiss him hard in reply.

At the entrance to my bedroom, I throw an arm to the doorframe, my other around his shoulders. "Say it. It's just need. Not a having. I can't be ... had again." There's so much behind what I'm saying, things he'll never understand.

He pulls back to find my eyes, diving deep into them. "It's whatever you want it to be, Ellis."

And it is what I want it to be, there in the comfort of dark. It's all the years we spent apart finally finding that one we spent together. It's the feelings from our past finding release in our present. It's only one night. Completely different from nearly every night of my marriage. It's a giving that I take, finally. A fulfilled need. Freedom in the dark that the daylight won't give me. It's not me warding off a punishment. It's not a manifestation of my self-hatred because of the things I'd do to make Oliver happy. Tomorrow, my facades will still hang in the closet of my mind, ready for me to don them so that my children will feel secure. My words will still be missing. I'll still no longer be an author. Wren will still need me to pull up her hurdles. Oliver will still haunt me. Panic will still have me.

But for this night, with Lincoln clutching my body to his, just fuck it all to hell.

I'm letting go in the dark and taking what I want until the light of day beats the warning drums of its approaching return.

Ellis Sloan Therapy Sessions

Gulf Tower
Pittsburgh, PA
September 2021

Dr. Parrish: Do you regret that night?

Ellis: I did at first. In the morning and the days after.

Dr. Parrish: And now, all these months later, him gone?

Ellis: I'm thankful we had it.

Dr. Parrish: Thankful? Interesting reaction. Why thankful?

Ellis: I thought it was just need, but I can see now it was clearly an expression of love.

Dr. Parrish: And with Oliver?

Ellis: With Oliver? I was trying to hold off punishments. It was him taking.

Dr. Parrish: Do you love him?

Ellis: Oliver?

Dr. Parrish: No.

Ellis: I think it's better if I don't let myself.

Dr. Parrish: Why?

Ellis: No good would come from it.

Dr. Parrish: Because then something bad would come along, right?

Ellis: See, you get it.

Dr. Parrish: No. I get you.

Ellis: And that's different?

Dr. Parrish: It's not the same.

Chapter Fifty-One

April 2021

"Ellis?" My name called out from downstairs wiggles into my sleep-clogged ears and knocks on my foggy morning-brain. "Your door was unlocked, dear. Ellis? Are you here?"

Much like when ten-year-old me shouted "motherfucker" in front of my preacher father, my genteel mother, my piano teacher, Cutesy the lounging cat, all my brothers, Lincoln Hale, and God himself, time halts to a stop, giving my brain the space it needs to process the situation I have found myself in.

The situation is this: I'm a slut.

I grabbed a man standing barefoot at my door and I dragged him into my house, kicked the door closed behind him like a horny Chuck Norris and used the cover of darkness to let my inner harlot out. And now here I lie, under my covers of the bed I've been alone in for nine months, with a man who sleeps with the peace of a million angels soft on his face, his arm thrown across my bare waist, an ankle loosely twined within mine.

I was right. I knew the light of day would shine harshly on me, and the Saturday morning April sun filtering into my window is doing its job—revealing in stark wattage what I don't want to see.

What I'd done. But I don't have time for shame or embarrassment at how I'd carried on last night and the things I'd let myself do and feel. Because Poppy Marks let herself in via the door I had kicked closed and never locked. *Damn you, Slutty Ellis, for being so irresponsible and not considering Saturday Mom's needs.*

My crystal ball tells me what will happen. My mother, never one for decorum or door-knocking, would walk into my bedroom. She would see me in bed, my hair tousled wildly on the pillow because another's hands had been all through it, and she would shift her gaze ever so slightly to see a body next to mine, at which point she would begin dramatically gulping in air that was trying to leave her body, and then she would see it was Lincoln and just like the time I handed her a porny bad grade in geometry, she would nearly gag herself on the rising disgust at the behavior of her daughter, the aforementioned slut.

I only have moments to save my reputation from my mother, the preacher's widow, lest she blast a prayer request for the "salvation of my only daughter" on Poppy's Prayer Chain. I don't need the kind of lifelong cackling abuse it would bring from Hadi and Christopher.

Time may restart now.

"Wake up! Wake up! Wake up!" I say each phrase with a smack on Lincoln's cheek and reach under the covers to throw his arm away from me. He pushes himself up with immediate awareness and flips onto his back, up on his elbows, the covers still over his body. "My mother," I hiss low and watch his eyes widen into frisbees.

"Ellis?" She's coming up the stairs.

"Shit!" Lincoln breathes out and leaps from the bed heading toward his clothes that had been left at the foot of it along with mine.

I throw my hands over my eyes. "Why are you naked?!"

"Because of the sex!" We are whisper-shouting at each other. He grabs his clothes into his arms and turns to me, not realizing my discarded bra is dangling from the pile he holds. "You're naked too, woman."

He's not wrong, I realize. I'm completely naked under the covers. I want to dissolve out of existence.

"Ellis?" Poppy is so close. Lincoln dives to the floor between my bed and the far wall just as I stand and wrap my entire bed comforter around my body until I look like a human face poking out of a cannibal giant's burrito. My door opens and I throw a bright smile at my mother.

"Ellis! There you are. You scared me." She lets her eyes take in my bedroom then looks at me cocooned within my tortilla of slut-shame. "Are you okay, dear? Not feeling sick again?"

"Oh, I'm great. Just enjoying sleeping in a bit. Chilly in here, that's all. Wren downstairs?"

"Yes. I'm off to a showing. Heard your book talk went great last night."

"Great. Great. Great. Yeah." I'm floundering. "Go ahead down and I'll get changed. Actually, would you mind taking Wren in the kitchen and fixing her some eggs? Too many Pop-Tarts lately, right?"

"Sure. Sure. I have time."

When she closes the door, Lincoln and I burst into frantic activity. Me flinging my comforter onto the bed and running my naked ass into my closet to find clothes to pull on in the dark while tripping awkwardly into the walls due to the pile of shoes covering the floor. Mrs. Doubtfire Mom seriously needs to do something about the closets at some point. When I meet Lincoln at my bedroom door, he's dressed again. His feet bare. The two Reizenstein high schoolers who regularly snuck into and out of the library will now need to sneak him out of my house without Wren or Poppy seeing.

At the bottom of the steps after a rushed and quiet creep, I hear Poppy in the kitchen trying to draw Wren into a conversation about her history project for school, without much luck.

"Okay, now!" I whisper and rush with Lincoln to the front door. I fling it open wildly and shove him on to the porch, but he spins back for me before I can close it on him. He grabs me into a hard kiss and then lets me go with a wriggle of his damn eyebrows. I resume my whisper-shouting. "No! Don't kiss me! This meant nothing! Go!"

"Whatever you say, Eller."

"Ellis!" I hiss after him before he closes his door with that infuriating half-grin.

"She did not want eggs," Poppy says as she returns to the living room. "Toaster waffle. Who am I to argue? She'll just win." She grabs her purse from the wing chair and joins me at the front door. "I'm heading out. We had fun. Did you know John Adams had a dog named Satan?"

"I did. Wren wants to get a black cat and name it The Prince of Darkness."

"Oh my. If your father were here. Maybe take her to church occasionally?" My mother pats my cheek. "Love you. Talk soon."

I wave her to the porch. "Bye, mom. Thanks again."

As she's about to lower her foot to the first step, she turns. "Oh, Ellis?"

"Yep?"

"I understand keeping it from Wren, but do tell that Hale boy he doesn't have to hide from me next time, love. Okay. Bye now. Sunday dinner this weekend. He's invited as usual."

For the rest of my life I'll never understand how I manage to widen my eyes as far as I do at my mother's retreating back without each of my eyeballs popping right out of their sockets and bouncing down the porch steps after her.

Ellis Sloan Therapy Sessions

Gulf Tower
Pittsburgh, PA
September 2021

Dr. Parrish: I didn't mean to laugh. I'm sure that surprised you coming from your mother.

Ellis: I'm not exaggerating when I say it was nearly as world-spinning as finding Chris and Hadi together in her laundry room. My mother. Poppy Marks. The widow of Pastor David Marks. The keeper of the Prayer Chain. The scolder of the profane. Not giving a rip that I'd done that?

Dr. Parrish: It's cool when people love us no matter what, right?

Ellis: —

Dr. Parrish: But that was it? You and he didn't settle into a romantic relationship?

Ellis: Absolutely not. There was just no way. I couldn't. Wouldn't. Do that to myself again.

Dr. Parrish: Couple of things. First, you didn't "do that" to yourself in the first place. It was done to you. Okay? You know that by now, but the language is important to remind yourself that you didn't create the bad. That's number one. Number two. Do what to yourself exactly?

Ellis: Trust someone to stay who I think they are in the beginning. Oliver was perfect. Even my family thought so. How he treated me. Doted on me. Look what he was hiding. What I didn't see. Anyone could be a monster, Dr. Parrish. I'm not going to poke at them to see what lurks underneath. I won't do that to Wren and Dunn again.

Dr. Parrish: Language.

Ellis: Fine. I won't allow someone to do that to Wren and Dunn again.

Dr. Parrish: Totally valid to feel that way. Trust is tricky. It's like getting a cavity filled. You get Novocain, but it doesn't take in the right spot because the dentist wasn't a good one, and you feel a nerve being hit and then there's pain. So, the next time you go to the dentist, you're waiting for the pain. Expecting it. Even if it's a different dentist.

Ellis: Exactly.

Dr. Parrish: So don't go to the dentist ever again, for sure. Let the teeth rot.

Ellis: I know what you're trying to do. It—

Dr. Parrish: Or maybe you go to the new dentist, and you say, this is what happened last time so I need you to be very careful and prove that you'll not hurt me. And the dentist hears you and understands and takes extra precautions and, over and over, he proves he's a good dentist and boom! You're no longer quite so scared or waiting for the pain. Not with that dentist.

Ellis: That's a lovely story, but there's a lot of chapters between where I was that night with Lincoln and where I'll need to be to get to the point where I'm not waiting for the monster.

Dr. Parrish: That's the story you and I are going to keep writing. I feel like we're getting close.

Chapter Fifty-Two

April 2021

"El, give me your hand."

The chaos of a Sunday dinner at Poppy's was made more interesting with the silent knowing looks Poppy kept ping-ponging from me to Lincoln to me to Lincoln. There are few things more mortifying than your mother knowing for certain that you had been naked in bed next to an equally naked man moments before she'd entered your bedroom four days earlier. Lincoln, for his part, kept making deliberate eye contact with her, as if daring her to blab the secret.

But Poppy Marks is nothing if not a woman of manners and restraint. Why, she'd never. Not even when Ash had noted the looks all through the meal and finally said, just as Poppy cleared Lincoln's plate with a wink at him, "There's weirdness afoot here."

Luckily Chris and Hadi were too distracted by the touches they were likely sharing under the table unbeknownst to the family to jump in and demand answers.

"No weirdness, Ash," I had said and then excused myself to the front porch. *Why, Ellis? Why? Why couldn't you have kept your stupid shirt on?*

It was only a few moments after I sat down to enjoy what seemed to be the first truly warm evening of the season, the air sweet with the perennials my father had planted along the house long ago, blooming annually in memoriam to their gardener, that Lincoln walked out and reached a hand out.

"El, give me your hand. Come walk with me. To the old house."

We walk with my arm linked through his because that's where he places it. We're comfortable—in, with, of each other. Like we used to be. Like we're meant to be. We walk through three backyards, through the narrow wood. We pass the spot at which I stood to grieve my father alone. The Hale house, which has a SOLD placard on the real estate sign in the yard, is dark. It won't be the Hale house much longer but will have a new family that hopefully lights it up like a Christmas tree every night for many years. I swallow hard, remembering my teacher. All the places in this yard she had lived her life, giving to the soil her hands, giving to the air her voice, giving to the stars her worshipful eyes.

Lincoln and I don't go any further than the walkway near the driveway. He watches his old home like it's a nostalgic television show. I can see him swallow as I had, trying to push down that damn knot of want and yearning for something lost. I pull my arm from his to take his hand.

He squeezes it and smiles. "You're good for me," he says after a moment, not looking away from the house.

"Good for you?" I laugh softly. "How so?"

"I don't know. I'm standing here looking at this tomb—that's what it is, right? A tomb of my childhood—and I'm okay. I'm not thinking about the bad stuff. I'm thinking about the good. Playing for my mom. Learning from her. Sitting on those steps with you. All the fun Christopher and I had."

"I'm glad."

"I wish I could be good for you." He says it with his gaze still on the house.

This is dangerous territory he's leading me into, and I know I need to steer us away from it. I lighten my voice and pull my hand away from his. "You are. You gave me my first real orgasm in seven years."

"Holy shit," he breathes at me and laughs in spite of himself.

"The mouth on you," we say at the same time.

But he won't let it go. "I wish I could help you like you've always helped me. To help you write again. You're so good. I wish I knew what you needed. But you won't tell me." He says it nearly sadly.

I grab his hand again and pull him to walk to Poppy's. He's seeking answers from me that I don't have. Wants to heal a wound I can't even find myself. "Not all of us can live as openly as you do, Linc," I say easily with a soft pat at his arm. "Some pain has to stay my own."

"But all of it?"

I link my arm into his and tilt my head to rest at his shoulder as we step into the trees. "For now."

Maybe for always.

Ellis Sloan Therapy Sessions

Gulf Tower
Pittsburgh, PA
September 2021

Dr. Parrish: So what happened then? You went back to status quo?

Ellis: We mostly did. A few touches he'd steal here and there, and I'd let him. I'm not a robot. But I was clear from that night on that it couldn't become more. Clearly, he was reaching for more from me and knew there were roadblocks. He suspected I'd gone through some bad stuff, you know? The most I could be to anyone was a friend. So yeah, we status quo-ed the shit out of it. But then he did a dumb thing and well, you know what happened.

Dr. Parrish: The fight.

Ellis: Right. It was going to happen sooner or later. Look at who he was. Then look at who I am. Maybe I did pick the fight a little bit to speed things along, but we were always meant to fall away from each other again. That's how stories work. Why not get it over with? Bad was coming; at least I got to control when it showed up.

Dr. Parrish: I want to verbalize how weird it is to hear you compare yourself to him in an unfavorable light. "Look at who I am." But to me, you're up here. With him. Beyond him. You're a published author. A huge accomplishment. It's clear you have a self-esteem issue.

Ellis: No shit.

Dr. Parrish: You were worth him, okay? We are going to work to get to the point where you start to look at people and ask if they are worth you. Like you finally did with Oliver.

Ellis: He wasn't.

Dr. Parrish: No, he wasn't.

Chapter Fifty-Three

May 2021

"What did you do, Lincoln?"

I shove at Lincoln's chest with all the pent-up anger I can fire out of my arms, pushing away the body I'd clung to so desperately three weeks ago.

He's taken by surprise and stumbles backward toward my front door that he'd just walked in through. "What? I was trying to help you, El."

"I didn't ask you to fix me."

"I wasn't trying to fix you. Help. Help you."

The phone call had stunned me. A literary agent and a screenwriting agent had conferenced together to call my cell phone. Seeking to speak with author Ellis Sloan. Seeking to perhaps talk to her about a second Luca book and approaching a few screenwriters to turn the first into a script. To look at a new writing contract, perhaps. Approaching a new publisher maybe. *We're really excited Kennedy called us about this possible collaboration, Ms. Sloan.*

Livid, I told them how mistaken they were, hung up and texted Lincoln to come over.

"You can't help this!" I point toward my head. "You can't make words come to me. Ideas. Plots. There's nothing there. Nothing to write. I've told you this! I've told everyone this. And then I had to tell those women that." I soften my voice and raise it a half-octave. "Oh, ladies, I'm so sorry. Kennedy is mistaken, you see. I'm still broken and haven't written a single word in nearly a year, thank you. Have a nice fucking day!"

Lincoln reaches for me, but I shove his arms away. He tries to soothe me. "El. The words are there. I thought maybe if you stopped drifting, you'd find them once you, you know, anchored down."

"There's no anchor to even toss overboard, you ass!"

"El. Calm down."

"I won't! You had no right! And to not even warn me. I'm not fixable. Why won't you believe that?"

Finally, I can see his anger ignite, growing hotter to match mine. "I was trying to help you," he says at a near-shout then deliberately calms himself again with a slow breath. "You can do this. You're not done yet. You're just afraid."

"Afraid?!" Hearing the truth finally come for me from outside of myself pushes my anger and volume higher.

"Yes! You're too afraid!"

"I'm too afraid?!"

"Yes!" We are stuck in a repeating loop, at full shouts, emotions winning battles over calmness, releasing us from the restraints that held back all the things we had long wanted to say.

"What am I afraid of?"

"What aren't you afraid of, Ellis?"

"How fucking dare you," I growl at him. "You don't know my life."

"Am I wrong? You're afraid to write. Afraid to succeed. Afraid to fail. You have mail piled up for weeks until I finally grab it for you, and look, it's sitting over there! You're afraid when Wren tries.

Afraid when she doesn't. You're afraid to be happy. You're afraid to try it again."

"Try what again?" I yell incredulously and with confusion.

"Me! Us!"

I don't want to acknowledge what that means so I rush past it to throw my own accusations. "You're afraid too. You're a coward. You always were!"

"I have never been a coward," he shouts at me. "I don't have anything to be afraid to lose!"

I can only glare at him, shaking with anger, tears beginning their trails down my cheeks. I hate that I'm crying in front of him again.

He inhales. "What do I have? Money? Fame? Stuff? My life? I'm not afraid to lose any of that."

"Only people who have those things say that!"

"Well, I mean it. It can all disappear tomorrow. Let it! The only thing I've ever been afraid to lose after my mother died was you and I fucking lost you anyway."

Exasperated, I throw my hands in the air and shout, "You didn't lose me back then! You threw me away!"

He explodes. "Because I didn't have a choice!"

"Stop it!" Wren runs into the living room from upstairs, screeching and crying before she even reaches us. She rushes at Lincoln and begins pummeling him in his stomach, shoving desperately at his chest. "Stop it! Don't hurt her! Stop it!" She holds the last syllable out in a scream that brings Dunn running down the stairs, fear plain on his face.

I'm immediately devastated. Laid to emotional waste. What I had worked to protect them from, this screaming. This discord. This emotion. It had all happened again. Wren trying to be my protector from shouted words that she feared would turn into fists. My hope forever: that she might never need to learn that words can hurt just as much. Dunn, a shadow in the room, wondering what the falling-apart he was watching would mean for him. All that I'd attempted to rebuild, this fragile lie of control and happiness, crumbled down and they had to watch it happen again. We are back where we started.

The three of us against the world.

"Wren. Wren. Wren." Lincoln is attempting to soothe her, grabbing at her shoulders but she's wild in her fury and fear. "Wren, I'm sorry. No."

She's too far past the point to gain control of herself. I pull at her shoulders. "Wren. Come. He wasn't hurting me. Wren." I pull her away from him and she whirls to fall into me, hugging me desperately, sobbing. Apologizing again and again, for what? I don't know.

"Wren. I'd never—" I hear Lincoln's voice catch. His eyes shine inside a face crushed with emotion.

"You need to go," I say slowly and calmly.

"No. I—"

"You need to go!" I shout it in frustration and anger and every other noun I can't see but that I hate, and then hold Wren closer when my shouting makes her cry harder. I lower my voice again to soothe her and glare at him over the top of her head buried into my chest. "Just go."

He does.

Chapter Fifty-Four

May 2021

"I don't even understand what I'm looking at here."

I stand inside the other side of the duplex—Lincoln's side—for the first time since he moved in seven months ago. But *moved in* is a terrible term to describe what I'm looking at. There's nothing here.

A piano. A wing chair with a neat stack of books on the floor next to it. There is no table in the kitchen. No tables anywhere. No couch. Not a single picture on the wall. It's a ghost room. I creep upstairs after flicking on the light at the top of the steps. An empty bedroom. Another empty bedroom. Finally, a bed in the last room. No dresser. A suitcase with neatly folded clothes, A closet of a few hanging shirts. Shoes lined neatly on the bottom.

It's not lived in. It's existed in. It's a room being passed through.

After two days not speaking and not hearing or seeing Lincoln, I'd knocked on his door in the early evening, wondering if I hadn't been angrier than I needed to be. When he didn't answer that day or the next, I tried the doorknob and found it unlocked. I opened it and walked in. It was dark. Silent. A tomb. What I was surrounded by stunned me and I'd texted Chris, demanding he come. It was time for answers. It was time to open the book on all this mystery and if Lincoln wouldn't reveal it, then Chris would likely have a key to it too.

"Like, what is this, Chris?" I turn away from the piano of my childhood to face him as he enters the dimly lit living room from the front door. He's strained. His features. His body. His eyes. He already knows a reckoning will happen and I can see it in his everything.

"El, sit down."

"Where, Christopher? Fucking where shall I sit? The couch? There's no couch!"

He points to the wing chair, and I lower myself to it while he sits at the piano bench, facing me.

I force calmness into my voice. "I feel like I've stumbled into a bad version of Narnia, so I'd like some answers before I lose my mind. Make it make sense."

"He's been at my place with me and Hadi for a few days. Giving you space from one another. He told me what happened." He sighs, his resignation even clearer. "He never meant to move in here, Ellis. I tricked him."

Well, there it is. The thing that's going to kick me to the asylum. The thing that's going to send my world spinning off its axis again, and so soon after I rebuilt it upon finding Hadi and Chris in my mother's "murdery" laundry room.

"You tricked him? How?"

"He mentioned he was going to be in town from California finalizing his father's estate, that absolute waste of air in Lincoln's life. I truly hated that man."

I wave a hand. "We all did. Off topic. Go on. The tricking part?"

"So, he mentioned he'd get a storage place for the piano and then put everything else in an estate sale. And I realized I had a chance to fix some things that I'd caused, and I realized this side of the duplex was empty, so I told him I had a place for him to store the piano."

"Here? What, he thought you were getting a storage unit for him?"

"Well, yeah. But instead, I gave the moving guys this address. And I gave Lincoln this address. And the moving guys I hired were not great, and they knocked the piano over. Lincoln calls me all 'what the hell' and I tell him to put the piano in here and that he could stay here for the few days he needed to work on the estate. That I'd put a bed and chair in there to hold him over. Just a day or two, right?"

"I have never been more confused in my life. That is seriously a half-cooked scheme."

"Just listen. He's frustrated, but because he's Lincoln, he's also chill about it and said, you know, whatever. I'll get the piano shipped and stay here a few days and we can hang out and catch up before I go back to California. But I knew, Ellis."

"First, no, Christopher, he was not 'chill.' He was mad. Screaming 'fuck,' and now I'm realizing maybe the frustration of your lie made him more angry than the fallen piano. But beside the point. What? What did you know?"

"That he'd see you and remember what you two used to mean to each other. I wanted you to find him again."

"Why?" I'm exasperated and throw my hands up before plopping them into my lap. "Why on earth would you ever care about something so silly?"

"Because of guilt."

"Guilt?"

"Forever guilt."

"Tell me."

"I'm the reason he didn't show for you on your prom night."

I don't speak and Chris knows it means he needs to press on because I'm not going to be able to form sentences while I'm processing the things I'm learning.

"He couldn't come for you because he came for me."

Loud rushing takes my head and my heart, throwing it wildly out of rhythm.

"I'd left him a note in his car." He looks ready to cry. "I tried to kill myself that night."

"No!" I rush to my brother, dropping next to him on the narrow bench, devastated at what I'm hearing. Nothing, not one of the pieces I pick up, is fitting into its proper space. I may have to toss this world aside and build yet another. "Why, Chris?"

"El, come on. Look who I am. Look how we were raised. Who our dad was. I was scared. I was full of hate for myself, you know? I didn't see how I was going to go through my life—because once I graduated, my life was really going to start—trying to not feel the things I felt. Things I thought were wrong."

I grab his hand in mine, my brain putting pieces in spaces that were empty for so long. Realizations. Possibilities. "Did you love Lincoln, Chris?"

He swallows. "Yes? No? Early on when I was still sorting myself out. But seeing you two together, seeing what could be. Happiness? Openly? Like you had when you saw him and like he had for you? I fell deep into some dark hole and couldn't get out of it. No, don't cry."

I nod despite my tears.

"I'm not going to tell you what happened that night. What I had almost done. What I nearly did before Lincoln got to me. Because I don't want you to have a mental image of it in your head, okay? Of your brother? No. You shouldn't know that. I just want you to know he came. He stopped me. He talked to me and pulled me up a bit from the hole. Saved me. Hugged me. He put me back together and then made sure I went home."

I remember that night in my bedroom, Christopher coming in so late. Unknown to me, experiencing the hardest night of his life. My father was right. We're all trying to reflect a still surface while deep down our currents run chaotic.

"It's remarkable he did that for you. You both were still so young."

"No. It's not remarkable at all. That's the other thing you never knew. Only Mom and Dad did because he talked to them about it, and me, because Lincoln told me that night. His mother wasn't sick. Not in that way. Mrs. Hale killed herself, El. Lincoln is the one who found her. I didn't know. He was stopping it from happening again, you see?"

I bend at the waist and lower my head to my hands. It's too much. Too dark of a secret. Too much of a loss. What he went through. What my teacher went through. Her body wasn't losing the battle against the shutter closing out the light; her mind was. I remember the sadness on her face when she closed her eyes and spoke Byron's words to me. I remember Lincoln at her funeral. On her birthday. I remember the perfect neatness of her home and realize what mess she was hiding—much like I hide my mess behind my personas and my closets and cupboards.

Christopher pulls me by my shoulder. "Ellis, listen to me. The guilt has held me for so long. I escaped to California, thankfully, away from you, but I always felt like I messed up your happiness. You met Oliver so young, two years after high school, and that asshole made you so unhappy. When Lincoln's dad died and you were here alone, I saw a chance and I took it, knowing Lincoln would find you again and stay another day. Then stay another week. Then a month. I knew he needed a break from his life. He'd said as much so many times."

"Chris. I love you. But look at this place. This is not a staying; this is a passing through."

"Because he's waiting to see if you'll stop him from going, El."

"From going where?" I can see Chris doesn't want to answer me, but I press. "He has chances, doesn't he? Don't lie to me."

"I won't. He's been saying 'wait' to project after project."

These are the answers I needed. The fog clears from my brain as quickly as it came. There's no need for a new world to be built.

Chris grabs my hand. "I know it's hard for you. To be with someone after Oliver. The problem is that when you decide to not give people a chance to hurt you, you also don't give them a chance to love you. I didn't give dad the chance to show me that. What if he wouldn't have hurt me? Maybe he would have loved me no matter what. Instead, I ran away. I'll never know because I stole that chance from him."

"Forget about me. Okay? Listen, did any of us really hold on to religion as much as Dad would have liked?"

"Probably not. Nathan, maybe."

"Nathan irons his underwear; Nathan doesn't count." Chris rewards me with a shaky grin. "And did ever once Dad make you feel like that troubled him? That he loved you or me or Seth or Lucas less? Did he sit us down and preach to us and judge us?"

Chris answers with a small slow shake of his head.

"No. And that means he'd never not have loved you; he would have loved you if he knew, and if we are to believe what he believed and taught us so fervently, somewhere, he's loving you right now."

Chris lets out a sob and hugs me tightly. "I hope so."

When we pull away and dry the emotions we've never let the other see, I swipe my hand at his cheek, catching a final tear. "Listen. Guilt relieved. Fully. Gone. Okay? Let's go back in time. Rewind. Lincoln shows up to prom and what happens? We go and we make out, maybe a little over-the-dress action, a couple of hickies, spend half a summer together, and then he goes to college and Hollywood, and we never see each other again."

"I want to say again, the mouth on you."

I chuckle and throw my arm around his shoulders. "Prom doesn't matter. Now doesn't matter. My problems and my awful ex don't matter. All I care about is that you're still here, you're finally happy, and when you're ready, I bet you'll still have all our brothers and our mother loving you. And you have Hadi, loving you as madly as I've ever seen him love anything, including money and everything that hangs in his closet."

"I really love him."

"You're welcome, and I'm never buying you another gift as long as we live."

We smile and look around the room. The sadness of it.

"What will you do?" he asks.

I stand. "We're going to sneak out of here like we were never inside. Then I'm going to fix it. All of it. I didn't have the information I needed to do so until now. Go home and send Lincoln here."

Ellis Sloan Therapy Sessions

Gulf Tower
Pittsburgh, PA
September 2021

Ellis: I did what you said.

Dr. Parrish: What's that? What's our victory today, Ellis?

Ellis: Wren. The school called while I was on my way here.

Dr. Parrish: What was the problem?

Ellis: She'd bumped into a classmate at lunch and spilled water on her pants. She was upset and wanted to come home. I had them put her on the phone with me and I talked her down some. They were able to calm her down the rest of the way and she's back in class, only missed one.

Dr. Parrish: Instead of four. I know sometimes you will

need to go get her. She is autistic, and I'm not diminishing that challenge. But in this instance, look what you showed her. She can handle some water and some anxiety that comes with it. Maybe next time, she won't even need to call you.

Ellis: Maybe.

Dr. Parrish: Well done. Reward her today for that growth. I wish I had a lollipop here to give you as a reward for yourself.

Ellis: Look at you with the jokes.

Dr. Parrish: You're a bad influence on me.

Ellis: There's more.

Dr. Parrish: I regret pulling out the lollipop joke so soon.

Ellis: Oliver flaked out on Dunn. Again. I didn't buffer it. Oliver had texted me and wanted me to tell Dunn that he couldn't take him to a Pirates game they'd made plans to attend. I knew he knew I would gloss over it if I was the bad news bearer. Protect him and protect Dunn and protect Dunn from him. Make it not seem like a big deal, right? I refused. Made him text Dunn himself, and then I went to Dunn and said, "I'm sorry Dad did that to you." Full stop. No making excuses for his dad's behavior. I took him to the game, we had a blast, and it was fucking amazing.

Dr. Parrish: It always is pretty life-altering when the Pirates manage to win a game of baseball.

Ellis: Oh! Two jokes. Put your fist out.

Dr. Parrish: It's like I don't even know who I am anymore.

Ellis: Oh no. It's contagious. I know a good therapist.

Chapter Fifty-Five

May 2021

Jane Hale's stars shine down on us from above.

"I remember we used to sit like this all the time," Lincoln says quietly.

"Yeah."

We sit on the top porch step to our front doors in silence for a minute. Lincoln waves to a neighbor walking a dog across the street. The light of the streetlamp filters through the tree branches, washing us in a golden glow even in the dark. Summer's promise hangs warm in the air already.

We try to speak at the same time. Him with, "El," and me with, "Listen."

I smile and pick up his hand. I can see he is surprised by the open show of affection. I pull it into my lap and clutch it like a mug of coffee I want to use for warmth, but really, I'm trying to draw some bravery from him.

"Listen," I start again. "I know."

"You know?"

"I know what you did that night. For Christopher." My chin shakes as emotions rush up at the renewed thought of my brother alone in pain, wanting to be away from his family and life forever. And Lincoln pulling him back to return him to us. Where would my life be if I hadn't gotten to live it with Christopher in it?

Lincoln looks at his hand in mine, then at me.

"I want to say first, even though they'll never know what you did, on behalf of my family, thank you."

He nods.

"I want to say that I get it now. I understand why you had to choose him over me that night and I'm so so so happy that you did. I understand why you couldn't tell me or anyone." I smile. "I understand you didn't throw me away."

"It killed me that you thought I did."

"I know that too. You remember teaching me to drive and you said about how you get to a point in your life where you realize how big things are? Well, I didn't know it then. My life was still small, and you and Chris were already seeing how big it could get. I'm glad you had each other to help." I squeeze his hand, willing myself on. "He told me about your mom."

I feel his fingers tighten around mine.

"It's too much. Nearly. I don't know how you survived."

He doesn't respond.

"I came to you before I left, you know?"

"What do you mean?"

"To your house. The night before I left for camp. I was going to confront you. Demand answers as only Ellis Marks could. I was so angry and hurt. But I got there, and the house was dark. Always dark. And you were playing the piano, right there in the dark. Remember that?"

"Yeah. 'The Tempest.' Beethoven."

"Wow. What a fitting name. You were soundtracking your life, weren't you?"

He grins.

"I listened to you play and I walked away, and I can see now, looking back, the pain you were dealing with. Your mom,

Christopher almost going as she did, your absent father, and then there was me and my stupid childish drama. All that on an 18-year-old? You're remarkably normal considering, right?"

He gives a rueful chuckle. "Maybe not. I still keep the house dark at night, wherever I am."

"Why? Why did you do that? The darkness seemed terrifying to me, you know? I'd have every light in the house on. I never understood it."

"Well, listen. I wasn't scared of the dark. Instead, it comforted me, because then I couldn't see what wasn't there. That's what was scary to me."

I'm stunned and saddened. "You mean *who* wasn't there, don't you?"

"Yeah. My mother. Hell, my father. A family. I couldn't—can't see that absence in the dark."

"Oh, man. You're killing me. I'm going to hug you, you basket case. Hold still." I wrap my arms around him at an awkward side angle and squeeze, hoping I'm drawing out some pain. I let go and again pull his hand into my lap. "I'm sorry your life was shitty."

"It wasn't shitty. Just a little lonely. Then you popped up in the library and made me laugh."

"I did, didn't I? I'm like the superhero of this story. Bad At Geometry Girl. I only needed a cape and a magic protractor that fires out right angles. *Pew-pew*!"

We laugh, then quiet once more. I still have so much I need to get out. "About Wren ..."

"I'm so—"

"No, Wren's fine. She's fine. Don't worry. She still thinks you're the moon and stars. I mean, she's for sure going to scold you for yelling at me, but she still thinks you're the good of every president rolled into one. I talked to her. And, you were right. And it's killing me to say that, and you know I don't do this. These damn emotions and these kinds of talks. I hate them so much." I chuckle at myself.

"But you're right. I need to let her start ... being. I never wanted to fail her."

"You're not. Didn't. Don't you see?"

"What?"

"Ellis, you've done everything right. You've learned everything about her to figure out the ways to lead her around the hurdles. You made her proud of herself. She'd never even be this ready if you hadn't done that perfectly."

I smile at him. "I really hate this."

"The talking."

"So much."

"Emotions."

"The fucking worst."

He laughs.

"Okay," I say. "Last big burst then I'll go in and tequila these emotions away. Ready?"

"Yep."

I inhale. "Everything you said was right. Everything. And it's remarkable that you could see all of it in such a short amount of time. Gold star for you." I chuckle at my own attempt to lighten a mood I know is about to get heavier. "I have become afraid. Of everything. Do you know the reason I'm afraid to open the mail is because I'm always waiting for a proverbial shoe to drop? Isn't that ridiculous? The mail! It fills me with dread. I leave it to pile up in the mailbox and then I leave it unopened on the counter for days. I don't understand why.

"I'm afraid when the phone rings. I'm afraid when the doorbell buzzes. I'm afraid to write, but afraid to not write because then, what the hell am I? I'm afraid to succeed. To fail. I'm afraid to meet my fans and disappoint them. I am afraid to be happy and that's the worst cliche ever, and it's absolutely true. I'm not going to sit here and explain it all to you, but I see the damage now. As I sit here with you, I don't believe I deserve happiness and if I get happiness, I'll be afraid it will be taken away because I didn't deserve it in the first place. It's an awful loop and I don't know how I got into it let alone how to get out of it, but I'm going to work on it now. Knowing how brave you always were, and how brave Christopher has been, it's time for me to step up and figure this out. To try to stop being afraid of everything, even the rain."

"I wish you'd tell me why you're so afraid of the rain."

Still seeking answers from me but I only offer silence. Some things I don't know if I'll ever be able to share with anyone.

I stroke the top of his hand and I hear him clear his throat. I hate what I'm about to say. "Lincoln, I'm going to work on all this alone because it's just not going to be fixed otherwise."

He looks sharply at me. I've stood in front of a mirror with devastation on my own face enough times to know what it looks like, and it hurts to see it flash even briefly across his. I smile in comfort.

"What do you—"

"I want you to go."

"You—" He swallows hard and shakes his head slowly.

"You're not leaving me this time. I'm telling you—asking you to go because I don't know when I'll be fixed. But for Wren and Dunn, I need to do it. For myself. I don't feel like I know who I am or was. Do you remember who I used to be?"

"Every minute of you. You're still here."

"Not really. No. It feels fake. I've been acting so long I don't remember me before I started playing this role of Ellis Sloan. So I'm going to find who I was, and there's something I want you to understand. You, being here, laughing with me again, showing me, yelling it right at me?" I nudge my shoulder into his with a grin. "It's what started it all. I'm only going to figure this out because you showed me it's worth doing. You made me miss who I was," I pause and smile at him, "because I had always liked who I was with you."

"But you want me to go?"

"I want you to live. Not sit here in a shitty duplex in Pittsburgh pouring into a broken friend and an out-of-tune piano what you could be pouring out for the world to see and hear. It's not fair to keep you here when I don't know when or, hell, even if I'll be ready again. I know you have opportunities. Chances. Take them and go. For me."

He studies my face for a long moment. "I'm going to say something and you're going to absolutely hate it."

"Oh boy."

"I love you."

"I can tell."

He grins crookedly. "You always have a way of yanking the feeling right out of a conversation, don't you?"

"It's my brand."

"It really is impressive."

"Gold star for me. Looks like we're tied."

He laughs up at the trees and I drink it in. I'm going to miss it. I am struck with a lonely sadness, knowing I'll have to let him leave in order to bring myself home. But it's bittersweet, because now that I can see a bit of my old self peeking out, I'm ready to draw her the rest of the way. I'm nearly knocked over by a sudden overwhelming wave of gratitude that he got me this far.

"I want you to do something," I say, surprised at myself for what I'm about to do.

He reaches his hand from my lap to run his finger along the scar on my chin, as if committing its pattern to memory like Braille. "Sure," he says, his eyes on the scar.

"I want you to kiss m—"

He doesn't let me finish and has crushed my lips to his. I feel wetness on my cheeks as I cling to him, and I don't know if it's from his eyes or mine. I don't think I'll like the answer either way.

It's a sad joining. It's a thank you. It's friendship that took a 21-year break before finding each other again. It's openness that grew out of secrets.

But most of all, it's the start of our goodbye.

He'll go live. I'll stay here and try.

Chapter Fifty-Six

May 2021

"Yes. I'm Ellis Sloan. I have an appointment."

"Have a seat. She'll be with you."

We said goodbye to Lincoln Hale on a Saturday. Wren offering him a real hug and a book on the presidents after the bestowing of a final name—Tyler. Dunn, looking pained, giving him a handshake. With his mother's piano already safely tucked into a reputable cargo truck heading to the West Coast where Lincoln said it would replace his baby grand piano, we stood outside Chris's car after watching Wren and Dunn head inside. The early summer air was already heavy with moisture even though the sun had yet to fully burn through the morning's fog.

He handed me a square box before pulling me into a hard hug and whispering his love for me one final time. He'd be in Japan in a few weeks. The other side of the world. Living big and loud and filming the role he'd wanted—an American pianist in Tokyo teaching an autistic piano prodigy who would be played by an autistic actor. Wren was delighted at the news.

I kissed his cheek and waved to Chris in the passenger seat then went into my house. I wouldn't watch them drive away. I placed the box on the kitchen table and considered not opening it—just putting it away as I had the divorce decree. Closed boxes and sealed envelopes don't release emotions. But my curiosity won, and I lifted the flaps of the box. Inside were two of the small daisy-adorned drinking glasses his mother had shared with me. I wondered what he'd do when he found the *Our Town* program he had autographed all those years ago that I had tucked into his bag without him seeing.

I called the office of one Dr. Willa Parrish on the Monday after he drove away to the airport, returning to his real life, her name given to me by Ash who said Dr. Parrish was the therapist the fire and rescue departments used. She would see me quickly as a favor.

Visiting the Gulf Tower in downtown Pittsburgh is an easy Parkway exit and a quick drive down brick-paved Grant Street, a lucky parking spot at a meter, and an elevator ride up 32 floors through one of the oldest, but most beautiful buildings in the skyline. Her reception area is small. Soothing. Boxes of tissues rest on small tables next to pairs of chairs rimming the room.

My stomach is knotted. I don't know what I'm doing here, but I know I need to start something if I ever want anything else to end. To change. There is wholeness out there. Completeness. My plea sent up is that she'll be the one to help me find it.

"Ellis?"

Willa Parrish is young. Younger than me, certainly. Perhaps only her late twenties. She's dressed in dark capri jeans pegged much the way I had once pegged mine, and a faded, clearly vintage t-shirt from the local rock station. "DVE ROCKS!" it shouts at me in large angular letters. Her shoes are white Chucks and her glasses baby pink and horn-rimmed. She's nothing at all what I expected. I expected grandmotherly Bea, but without the aura of Beelzebub and snakes for hair.

Dr. Parrish leads me into her large office. It's minimalistic and she looks out of place with the quiet simplicity pushing hard against her complicated realness and her loudness of being. Like she's a child playing "therapist." *Paging Dr. Lucy Van Pelt. Help, 5 cents.* Her wall of windows looks out onto the Allegheny River, the yellow brightness of the Rachel Carson Bridge glowing stark against the brown-green hue of the water Ash will tell you is cold, fast and unforgiving.

I settle into the beige couch she gestures me toward as she plops herself easily into her large sea green armchair with a light bounce, folding one of her legs under the other.

"Ellis," she says breezily, "good to meet you. I should tell you I loved your book."

I don't know what I've begun or what path I'm about to take my first step upon, but I sure hope I like where it ends.

"You've read my book?"

Ellis Sloan Therapy Sessions

Gulf Tower
Pittsburgh, PA
September 2021

Ellis: I'd gone with him to San Diego. I had three wines at the faculty reception the night before the conference and I told the most hilarious Nero joke—a bit purple one at that—and it got a huge laugh. I had the best time. With history professors! Imagine it. But they were so interesting. I laughed so much, as did they, and I thought Oliver was enjoying it. But afterward, he asked to take a walk with me. He lit into me. How embarrassed he was. How I'd shamed him. People were staring, he got so loud. He walked away and told me not to follow him. He didn't return to the hotel that night. When he finally did, I was angry, and I confronted him. We fought and he told me he wanted a divorce. Said we weren't having sex anymore.

Dr. Parrish: Were you not having sex?

Ellis: We were. I think he was just searching for something to be angry about.

Dr. Parrish: So what happened after he said he wanted a divorce?

Ellis: We talked it out. I forgave him.

Dr. Parrish: Did he ask you to?

Ellis: —

Dr. Parrish: Did you have sex with him soon after?

Ellis: Right then and there. I initiated it. I felt guilty, and I was miserable. I didn't know how to be happy if he wasn't happy. I needed to make him happy so I could be too.

Dr. Parrish: And there's your damage.

Ellis: Holy shit.

Chapter Fifty-Seven

September 2021

Wren is crying somewhere.

I hear the low moan and the guttural sobs. Muffled. Wren is crying somewhere. Beneath something. Under something. Inside of something, maybe.

"Wren is crying somewhere."

I sit up in my bed, my room dark, to find Dunn silhouetted in my doorway with the hallway light glowing behind him. I look at my phone. 3:32 a.m. "Yeah. I hear it too. Her bedroom?"

"I already checked. Was going to see if she's okay."

"That's amazing of you, Dunn. I'll go find her. Go back to bed."

"I'll go with you."

I join him in the hallway and look up at him. So tall. Strong. Almost seventeen now. "You're too good. Where'd I go right?"

He doesn't answer as another of Wren's wails finds us.

"Downstairs," I say, placing the direction of the sound.

Wren is crying downstairs. In the messy coat closet. Crouched low and surrounded by tossed shoes. The fists she holds clenched tightly to her mouth do nothing to mute the sounds of her inner torment. She twists away from the light when I open the door with Dunn by my side.

"Wrennie. What is it?"

"Leave me alone," she gets out between gasps.

When we finally cajole her out of the closet to sit on the couch, it takes another ten minutes of Dunn and I sitting on either side of her, careful not to touch her, instead using only our voices to soothe, to finally calm her down.

"Tell me what's wrong, Wren."

"Nothing."

"You'll feel better if you tell us," Dunn offers, draping his arm behind her on the couch cushion, again careful not to touch her. She eyes him, but hunches further within her shoulders.

Often when Wren is upset, I have to guess close to right before she'll finally unload what she's pent up inside. "Something with school today? Something happen on the bus? Someone upset you in the halls? Lindsey say something to upset you? Did I do something?"

She shakes her head no to all those things.

"Did I do something?" Dunn asks, and I want to hug him.

She shakes her head again.

I try one more. "Is it dad?"

She doesn't speak or shake her head. I'm close. But she hasn't seen Oliver in nearly a month, so it's likely not something he's done, but rather something he hasn't. Which guts me. It's hard to heal absence. Lack.

"He'll be here next week," Dunn assures.

Wren's face bunches at this and she begins crying anew. "I don't want to be like Uncle Edward," she wails out.

"What?!" I can't place the emotions inside me. Confusion? Surprise? Devastation? I grab her in a hug that she immediately pushes away, reminding me that touch does not soothe her. "Wrennie. Wrennie. What do you mean?"

"I don't want you to have to hide me away. Because of the stuff

I do. To make dad leave. To make Lincoln leave. I don't want to grow up to be hidden too because I'm bad."

Because I'm bad. She thinks she caused it. All of it. Oliver and me. Lincoln going away. And she knew, all the times we visited Oliver's family, all the times she never said a word, that her Uncle Edward was there, hidden away. Lincoln has been gone four months already. How long she's been suffering with this. "Wrennie. Can I hold your hand?" She shakes her head no and clutches her hands together in her lap tightly, working her fingers. "You'll never be hidden."

"Uncle Edward is hidden."

"Listen to this promise: you will never be hidden. You're perfect. You didn't cause dad to leave. I did. Me. Only me. And you didn't cause Lincoln to leave. I did. Only me."

"Why? Why did you make them leave?"

I catch Dunn's eyes. They are asking me the same question. "Well, dad and I are better apart. And Lincoln? Well, he didn't belong here. I was just letting him go do the big things he needed to do. The movie. You'll be so excited to see it someday. To know you know him. To see that it's about people like you. And you're perfect. You defend me. Every time. When no one else will, you stand up. That will never be hidden. You will never be hidden. I promise you."

I eye Dunn again. He has managed to pull his arm down slowly and softly enough to rest it around Wren's shoulders without her pushing him away. He looks pained. He looks how I feel.

Wren inhales on a gasp. "I bet they used to promise Uncle Edward that."

Sitting there on my couch in the dead of the night, listening to my sobbing daughter tell me she's afraid she'll grow up to be hidden away, I realize she took on more damage than she'd ever let on. That perhaps, like me, she'd been putting on her own facades to hide her pain. But unlike my phantom damage, I know where Wren's is, and I know I can help fix it.

And I'll start tomorrow by loading her into my car after I send Dunn to school. It's time she and I took a quick daytrip to the Sloan Winery.

Dr. Parrish's voice echoes in my ears.

Bravery is the prescription.

Ellis Sloan Therapy Sessions

Gulf Tower
Pittsburgh, PA
September 2021

Dr. Parrish: You spent seventeen years trying to make him happy, Ellis. Do you see that? You spent all that time trying to make yourself happy through his happiness, because he manipulated you into doing so. If you were happy, he would become unhappy, knowing it would negatively affect your happiness. So the circle starts again and you try to make him happy, you do, you feel happy too, he sees this, he finds a way to become unhappy and round and round you went. It was him taking control, so that you couldn't. It was always about control.

Ellis: And now?

Dr. Parrish: And now it makes perfect sense that you've been conditioned to believe you don't deserve to be happy and that if you are happy, a bad thing will come along on its heels because that's what always happened. So it's easier to not be happy to keep the bad stuff at bay. Maintain the status quo. But Ellis, all that time, bad things weren't coming along. He was—

Ellis: He was sending them to me.

Dr. Parrish: Here. Take a tissue.

Chapter Fifty-Eight

September 2021

"Ellis?"

The surprise on Oliver's face—that face I still inexplicably love—is expected. I watch the emotions I've long been able to read on him wash in and out like waves. Confusion. Recognition. Sadness. I recognize all the questions he wants to ask. But they will not be asked. I will not allow them to be asked because I'm as surprised at myself as Oliver is.

I, Ellis Robin Marks Sloan (the Third), put my daughter in the car at 6:30 this morning and drove straight to Sloan Vineyards and Winery, past the shop, past the stables, past the turnoff to the gardens and the tennis court, and I did not stop until I reached the front of the huge Georgian mansion that's been in the Sloan family for a century.

I, Ellis Robin Marks Sloan, knocked on the door of the Sloan estate with my daughter standing next to me and I jutted my chin up and straightened my back and set my jaw, my gaze, and my nerves.

I, Ellis Robin Marks Sloan, would kick the door down for Wren.

"What's— Wren—" Oliver stammers.

"Hi, Dad," she says shyly, almost as if apologizing that her mother has become the kind of woman that does these rash things, and nearly overnight.

I grab Wren's hand and pull her with me past Oliver to enter the large foyer, my eyes on the long staircase that winds up and around before disappearing beyond a high wall adorned with artwork that probably cost more than even Lincoln's possessions. I turn to Oliver and take three steps toward him to smack the project folder I'm holding into his chest and wait for him to grab it.

"What is it?" he asks. "What's wrong?"

"I'd like you to take a look at that. That's your daughter's history project from last year. She was in seventh grade, Oliver. That's a 20-page look at the changing powers of the office of the presidency. And then I want you to flip to the last page and take a look at her bibliography. And I want you to see that every source, Oliver, every single one is yours. One of yours. A book. An article. You look at that and we'll be back. Wren, come."

We leave Oliver standing there in the bright foyer of his family home, slowly opening the cover of the folder. We head for the stairs. Up. To where I remember. The place I recall. The set of rooms. Down this hall. To the right. I knock and wait four seconds before opening the wide oak door.

Edward Sloan. Thirty-five. As handsome as ever. Dressed in a dark blue jogging suit. Sitting by his window reading while his in-home aide, a small woman about my age, pauses her task of putting away folded laundry. His room is huge and meant to be lived in. A full bathroom at the far wall. A refrigerator and sink with a cupboard for his dishes. An area of soft floor pillows. Books everywhere. So many books. An art corner with an easel. A desk with three computers and multiple gaming systems.

He finds me and I watch as recognition dawns on his face. "Ellie?"

I could cry.

"Ellie? Are you here to be with Oliver again?" he asks with too much hope as he stands to walk toward me.

"No, Edward. I'm here to be with you. We've come to take you to lunch, you see. We've missed you. Would you like to come with me and Wren to get some lunch?"

Edward looks from Wren to me, his eyes large and bright. "Oh, I would, yes!"

His aide starts toward us, but I don't give her a chance to interfere, and hold my hand out to my former brother-in-law. "Can I hold your hand, Edward?"

He nods. Wren reaches him before I do and grabs at his hand.

Edward turns toward his aide and says loudly, "Millie, this is my family. I'm going to go with them."

She starts toward us again, and I eye her quite seriously in warning.

"Wait," she says, holding her own hand out toward us.

"I'm going to lunch," Edward says, letting Wren pull him toward the door.

"But wait," Millie says as she pulls open a door to disappear into a large closet. When she reappears, she's holding a pair of black Crocs. "You'll need your shoes."

Wren beams. I smile. Edward heads for his shoes.

When we reach the bottom of the steps again, Oliver is no longer alone. His mother, dressed in a green pantsuit, stands next to him, and watches us descend. My nerve takes a small ding to its armor, but Wren pulls Edward ahead, determined. She needs no prescription of bravery. She has it in spades.

"Lisa," I say, putting familiarity I don't feel into my voice. She's a stranger now. "You're looking—"

She takes one step. "No. You're not taking Edward anywhere. Edward, go back to your room. It's nearly lunchtime. Then maybe you can have a walk in the garden for a bit."

Wren looks at me for help, her eyes shining. Wet. Her chin

dimpled with a quiver. I inhale. "We'd like to take Edward for lunch. We'll get him back safely. Just an hour."

Lisa Sloan walks purposefully toward me, her shoes echoing throughout the high foyer, bouncing off the walls, the art, the cold hard floors, the vases overflowing with flowers, the huge windows letting the late morning light work their magic. "You don't have permission. You're not family anymore. Edward, go to—"

"They'll be taking Edward to lunch, Mother."

I snap my head to find Oliver behind her. He's staring down at the last page of Wren's project. Her sources. His name repeated. *Sloan, Oliver. Sloan, Oliver. Sloan, Oliver.* When he looks at us, his face is wrought with something I haven't seen in years. Some distant emotion is pulling at him, trying to surface. He works his mouth and then eyes his shocked mother.

He repeats, more slowly this time. Deliberate. "They'll be taking Edward to lunch, Mother."

"Oliver, no, they—"

I expect the explosion. It will come now. Arguing with Oliver. He will light up. Yell at her. Kick over the table with the vase on it. I hope Wren and I won't be caught in his line of fire.

Oliver approaches his mother until he's mere inches from her face, looking down his nose at her. "He is thirty-five years old. They are taking Edward to lunch." He says it calmly, tension evident only at his jaw. He addresses his brother while still staring down at her, "Edward, go with Ellis. Go have—"

Oliver stops speaking when he feels Wren move next to him to grab at his hand, pulling him away from his angry mother whose face is stony. Clutching her project to his chest, he looks at Wren, and I see him working his mouth once more, fighting so hard to hide things he's feeling.

"You can come too," she says to him, "but you have to give me back my project. I'm not giving it to you. It's mine."

I lift my hand to cover my grin. *Atta girl, Wrennie.*

Edward lights up. "Where are we going, Ellie?"

"You get to pick."

"Anything but shrimp," he says.

"Great," I smile at him. "We'll find a quiet place that serves lots of things that aren't shrimp."

We leave his mother standing inside of her anger like a statue, Oliver closing the door softly on her. Not a slam that screams, "You're wrong!" but a gentle latching that whispers, "This is the way it will be."

He gives me a weary look. A sad look. An open look. I only turn away and smile at his brother instead. Oliver deserves nothing from me. I want nothing from him. Forever. But if there's anything good I can get out of him to give to Wren, I'll find it because she deserves every ounce of it.

Ellis Sloan Therapy Sessions

Gulf Tower
Pittsburgh, PA
September 2021

Ellis: So how do I fix it?

Dr. Parrish: Well, knowing what caused this is going to free you some, because you're going to see the truth when you look back on those memories. Give it time. But first, you need to start taking small steps in bravery, okay? Put away one of your small anxieties. Get the mail and open it every day this week. Try to say yes to more things you once said no to and see if anything bad happens, or if maybe, rather, you find yourself being perfectly fine. You've got the book reading next month. Keep going. Open yourself up with a little less fear. Try to. Bravery is the prescription I'm writing for you. "Take small braveries."

Ellis: Ok.

Dr. Parrish: And when you find yourself waiting for the bad, I want you to try to write the good that led you to the psychological bench Oliver created for you to sit at while awaiting the bad. Write it and read it and realize that even if some bad does come along, it won't have been sent to you as punishment because there is no longer a punisher in your life. And soon you'll see the happy parts are deserved. And the bad parts? Well, that's just life, Ellis. It sounds like you have the choice whether you go through the rest of yours alone. I think it's good and important for you to have decided for yourself to be alone for a while, so you can heal. But when you're ready? Take a bigger bravery. If I may? Grab what makes you happy and kick the door closed behind it.

Chapter Fifty-Nine

October 2021

It's too much.

I'm a little taken aback at the turnout and look pleadingly at Bea who offers no sympathy, but instead adjusts the lay of my striped scarf Hadi paired with white jeans and an army green jacket. Add to this the wedge booties and I'm feeling quite out of my comfort zone. Add all that to the 120 or so who showed at the Wander Bookstore for what had been promoted on social media and even the print media as "A Rare Reading and Signing: Ellis Sloan with *Luca Rex*." I was expecting maybe 25.

Bea had been telling me that my refusal to acknowledge the existence of my heroine Luca Rex since the first book tour, before word-of-mouth launched it into greater popularity, had resulted in a fan base frantic for any appearance. My brave new existence meant saying yes to this event, my first appearance in two years. But eyeing the tittering and humming crowd from a side room had sent my courage scampering away.

Bea wasn't having it because Bea doesn't deal in weakness. Bea deals in unrelenting fortitude only. "Listen to me. This is nothing," she reassured without sounding at all reassuring. "You go out there.

You smile. You read a bit of *Luca Rex.* You sit in a chair at a table, ask these lovely people their first names, feign interest in their lives, sign their books, of which several dollars goes in your pocket, and then you go home. Time to give the people what they want. They want Ellis Sloan, and you need the money."

She looks me up and down. "Your outfit is lovely. Whose work is this because I know if it was your choice you'd be in old leggings and a ratty t-shirt."

I laugh. "I cannot tell you who dressed me because then we'd violate Bechdel again."

"So it was a—"

I hold my finger to my lips. "Shh. Bechdel."

Bea smiles as a smattering of applause signals I'm on. She gives me a small pat on the cheek. "Off you go. Pretend you're human for an hour."

"Beep boop," I say in imitation of a robot.

"No, I meant like an alien. I'm always expecting you to rip your own face off to show me what's under that facade."

I'm still laughing lightly when I reach the lectern to applause and a sea of eager upturned faces, a clutched copy of my book in every lap. Some teenagers with their mothers. Lots of twenty- and thirty-somethings. A few teenage boys who I make plans to hug later.

"So, it's been a minute, huh?" I say to them, to which they laugh and offer a few additional claps. "You're all lovely and let's get right into it, right? Right. And you know, I should have picked what to read to you before I came up here, but I didn't because I'm terrible, so let me flip through here. It's been so long since I've read my own work." This pulls another round of laughter because they think I'm joking but I'm serious. "Ah. This looks good. The beginning! Page 1. Here we go."

I read:

Lev had never seen so many colors.

He'd never seen them so electrically alive either. Reds, zapping like lightning from her eyes. Magenta exploding into fireworks all around her. Blinding silver so intense he wanted to shield his own eyes. Violet. His least favorite. He tasted that one. The bitterness of it churned his stomach.

He bent down intent to pick her body up, her mangled ankle not looking to be able to support any weight. He knew it wouldn't. The plan was ... it wouldn't.

"Don't touch me." She spat the words as individual daggers of violet. He saw them, letter by letter, push through her swimming colors to attack him.

He ignored them and straightened to his full height. "You can't walk, Luca."

"Because of you*."*

"Well, yes, that's true."

"You could have killed me."

"It is literally impossible for me to kill you ... even if I wanted to." He winked, knowing were she not splayed like a tossed rag doll, she would leap wildly for his jugular.

A wave of snickering trails through the crowd.

I read longer than I intend to, finding myself falling into the world of Luca Rex again, flipping through chapters to re-discover passages I barely remember writing. It's almost as if I'm reading someone else's work. And I weirdly don't hate it.

A plea sent up to no one. Just ... up. Into the dark sky. Into the nothingness above. A plea that for just this once, could something not suck? Could something not fall apart? Could something not hurt? Could something decent come down? Could she have something good? And whole? And un-wrong? And hers?

I swallow hard at this passage, remembering the pain I felt

when I wrote it. We'd fought. He'd yelled. So harshly. "I don't feel you've been giving me what I need," he'd said when I begged him to explain what he was so angry about. I wrote that passage deep into the night while he slept, tears falling on my hands as they typed out pain at my own unworthiness. I can see it now for what it was. Lies. That I believed for a long time.

I take a sip of water and then turn to one of the most beloved chapters in the book, according to Bea—when Luca finally understood that she was speaking to an angel and began to demand information:

"Do you pull rabbits out of hats?" She was only half-joking.

"That's magicians."

"Spells?"

"Wizards."

"Wishes?"

"Genies."

"Teleportation?"

"The crew of the starship Enterprise." He saluted.

"Water into wine?" She waved her half empty water bottle in his face.

He grinned, his steps refusing to falter. "Jesus."

"Is that a swear?"

His grin turned into an appreciative crooked smile, but still his pace quickened as if he was desperate to escape, leaving Luca looking at the back of his head. She groaned and half jogged to catch up.

"So, no wine?" she asked.

"No wine."

"Well, hell."

He side-eyed her. "Is that a swear?"

She was very near breathless. "Always. Can you fly?"

"Superman. Fairies. Birds. Insects. Planes. A specific set of squirrels. Childhood-ruining movie monkeys."

Luca felt disappointment knock at her heart but continued with her line of questioning. "Does the sun burn you?"

Lev pulled his hasty pace to an abrupt stop, causing Luca to move a few feet ahead before she could rear up. She turned to look at him and used the blessed rest to catch her breath. He was infuriatingly having no difficulty with his own breathing.

He crossed his arms and cocked his head to the side. "That's vampires. In fiction," he said, then narrowed his eyes. "You know vampires aren't real, don't you? Please tell me you know vampires aren't real. I need to see the words come out of your face." He stared hard at her lips.

I glance at the rapt crowd and say with unabashed delight, "Well, that is fucking hilarious if I do say so myself." I drink in their laughter and continue reading random passages, reacquainting myself with friends I had long ago tossed away as my most worthless creations.

Then finally, near the end of the book, the chapter I wrote first:

Then she saw her colors as Lev saw them. She was surrounded by them. Her yellows and blues swirling into soft green. Her senses lost meaning as she tasted what she used to see, saw what she used to smell, felt what she used to hear.

Ever up they went, straight toward the sun. It grew as they neared, a blinding fire whose intense heat beckoned her, welcomed her and soothed her. Growing closer and stronger until her clenched eyes were filled with a pulsing curtain of impossibly intense white. She saw only light. It filled her and surrounded her until she was sure she was inside the sun, 93 million miles from life on Earth. Part of it. On fire, but not burning up. Aching, but not in pain. Alive, but dead. Broken, but whole. Terrified, but safe. Nothing. Everything.

She briefly clung tighter to Lev, the only sure thing she knew she could hold on to in this disorienting piece of time and space.

Then she heeded the whispered command echoing in her head. Because she knew with absolute certainty it was why he took her there. To let go. She let go.

She fell fast with her back to the Earth, down and away from the light, the fear, and the anger. Down and away from all her colors. Down through the nothingness, away from Lev. Faster and faster she rushed. Fearless. Open. Ready. For "Next."

I close the book softly, nearly reverently, and see my face looking at me on the back jacket—my smile hiding damage. I am no longer that woman, I realize. When I look at the faces in front of me, my emotions are nearly succeeding at breaking the surface, but I push them down with a shaky inhale. My raised hand requests a silence to their applause and they oblige quickly. I could get used to this power because I certainly don't have it over my teens.

I'm not sure where to start. "I want to tell you, I thought I hated Luca Rex. Cards on the table? I've hated her for a long time." This draws the expected shock, but I add, "I thought I wrote a garbage book about things that don't really happen. Bad doesn't become good. Pain doesn't ever go away. Sometimes life doesn't get better, and it just stays really really shitty, you know? I thought I wrote a book that told you a funny and handsome angel would come and save you from your troubles." A few heads shake no in clear disagreement. "Now that my life is different, and I've now gone back to read some of this," I hold the book up, "I see, no, Luca was quite strong. Look what she did, you know? She wasn't saved by a man. She wasn't saved by an angel. She saved herself. She just needed someone to show her where to start, right?" They nod. "Then the dominoes to happiness fall from that.

"I forgot how much I loved her. I loved creating her. I wish I could explain what happens to a writer, or maybe some of you know, when you create a character and you build them from literally nothing, until they're nearly alive and walking the Earth with you, but they don't exist, except in here," I tap my finger to my temple.

"But maybe you all know you're not waiting for an angel. You're simply learning to do what she did. Open yourself to another's help and then use it to get stronger so you can change things in your life, and maybe help others. So Luca might not walk the Earth with us, but I'm pretty sure she made the jump from here," I tap my head again, "to here." I lower my hand to my heart. At once, realizations and certainties crowd my brain, demanding acknowledgement.

"I have news. First, my next book is going to be different. It's a highly fictionalized account of my teenage daughter. A funny look at life as an autistic middle schooler and all the lessons we can learn from wonderful people like her. It's to be titled *Labeled.* I hope you'll read it and learn something, and I promise you'll laugh and cry and want to become her best friend as much as you did Luca's."

With a quick glance thrown at Bea, I make a decision. Perhaps rashly. "But that book is written. It will be ready soon. It was the easiest book to write because it was inside me for so long; I just didn't realize it. But now, I'm ready for "Next," like Luca. I'm going to start writing the rest of her story for you. We'll call it, hmm, let's see, since this one is *Luca Rex: For Now*, and we left her story with her being ready for "Next," how about, *Luca Rex: For Ever?*

Bea sends me a wink and I smile while the sounds of excitement and happiness swirl around me, punctuated with the staccato of shutter snaps popping from the camera of a local journalist who I assume filtered in unnoticed at some point.

I widen my smile and mean every stupid toothy inch of it. Somehow, reading my own words—words I'd forgotten I had ever felt and loved, but that I'd poured my entire soul into—opened something inside. Unlike the window shutter that had once closed on Jane Hale, mine had been slowly opening for months and it finally let the light flood in. Reading about a strong girl who thought she was weak and lost, but who only needed one small moment to set in motion a ripple of change that would allow her to take control and live fearlessly, opened my eyes to see that I had created something good, valuable, worthy.

And I'm reminded of a small moment in my own life that sent similar ripples outward. It all started with one shouted word that drifted into my bedroom a year ago, waking me when all I'd wanted to do was sleep away my lonely pain.

And that word was "fuck."

Ellis Sloan Therapy Sessions

Gulf Tower
Pittsburgh, PA
September 2021

Ellis: Something happened.

Dr. Parrish: You want me to beg you?

Ellis: Something gave. Broke.

Dr. Parrish: Good broke?

Ellis: I'm writing.

Dr. Parrish: Ah. The dam broke. What did it?

Ellis: I did what you said. Wrote down the good thing, Wren had a friend over. I know that seems small.

Dr. Parrish: It's big. I get it.

Ellis: And it went great, and I was waiting for the bad. You know? What's coming? What's going to negate this? Terrible anxiety. So I typed it into my damn blank Google document. Then I wrote another Wren thing. And another. And I realized, I can tell Wren's story in a way that will reach people, especially middle schoolers. Teach them. Make them laugh. Maybe open their minds. It's told from her viewpoint. I already have 25,000 words.

Dr. Parrish: Wow. When your dam breaks, it really breaks.

Ellis: I feel so free. I sent it to Bea. She's over the moon. I'm terrified that I do, but I feel free. I'm not even too nervous about the *Luca* reading in three weeks. Shouldn't be too big of a crowd. I'm going to do it and do it knowing I'm still an author, you know? I'm a little bit more me again. I'm Ellis Sloan. Not a person who play-acts her so her kids don't realize how messed up she is. You made me a little less messed up.

Dr. Parrish: Can I steal that for my website? "Dr. Willa Parrish: Makes you a little less messed up."

Ellis: I'll invoice you.

Chapter Sixty

October 2021

It isn't until I sign every last book, hug every dear person who asked for one, and give an interview to the *Post-Gazette*'s reporter in which I accidentally say "fuck" two times, much to Bea's amused horror, that I notice a vase resting near a table at the inside of the front entrance. It is nearly exploding with daisies.

Bea follows me to it. "Oh, Miss Sloan," the quite young and overly eager bookshop owner Lily says to me, "those arrived for you earlier. We were instructed to give them to you right before you left."

I can't rip my gaze from them and Bea notices. She deftly guides Lily away from me with a gentle arm, offering thanks for the invitation and platitudes for a well-run event. I'm already overrun with emotions, and I know when I look at the card tucked into those daisies, I'm going to be confronted with more. I hesitate over the small white rectangle. I play it out in my mind. I will flip it over. Like at my father's funeral, it will simply say "Lincoln." My heart will feel feelings and I'll go home and go to bed missing his laugh. Then I'll wake up tomorrow and bury it all down and start fresh. Luca's story is my job now.

I consider not reading it, but then remember I'm supposed to be working on my fears, not letting them work me. I inhale and grab the card before I can change my mind.

Just go. I promise it will
be worth it.

I read the card four times trying to solve the riddle, but dawning realization doesn't come. Just as I deduce that the wrong card had been placed into the flowers and that somewhere in Pittsburgh a woman was equally confused while reading a card that said "Lincoln," the bell on the door to the shop rings out an arrival.

A middle-aged man in a black suit enters and eyes me. "Ellis Marks?"

I smile at my old name. "Yes, that's me."

"I'm here for you, ma'am. The car service." Past his shoulder, out the window to the road, I can see a black Town Car idling.

I spin around to find Bea standing behind me, then turn back. "I didn't hire a car. I came with my agent here. Perhaps this is a confusion?"

"No, ma'am. Ellis Marks, if you would come with me. Mr. Hale sent us, and we have instructions." He smiles and holds the shop door open in a beckon to me.

Bea shoos me forward. "It seems that a lovely gentleman has done something for you, and yes, I'm ruining your attempt to live your entire life by the Bechdel test, and I don't give a flip. Go get in that car. You've had a marvelous night. It's beyond me why it should end so soon. I'll see you in a month. I'll want twenty chapters."

I smile at her then say to the waiting driver, "I guess I'm going with you."

Twenty minutes later, we've crawled through a few neighborhoods and are now climbing a narrow, wooded road with no streetlights. I'm concerned. I've resigned myself that I've been conned and am being taken to the eventual site of my murder and will become the subject of a viral Netflix documentary called *This Stupid Woman Just Like Got Into Some Stranger's Car No Questions Asked LOL*. #thisdumbbitch will trend on Twitter.

I consider texting Lincoln, but I don't know what time it is halfway around the world. Just in case this breaks bad, I start composing a text message to Christopher and Hadi explaining that they should track my phone location and dispatch the police after me. I'm nearly ready to send it with a bunch of scared-face emojis as well as a knife emoji when the driver says, "And here we are."

Outside the window, a tall three-domed building appears ahead, its white stone lit eerily by the car's high beams. "Where exactly?" I ask, expecting the answer to be along the lines of, "Why, the kill room of course, ma'am."

"Allegheny Observatory, ma'am."

"The observatory! But why?"

He doesn't make any indication that he heard me as he stops the car in front of the main entrance that stands above several dozen wide stone steps. Lights shine from behind glass doors nestled between two large ionic columns. "I'll be waiting out here when you're done, ma'am. To take you home."

As he pulls my door open to allow me to exit, I consider telling him how exhausted he's made me about the word "ma'am." I smile instead.

A woman with a short dark bob and thick-framed black glasses walks out with her arms open in greeting. "Ellis," she calls down from the top of the steps that I'm hesitant to climb. "Welcome. I'm Gloria Pace. The director here. We've been expecting you."

Fight or flight. I choose bravery instead. "You have?" I ask her once I've climbed the steps. "I'm not sure what I'm doing here?"

"Mr. Hale is a friend to the observatory and quite a generous one at that. His mother was an astronomy student at the University before she shifted to music, did you know? We pretty much would move the stars we study for him." She pulls one of the glass doors open for me. "Consider this as us, well, nudging a star a little."

"I see how you aren't answering my question," I say with a laugh.

"As we say in the astronomy field, 'How observant of you.'" She chuckles at her own silly joke. "This way. I must tell you, my daughter is a big fan of yours. She's extremely jealous of me right now. I'll beg you for an autograph before you leave. Turning here. Here we go. This way up these steps. In here. It will be chilly. It's important we keep our observation domes the same temperature as outside."

She leads me to a circular room capped with a high domed ceiling with a curved rectangular section of the roof open to the night sky. A towering telescope in the center is pointed at a tilt toward the heavens, seeking out answers and beauty in the cosmos. "That's our 13-inch Fitz-Clark. Once the largest, now our smallest."

"It's beautiful."

"Would you believe it dates to the Civil War?"

"Wow. Never would have guessed."

"Oh, yes. Science is as old as nature. We forget that sometimes."

Memories of Jane Hale knock at my heart seeking safe quarter. I let them in. Mrs. Hale regularly pointing out constellations holds new meaning.

A technician standing beneath the telescope sends a thumbs-up to Gloria who says, "That's one of the university astronomy students. Rachel Chambers. She's got it all ready. Go on. Take a look."

I slowly approach with uncertainty, but at least it doesn't seem like I'm here to be murdered. Rachel seems shy and wanting to shrink away from me, but points to the eye piece. "You can look in there. It's set."

"Okay, then. I'm confused, but okay." I push my eye into the

opening and am greeted by a pretty unimpressive orb with a slight glowing haze. "What am I looking at here, ladies?" I ask.

Rachel answers, "That's C 2020 F3. The comet known as NEOWISE. We were told you wanted to find it?"

The comet. The fucking comet. I am stunned and touched as I stare at the jewel of heaven. A jewel I thought had gone too far away to ever see is right there in front of me, streaking free through the galaxy. He had them show me the comet I couldn't ever find.

"Hello, NEOWISE," I whisper too low to be heard, "you elusive bastard." The second part is loud enough for Rachel and Gloria to hear, and their laughter echoes low in the dome and then rises to escape out the gap in the roof to try to reach the star-holding heavens.

"Not the scientific descriptor, but it'll do," Gloria says.

I can't tear my eyes away. "I thought it was gone."

"Never gone forever. Everything living on Earth dies, but most everything in space goes on for near eternity, stars only burning out after billions and billions of years."

"Our solar system is thirteen billion years old. Imagine that," Rachel says in a worshipful whisper, her eyes cast to the stars, every syllable dipped heavily in the awe of the majesty of the celestial bodies she studies. "There are a billion stars in our galaxy. A billion galaxies beyond ours. A billion stars in probably every one of those galaxies."

NEOWISE remains before me on the black canvas, moving on, even in its seeming stillness until 7,000 years from now when it returns to a changed Earth on which I no longer stand and haven't for millennia, all my seemingly big problems and fears during my brief existence in the cosmos washed away by the passing of unimaginable time. I'm so small. A tiny blip. Sitting here looking at time and space and realizing maybe the big things aren't as big as I've made them to be. Maybe life needs to be lived in full while it can be, not timidly while finite time ticks by.

When I'm outside again, after drinking in the majesty of the stars for as long as I could, and after handing Gloria a signed copy of *Luca Rex* that had been in my bag, and promising to mail one to Rachel, who in her aching shyness revealed herself to be a fan, I find the car and its driver at the bottom of the steps, waiting as promised. A rumble of thunder groans in the distance as I reach him, but when I look up, the stars still return my gaze.

"There's a short but strong storm coming, ma'am. Would you like the keys?" He holds the keys out as if what he has done is normal car service etiquette.

"The keys?" I say with plain surprise.

"Yes, ma'am. We were told that if would storm, we were not to drive you through it but should offer for you to drive the car yourself. It's all been arranged. I've checked the weather radar and we're seeing a fast-moving burst pushing through in a minute or two. We can wait it out, or would you like to drive?"

I nearly stagger. It's all too much. This night. The reading. The lovely fans. This kindness. It's all too damn much. I could sit down on this bottom step and sob my eyes out. I smile at the driver instead. "You know what? What's your name?"

"Brian."

"Brian. If Mr. Hale trusted you, then I'm going to trust you so I have some progress to report to my therapist next week. I'll trust that you'll drive safely through that storm and get me home to my children? Not speed or take turns too quickly? And if I say to stop and pull over, you'll do that and we'll wait it out, right, Brian?"

"Of course, ma'am."

"Please stop calling me that. I'm Ellis. Like the island."

"Okay, Ellis Island," he says with a grin, "I'll get you home."

In the car again, as the first hard raindrops start to pepper the windshield, he hands a small white card to me over his shoulder. "For you."

It's similar to the one from the flowers and there is no hesitation from me this time.

I hope you found
what you were looking for
Love, Lincoln

I bring my hand to my mouth to cover what I'm sure is a quiver pulling at my chin. The inner edge of my finger brushes along the scar that once only reminded me of ugliness and terror in the rain, but now evokes memories of a soft touch. I tuck the card into my bag as the car starts down the hill, the rain suddenly pounding its torrential anger on the rooftop. Lightning momentarily flashes brightness into the trees outside my window.

"You be careful up there, okay, Brian. I have stuff to live for."

"Always am, Ellis Island. I got you."

I smile at him in the rearview mirror then reach for my phone. I send all four of my brothers and Hadi a text.

Sometimes the wagons circle you when you aren't even looking. But sometimes you have to summon them.

Chapter Sixty-One

November 2021

It was a plot.

A good old-fashioned plot I came up with, and it required nearly all my wagons.

Chris and Dunn to help me research, because truly my son can find anything online. We found names, phone numbers, addresses, dates, schedules. The internet is terrifying.

Hadi, to use his dearth of dollars to bribe a staffer at the movie studio to confirm the filming in Tokyo remained on schedule to wrap final reshoots four days before Thanksgiving.

Celeste, to create an official-looking court request sent to Lincoln in Tokyo via his agent, whose information Chris obtained, informing Lincoln of a claim against his father's estate, requiring Lincoln to return stateside for a deposition that would take place two days after Thanksgiving, rather than him returning straight to California.

Chris, armed with Hadi's money as a bribe, to contact Lincoln's assistant to be sure his arrival would fall on Thanksgiving Day, meaning lots of claims that flights were simply sold out, leaving no other options. Money really can buy anything, I learned. No wonder Hadi worships it.

Ash and Seth, to use their contacts in the police department to send a trio of officers to escort a confused Lincoln directly from the security exit at Pittsburgh International Airport to the black SUV waiting at the arrivals curb. A few passersby recognized him and snapped photos, thinking he'd likely obtained a security detail for his arrival. Inside the SUV waited every brother and a delighted Hadi. Nathan at the wheel.

Poppy, to set an extra place at her table.

To hear Chris tell it, Lincoln's first question when he saw who was in the SUV was, "What the hell is going on?" and his second question was, "Is Ellis okay?"

To hear Hadi tell it, "That boy thought he was getting taken to be tossed dead into the confluence, is what I saw."

To hear Lincoln tell it, "I wasn't scared. I was jet lagged out of my mind. The Marks brothers don't frighten me."

To which Hadi had shouted, "The Marks Brothers! I just now hear it. I'm never not saying it like that."

They arrived at Poppy's around 3:30, the atmosphere inside already chaotic with laughter, commotion and the shouts of children. They'd filed out of the SUV as I watched from the window, one after another, these men of mine. Nathan. Chris. Hadi. Seth. Lucas.

Lincoln.

Lincoln who deserved words from me. Lincoln who created celestial and healing magic for me from halfway around the world. Lincoln who found a way to help me no matter how many times I told him there wasn't a way for him to do so.

They filed into Poppy's house, and I caught his eyes and his confusion. Serves him right for letting me think I'd been kidnapped.

Nathan grabs his elbow and guides him to the table, ordering him to sit at one end of it. And my family, as I've instructed them to do, immediately returns to their normal pre-dinner tasks as if he'd never not been sitting right there. One of us.

Chapter Sixty-Two

Thanksgiving 2021

Seeing Lincoln at the table, surrounded by the rushing bustle of my family, pulls at my breath. I'm careful to mask it. I don't need or want an audience for the rush of emotions I feel burning up my neck. It has been so long since I've seen him. Six months.

I want to grab his hand and pull him from the chair so I can drag him outside into the cold air to feel the contrast of his warmth against me. I want to explain things to him. Share things. Thank him for things. Tell him where I'm at now. Who I am now. To find out where he is now. Instead, I busy myself with the task of placing folded napkins on the plates as dishes of steaming food are plopped down by Ash, Maddie and Celeste. My beautiful Hadi catches my eyes and winks before heading into the kitchen, from where I hear my mother warning random children about random infractions on noise level, running speed and potty words.

This was what I needed. To bring him here without spilling my guts out to him—a place I'm simply not at yet, despite all my work with Willa. To fold him back into my life if he wants to be there. Slot him into the emotional space he vacated at my request in May.

Like returning a book to its nook on the shelf. Nestling it into its waiting home.

As I circle the large table, plate by plate, I watch him with one eye. Nathan grips his shoulder briefly. Lincoln chuckles at something Dunn has said or done. Maybe both. He gives Wren a small salute and warm smile. I am a few plates away from him. I feel him watching me and bask in the renewed warmth it gives me, as if he's put a hand on me.

I remember that day I went to him long ago when we were young, when I was in so much pain, wracked with confusion. I remember him playing out his pain in the dark. I remember being too wrapped up in myself to wonder if pain had taken him too. I am a plate away, and I remember the daisies he sent to my father's funeral. I remember that he saved my brother's life and never said a word and let me hate him to protect the secret. I remember him protecting my daughter from a symphony while at the same time teaching her not to fear it. I remember the comet and what it's like, after all that time, to finally find something, even if it's only because someone had to show me where to look. He wasn't going to allow me to be driven through a storm. I am standing next to him, with my heart screaming out words my mouth will never be able to say.

He looks at me. I hope he knows. I hope he feels my gratitude. I hope he sees my heart and the room I have now been able to make in it for him by throwing a little fear away.

I swallow away the knot in my throat and reach down to squeeze his hand resting on his leg, because I am desperate to touch him and to somehow send all my thoughts to him. I offer a smile down at his open face, and I'm more sure than ever that I'm ready for all the nouns I cannot see.

Ellis Sloan Therapy Sessions

Gulf Tower
Pittsburgh, PA
October 2021

Ellis: How will I know I'm healed? And ready?

Dr. Parrish: I can't tell you that because only you will know, but I promise the answer is a story you're absolutely going to tell me one day sitting here. Or maybe it's one you'll write for others to read. And I'll buy it.

Epilogue

Thanksgiving 2021

Lincoln Hale was surrounded by barely reined chaos.

The adult Marks children were circling the long dining room table, haphazardly plunking down steaming dishes of turkey, stuffing, yams, beans. A basket overflowing with bread rolls plopped down an inch from the plate Lincoln was seated behind at the head of the table—a place he didn't feel should be his. He was uneasy with having been deposited there, but that was where he was ushered and commanded to sit and truth be told, he was too afraid of Poppy Marks to make a show of protest.

The three wives and the one Hadi of the Marks children were attempting unsuccessfully to herd the younger children to two smaller tables covered with craft paper rather than tablecloths. Crayons and markers scattered over traced hand turkeys and illegibly printed letters. The older children were scattered already around the larger table.

From the kitchen, Hadi could be heard observing loudly, "This is too many children! What am I marrying into?"

He could hear Poppy Marks calling orders from the kitchen—mostly about behavior. Two dogs sprinted through the room.

Lincoln watched Nathan silently pour a red into a wine glass in front of him. Nathan brought his hand to rest atop Lincoln's shoulder, then continued away, leaving Lincoln to translate its uncertain meaning.

Half the table away, Dunn sat with his own glass outstretched toward his approaching wine-toting uncle, only for Ellis to swish by and cancel the transaction with a stern shake of her head and a remark that pulled a loud laugh from a passing Ash. Nathan directed Dunn to the water pitcher on the table instead and was rewarded with an eyeroll from the teen.

Next to Dunn was Wren. She was like Lincoln. The quiet place. The still place. She sat with headphones over her ears, her eyes on her phone screen in her lap while her family swam around her. She was drowning out the noise Lincoln knew she couldn't handle. She looked up suddenly at him, as if he had called to her. He was warmed by her unexpected smile and gave her a small salute in return. She returned her attention to her phone with no further acknowledgement. He would take what he could get, and it would be enough.

Christopher clapped his back as he passed by with someone's squirming and squealing toddler in his other arm, who he then handed off to Hadi with a kiss. Hadi dutifully carried the small flailing human away, holding her as far from himself as possible, as if she were radioactive.

Lincoln watched the movement around him—this dance they all did without realizing they were doing it. Swerving. Circling. Encountering. Sidestepping. He listened to the music they didn't realize they were making—laughing. Scolding. Offering. Taking. Thanking. Teasing. Barking.

He wished Wren could hear it and not be pained by it. He wished he could guide her safely through it like he could Tchaikovsky. Pointing out the beauty parts, shielding her from the painful ones.

He found Ellis's curl-framed face in the chaos and took hold of the familiar warmth he felt, not wanting to let it go. She was circling the table, dropping folded napkins as she went. He watched her features. Saw the symmetry of them. The angles and math. As she neared, her voice cut through the swirling noise. He heard the music of her. The ever-present irreverence. The flippant word. The unleashed laugh. Trying to pull laughs from others around her. Succeeding every time. She was her. Who she'd always been, but at ease with herself like he remembered her from before. The lightness of being that always drew him to her.

He knew she was why he was there but wondered what it meant that she wanted him there. He supposed he would find out later.

She arrived at his chair and set a napkin on his empty plate. Lincoln looked up at her. She reached down to squeeze his hand. She didn't like words or emotions—he knew that about her. She probably didn't understand, though, how much she conveyed with the squeeze and with the plain emotions written across her face and the small intake of breath she pulled before she let his hand go and moved to continue away from him. To disappear into the swirl.

He couldn't let her.

He caught her retreating hand with his and pulled, dragging her down toward him. He watched the confusion on her face transform into soft knowing as he caught her. He captured her lips hard and pulled her across his chest until she was in his arms across his lap. He felt her twist her body toward his. Felt her melt slightly against him as she reached a hand up to cling to the front of his shirt. Felt the pull at the fabric clutched in her fist and heard the desperate unspoken words behind it. He remembered untangling those same fingers from a shivering wet head of hair in his car. Remembered the feeling of helplessness he confronted that day as she fought something much bigger than either of them. He thought of their night and the touches that followed and wrapped her closer at the memory.

He heard Wren. "God, Lincoln."

"I mean honestly," Hadi said in snarky agreement.

Lincoln pulled his face away from Ellis's and chuckled at hearing his real name finally come from Wren. He let Ellis wriggle out of his loosened arms to stand. She tugged and smoothed her crumpled sweater. He did the same to his shirtfront she had been clutching. "Yes," Ellis clucked at him, "God, Lincoln. It's only a napkin. We're going to feed you too."

As the room dutifully returned to motion, and bodies began to sink into their assigned chairs, toddlers deposited into theirs, he saw Ellis wink down at him with a light laugh before she moved away to continue her task. He felt her hand trail lightly across his shoulders as she passed behind, a silent statement of mutual possession.

He breathed in her music and her math and thought of his mother, lost long ago, who taught him how to find them before she took her own away.

"Had sigh'd to many, though he loved but one."

He felt fortunate, for in his life, he had gotten to love Ellis Marks twice.

Acknowledgments

My parents, Terry and Donna, for never once hinting at a single limit for my life.

My "Sestras," Stacey Davis, Marcia Larson, Terri Hurt and Tammy Barnett, for reading my words, offering encouragement, and maintaining the fiercest of loyalty. Additionally, Marcia, for editing my first draft and being my unwavering support system during the writing and publishing process.

Michael Dolan and Winding Road Stories, for taking a chance on me, leading me carefully and kindly through this journey, encouraging me at every turn, and editing with patience and love for this story and its characters.

Mike Woycheck and Jonathan Wander, for time and again demonstrating what true friendship looks like. Without them, I would not be the writer I am today.

My book (wine) club girls, Nancy Angus, Maureen Mahoney Hill, and Lynne Marchese, as well as Megan Amster, Barbara Bridge, Patty Broderick, Patti Coyne, Ellen Gamble, Jackie Gasdick and our lost but never forgotten Joan Tumbas, for listening, laughing, and forcing me to read books I didn't love so that one day I could write one I did.

Tyler Rupert, for my author photo, and to the whole Rupert clan for being my second family. Additionally, Duke Rupert and Michelle Rupert, for saving my life more than once in two very different ways.

Joy Krumenacker, for giving me permission to be proud again.

Comet NEOWISE C/2020 F3, for the inspiration. Louis Coban at Allegheny Observatory, for giving me permission to take some celestial liberties in the name of literary fiction.

My childhood neighbor Paul, who I tried to kick when I was 10 years old during a regular neighborhood tiff, but he caught my foot and I fell backward onto a gravel driveway. That very day, the two of us and our warring sibling factions found ourselves facing disappointed parents. And thus, I reveal the origin story for this book. I did not scream "motherfucker" during the peace talks. This is entirely a work of fiction.

And most importantly, my children Noah and Isabel, my prides and loves. I'm a writer at a loss for words, but I know you both can hear what my heart is shouting out to you right now, for always, no matter what.

About the Author

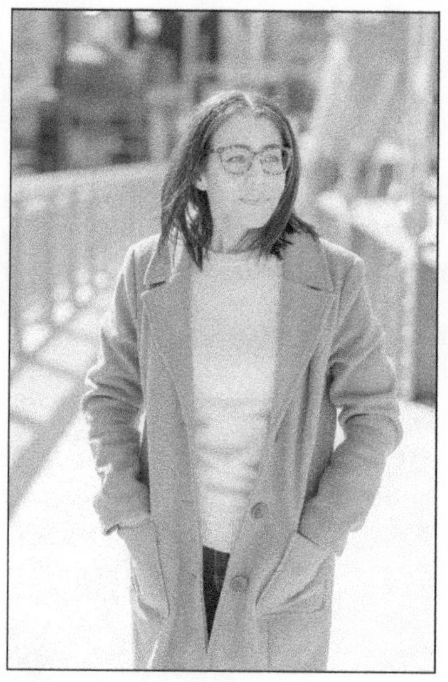

Virginia Montanez is a columnist, essayist and a writer of humor and history. A lifelong Pittsburgher, she has been profoundly hearing impaired since birth. *Nothing. Everything.* is her first novel.

Printed in the USA
CPSIA information can be obtained
at www.ICGtesting.com
CBHW022322110924
14436CB00025B/194